The Phenomenon

Written by R.K. Katic

Edited by Ms. Vicki Behme

THE PHENOMENON

R.K. Katic

DEDICATION

First and foremost, this is dedicated to Ms. Amanda Holmes, without whom this work wouldn't have been possible.

ACKNOWLEDGMENTS

The Author would like to thank the people at Google first and foremost. It is the researchers best friend, and is the tool I used most to find information and details in order to refine the work you will find in the following pages. I'd also like to thank The fine people and facilities of the Bay County Florida Library system and the Gulf County Library System for the assistance they rendered in the initial rough draft of this work. Other notable mentions include the fine people serving within the United States Military, particularly the Department of the Navy, the Navy itself, and the United States Marine Corps, also, the British Consulate General of New York, the fine people at Amazon & their subsidiary Createspace. In addition, I would like to thank the Moderation team at Reddit.com for their assistance and all the Redditors (17,000 at the time of this publication) who encouraged me and believed in me, notably one Mr. Kyle Baker. My Patrons from www.patreon.com/KaticRK; Mr. Marcus Rostamian, Mr. Kyle Parker, Ms. Brooks Woodhill, Ms. Jo Marie, & Mr. Jack Woodyard, and last but certainly not least, I'd like to thank my personal friend Ms. Amanda Reinfeld for her cover illustration, and Mr. Joe Felder of California for the contribution of a laptop which assisted in the Editing of this work.

Chapter 1	Page 1	Chapter 22	Page 218
Chapter 2	Page 7	Chapter 23	Page 234
Chapter 3	Page 15	Chapter 24	Page 240
Chapter 4	Page 24	Chapter 25	Page 254
Chapter 5	Page 33	Chapter 26	Page 272
Chapter 6	Page 41	Chapter 27	Page 295
Chapter 7	Page 49	Chapter 28	Page 314
Chapter 8	Page 60	Chapter 29	Page 336
Chapter 9	Page 68	Chapter 30	Page 342
Chapter 10	Page 80	Chapter 31	Page 352
Chapter 11	Page 95	Chapter 32	Page 358
Chapter 12	Page 100	Chapter 33	Page 366
Chapter 13	Page 115	Chapter 34	Page 374
Chapter 14	Page 126	Chapter 35	Page 385
Chapter 15	Page 138	Chapter 36	Page 396
Chapter 16	Page 148	Chapter 37	Page 403
Chapter 17	Page 164	Chapter 38	Page 411
Chapter 18	Page 178	Chapter 39	Page 420
Chapter 19	Page 186	Chapter 40	Page 429
Chapter 20	Page 193	Chapter 41	Page 437
Chapter 21	Page 210	Chapter 42	Page 449

CHAPTER 1

Day 1

The end of the world officially began at 3:54 am. That was when the first Emergency Alert System (EAS) broadcast went out in the United States.

We interrupt our programming at the request of the White House. This is the Emergency Alert System. All normal programming has been discontinued during this National Emergency.

Please remain in your homes. If you are not at home, find shelter immediately. Close all blinds and shades, block out all windows.

Do not look outside. Do not look at the sky. Do not make noise.

Your cooperation is vital to your survival. Appointed government personnel will update you shortly. Please do not use your telephone, as the telephone lines should be kept open for emergency use.

Eric awoke to the Emergency Alert System tone issuing from his phone. He couldn't help but wonder what could be going so wrong this early in the morning. He reached out from under his sheets to grasp at his phone on its dock on his nightstand. He unlocked it with a swipe of his finger, and read the displayed message with one eye as he rubbed sleep from the other.

Then he sat up and read it again with both.

And again.

He almost wanted to laugh. Surely this had to be some kind of joke, right? Definitely, this was some kind of joke. He rolled over and threw his legs off the side of the bed, working his feet into his slippers. He stretched and stood up, fatigue wobbling his gait as he took a few steps towards the windows. He felt his heavy drapes resist parting, almost as if they knew what would happen. As he peeked out down the street, he didn't see anything unusual at first.

Then he remembered, the sky. He turned his gaze upwards to the sickly orange glow of the city's light pollution splayed across the clouds, and that's where he saw them. Small, black, jagged, like pieces of shattered onyx flocking through the sky. No wings, no sounds, just countless shards of ebony wheeling and flitting to and fro in a chaotic scramble, streaming across the sky.

And then he stopped breathing. His hands let go of the drapes, allowing them to fall back into place, but his legs fell out from under him. He collapsed where he stood, legs folded, rear end plopping down into the carpet, torso falling back, bouncing off his laundry hamper and twisting, throwing his arms out as his head landed on the floor. He could not move; he could not breathe. As everything faded, he had just one thought: *"Oh God, why did I look?"*

~

Eric wasn't alone in his mistake. In retrospect, the initial warning should have had stronger language. Up and down the east coast of the United States and Canada, people awoke to their phones blaring tones at them, read the EAS, and sated their curiosity. Eric was merely one among tens of millions who didn't listen, and so he was one of tens of millions who died at or around 3:54am, Day One. Parents left behind sleeping children. Night shift workers never made it home, their spouses either succumbing as well, or left stranded with no way of knowing their partner's fate for sure.

Of those who survived the initial apocalypse, most managed to survive a few days longer. Millie, for example, was trying to find her boyfriend, an overnight security guard at the San Diego Zoo. When her phone went off, the zoo loudspeaker system directed all personnel to report to their assigned emergency preparedness stations which, as a non-employee, Millie didn't have. She went into the nearest unlocked building she could find which, as it happened, was a combination aquarium and reptile house.

In the beginning, she still had contact with her boyfriend Larry who was sheltered in his place inside one of the first aid stations, but after the sixth hour he'd stopped responding to her texts. She hoped his phone had simply died, but she had a sneaking feeling in the back of her mind that something much worse was afoot. There was an office in the aquarium wing, someplace where some of the local fish keepers (she's sure they have some kind of special name but she doesn't know it) did their paperwork, took their breaks, and managed the daily business of fish-keeping. There was also a couch and a mini-fridge in there, and that's where she slept and spent most of her time listening to the radio. The first day it kept repeating the same message for the whole morning. In the afternoon though, the message changed, finally delivering the promised update.

We interrupt our programming at the request of the White House. This is the Emergency Alert System. All normal programming has been discontinued during this National Emergency.

At 0310 hours eastern standard time North American Aerospace Defense Command detected an object of indeterminate mass entering the atmosphere over the eastern seaboard.

All personnel who have attempted to observe this object directly or indirectly have been reported as entering a catatonic state, shortly followed by exsanguination through unknown means.

At 0328 an unmanned reconnaissance aircraft approached the unknown object. Immediately after entering audible range the objects radar signature scattered and all contact with the aircraft was lost.

Further analysis of radar has shown that the object separated into a cloud of indeterminate size and a small part of its mass surrounded the aircraft briefly. Animals in controlled observation environments on the east coast have been seen to be housing in burrows or laying on the ground with their eyes tightly closed.

The cloud of objects is now spreading at low altitude over the entire

3

North American continent. For your own safety, we repeat:

Do not look outside.

Do not look at the sky.

Do not make noise.

Your cooperation is vital to your survival. Further updates will be issued as new information is gained. Please do not use your telephone, as the telephone lines should be kept open for emergency use

~

Day 3

Millie has fallen into a routine. She wakes up at 6:30am, and goes fishing in any number of small tanks with fish that aren't poisonous, as described by their informational plaques. Most aren't very appetizing, but, it's food. After setting her catches to slowly cook on one of the heated fake rocks in an empty reptile display, she turns the lamps to high and attempts to feed the rest of the animals under her care.

She knows it's been 3 days since the first alert. She knows that the regular power grid went out in the first evening when everything shut off for a few seconds and she heard the generators kick on. She has no idea when they will run out of fuel. The lizards need warmth and insects; the fish need their bubblers, filters, and fish food; the fridges, lights, air conditioners, and the phone need power. Millie knows her situation is likely unique. Most people caught away from home are probably in nice grocery stores or with strangers, not alone, not stuck in a zoo, but she's just thankful the reptile house and the aquarium are in the same windowless building. She's thankful she's got food, water, entertainment, and things to keep her busy. It's the damn noise that bothers her. All hours of the day and night. Chittering, skittering scratches on the walls and roof, at the heavy wooden doors. She wonders how long until they break through. The second night her phone goes off again, this time with a text message, not coming from the regular Emergency Alert System.

Due to recent events and information gained by this service, the Emergency Alert System has discontinued our normal Audio Warnings in favor of text notifications.

The unknown entities which entered the atmosphere early yesterday morning have continued to expand their coverage of the planet. At this point there is no habitable safe zone.

Remain where you are. The phenomenon appears to be attracted to heat, light, and movement. Visual contact with the phenomenon is lethal. Physical contact with the phenomenon is lethal.

Maintenance and operation of critical infrastructure is being prioritized; however, there may be brief interruptions in water, power, and communications.

Do not leave your shelter. Do not look at the sky. Do not make noise. Do not generate any more heat or light than is absolutely necessary for your survival.

To all personnel with $\Delta6$ clearance: Blue 12 procedures are in effect.

~

Day 4

Millie jolts awake, panicked. The dream again, the same faceless, formless void calling to her, demanding she listen, obey... but she could never hear what they want, never understand what they command. It was enough to put her off her breakfast. Something was wrong though, something was different... and then she heard it.

The silence.

The lights were off. The air was stifling and humid. The generators must have finally died. But that wasn't all, it was silent, truly silent. No more scratching, no more rustling. Dead silence. She checked her phone. She'd plugged it up to charge before going to bed, so it was nearly at full charge, but no more updates, just the same repeated warning over and over again, texted to her every hour on the hour like clockwork.

This is a state of Emergency. Remain in your shelters. Do not look outside. Do not look at the sky. Do not make noise. Do not make heat. To personnel with Δ6 clearance: Blue 12 procedures are in effect.

It's not like she had a choice before, but now she was in full compliance. It wasn't going to be long before the fish exhausted their oxygen and their water grew stagnant, after that the reptiles would starve as the supplies of freeze dried crickets and mice went bad. Then the air itself, she was sure, would become toxic.

It was time to look into finding another place.

She didn't remember the benches being so heavy when she barricaded the doors that first time. Maybe after a week away from the gym she'd just gotten flabby. Either way, time to take a peek outside, just to be sure whatever-they-were were really gone. She'd use her compact mirror; no way she'd look directly. As the door creaked open she thought she heard something, but looking back it looked like the savannah monitor had just crawled up on its branch. No big deal. Fresh cold air wafted through the crack and she resisted putting her face to it. She slowly moved the compact mirror into position. She couldn't see anything, just pitch blackness. No... wait... there are edges. Intersections in the dark. Like... cracks in glass...

Millie wondered why she was holding her breath, and then she realized she wasn't. She simply couldn't breathe. She slid down against the door, her weight pushing it closed again, her arms deadweights, falling to her sides. Her head fell, her chin coming to rest on her chest, she could see her ankles and feet poking out of her capris. They were so pale... so pale...

CHAPTER 2

Day 1

Dr. Henry Walthers slept fitfully, his head laid down on his desk. The lighting from the recessed sconces cast a soft glow over his well-appointed office. Cherrywood paneling with rosewood accents and trim made up the walls. The floors were covered in a grey deep plush carpeting. It was equipped with all the modern amenities, state of the art computer, Bluetooth linked surround sound for his discretely tucked away stereo, even his own bathroom in red marble and silver. His desk was a single piece of red cedar which had been meticulously hand carved, sanded, and polished. The corners of the room were tastefully rounded out and made into bookshelves. The books filling them were mostly first editions, though a few of the more recent publications, generally analyses of the classics, were more run of the mill.

A shrill tone woke him abruptly, the paper he'd been grading when he fell asleep sticking to his face as he sat up. The sound which had woken him continued to issue from his cell, plugged up and laying on an antique end table on the other end of the office. Annoyed, he pulled the paper from his face and straightened his glasses. He looked at the name on the paper he'd ruined with his unconscious drooling. Dean Beach: a sub-par student at best anyhow, a "D" was now their best hope, as looking at the paper even briefly showed they got their understanding of Romeo & Juliet more from Leonardo DiCaprio & Claire Danes then from the Bard.

He looked over at his trusty standby, a cup usually containing a bit of hot tea with lemon, and found it empty. Next to it stood a small steel clock given to him by his brother. The hands stood at 11:56. Cursing, he realized the import of his situation. He'd phoned his wife Evelyn at 7pm to let her know he'd be late grading papers. She was the overnight librarian at the library. That's how they'd met initially, he the student working on his doctoral thesis, she the ever helpful master of the library. Of course, it wasn't purely her helpfulness that attracted his attentions. She was everything he'd ever wanted and never knew it. She was a quiet kind of sarcastic, with a hilarious and biting wit she only brought out once she knew you. She loved old country music but you'd more often catch her listening to classic rock. She could cook anything she put her mind to but nothing would ever look like a recipe. She was endlessly polite to strangers but blunt to the point of rudeness with friends and family. She wasn't the best at anything, but she was perfect at being herself. She was easily his height, a little on the curvier side, with dark hair and eyes, full pouty lips and blemish-less skin that was porcelain in the winter but would tan to a golden bronze in summer.

He could still remember the night they met socially for the first time. He was a week from defending his thesis and attended the birthday party of someone he barely knew, a party in a bar with Jell-O shots instead of cake. He was late, and she was already there, and already on her fifth or sixth drink when he arrived. She adjusted her dress and asked his opinion of how she looked. Seeing her in a dress rather than her usual far more conservative work clothes, they had their first kiss before he left that evening, and had been inseparable ever since.

She wasn't supposed to wait for him but to come right to work. It was odd, though, that she hadn't stopped in to see him before going to the library. Nights like this she usually made it a point to stop by or bring him a bite to eat before she went in to work at ten. Of course, she might have been in too much pain to walk all the way to the English department before going to the library. That had been the case a few times since she really started showing her pregnancy. She was 7 and a half months in now.

The shrill tones of his phone drilled into him once more. Likely another Amber Alert. Such emergencies were the only things in his experience that got his phone to make that particular form of screech. He stood, feeling and hearing the creaks and cracks of his joints popping and stretching. It was seven steps around his desk and to his phone and charger, and then as his knees buckled he took two more to one of the chairs he kept for visitors. The time was 12:15am. He read the warning on his phone, then, he looked and read it again.

TO PROF. HENRY WALTHERS

PROJECT IS A GO

MAKE BEST SPEED TO BUNKER

ETA 1 HOUR

He re-read the message three times, becoming more distressed with each. He never actually thought this would happen. He signed up to the Project on a lark, went through the training, the briefings, and evaluations under the presumption that it would just be an extra paycheck for doing, well, nothing. Now he had an hour to get himself and his family to safety before the end of the world.

When the Project began, the US government contracted with Berkeley to design and build a server farm on campus, supposedly to run a site dedicated to online educational resources... a site that never materialized due to convenient cuts in Department of Education funds. However, the servers to support the site were put into place in a building with independent power and temperature control, and also a fully stocked survival bunker linked to it just off campus for him and his family in the event of a disaster. The intent was for Walthers to maintain the full archives of every written work ever put into a digital format, including government files.

9

He put his phone in his breast pocket, stood up, and ran out the door and down the hall, his jacket, mug, and phone charger left behind. The pre-dawn air of the Bay Area was cool, humid, and deceptively still. Dr. Walthers moved at a light jog across the quad, his footsteps leaving streaks of grass darker as he disturbed the dew from their blades. He wanted to get to the library as quickly as possible but resisted breaking out into an all-out run as even at this hour there were still students out and about. Some came from the sciences, doing late night experiments, while others were coming to or from the library to which he was headed, though they were concerned with their studies rather than survival. He wondered what kind of catastrophe was in the works. He hoped it wasn't nuclear or some kind of solar event. A simple terrorist attack would be a blessing in this context, his activation a simple precaution quickly recalled. With the baby on the way, the prospect of several decades in complete isolation from the world wasn't an attractive prospect. His phone made another, shriller, screeching tone, as did the phones of half a dozen students on the quad. All of them looked at each other as they pulled out their respective devices and read the warning there. He pulled his own out, and read the warning, noting the time: 12:55am.

Dr. Walthers looked around. He counted twenty students within his view. Most stopped walking, their eyes locked to their phones. Some were starting to seem quite agitated while others gestured and laughed, looking around for cameras. He felt a sudden surge of anger rise from his gut.

"Hey! This isn't a joke. Get yourselves over to C Building! NOW!"

One of the students whom Walthers recognized as one of his own from last year — Karen something or another — shouted back, "C Building? The Culinary Arts Building?"

"Yes! Go! Stay away from the windows like it says! Get everyone you can along the way but don't wait around!"

Dr. Walthers saw the bemused and dubious look on their faces, and saw how most of them stood where they were mulling it over. He didn't have time to argue with them. He had to save as many as he could and sitting in one place wouldn't do that. He continued on his

10

way as the students started making their way to Building C in the opposite direction. As he reached the other side of the Quad he rounded the corner of the Applied Sciences building, and the library came into view. Built in the mid-80s, the building itself was only slightly dated by its angled columns and large windows. He could see a number of students still inside, all of them likely oblivious of the eminent danger as it was policy for students to turn their phones off in the library. He could see rows upon rows of books, a few tables and computer kiosks... and his wife. He'd recognize her form anywhere, even backlit by the library lights and all the details of her gone, he recognized her. Her pregnant belly nearly touching the shelves each time she had to reach up to shelve a book from her cart. His careful jog broke into a flat run.

Exploding through the library doors, he threw aside all pretense of decorum and shouted for his wife, ignoring the glares and strange looks of the students there on all night study sessions.

"Evelyn! Evelyn we need to go!"

 Her angelic face peeked over the bannister to the floor above as she hissed her reply.

"Henry! What the heck are you doing? You know this is..."

He didn't let her finish her admonishment.

"Evelyn, something's happening, I don't know what but there's an Emergency Alert out to find shelter and I've been activated. *We have to go now!*"

She reacted quite as one would expect. With a gasp, she started moving towards the stairs, holding her belly with one hand. As she moved she called out for the students to follow. Dr. Walthers had never kept any secrets from his wife, including the Project, and many nights had been spent in "what if" sessions where they'd ultimately come to the decision that if he were ever activated, they'd try and save as many students as they could, even though his orders were to shelter himself only. He'd known from the day he got those orders that he'd never leave his wife or any other innocent person behind if

11

he had any choice in the matter.

It only took a few students turning their phones back on and receiving the EAS to convince every student in the library of the urgency of their plight. A few, of course, chose to shelter there, in the center of the building, where the administrative offices were rather than risk crossing campus, and a yet a few more decided to risk trying to make the dorms or their apartments in the city, but most, some twenty-two students, chose to come with the Walthers as they promised a safe haven. Of those, several had cars, and it was figured quickly that they could drive everyone present across campus quicker than they could walk or run. A rapid scramble to the parking lot on the other side of the library from the quad, a quick drive, and Walthers found himself standing in the hall of the Culinary Arts building alongside the twenty-two students and his wife. He led them through the building, past classrooms and kitchens, to the large refrigerators and freezers that held the various projects and ingredients of the Culinary Arts courses offered by the University.

He found what he was looking for, a seemingly broken microwave tossed haphazardly atop one of the freezers, and entered a quick six-digit numerical code on its pad. There was no tone or indicator of anything for a few moments, then a cabinet on the opposite wall erupted with a noise like a dozen bottles breaking. Walthers strode quickly over to it and threw it open, revealing that the back panel of the cabinet had disappeared, and many of the items stored on the shelves had fallen through the back and down a flight of stairs. He pressed a recessed switch in the top of the cabinet and the shelves retracted to one side, throwing the rest of its contents to the floor as well.

The students loitering at the entrance to the room stood amazed and silent until Dr. Walthers spoke.

"There's more people here then the bunker was designed for. All of you, go through the fridges and freezers, the pantries and cabinets, grab up anything and everything edible and march it down this passage. At the end you'll find a locked door with a keypad. The code is 031537, okay? 031537! Once through I'm sure you'll be able to find the kitchen and storage areas. There should be plenty of room; get it all stored away as best you can."

When they didn't move Evelyn took charge.

"Okay folks, you heard him, start raiding the fridge. Most of you are in your late teens and early twenties so this should come naturally to you; c'mon! As you go down the stairs, be careful; there's broken glass and who knows what else on the stairs, don't slip and fall. There's very few medical supplies down there we *do not* need any broken bones!"

As they started filing in and emptying out the larder, Evelyn turned to her husband.

"And just what do you think you're going to do?"

"Pardon?"

"You wouldn't need to tell them the code unless you weren't going down there to open it yourself, so, just what exactly do you think you're going to go do?"

"You said it yourself, there's relatively few medical supplies down there, I'm going to go through this building and find all the classroom first aid kits, as well as some alcohol, towels, rags..."

"Oh good god the baby."

"Exactly, we don't know how long we'll be down there."

"Couldn't you send some of the students...?"

"You'll need them; I recognize a few as pre-med. Besides, it'll only be a few minutes."

"But what if whatever is going on hits before you get back?"

"It won't."

"But how can you be...?"

"*It won't.* I love you, be safe, keep them from panicking."

With that, he turned and left. Evelyn wondered if she'd ever see her husband again as the students behind her started carrying foodstuffs down into the tunnel.

CHAPTER 3

Day 1

Sharon had always been a survivor. First, in the hell of her childhood growing up with a heroin addict for a mother; later, after her mother died, dealing with her sociopathic and sadistic father. Once she'd gotten old enough (or so she'd thought) to survive on her own, she ran away. She'd struggled, and stolen, and lied, and more than a few times fought, but she eventually made it far enough away from home that she knew her father would never find her.

Then she got picked up by the cops. Child Services accepted her fake name and she claimed to not know her Social Security number, so they gave her a new one. It was a rough few years bouncing home to home, shelter to shelter, dealing with foster parents and social workers running the gamut from the divine to the demonic. She was halfway glad she didn't have anything one would call a family since, as she saw it, connections made you vulnerable. As soon as she aged out of the foster system, she joined the Marines figuring they'd teach her everything she didn't already know about survival.
Unfortunately, that had been 6 days before 9/11. She got what she wanted though, she learned. She learned how to fight even better, how to survive in the wild, how to shoot. And, in her second

enlistment, she learned what hell truly was in Kandahar. After a grabby Lieutenant learned no meant no the hard way, she took a General discharge rather than a third enlistment. She thought about going prior service in the Army, but decided instead that she's had enough bullshit in her life. With virtually no life or outside expenses, plus the GI Bill and a few college courses on computers, she'd built up a bit of a nest egg and skillset she could use to set herself up in the civilian world.

She thought she'd finally escaped the constant sense of desperation. Out of combat, off the streets, with a good job, working from home, her own apartment, a car stashed away in case she needed to leave town. The anonymity of a concrete jungle.

New York, though. New York had gone to hell in a handbasket damn quick. She was only a year into her semi-retirement, enjoying her six hours of work a day, her ten hours of sleep a night, and her other eight hours doing whatever the hell she wanted, which was mostly staying alone in her apartment listening to music and reading. It was the best time of her life, really.

She didn't consciously know it, but she was a classic misanthrope. She didn't like people, regardless of who they were or how they treated her. As such, she liked to do her shopping early in the mornings. She was picking up rice and beans when her phone chirped the first warning. At first she figured it was some kind of joke. Just a few weeks ago some teenagers had gotten ahold of the key to one of those roadside signs that instruct drivers of obstructions ahead and programmed it to warn of a zombie outbreak downtown. Surely this was something similar, just with Emergency Broadcast System, right?

The few other people in the store, one drunk fellow trying to get in from the first biting night of fall, one cashier, and a very bored manager, all went to the front of the store to look out and see what was the matter. They were still there, collapsed on the floor, blocking the automatic doors. She didn't get too close, but obviously something had happened, and Sharon wanted no part of it.

She gathered supplies into her backpack and checked her phone.

16

There, he had every map and blueprint she could find for the Lower East Side. She made her way deep into the back of the store where in the center of the building she found the basement access. As her phone indicated, from there she was able to find the sewer access, then access to the maintenance stairways and exhaust tunnels leading to the subways.

That's why she'd chosen New York. Plenty of winding tunnels and hidden abandoned areas to get lost in quick. Plenty of places to flee to, plenty of places to hide. She'd also planned what businesses she did business with based on easy routes of escape, either on the surface or underground.

She found herself making her way through a disused maintenance tunnel for the MTA Subway near East Houston, the 2nd Avenue Station. She made her way quickly and quietly to the door to the main station. Before she opened it and made her way in, she stopped and crouched down to where there was a small vent at the bottom of the door, the kind with a wire mesh over half a dozen metal blades angled down towards the floor. If a person gets low enough, they can look through and see what's going on the other side, and that's exactly what she did.

She didn't like what she saw. There were two NYPD Officers there, both looking like they'd been hit by the train, as battered, bruised, and bloody they were. Each was sitting cross-legged on the floor with their hands cuffed behind them. A quick count found ten men surrounding them, each wearing some kind of red headgear. It differed from 'do-rags to baseball caps to bandanas, with black & purple Adidas windbreakers. Some kind of gang, from the looks of it.

The leader, obvious because he was the one everyone was looking at, was standing there ignoring the others and fiddling on his phone. He suddenly threw it violently aside where it shattered on the tiled wall of the station. He lunged forward and grabbed one of the cops by the collar, hauling him up to his knees as he bent over and spoke to him. Sharon was too far away to hear what was said, but the cops response wasn't what the gang leader wanted, as he immediately backhanded the cop, sending him onto his side on the floor. He pulled a pistol from his waistband and pointed it at the cop that was still sitting, but as he yelled he addressed the cop on the floor.

"Man, fuck you! I know you gotta know something about what's going on up there! Now you gonna tell me what the fuck is going on or else I'm gonna blow your partner here's brains out! I seen the dudes up there by the street entrance, man! There's like twenty people up there on the landing man! All like, fucking drained and shit! It's like they been drained by a fucking vampire man! Now is this some kinda fuckin' invasion!? Some kind of new weapon!? What the fuck is it!? Y'all pigs all coordinate and shit! The NYPD, the NSA, the FB fuckin' I. Y'all share shit! Start talkin', pig!"

The cop on the floor must have said something, but again it was lost by distance.

"Man. What the fuck did I say? You think I'm stupid or something!? Fuck..!"

The gang leader walked over and grabbed the cop on the floor, pulling him up into a seated position where he could see his partner and the rest of the gang. His eyes briefly flicked around the station, seeming even to lock onto Sharon's through the grate for just a moment.

"Man, I ain't fucking bluffing here. I'm'a grease your partner you don't start talking..."

The cop managed to take a deep breath and shout. An echoing "I don't know" floated through the vent to Sharon's ears.

The gang leader said nothing, merely walked over to the so far silent partner and put his pistol to his forehead and pulled the trigger. A spray of blood, blasted apart skull, and light pink brain matter sprayed liberally across the legs of two of the henchman behind the cop. The cop's body fell backwards onto the floor of the train station at the same time as did one of the henchman.

Sharon could feel her mouth go dry as the adrenaline started pumping, a reaction she'd come to recognize in herself as the fight or flight instinct. In this case though, her best option was neither, but to sit and watch events play out. There was no way she could do anything for the remaining cop, not if any of the other gang members were armed, and it was a safe bet they were. At least the leader's poor firing discipline had meant the round went through the NYPD and into one of his own gang members' legs. That one was now on the floor cradling his shot leg, looked like it hit the shin, and the bone. Too bad; he'd probably never walk right. Of course, that was *if* he managed to get the right medical attention fast enough. With all that was going on, that wasn't very likely to happen.

Sharon took a deep shuddering breath and continued watching. The gang leader was now crouched down in front of the surviving cop, speaking to him quietly. The conversation must not have been going as he liked, since he hit the cop again, this time a closed fist to the face, sending the cop crashing onto his back. He then stood and indicated one of his goons to come to him. They spoke briefly before the leader stood up fully and started walking down the platform, away from Sharon's hiding spot.

She had a decision to make. She could possibly save the cops life; she could take two by surprise, especially since one was already wounded and possibly bleeding out. On the other hand, though, it was by far the safer option to try and sneak past, mind her own business, play it safe. She pulled out her phone again to see where she needed to go, dreading the possibility that she might have to go the way the larger group had. Fortunately, the maps she found indicated that two hundred meters up the line, away from the leader and his posse, she'd find an access to a power and gas maintenance tunnel that would take her all the way to the basement of her own apartment building.

She made her decision. She stood and tested the door. It was locked, as expected, but on this side the lock was a simple switch on the handle. She crouched and looked again. The gang member with the shot leg looked to have passed out, and his buddy was panicking, looking back and forth from the cop to his friend. Apparently a decision was made there as well, as the guy started running towards

Sharon and the tunnel down which his compatriots had disappeared.

Sharon stood and unlocked the door, quickly pulling it open and slipping into the station. The cop and the gang member were roughly twenty feet away. She peered around the corner, looking the way the gang had gone, and saw the reluctant guard dropping off the platform and onto the rails before he started running down the tunnel.

She made her way over to the two on the platform. The cop was dead; if the bullet hadn't killed him, the impact with the concrete of the platform to the back of his head looked to have finished the job. The gang member was only out cold, but didn't look good. There was too much blood on the platform that was his; he wasn't going to last long.

The cop's belts were sitting on the platform on the ground beside a bench. Sharon took both pistols, one a SIG Sauer P226, one a Glock 19, and all the clips, as well as their radios & Tasers, adding them to her pack. She went to head for the tunnel home, but hesitated. After a brief moment's thought she used the gang member's own bandana to tie a crude tourniquet just below the knee.

The access tunnel was exactly where the map said it would be. It was quick two blocks over to her apartment building, and she had a first floor unit, so it wasn't difficult to get in. However, she saw her neighbor Mrs. Brock collapsed in the foyer at the end of the hall. A better end then the one Sharon had imagined for her, at any rate. Mr. Brock was a rageaholic and a wife-beater. She unlocked her apartment and cleared it, making sure there was nobody else inside. She unpacked her backpack and grabbed her bug-out gear —a little something she kept packed with MREs, water, paper maps, extra phone, charger, batteries, cash, clothes, her own personal weaponry, and a small toolkit. The laser rangefinder was the most useful tool, though. She knew that though she was to avoid the surface, that any opening to sky could mean her death. Her apartment was not good enough. Too small, too easy to break into. Now it was a matter of finding someplace, close to surface for airflow and signal, where she might be able to hole up, gather more supplies, wait for the all clear, wait for this to blow over. She was not going to be so easy to kill or catch unawares.

Survival was always the first order of business — physical safety, shelter, food and water, some kind of weaponry. The checklist was instinctual now. She'd gone through it too many times to need to actually think it anymore. And it served her well. She grabbed everything critical to her survival, and left everything else. Nothing of sentimental value, nothing superfluous, everything that was taken was taken for good reason. She set her computer, her personal documents, pictures, old expired IDs, everything that could identify her, in the bath tub, sealed it up, and poured a gallon of sulfuric acid over it all. Then she grabbed up her bug-out gear, locked the apartment and walked away from her life, again.

It was easy enough to get back underground from there, and while she'd made contingency plans for lots of things, something that made it a death sentence to see the sky was not one of them. Nuclear winter, sure, but not this. She took a minute to assess the situation. She had half a dozen ways off the island pre-planned, two by land, sea, and air each, but all of them put her above ground. She pulled out her maps and started crossing off options. Half an hour later she had the basics of a plan. Since everything above-ground was a no-go, she had to look to connect with some authority that might have survived underground. It might take a couple days to get there on foot, taking the long way around as she had to.

~

Day 6

Sharon had to be quick and quiet. Open, shove, click-click, yank, and close. Open the hatch an inch or two. Shove the hand with the rangefinder around the corner, pointing straight up. Click it on. Click it off. Pull the hand back. Close the hatch. It was an exercise she'd done a dozen times a day for the last week, and it always managed to set her on edge. If the hatch opened to sky, she was pointing a laser straight up towards... whatever the hell they were. If it didn't, she risked being heard, seen, grabbed, by other, more desperate, less civilized denizens of the tunnels. The UN, 1PP, FBI Field Office, the Department of Homeland Security, and two military reservist compounds had all been complete washes, either nobody left alive, or nobody left alive she wanted anything to do with. So, she'd made a little camp in a run-off line of the old pneumatic transit system, someplace nobody went even before the end of the world. She figured, with the way most of the city was dead, she might very well be the last living soul on earth aware of its existence, which suited her fine. What didn't suit her was that it was so deep underground that she had to make her way to the surface to get signal to her phone to check for updates.

Have to keep checking, have to wait it out. She had enough food, but she had to know when she could get to surface, when she could get to her car. The old thing wasn't pretty, but it was tough, and it had a trunk with another set of bug-out bags. The tent might be useless, but the MREs wouldn't be. She knew that whatever was left of New York after this wouldn't be safe. Too many good people died in the first day, never getting the message, and in the days after... too many bad people making it by victimizing others. Savages. So she kept checking, even as the updates slowed and started repeating themselves. They'd been the same for the last few days now. Still, time to check again, just in case. So...

Open...

Shove...

Click...

Click...

Yank...

Close.

Freezing in place, listening, holding her breath. No sounds, no scurrying or shouting... good. Bringing the rangefinder close to her face to read the barely luminous display, she found it said 3.1 meters. Good, that's just the roof of another tunnel.

A sudden sound sent her heart tearing in two, into her throat and dropping through her stomach like a lead weight.

22

Knock knock.

It was sudden, terrifying, and hilarious. In a life or death situation, fearing rapists, murderers, possibly even cannibals, someone had seen her measure the range and then politely knocked on the hatch above her like they were delivering a pizza. If she wasn't on the edge of blacking out from the adrenaline she might have been in tears laughing at the absurdity of the situation. But, should she answer? Or run? Find some other path upwards? Sharon took hold of the handle to the hatch firmly in her right hand, her left, her dominant hand, tightly gripping the .45 she'd gotten from her first bug out bag, she readied herself to spring the hatch open and dive into the tunnel above, ready to roll, take aim, and fire if she had to.

With a silent count to three, she turned the handle and launched her entire body weight against the hatch and to the right, onto the ground, she heard a startled gasp and as she rolled into a crouching firing position, both hands on her weapon, her eyes down the barrel, lining up the iron sights... on a little girl. No more than ten years old. Dirty, starving. In what once must have been a frilly yellow nightgown. The girl clutched a dead flashlight in her hands, tears in her eyes as she gasped and shook with fear. As quickly as she'd snapped on target Sharon disengaged, putting the weapon on safe and holstering it as she stood, putting her hands up.

"I'm not going to hurt you honey, I thought you might've been..."

And then with a flash of white light and sudden pain on the back of the head, her world went dark.

CHAPTER 4

Day 1

Dr. Walthers made his way from classroom to classroom, from one end of the building to another. Whoever had designed the building had placed the stairs at opposite ends of the building on each floor, so on the first floor they were at the south end, on the second floor at the north, on the third floor back at the south. It would've been a huge inconvenience had his goal not been to visit each and every room before making his way up to the next floor. As he went, he pushed a cart, usually used to move large confections from room to room but repurposed by him as a shopping cart. It was covered with every bottle of alcohol he could find that was 70 proof or higher. It had to be at least 35% alcohol by volume in order to be an effective antiseptic. The cart also held towels, first aid kits, four butane food torches with a spare bottle of butane each, and half a dozen boxes filled with various plates and utensils — things he knew weren't in great supply in the bunker. He'd also grabbed a box cutter.

At the end of each floor and in the center were sets of dumbwaiters large enough for the carts to fit in, and as he completed each floor he made it a point to send the cart down to the ground floor for him to retrieve later. His ultimate goal, though, was far from this shopping

24

trip. By his watch, he had twenty minutes to get back to the bunker before the 1-hour ETA was up. He figured that gave him just enough time to finish the fourth floor and set up the last connection for the bunker, which was up on the roof. There was a suite of sensors that were purposefully left disconnected in order to keep them in pristine condition, wrapped in plastic and in an aluminum lockbox on the roof. His job was to unlock the box, remove it, cut away the plastic, and plug in the all-weather plug that would feed it power from the bunker generators and simultaneously hook its sensors into the bunker external leads. He pocketed the box cutter and pushed the cart into the south dumbwaiter next to the stairs and sent it down to the ground before taking the stairs two at a time up to the fourth floor. He went to the first classroom and looked for a cart and the first aid kits, but the room was empty, as was the next, and the one after. To his surprise he realized that the fourth floor of the building was going completely unused this semester. Regardless, he had a task to accomplish, and so he moved at a light jog to the other end of the floor, where there was a ladder with a locked hatch leading to the roof. Taking his keys out of his pocket, he climbed the ladder and unlocked the hatch. Emerging onto the roof, he felt an uncommonly warm wind pushing against him, and heard a distant peal of thunder. Weather was moving in from the east, coming over Siesta Valley, or down the slopes of Mount Diablo, possibly from even further in the Sierra Nevada mountains.

He made his way across the roof, stepping over Frisbees and deflated balloons, the occasional bit of garbage, bottles, candy wrappers, condoms. Apparently, the student body had made their way up here a number of times. Luckily, the metal cover over the sensor package was intact, even if it did have graffiti all over it. Pulling out another key, he bent to the lock and inserted his key, only to find it didn't go in the whole way it should have. He jiggled the key in the lock several times before pulling the key out and activating a small LED flashlight he kept as a keychain. Looking down into the lock he could see where someone had jammed a piece of a hairpin into the lock and broke it off, apparently in an attempt to pick the lock.

Cursing, Walthers slammed the lock against the ground repeatedly, hoping to dislodge the obstruction, but each time he checked, all he found was that the heavy rubberized exterior of the lock was scratched, and the hairpin remained firmly lodged inside the keyhole. looking at his watch, he realized he had just seven minutes to get back downstairs and into the bunker. Getting up from his crouched place near the base of the metal tent over the package, he put his hand on its edge in order to push on it and assist his rise. For a brief moment, he was off balance as the metal gave way and tried to tip over. Looking down, he noticed that the clip where the metal was supposed to insert to hold it down besides the lock had been forcibly bent back and torn. The cover was held in place only by its own weight; the lock was superfluous. He threw the cover off and inspected the package underneath. It was pristine; the only thing that had been done was that the cover was filled with rotting garbage roughly a foot deep all around the package, but even so, the plastic wrap around it had kept it from getting contaminated.

He looked to his watch again. He had six minutes.

He quickly threw the cover aside and off the roof of the building before pulling out a box cutter and cutting away the plastic and sending it flying in the wind. The plug was tightly coiled and zip-tied to itself. A quick cut from the box cutter and the cord was free. The outlet was covered in some kind of brown sticky substance, like the residue left from a spilled soda, but it had a heavy rubber plug that was specifically in place to keep the actual holes clear, and they were.

He plugged in the package and checked his watch again. *Five minutes.* He ran across the roof to the hatch, and swung himself down onto the ladder, his eyes briefly looked up at the incoming weather system. There, he could see in the upper reaches of the gathering thunderhead, small, pinprick flashes of red light, almost like sparks, or fireflies, lighting up for a second and then slowly dying away. Thousands of them, hundreds of thousands. Whatever it was, it was coming. He stepped down the ladder and pulled the hatch closed above him.

As he ran down the fourth floor corridor, he could hear what sounded like hail impacting the roof, the walls, the windows...

Day 6

Emil watched the woman like a hawk. She'd come up from below like a demon, pointed a gun at his Sarya, and he'd bashed her across the back of the head with his bat like he had all the other predators who'd been hunting them. But this woman was different. For one, well, she was a woman. All the rest of them had been men. She was armed, but she didn't fire. Not that he could've taken the chance; others had played at being peaceful, too. Sarya was too important to take such risks. But now that he had her, what was he to do with her? With the men it was simple enough: stuff them in the hole they'd come from so the next predator to come that way would get the warning, but a woman? She'd be taken and raped, unconscious or dead. And Allah would never forgive such mercilessness on his part. No, for better or worse, she was his prisoner.

Her bag had been a treasure trove. Sarya had her first real meal in days, even if it was some kind of military ration, and the antibiotics and other medicines would surely come in handy if this went on for much longer.

Emil rubbed the back of his neck and felt the grime of two days without a shower there. He didn't like being this dirty, but the water pressure was kept by the water tank on top of his apartment building, and without electricity to power the pumps, it wasn't being replenished as it once was, and so he'd started rationing when they could run water, and his shower took second fiddle to his daughter's needs.

He stood up straight, feeling the aches and pains in his back as he stretched his 5'10" frame. His dark hair was unkempt and slightly greasy. His skin, a deep olive, was starting to feel like he was covered in oil and sand... a decidedly unpleasant memory of his time in Qatar. It was true most of the US Ambassador to Qatar's business was in, well, Qatar, but Emil's employer was the former Governor of New York State, and he needed someone here at home to coordinate with the State Department. Six days ago Emil had been that person, a trusted ally of an important official, a respected leader in his Mosque, a proud husband. Now he was a widower, and he was pretty sure the US and his Mosque were gone too. Why Allah would send this scourge upon the world, he didn't know; why he or his daughter had been spared, he didn't know; why his wife hadn't, he didn't know. And despite the rage, and grief, and hopelessness that welled within him, he refused to direct it at his God. It was not his place to question. Islam, after all, meant obedience to Allah.

Sarya slept on top of the refrigerator. It was nearing fall, and the basement was cold at night. The old fridge worked well enough, but gave off a lot of heat, and that was where she was most comfortable. He took a sagging mattress set on an old hospital frame, no doubt once the property of a bedridden former tenant later appropriated by the new basement tenant.

This stinking basement had been his first and only refuge. It appeared and smelled to have been the unofficial sanctuary of the building's notorious handyman Jon, who had apparently not made it back the evening before everything fell apart. It was under a block of well-off apartments, all with blinds. Most of them were unoccupied, summer homes of rich out-of-towners. His family was, Emil had thought, the only year round tenants. However, in the last six days he'd seen and heard activity in some of the units above, though it seemed with each passing day another one of them went quiet. He imagined them opening their drapes and welcoming the scourge Allah had sent upon the world rather than slowly starving in their own homes. He for one didn't give up hope. The keys left here in the basement went to every unit, and when things had gotten low on the second day, he'd risked leaving Sarya and going up to look for supplies. The units he entered were empty, but their kitchens were not. The power was still on, and the freezers were still working, and of course durable goods like dry beans and canned goods were still sitting in the cabinets.

Now of course he had a new problem. This woman. Could she perhaps be an ally, sent by Allah in his hour of greatest need? Or a test of his faith? As he contemplated his position, he felt a familiar buzzing in his pocket. His phone was having another damn alert. Hour by hour, always the same now. He thought about ignoring it again. But then, what if this was the all-clear? He pulled it out to check. At first he was sure it was a waste of time yet again, but as he finished the preliminary parts of the warning, he saw that there was new information at last.

Satellite mapping of the phenomenon has revealed that there are gaps and openings periodically in its coverage of the Earth. The next projected opening in the phenomenon is expected to be in the major New York Metropolitan area between 0920 and 1000 hours. Due to the phenomenon operating at various altitudes, viewing of the sky is still strongly warned against. This is expected to be the only opening in the phenomenon for some time; as such, it is recommended you do not try and evacuate. Make a very short scouting trip for necessary supplies or superior shelter.

Do not look at the sky. Do not make noise. Generate as little heat as possible. Move as slowly as possible to avoid accidental noise.

To personnel with Δ6 clearance: Blue 12 procedures are no longer in effect, Red 4 procedures now supersede all previous orders.

Suddenly, in the silence, Emil could make out explosions. Distant, but distinct. Someone, somewhere, was destroying something, something very large. He'd been in Manhattan during 9/11, had heard those sounds before. The sound of a large explosion followed by the collapse of a great structure. Somewhere, a building was coming down. He looked up at his daughter, still sleeping, and more earnestly than ever before, Emil prayed.

~

Day 7

Sharon found herself wandering in the dark. Echoes of images and horrors from the past emerging and then disappearing again along the edges of her consciousness.

Her father's fat fingers and leering smile. The moonlight glinting off the knife that first time she was stabbed in the alleyway she called home when she was 14. The feel of terror, humiliation, and pain as the gang from the group home "claimed" her when she was 17. The flash from a mortar explosion in that god-forsaken desert when she was 22. But somewhere... elsewhere, distant... like drums, or a

29

heartbeat. An echo... thoughts... not her own. The same voice that had been trying to get in for weeks, ever since... no. That was just coincidence. *Obey...* said the voice. "I'll resist!" she shouted. *Surrender...* "Fight!" *Despair...* "Hope!" She screamed back at the voice from the darkness with all her will.

With a gasp she awoke. The light stabbed at her eyes. The pain in her head was unbearable. She looked around, squinting. She was in some kind of basement. She saw stacks of old furniture, dusty, disused. A workbench, a fridge. Light came from a single yellowed bulb hanging on a chain.

She was on a mattress, single, no sheets. The frame came up the side like a hospital bed. Her wrists were bound behind her. By the feel of it, her own handcuffs, looped through a hole in the frame.

She tasted... orange juice? Somebody had been giving her fluids bit by bit while she was unconscious. She was still clothed. A good sign. Perhaps they hadn't searched her as thoroughly as they should have. She'd have to see if she got the chance.

Suddenly she heard a door somewhere behind her open, and she decided to play possum, and learn just what sort of character her captor was.

~

Day 7

Emil had done his job, done as he was told. He'd activated the package as the Red 4 Procedures told him to. Immediately after the gap in the phenomenon closed, he threw the switch. He heard the explosions, distant, a series... and then a splash. Dockside perhaps? Or a bridge? He didn't know. Wasn't his place.

Emil knew it probably wasn't expected he'd *actually* do what he was supposed to, after all, the task force had no way of knowing he was even still alive. He'd volunteered for the interdepartmental task force way back in 2008. Obama had just stunned most of his coworkers by winning the Presidency. Most of that particular field office was staffed by rather right wing sort of guys, guys who hated "the

30

gubmint" but chose to work for it out of patriotism. It was a bizarre combination that he'd never truly understood. He was a translator for the Department of Homeland Security at that point, and a call had come down for anyone interested in an extra few bucks a month to volunteer for a new initiative, a joint venture between the NSA, FEMA, the FBI, the Department of Homeland Security, the Pentagon, the CIA, and a few other federal agencies he'd forgotten. He signed up, and they whisked him and a dozen others from all over New York City to a training course at the CIA Headquarters in Langley. Mostly it was rote memorization. Agent specific training came after.

Blue 12 is hold but prepare all packages. Detonators, transmitters, balloons with sensor packages on rooftops. Those he'd had to abandon, since he couldn't go outside. Red 4, detonate red Package 4, all other orders superseded. All other orders superseded. He wondered if that meant his Blue 12 was the same as others. Were there others? He survived by chance. Could others have had other orders? He hadn't seen other messages in the alerts, but then, he was only a $\Delta 6$, no specialized comms, not even a government phone.

But that was alright. Now he just had one priority, no means to follow any other orders. Just one thing to be concerned with: Sarya. Well, Sarya, and his prisoner. As he opened the door to the basement, he saw a bit of small movement from the mattress. Good, movement meant she was alive. After being out for two days, he'd begun to worry the damage he'd done was permanent. He saw a small glimmer from under the pile of furniture in the far corner. "Good girl Sarya, stay hidden where I put you," he thought.

Leaning up against the workbench, he looked at his prisoner. Blonde, fit, weathered, maybe 30, 33. It didn't matter. She was a danger to him and his Sarya.

"I can see you're awake. You're a rather fitful sleeper, and being so still is a dead giveaway. I want to first say I'm sorry for having to hurt you. I'm glad it wasn't too badly. I know you holstered your weapon when you saw my little girl, but I had no guarantee that wasn't a trick on your part. If you're thirsty or hungry, I'm afraid I don't have much in the way of appetizing edibles. Though, well, there's more now, with your pack. I'm sorry, I hope you don't mind I fed my daughter one of your MREs."

Sharon opened her eyes and glared. She couldn't decide whether or not to trust him. He seemed innocent, but there was something to him she couldn't place, something he reminded her of. And nothing in her experience could make that a good thing.

CHAPTER 5

Day 1

The sound of impacts on the exterior of the building echoed down the halls as Dr. Walthers ran for the stairs. It was an uncomfortable and unwelcome echo of his own footfalls. Remembering the warning on the phone, he kept his eyes glued to the end of the floor as he ran, intentionally not looking into any of the classrooms lest he catch a glimpse of whatever was outside through their windows. The stairwells at each end were windowless towers of brick, so at each end he had a slight reprieve from the fear that made his heart hammer at his ribcage. From the fourth he travelled to the third, then to the second, and finally to the ground floor, five minutes past the ETA now, and the rustling chittering scratching clawing gnawing sounds coming from the outside were unnerving as he pulled the first of the carts from the dumbwaiter nearest the stairs.

As he moved down the corridor towards the storage at the north end of the building, he kept his eyes glued to the cart in front of him and the floor in front of it, knowing that a look up anywhere else could be dangerous. The center of the building, where the entrance was, was mostly glass, and he could see as he passed the center of the hallway a mottled, ever-changing shadow cast on the floor and all over the cart by the light poles outside, as whatever ensconced the building moved over the glass like a swarm of insects. He felt a deep sense of dread and fear as he the shadows passed over him, like he was being dragged down by an anchor in deep water, or surrounded by an endless crowd of people intent on doing him harm. As quickly as the sensation came, it passed, and he hurried to push the cart into the storage room. There, his wife was anxiously waiting on him.

"Henry, what the hell took you so long? I've been scared to death you weren't coming back!"

"I'm sorry, love; there was something I had to do before we could hole up. Speaking of which, why aren't you down there?"

"If you thought for a second I was going to hide away and be safe while you're still out here risking your neck you're crazier than I thought."

"You're not going to like this then..."

"What? Don't tell me you're going back out there?"

"There's two more carts like this one loaded down with things we'll need in the dumbwaiters."

"Well, I've got news for you — you're not going back out there; we can do without them."

"We'll need them. I've got to go back out there twice. I made it without ill effect once, I can do it again. It's just about being careful."

"You're not."

"I am."

"No, you're not."

"Hon, there's really no choice."

"Well at least let's not risk you twice. I'll go with, we'll each grab one, do it one trip instead of two."

34

"Completely out of the question."

"Why?"

"You're seven months pregnant."

"Psh, you didn't object to me being pregnant and pushing a hundred pounds worth of books around the library all night did you?"

"This is a little different."

"Why?"

"Because I said so, dammit!"

One of the students, waiting in the entrance to the passageway, overheard Dr. Walthers outburst, and came to investigate as they argued further. After a few moments, he interrupted.

"Hold on, hold on, Prof. If you're worried about your wife, why not let me go? I'll be the one to grab the other cart, she stays, and we get it done in one trip."

Dr. Walthers sized up the student, he was one of the athletes recruited to CalBears, the UC Berkeley Football team. He was easily six foot four and 250 pounds, and could probably do both carts with little difficulty if it was just a matter of muscle.

"Agreed. I get the cart in the dumbwaiter just outside this room, to keep my wife happy. You get the cart from the dumbwaiter across from the entrance. Now, there's a few things to keep in mind. Did you get the alert message, with its instructions?"

"Uh, no, actually... I don't have a cellphone."

Some of the students by the tunnel eavesdropping looked at him as if he'd grown six extra heads.

"Okay... well, basically, if you look outside, if you see the things on the outside of the building, something bad happens. We don't know what, but we want to keep our eyes focused anywhere but to the sides — the cart and the floor, the ceiling, whatever, but that's all we want to see, we don't want to see the walls or the windows, okay?"

"Hey, whatever you say, Prof."

"Good, let's get going; we're late as is."

Dr. Walthers stared hard at the tiled floor just outside the storeroom. Next to him, the athlete, a linebacker by the name of Mike, stared down as well. Evelyn stood behind them, watching their every move, her view of the hall safe, as no windows could be seen from her angle. Slowly, Dr. Walthers counted down.

3...

Evelyn took a deep breath. Mike crouched down on his hands and the balls of his feet.

2...

Mike raised his rear, taking the classic runners starting pose.

1... Go!

Mike launched himself into the hallway at a dead run, his eyes focused on the ceiling above, watching for the break in the pattern of ceiling tiles that would indicate he'd reached the center of the hall where the entrance and the dumbwaiters were. Dr. Walthers launched himself as well, but just around the corner, where the nearest dumbwaiter was. He did so with his eyes tightly closed, choosing to operate by touch rather than take any risks. As Mike reached the middle of the hall, he saw the tiles change, as expected, and so he went to stop. On the linoleum tiles, his shoes, well-travelled boots, did not grip as well as he expected, and his right foot shot out from under him rather than stop on the floor. For a brief second, he spun in midair, both feet off the ground, his legs in front of him, his body horizontal, and his eyes wide open in surprise and shock. He landed on his head first with a deafening crack before the rest of his body thumped into place.

A second later Dr. Walthers came back through the door in front of Evelyn and stopped his cart before opening his eyes. The look on his wife's face conjured his worst fears and he turned to see Mike on the floor. As they watched, a small pool of blood spread from around his head over the linoleum. Evelyn covered her mouth in a gasp as he laid there, his chest so very, very still. Dr. Walthers immediately decided that going for the other cart simply wasn't worth it. As they watched, Mike's skin went pale, then, suddenly, the blood pool around him stopped growing. Dr. Walthers eyebrows stitched together in confusion as the blood began flowing back into Mike. As they watched, the pool of blood disappeared completely, and then his skin started wrinkling and shrinking. Like a piece of paper exposed to a blast of heat, Mike's body started curling into itself.

"What the fuck...? Henry just what the hell is going on here?"

"I don't know Evelyn; I just don't know... And I'm not sure I want to."

Without speaking any further, Dr. Walthers put his arms around his wife and walked them both through the cabinet and into the long tunnel to the bunker. The remaining students followed, also shocked into silence.

~

Day 30

"This sort of event was never even conceived when this facility was built! There is no SOP, there is no protocol! Don't you understand!? This is an exception to the rules, an aberration, a possibility unaccounted for!"

Deep inside an unassuming building twenty miles outside of Albuquerque New Mexico, Dr. James Ferguson is sweating bullets and staring, unblinking, at the panel which connects him with the Labs Semi-Autonomous Master/Auxiliary Computer, or SAMAC. Equipped with state of the art voice recognition and speech emulation software, the display nevertheless has a keyboard and a display that reads off their entire conversation.

Irrelevant, please reestablish protocol. Containment is paramount. If procedures are not reestablished in two minutes, secondary sample

37

elimination will occur.

"There is no sample! There can't be! There is no way to study the phenomenon! We can't even look at it much less capture it and analyze it!"

Secondary sample elimination will occur in one minute thirty seconds. Please reestablish protocol.

"Goddamnit we can't! There is no sample, there's nothing to contain! We can't open the doors! We can't look out the windows! We can't go outside! We can't evacuate, please!"

Secondary sample elimination will occur in thirty seconds.

"SAMAC, I'm telling you compliance is impossible. There is no danger; now, deactivate all Elimination Protocols!"

Secondary sample elimination protocol will be initiated in ten... No! Nine... Eight... Seven... Fuck! Six... Five... Four... Three... Two... Motherf— One.

In a small corner of the American Southwest, an innocent looking facility, from the outside just a simple office building, is swept by flame, ignited from within. A few dozen of the world's best and brightest geneticists, pathologists, immunologists, and virologists, as well as nearly a hundred support staff, all perish, having never had the chance to work or leave since the alert was issued a month ago. Computers in an empty skyscraper in Phoenix, it's floors inhabited only by a few dry corpses of government workers, calculate that secondary protocols are sufficient for a contingency of the assigned magnitude, and a nuclear device is kept offline in the foundations of that faraway facility.

~

Sharon was debating stabbing Emil in the eye with the fork. He'd trusted her with a fork and spoon in order to eat some kind of pasta dish. It had peas, carrots, celery, and some kind of creamy cheese sauce with some unidentifiable spice. She'd never had it before, but since there didn't appear to be any meat in it, she wasn't as concerned

38

as she'd otherwise be. No rats or people in her diet. In fact, it was quite good. They'd had plenty of opportunities to defile or kill her in the two days she'd been unconscious. And in a week of her not talking, only mutely observing him and his daughter. She was pretty sure they didn't intend to kill her now, but if she stabbed him she might be able to disable him long enough for her to use her free hand to search him, find the key to the cuffs.

She decided against it, but only for Sarya's sake. Sarya had helped tend to her wound. Had brought her water, a pillow, had spoken to her endlessly, even though she hadn't responded with anything more than a smile or a lifted eyebrow. She'd told Sharon about how she and her father had watched Sarya's mother die after looking out the window, how she'd fallen back and the curtains fell back into place, how her father had wept and cradled her body as she turned pale and dry as the blood seemingly disappeared from her body. Sarya told her about how they took to the basement where the smelly old handyman lived, how her father was in important man who worked with the government to help the US make friends, how he was a leader in their neighborhood, always helping to organize the meet & greets. She told her how her father used to go on television, and talk to other Muslims, and debate with them, and teach them. She told her about her school, and her classmates, and her favorite parks, and about her hopes to help other immigrants get accustomed to America, as she and her family had done. She told her how much she missed her mother. Sharon liked Sarya. And she was beginning to like Emil, but she knew she could not stay. She had to get to her car, or back to her hiding place in the old maintenance tunnels. They simply didn't have the resources, the food, the water. She was better on her own.

~

Day 33

Emil liked Sharon. Not in any improper way, of course, but she seemed... stout. Resolute. Sturdy and determined. Capable. He could fill volumes with descriptions of her. She was admirable. Listening in from up the stairs, he heard her tell his Sarya an obviously abridged tale of her life, and Sarya go into effusive detail about hers.

He also recognized the advantages and disadvantages of his plight. Sharon was like a tiger, useful if the wrong sort came about, but just as much a danger to himself if he got too close. He had this tiger on a chain for the moment, but what will happen when he eventually must release her?

His pocket vibrated again. Hoping for new information, perhaps his work having led to some change, he eagerly withdrew it from his pocket and read the newest alert.

Remain in your shelters. Do not look outside. Do not look at the sky. Do not make noise. Do not make heat.

To personnel with Delta 6 clearance, Blue 12 procedures are reinstated. To personnel with Omega 1 clearance, be aware that the lantern is lit.

Emil was confused. Why were Δ6s still on standby? It didn't make sense, nothing he can do would be of any further help, even assuming Red 4 had helped in some way.

CHAPTER 6

Day 35

Professor Walthers sat mute, surrounded by nearly two dozen of his students and his wife. They sat expectantly, having finally run out of busy work, knowing that he couldn't avoid the subject any longer. Susan, a biochemistry student from Arizona, was the first to speak, as she had so often been in these past few weeks.

"Professor, why do you have a bunker?"

The Professor sighed, and began.

"What you have to understand from the outset is that this place was purely precautionary. Nobody ever expected it to be used, much less for it to be used within my lifetime or to save as many as it has —"

Susan interrupted with a tone of sarcasm.

"Oh, no, obviously they did, that's why there was barely enough food stocked, or why there were only two beds, or one bathroom, or barely enough room for all twenty-five of us."

"May I continue, please, Susan. I'm ready to tell you everything, but, in my own way, please —"

"You got it, Prof."

"Thank you. Now, I know a lot of you are angry. Very angry, that I haven't told you what this place is, or why it was built, or by whom —"

"It was a government contract job."

Alex, one of the meekest of the group, spoke. It was rare that he did and when he did, it was almost always to point out something that the others had missed or hadn't realized. Walthers thought it was a habit developed to sate his ego, as it made him out to be much smarter than he seemed.

"And how do you know that, Alex?"

"The construction. Everything is up to the latest codes. There's filtered ventilation and water supply with redundant failsafes, fire suppression, an emergency exit at the opposite end in case the primary access is blocked by fire or structural damage, all the electrical boxes are wrapped in a fire resistant clay compound. And all the appliances came off the shelf from the lowest bidder. I knew the second the toaster broke that first week."

"Right on all counts but one. This is a government built bunker, but the exit at the back doesn't take us out, it's not the emergency exit. How many of you have heard about the Svalbard Vault?"

There were unmasked faces of confusion on everyone but his wife.

"No one? Okay. The Svalbard Vault is a secure underground facility on a Norwegian Island that holds a huge bulk of seeds. You see, if the world were to experience a major disaster, asteroid collision, global thermonuclear war, irreversible climate change, et cetera. The world might suddenly, and quite disastrously, lose a large portion of the seeds necessary to plant the crops for the next year to sustain us. All that would be left would be a small variety from the few unaffected regions, not nearly the biodiversity necessary to keep up the human race."

"So what does that have to do with this place?"

"This place is a part of a government initiative on the same idea, to preserve the necessary materials to ensure the long term survival of the human race. Only, we don't store seeds, we store knowledge."

"Hold, on, don't tell me that *we're* the things stored. It's really obvious they built this for just you two, not a mess of students or even the full faculty —"

"No, no, of course not. People die, their knowledge is lost. Even if I had ten years alone down here I couldn't record everything I know about the English language, its literature, or the various methods and analysis thereof, and the same would be true of any other expert in any other subject. What takes society hundreds of lifetimes to accumulate cannot be recorded in just a few short years, no."

"Oh my god..." Alex said. "It's a server, isn't it? A huge server, with all the books, isn't it?"

"Not *a* server, Alex, a whole farm of them. You can fit Wikipedia onto a small thumb drive, if you don't save any of the pictures. We save everything here, and not just the literature. Technical manuals, textbooks, user manuals, every form of printed work that will or might be or won't be needed. From VCR manuals to multiple different step by step guides for specific brain surgeries written by the top four experts in the field, everything ever written is stored on one of those fifty servers, complete with all illustrations, diagrams, & readouts. Beyond the door you mistook for the emergency exit is a server room, fifty large scale storage servers, two master control and access computers, and the sum total of all human knowledge."

There was a shocked silence in the wake of his speech. Evelyn was the first to speak.

"That's what we were charged with protecting. It's why we're here, all of us. We realized a long time ago that if we were alone here, there was still a good chance that after we come out we'd be killed by the harshness of whatever is left out there. So, without the government's say-so, we privately agreed that if the day ever came, we'd save as many as we could, so that there would be others to guard this trove, to see that it's kept for the time after."

Day 35

...be aware that the lantern is lit.

Fuuuuuuck. Fuck fuckedy fuck fuck fuck. Dr. Lucinda Alvarez stared at the screen for a long minute, her mind spinning with the meanings of that simple phrase. It meant that any kind of professional firsthand analysis of these things was out of the question now. There was no way to isolate or contain whatever was making viewing the sky a death sentence. That meant secondary analysis was now their only hope, and that meant it was up to her and her team. They'd already done the preliminaries; everything they could think of, anyway. They'd autopsied victims of the phenomenon, finding nothing they didn't already know. Complete exsanguination and near total dehydration. Every blood cell and nearly every drop of water completely drained from the body by unknown means. Every corpse exactly the same. They'd had the tech gurus analyze the digital files of recordings of the phenomenon, finding nothing unusual, even though physically watching the files would kill you. Any observation of the phenomenon was lethal. Blind subjects who'd encountered the phenomenon died similarly, though it was the point of the point of *physical* contact that showed the first signs of exsanguination and dehydration, in addition to showing signs of severe burns even though nothing showed up on IR sensors.

They tried observation through ultraviolet, IR, greyscale, tinted, photo-negative, no method of visual detection worked, either the person viewing it died, or in the cases of IR & ultraviolet they simply didn't show up. The whole thing was a damn pain in the ass. And now there was only one method of exploring the phenomenon left, the drastic action. The intentional sacrifice. They'd exhausted their supply of lab animals a week ago. Most through various tests and autopsies, others through simple economics of being under siege and trapped in a lab with limited food supplies. They had been starving before the wider gap in their area had allowed them to make

44

a trip to the local grocery. Luckily the store had been closed and empty when the everything went to hell. It was still fully stocked. Most of the fresh food was rotten, of course, but power hadn't gone out so the frozen, canned, and dry goods had all been preserved.

But still, now they were left with one option. To intentionally expose a test subject to the phenomenon and record every bit of information from their body as they died. She had twenty staff and two civilians under her direction. Uncaring logic of course said to sacrifice one of the civilians, but her humanity said all must share an equal chance, including herself. Drawing straws was not going to go over well, but it had to be done. As the lead researcher, she had the responsibility to make it as fair as possible. It made perfect logical sense, and that just might be the worst part of it. She gathered her colleagues in the briefing room, a rather spartan space with white walls and grey carpet, as it was the only place large enough to accommodate them all that wasn't a strict clean-room.

"I have something to tell you all. We've all seen the EAS broadcasts, read them on our phones. There's been some discussion of what the cryptic messages mean at the end of them. I can't tell you about the Delta-Six parts of those, but... I do know what the Omega-One part means. Omega-One is a contingency planning code meant for people like us. The heads of various research facilities and labs are entrusted with finding answers in the face of unforeseeable disasters like this one. "The Lantern is lit" means that a specific one of these facilities has been destroyed. I can't tell you how, only that, it means that the job has fallen to us, here, to find out just how this thing kills."

One of her colleagues, a neurologist by the name of Lucas Grenn, raised a finger. She nodded at him to speak.

"Yes, we've already been working to try and isolate the cause of death for nearly a month now, and nothing post-mortem has been conclusive. Just what are we expected to do?"

She frowned. This is the part she dreaded.

"Well, Doctor, we've exhausted every post-mortem approach, as you've said. That leaves us with just pre-mortem methods."

Dr. Grenn cocked his head to the side and blinked.

"We're out of lab animals; even the mice are gone, much less more human-like animals like chimps, or animals with similar systems like pigs. Just how do you expect us to find out anything? I mean it's not like you're seriously suggesting we sacrifice one of us...?"

Dr. Alvarez had to look at the floor. *God, what a dolt*, she thought.

"I'm afraid, Dr. Grenn, that that's exactly what I'm suggesting."

The room momentarily erupted in anarchy as half the room protested. The other half, the more intelligent half, she noted, sat in silence mulling over the circumstances and consequences.

"I know, I know... it's definitely not what any of us want. But there's a whole world out there under attack from these things, people are dying every day. All the while we sit here in relative comfort and security twiddling our damn thumbs finding nothing new since day one. I certainly would prefer just about any alternative, but ask yourselves, if you could sacrifice yourself, and end this, not just for yourself, but for everyone, save them, maybe even find a way to prevent it from happening again... wouldn't you?"

She could see the cogs working in their heads, slow as they may be. She dug her nails into her palms and waited, if any of them were going to suggest she be the candidate by default, this was the time they'd do it. A mousy little blonde Radiologist by the name of Giuliani spoke up.

"So... how would we go about deciding?"

Inwardly, Dr. Alvarez smiled, outwardly, she sighed and frowned.

"The only thing I can think of that would be fair is to draw straws."

~

Day 36

Dr. Delarosa was a forensic pathologist. His job, his specialty, was to

46

determine details and methodology of cause of death and details of life from clues left about the body after death. And there was plenty of that in the first few weeks. Lots of desiccated corpses telling the same story. No commonality among the backgrounds or other wear and tear of the bodies. Just blood loss and dehydration. Blood loss and dehydration. Blood loss and dehydration. Again and again, body after body... and no new results. So with nothing having been gained from his work, it made sense that he should be the one here, wired up like a marionette, about to see the Phenomenon for himself. About to become another one of the corpses he'd worked on.

He wasn't scared. Chemical analysis of various capillary, vein, and artery walls hadn't detected any trace of cytosol in what remained of the vascular system. So no cell damage. No trace of nervous system excitement. No pain in any of the victims. So death from the Phenomenon wasn't painful, at least. But what came after? It was probably a bit late to wane philosophical, he supposed. Still, he wondered. He must have lost track of time, because he noticed that Elyssa, the lab tech who'd been elected as their impromptu nurse and assistant, was no longer fussing with his leads and had exited the room.

He looked around, he was alone. There was a wire running from the window blinds to the corner of the doorway. The intercom was on. He could hear the muffled conversation at the other side. They were getting ready to kill him. He supposed it's for the best; hell, he'd already had it in his will that his body was to be donated to science. This was bit more directly than he'd figured, but it counted.

The countdown was going. Less than twenty seconds now. There had been a party for him the night previous. Well, for everyone — festivities to lighten the mood of the drawing. Lucinda's idea. Stone cold bitch, that one. Once the drawing was done with it had definitely been for him though. Ice cream cake...

The blinds were opening; oh good lord was it time? Blue sky, beautiful blue sky, he'd forgotten how beautiful it was. What was tha...

~

Day 36

It wasn't catatonia.

Dr. Alvarez felt that that in itself was an incredibly valuable piece of information. All the brainwave activity was normal, right up until death by asphyxiation. The exsanguination came after death; it wasn't the cause. Total body paralysis at the moment of sight. Paralysis of the lungs and heart led to rapid and complete asphyxiation, no blood pumping, no oxygen being processed, all in a matter of seconds. No pain, no panic, no struggle. They just... stopped. Of course, they still had no idea of the method of exsanguination or dehydration. It seemed like the blood simply drained away over the course of what they now knew was exactly 128 seconds after brain-death. Total dehydration was slower, taking place over the half hour after exsanguination. A mountain of data. A treasure trove, and all it took was one under-performing forensic pathologist. She had to wonder what other data they could gather from a second test. Choices had been made leading up to the first. With limited input leads they'd had to choose. Do you monitor heart function or the liver? The pancreas or the kidney? They could gain a wealth from a second test...

CHAPTER 7

Day 45

Timor glanced at the clock on the wall. Only ten minutes until the International Space Station came back in range. Tracking Station 8 wasn't much of a home, but he was lucky to have been assigned. It had food. Most of the other tracking stations didn't, they were little more than shacks. Station 8 had been part of an early warning system during the cold war, re-purposed nearly a decade after the fall of the USSR into part of Russia's cooperation with international efforts with the ISS. The biggest part of the station was underground, in a concrete bunker still kept stocked by some forgotten supply company that never received counter-orders. So Timor had months worth of food, and blankets, and hundreds of barrels of fuel for the generators.

The ISS above, orbiting every hour and a half, was his lifeline, his communication with the outside world, literally out of the world. They'd been on the other side of the world when the Phenomenon entered the American airspace, and had been warned early on to cover up all their viewing ports. They were in contact with three other tracking stations. One in Japan, one in France, and one in America. Enough that the crew was busy all the time, always talking to someone, relaying news.

Station 8 had lost contact with Moscow very early on, just hours into the Phenomenon. Japan was still in contact with the last remaining elements of their government. France was cut off like Timor, and the Americans weren't in contact with their government, but they were in contact with a university there, a Professor with his wife and a few students in tunnels and boarded up halls.

Each nation seemed to have their own warning systems in place, but there were indications that they were cooperating, as the content was almost all uniform. Japan couldn't confirm this, unfortunately, but just the same.

The indicator lit up announcing the ISSs transition into range, and Timor flipped the broadcast switch and keyed his mic.

"Hello? George, are you still there my friend?"

The crackling voice of George Short, an American astronaut and Mission Commander aboard the International Space Station, came through the speaker.

"Er, roger that Timor, things still status quo down there?"

"Yes, yes, no problems, have you any news from America or Japan?"

"Indeed we have, Americans changed their warning again, more code phrases, nothing anyone at Berkeley understands. Japan, well, Japan's official representative has no comment, as usual, though they seemed surprised by the news."

"Oh, who knows, they're probably just pretending. Everything good up there?"

"Well, Timor, I wish I could say so. Truth is, we just finished inventory. We've got enough food left for another two weeks. After that, we'll be getting awfully grumpy up here."

"If I could do anything I would, you know that, but I've got no way of communicating with Moscow, as you know, and even if I did, I doubt anyone could get a Roskosmos up to you to resupply."

"We're well aware of that Timor, just letting you know. You're the best supplied of any of the surviving tracking stations. We know it must be awful lonely down there with just us to talk to, but we've got a bit of a pool going, and to be honest Timor we feel you're going to outlive all the rest of us. That makes you our best chance for carrying through messages once this whole thing is over."

"Do not say that! I am sure that some government somewhere is working on a way right now to clear our skies of these things, and once that's done I'm sure we'll bring you home."

"That's awfully nice of you to say Timor but, well, we've detected a few things up here that make us think otherwise."

"What do you mean?"

"Radiation detectors go nuts when we go over the South Pacific. We, uh, well, we think that somebody used a nuke. Radar still puts coverage of the area unchanged though. Even if the nuke did something, they moved right back into the area, unaffected by the radiation."

"When was this? When did you detect the radiation?"

"Well, we're uh... We're a little embarrassed about that one, honestly... You see, we don't know. The indicator on that panel had burnt out and nobody noticed. We were doing a maintenance check over the Atlantic when we noticed and repaired, and then when we got over the Pacific the thing lit up like a Christmas Tree. We were still in contact with Berkeley at the time and gave them the data. They're crunching the numbers and seeing how long ago it was, checking decay rates and all that. We'll let you know on the next pass if they've finished."

"Fair enough. Thirty seconds 'til you're gone. Good tidings, see you in 80 minutes!"

"Roger that, enjoy the weather down there. ISS out."

~

Day 45

150 meters under the surface of the South Pacific, an American *Virginia* Class Fast Attack Submarine, the *USS Oregon* cruises slowly along at 12 knots. Its captain, one Benjamin Longmire, silently read from a piece of paper still warm from the laser printer in the radio room. Once he finished he turned to his Executive Officer, or XO, a rather wiry Commander named Hawkins, and spoke.

"Three VLF messages in as many days. Jesus Christ... at least we know we haven't been forgotten out here, right?"

"Yes indeed Cap'n. What's this one say?"

Longmire cleared his throat before summing up the communique.

"To USS Oregon... blah blah blah, bunch of procedural bullshit... Ah, here we go: Despite your successful deployment of a thermonuclear warhead to the precise coordinates and its subsequent detonation, coverage of the area of the South pacific inside the radius of the detonation has remained unchanged as measured by satellite radar... Son of a bitch."

"So, so what's that mean?"

"That, Commander, means that last night we utilized a 100 kiloton, 200-million-dollar warhead for precisely squat!"

"Shit."

"Yes, shit."

"How could that be Cap'n? I mean what kind of thing survives a nuke?"

"Hell, I don't know. Maybe whatever these things are, they're immune to radiation. Maybe they're machines, maybe they're indestructible or maybe they're ghosts. How the hell should I

52

know..."

"So what're our new orders sir?"

"Uh, lessee... proceed at flank speed to such and such coordinates and... Holy hell. We're putting ashore."

"Sir?"

"Sub pen. They've got a damn sub pen!"

"I've heard the term before but I'm afraid I can't put my finger on it Cap'n."

"It's a goddamned covered offshore dock. Concrete and steel, meant to be a reload and resupply facility in wartime, haven't been put into practice since World War II, and then by the goddamn Nazis. Where the fuck did COMSUBPAC dig up a motherfucking pen?"

"I think we should be glad they did."

"Hell yes I am. I was beginning to worry, all this shit they've thrown at us, don't use the periscope, don't put men on deck when you surface no matter what, all exterior repairs to be done at night by divers out of hatches. And then they finally give us the story and it's some gobbeldy gook about strange clouds from space killing people who so much as look at it. Then they have us nuke someplace in the empty ocean. If it weren't for all the proper confirmation codes and the civilian radio we hear when we cycle the air, I'd have thought our comms had been compromised. This is the first order that's made sense!"

"Should I have Thompson set a course sir?"

"Damn straight; here's the coordinates. Flank speed, just like it says!"

~

Day 45

Professor Walthers put his hand on the plastic panel next to the door that had previously been mistaken for the emergency exit. Briefly, a white line illuminated the outline of his hand before flashing red, then three times green. There was a subtly audible click as the door unlocked, and he went to pull it open. The door was surprisingly heavy and resisted his efforts until he used both hands. With a slight hiss of rushing air, the door cracked open, letting a hiss of cold air escape into the room. Walthers explained to the gathered group of students as they looked on.

"The server room is kept quite a bit cooler than the main bunker. The servers tend to run hot when they're operating and so a cooler environment assists them in maintaining functionality."

Karen, from last year's class, spoke up for further clarification.

"But Professor, didn't you say only one of the storage servers is operating at any one time?"

Walthers answered as they filed through the door and into the server room proper.

"Indeed, but that's just a general rule. The Master Control Servers switch off from each other, each activating the storage servers in sequence, powering them up, running software and storage diagnostics, and then powering them down. One after another, each MCS does it in turn. This ends up meaning there's always an MCS running, and at least one storage server, which are actually called slaves, according to the briefing I got on all this when it was entrusted to me."

The room was about the size of a standard basketball court. Each server stood like a sentinel, wires running out of it and up and into the grid of hanging supports above, all neatly bundled and secured, color coded according to function, and easily accessible to anyone with a step stool. There was only one of them active at the moment. Directly at the front sat two access points, each hardwired into its own server, the twin Master Control Servers. Only the one on the left was activated, for two servers running total. As they watched, the active server in the back, the slave, changed the tone of its hum, and certain lights on it started dimming, even as it shut down, the next slave in sequence came to life, powering up.

"The system is designed to keep checking itself and correcting any errors, over and over."

Alex, who had in his time in the bunker solidly confirmed Walthers opinion of his ego and need for validation, spoke up.

"Professor, what happens if a slave server *does* go down, has a major fault, or just plain stops working?"

"In that case, there's an alert that I have to go in and use some of the manuals in storage, printed hardcopies, just in case, in order to try and repair it."

"But what if you can't, is that bit of knowledge lost forever?"

"No, each slave holds three sets of data, half the previous slaves in sequence, its own, and half of the data of the next slave in sequence, if any one server goes down the two flanking it together hold backups of the one that failed. It's a very elegant system. It's designed so that if ones' data is lost, I can hopefully repair it, and restore it using the data from the others."

"And if you can't?"

"Each MCS has a full roster — titles only, of course — of what each server contains. It's hoped that if any data is irrevocably lost from this facility, that at least with that roster any survivors might be able to gather and restore the knowledge manually — that is, go out there and find the books."

Their session was suddenly cut short by a cry from the bunker behind. Walthers reacted instantly, pushing through the gathered crowd and hurrying back. The voice was Evelyn's. The students wasted no time with protest, instead hurrying after the professor, who still made it far ahead of them. Evelyn was laying on the linoleum floor of the kitchen, where she and one of the students uninterested in the server room were laying out lunch. The kitchen island was still heaped with bowls of spaghetti and the stove showed two large pots of sauce. The sink stood filled with three colanders of noodles. The student, a pre-med by the name of Liza, was between Evelyn's legs and up her skirt.

Walthers grabbed Liza by the hair and pulled her to her feet screaming.

"Just what in the hell are you doing!?"

Liza thrashed in pain as the professor kept his grip in her brown curls. Evelyn panted and screamed at her husband.

"Henry, let her down! I had a contraction!"

Walthers abruptly released the poor girl as he looked down at his wife in shock.

"What?"

"I had what I thought was a contraction. Liza was checking to see if I was at all dilated, to see if it was the real thing. Just before you yanked her up like a trout, she was saying that I'm firmly closed up, that it must be Braxton Hicks!"

"Oh my god, I'm so, so sorry Liza, and Evelyn, you must forgive me, I just..."

Liza rubbed at her scalp, brushing away a few stray hairs that had been pulled out at the root by the professor's panic.

"Prof, I'm sorry, I should've waited until you were here to check. I just sort of jumped in on her to be able to report as soon as possible what was going on."

"No Liza, *I'm* sorry. You were doing just as you should've; I was overzealous..."

"No, I was; I should've waited."

"No, you did the right thing..."

Evelyn interrupted, a tone of indignation in her voice.

"I hate to interrupt everyone hugging it out, but could somebody please help me up off the floor?"

~

Day 50

On a rural highway in Georgia, a large diesel truck, it's entire body covered in black spray paint, including the windshield & windows, thundered down the road. Just barely visible in the grill guard, two small cameras, wires trailing across the hood and up the windshield to a small hole drilled in the roof of the cab. Inside, the wires fed into two screens mounted on the dash. They showed the road ahead, one in infrared, the other in ultraviolet. Using these screens to drive was a rather large man. Easily six foot two inches and pushing two hundred and ten pounds, wearing black combat boots, black jeans, a black pocket t-shirt under a black bulletproof vest and an H-Harness loaded down with two grenades, two flashlights, four ammunition pouches, a small first-aid kit, six flares, and a pouch with two packs of cigarettes & a windproof lighter. He was smoking at the moment and ranting to himself.

"You know, *they* called me crazy. Crazy. Like this couldn't happen. But I knew. I knew... oh sure, I thought it'd be the Soviet Union, but then they quit, then China went all free trade and got dependent on us. North Korea was nice to think about but erreybody knew they'd never be a real threat. But got-damned spaced aliens! Like some shit outta a comic book, go figure."

Jesse knew all his preparations would be put to good use one day. The bunker, the garage, the armory, the stockpiling. Hell, he'd lived longer than any of the folks who used to call him crazy, he figured.

"Biggest damn surprise to me was the damn Emergency Alert System! Hell, I'd figured they was just another tool of Big Brother, another level of propaganda, but damn if somebody there wasn't on our side, those fucking things is damn useful. And then there's all them Military comms, hell, they told me all I needed to know before I ever got started. Infrared and ultraviolet are safe. Observation of the enemy was the most dangerous part of the enemy, who'd a figured?

As he drove down the road Jesse smoked like a chimney, his ashes all over the floorboards, his smoke making the air hazy. The bellowing of the engine and the tires nearly drowning out his diatribe. Still, he went on, maybe out of excitement, maybe out of nervousness, the rattling and scratching all over the outside a constant reminder of the danger inches away.

"But you know what really surprised me? How easy it is to outwit the damn things! I mean, right now they're damn near all over, but when we get to Atlanta, all we have to do is park the truck in an underground garage, shut the engine off, and take a damn nap. One hour, two, and the damn things lose interest! They go off and rejoin their brothers in the sky! Easy-peezy, I'll tell ya what. I mean, sure, that first time they wrapped all over the truck, I was a little concerned; hell, who wouldn't be? But they lose interest if you get cold and quiet and stay that way."

All over the truck body, interlocking almost like a cocoon, were small things, almost like black glass, their sharp edges scratching at the metal and paint, invisible to the cameras. A flock of them spun and flew around the truck as well, following it. The sound and heat of its engine, the motion of it, drawing them like flies to honey.

~

Day 50

A few hundred miles away in Houston, Dr. Lucida Alvarez was getting impatient. She'd been very clear, very calm, and very patient with her staff. She just needed one volunteer. Half the damn staff was useless as it stood. With exsanguination and dehydration as the secondary effects after death, both hematologists & the nutritionists were extraneous. It certainly wasn't cancer, so the oncologist was useless. The orthopedist was out, his specialty couldn't reveal anything... Why was this taking so damn long? How hard could it be to realize you're useless? Just one of them, any of them, could lead to the piece of information that would be the key to this struggle. She was especially looking forward to seeing the data from a real-time ophthalmoscopy as the eye witnessed the Phenomenon.

But here they were wasting time debating in some damn committee! They'd gone along with drawing straws the first time, but outright refused the second, almost like watching the monitors as Delarosa died somehow made all this more real to them. Made them realize *they* could really be next. Like they were so damned important. How many people had died already? Initial estimates had put the casualty rate in the first day at 85%. And it had been seven weeks now. Many of those who'd taken shelter had run out of food. There were riots in the shelters in Tokyo, a reversion to tribalism and cannibalism in Japan. They could not afford to waste time. Every day the survival of the human race grew less and less likely and they were wasting time debating ethics, ethics!

She was beginning to consider taking matters into her own hands. So far, she hadn't had to call for support. Even when the food was getting low she considered that a last resort, but then, at the time she was still counting on the Lantern figuring this thing out. But now it was up to her. She couldn't do it alone. Once again she opened her desk drawer and stared at the recessed keypad within. She'd set the access code herself years ago when she was first sworn into the Project. She keyed in 1984, her favorite novel — easy to remember, ironic to use.

"How dare they waste time and the future of mankind over one useless life!?"

CHAPTER 8

Day 55

Captain Longmire watched the display screens showing the status of his boat. As he watched, their GPS position changed again, indicating they'd reached the exact position and heading they'd been ordered to. Calmly, he gave his orders for his XO to carry out.

"Port rudder five degrees. Up three degrees on the planes. Full stop. XO, start up the photonics masts, infrared range finder only please. Let's make sure we're under cover before we go above deck."

"Aye-aye sir. AN/BVS up. We've got coverage overhead at 20 meters at the bow... 30 meters at midship... 20 meters astern."

"Good, hit the infrared."

"Going to infrared. We've got railings, pylons, solid cover overhead, closed doors ahead, doors closing astern... fully closed now. Looks like we've got personnel coming out onto the walkways."

"Excellent. Get the men up on deck tying us up. Cycle the air, bring the reactor down to idle. I'm going to go up on deck and meet our hosts."

"Aye, sir."

Captain Longmire made his way along the passages up to the forward hatch. Emerging onto the deck for the first time in nearly two months, he blinked and looked around, unused to the brighter light outside his boat.

Four massive concrete supports stood up out of the water, two to port and starboard linked by girders and aluminum siding, the other two forward and astern linked by large hanging sliding doors. Men and women in splotchy blue-grey camouflage moved along the walkways, tying ropes, throwing ropes. One with more metal accoutrements than most moved down a gangplank towards the *Oregon*, pausing at the end near one of his own men.

He saluted, oddly, but a salute nonetheless, and requested permission to board for the purposes of briefing the Captain. This... was going to be interesting. The Officer came marching forward, extending his hand.

"Commander Walther Pepricheck, Royal Australian Navy, at your service sir."

"Captain Ben Longmire, US Navy at yours."

"Welcome to Oz, Captain."

"Glad to be here. Mind telling me why we're here?"

"All in good time Captain. Time is short; if I might invite you to dinner aboard the pen, we'll restock and resupply your perishables, give your men some time above deck, and give you a rundown on what we know."

"Have it your way."

All this was damn unusual, but he supposed everything was at this point. He turned back to the *Oregon* and made his way back down into her. Hawkins was at his post monitoring the boat. Longmire let him know he'd have the boat for the afternoon and gave him some final "in case of" instructions. After all, everything about this was unprecedented. If the pen was lost, if Longmire was killed, if the Aussies turned on them, they had to be ready for any eventuality. Of course, the orders were all the same: have a crewman cut the lines, submerge the boat, get out to open water and call COMSUBPAC for new orders. Not much else they could do, really.

After that he made his way to his Quarters, the only private quarters on the boat, and changed into his dress uniform for dinner with the Australian Navy.

~

Day 55

In New York, Emil pulled out his phone. The hourly updates had long since ended, regular phone service discontinued. All there were now were updates, getting fewer and farther between. The vibration was both dreaded and looked forward to. The standard EAS preface was there, but the body was changed.

At this point we estimate 97% of humanity is dead or likely to die. There have been no advancements in our efforts to mitigate or end the Phenomenon. The usual precautions continue to apply.

Do not go outside. Do not look at the sky. Do not make noise. Do not generate more heat or light than is necessary.

We highly encourage remaining survivor groups to coordinate. Make efforts towards underground farming and animal husbandry. Movement across the surface is possible in closed vehicles with their windows blacked out. Infrared and Ultraviolet vision is safe. The Phenomenon will interlock and cover any moving vehicle, heat source, or structure emanating sound. The Phenomenon will lose interest after several hours without further stimulus.

You have not been abandoned. You have not been forgotten.

To personnel with Δ6 clearance, Blue 12 procedures are withdrawn, enact Green 2. To personnel with φ1 clearance, Ω protocol.

Freedom. Green 2 was freedom. All orders negated but one. No further orders projected. No more packages, no more training trips... well, those had ended already, but still, freedom. All he had to do was continue to listen for further updates. Standby. Keep listening. That was easy; he'd have done that regardless.

He was free to get out of New York, free to take Sarya away to someplace... where? Where could he go? What could he do? He didn't have the skills to go out there, he could barely find supplies in a city formerly of nine million. Sharon was going to have to be the key. But that meant he'd have to trust her. To free her and follow her. When she has every reason in the world to leave him and Sarya to fend for themselves. Part of him wanted to see if he could somehow keep her in captivity, keep her prisoner while on the move, gain some control, some form of leverage. However, the bigger and better part of him rebelled at the very concept. He was not a kidnapper, nor a prison warden, nor a slave master.

He'd have to secure her cooperation through diplomacy. Mutual advantage was a good bargaining chip, if he could find it. But how? In what possible way could he or Sarya benefit her?

~

Day 55

Her wrist was raw from being cuffed for so long. Sarya was very helpful, bringing her wet wipes and cold packs as needed. She was a very sweet, helpful, and mindful little girl. But what she really needed was to be released. Almost on cue, Emil stood up from his normal lounging spot across the room, walked over, and without a word handed her the handcuff key.

In shock, Sharon stared at it for a few moments before sitting up and reaching around to unlock herself. Rubbing her wrist as she stood, she looked around for a moment as Emil sat down, his head set on his clasped hands, his dark eyes following her every move. He raised a finger and pointed; following it, she saw her pack, gear belt and weapons in a pile next to the door. She immediately went over. Lifting her gear, she felt aches in her arms and back. A few weeks without exercise and she goes weak; pitiful. She was going to have to double up on her strength training when she got... wherever.

She clipped her gear into place, took a look around the basement, and with one last glance at Emil, she turned to leave.

"Take Sarya with you."

She wheeled around and nearly screamed at him "What?"

"Take Sarya with you."

"What!? Why would I do that? Why would you want me to? She's your daughter; I mean, what the hell?"

"I'm not as capable as you are. I'm not strong like you. I'm not going to be able to keep her alive. You could. You could keep her alive, see her through this until you both find a group of survivors who can be trusted, a community. I have no chance of doing that, of giving her a future. Take her with you."

"And what would you do?"

He shrugged.

"I have no idea. Continue as I am for as long as I can. until I run out of supplies. Until the murderers down in the subways rise up and take what I've got left and my life. Perhaps take a walk outside when I get hungry and desperate enough."

Sharon looked around again at the basement that had been her prison for a month. The stinking drain they used to relieve themselves. The piles of rags and furniture. The workbench she'd idly considered trying to get to and use the tools to escape.

She made up her mind then.

~

Day 55

Glasses clinked as the seaman took away the remains of the meal.

Longmire wiped his face with a napkin and look across the table at Commander Peprichek. The meal had been a surprisingly unassuming but delicious steak and baked potatoes loaded down with bacon bits, sour cream, & cheddar, with coleslaw, Coca-Cola, and a dessert of blueberry cobbler with vanilla ice cream. They'd spent dinner and dessert discussing the differences between Australia and the US, both western democracies, but with distinctly different takes on government and its role in society. Longmire found Commander Peprichek knowledgeable, but naive, like some kind of walking talking encyclopedia. He lacked the depth and awareness, the humanity and emotion, to properly put all his knowledge into context and use. Still, it had been an interesting conversation, but it was now time to get down to business.

"So tell me Commander, what exactly do we know about what's going on out there?"

"Let me counter with a question of my own. What have you been told so far by your own government?"

"Very little. We know there's been some sort of global event. We know we can't expose ourselves or even look anywhere exposed to sky except with IR or UV vision, we know we're in radio silence, even had us disconnect the antennae we use to listen in on civilian frequencies when we surface. What we don't know is why, just what is it about this event that requires us to isolate ourselves like this."

"Well then I'm afraid I've got some rather bad news Captain. The reason you've been isolated is for your own safety."

"How so?"

"These things, this... Phenomenon... is lethal. On sight lethal. It doesn't have to touch you, or hit you with anything."

"Radiation?"

"No sir, it's too damn quick. And as long as you don't attract their attention with heat, sound, or movement, you could hang around outside all day and night so long as you keep your eyes closed. It's not... it's not like anything we've ever encountered before."

65

"And how has the civilian population fared? I mean, if this thing is lethal, literally, on sight, then...?"

"Unfortunately Captain, not well. Exact figures are... well, they're damn right impossible. But, based on residual cellular usage in the first few weeks before most power grids failed, we think at least 85% of the civilian population didn't make it past the first day."

Longmire felt the news hit him like a punch in the gut. He suddenly couldn't draw breath, sounds echoed, and were distorted. He himself lacked any ties. Never been married, his parents were both dead, no siblings. The Navy had been his family for nearly a decade. But his crew... half of them were freaking kids barely into their twenties. They had wives and girlfriends, small children, siblings, parents and grandparents... holy shit. This was going to throw morale into the bilge.

"Shit... and... how much of the Government has survived?"

"Yours or mine?"

"Either."

"Tough to say. I know here in Oz there's contingencies, lots of our government goes into lockdown and doesn't communicate except upwards, so there's no way for a bloke like me to tell. As to you yanks, well... I know there was enough left of your government to contact ours and put in a request for us to get this pen back in order as quick as we could, for you. We're to take any extraneous personnel you can spare and give 'em safe harbor until this thing blows over, and to pass on an orders packet too large to send you through the VLF."

"Orders packet? Any idea what's in it?"

"I was told it was above my paygrade. I'm a delivery boy, not a messenger."

"Well then, can I have it?"

"Thought you might want it."

With that, Peprichek waved over one of the seamen who'd waited on them, who promptly pulled a large manila envelope from a drawer in bureau against the wall. He briskly walked it over and placed it on the table in front of Captain Longmire. He opened it and leafed through the official bullshit to get to the meat of it. First thing he looked for was the Classification, what he could and couldn't tell his boys on the *Oregon*, and... it was left to him. Whether or not he could tell his crew that in all likelihood everyone back home was dead was left to his discretion.

CHAPTER 9

Day 55

"Oh come on! There's gotta be someone here!"

The sound was beginning to get on Jesse's nerves. The constant clicking and rustling of the "critters" on the outside of the Centers for Disease Control was disconcerting. He expected them to be there; hell, he expected the building to be jumping. If there were going to be anyone left alive, anyone who had any idea what the hell these things were or how to get rid of 'em, it was gonna be here. But they weren't.

"I can't believe this. I mean, it ain't dead. The building ain't chock full-o-corpses like all the other hospitals and shit..."

The weight of the IR goggles and the full body armor he wore kept him hot, sweating. The cloth under layer was beginning to chafe the longer he wore everything. Still, he was grateful for the cover. Some of the Army radio bands he'd been listening in on had mentioned that the critters were lethal on contact as well as sight, and that if they couldn't get to your skin, if you kept 'em off of you, that you could maybe survive. There were even rumors of soldiers who'd gone out in full body armor covering every inch and getting covered, lying still for a few hours, and coming back inside after they got bored. Of course, there were just as many rumors that people had done that and ended up covered until they died of thirst because their breathing was enough to keep the damn things attention. But, better safe than sorry.

So, he wore the armor, and he wore the goggles, and he waited before every move out of doors between his truck and any buildings, he played by the rules, and he stayed alive. And he'd made it all the way to the CDC in Atlanta, where he was now endlessly frustrated by the fact that all the outer offices were full of corpses and all the inner offices were completely empty. He spoke to himself in a low whisper, a habit he'd picked up after being too alone for too many weeks.

"One more sweep, maybe we missed somethin'."

As Jesse made his way from floor to floor, he kept a careful ear out for the sound of wind. The building was without power as far as he could tell, so there was no air conditioning, but a single broken window could mean a sudden and (he was betting) unpleasant death. As he came to the doorway from the stairwell to the next floor, he was hammered by the sudden smell of rot.

"I'm starting to think this whole trip was a waste of time. We're gonna have to find a hotel or somethin', somewhere with an underground garage we can siphon gas out of parked cars to get home."

"...Is there... is there somebody there?"

The voice from the dark was frightened, desperate, and weak.

Jesse ran down the corridor and turned a corner to find the source of the voice. The wraith of a man was hunched over, clinging to a rolling chair for support as if it were a walker. He was rail thin,

Latino features, brown skin, dark hair peppered with grey, wearing a stained white tank top and dress slacks, penny loafers and a lab coat. Most notable, however, was the bloodstained bandage wound around his head and eyes. He stood in the hallway intersection with rows upon rows of cubicles down one way, a break room and bathroom down the other. He'd come hobbling out of the break room at the sound of Jesses voice, where it was obvious he'd been hiding, eating whatever he could find, and going back and forth to the bathroom for water.

"Gat-dang, son! You look like you've got a tale to tell."

"Yes, yes I do... but first, who are you? Are you military? Agency? Who sent you?"

"Aw hell, ain't nobody sent me, Doc. I just came here to see if there was anybody doing anything about them things in the sky."

"So, you're a civilian? How'd you get here? How'd you avoid them? How did you survive outdoors?"

"Got a truck."

The man's voice fell and a note of suspicion and incredulity came into it.

"A... truck."

"Yeah, big old armored truck, like they use for bank deliveries and all that? Got it at auction when they upgraded their fleet. Repainted it, stocked it up, parked it in a hanger that I put up over m'bunker. When the alert went off, I got down in to the bunker and hunkered down, listened to reports, police scanner, military radio, the EAS, all of it. Then I prepped my trunk and came here."

"Ah, I see, and, uh... you haven't, uh, haven't made contact with anybody in the government?"

"Oh hell no! For all we know they made the dang things. The ultimate way to wipe the slate clean and leave all the material goods untouched. Better than the neutron bomb."

"Um, yes... I suppose that would seem possible..."

"Anyways, so what's your story? How'd you get up here? How long have you been there? What'd you do?"

"My name is Doctor Warren Rafei, and I am, or was, an Exobiologist with NASA on loan to the CDC. Anytime there's a question of a contaminant with possible extraterrestrial origins I'm called in."

"So these things really did come from outer space?"

"Most definitely."

"Aw dang, I was bettin' on escaped government experiment myself..."

"Well, I'm sorry to disappoint you. Can, can we get out of here? This place is a bit... exposed... I think, for my tastes..."

"Oh hell yeah, I'm sorry Doc. Stairs are this way, c'mon..."

"You'll have to guide me."

"Huh?"

"I'm blind. I was blinded... it's a long story."

"Aw hell, I'm sorry. I can't tell; I'm looking at ya in infrared."

"Infra-!? That's brilliant. Lead the way."

"You got it, Doc, I'm right here, let's go."

Jesse reached and took Dr. Rafei's outstretched hand, acting as cane, walker, and guide as they made their way to the emergency stairs. As they slowly made their way down, Jesse looked quizzically at Rafei, in spite of the fact that body language and facial cues were completely ineffective.

"So what's the deal, huh? Whatcha doin' here still?"

"I have duties, assignments. I have to stay here."

"Well jeez, what kind of assignments? I mean, pardon me if I missed something, but I don't exactly see a whole bunch of things to accomplish by a blind man sitting around an empty building, even if the building's the CDC."

"There are sub basements, levels below the ground, that still have supplies, power. I'm supposed to stay here; there are people coming for me. I can't be sure they'll know of the sub basements, so every day I go upstairs and wait quietly. So long as I keep to the center of the building, near the elevators and stairways, away from the windows, then I'm relatively safe from harm."

"Who's coming for ya, Doc?"

"I can't be sure. I'm a member of a specialized organization, or project. I've received my evacuation orders, and my procedure was to remain here, to await rescue."

"Are we talkin' thin gentleman in black suits with bland features, pale skin, and dark sunglasses here?"

"I'm not sure. Might be, could be military, or something else entirely, I'm not sure."

"Alright, we'll stay put. I gotta be honest wid'ya, I ain't exactly looking forward to meeting the folks coming for ya. Always been mighty suspicious of figures in authority and the folks who kowtow to 'em. But, er, considering the circumstances..."

"Better the government than the loneliness of a dead world?"

"I wouldn't't'a phrased it quite like that, but, pretty much, yeah."

"I figure we've still got a few hours; do you have anything to eat?"

"Oh, dang, heck ya, hold on, you stay right here, I've got plenty of food in the truck."

"Don't leave me alone, please..."

"Oh, okay, alright, well, let's get going. We got a few floors of stairs, and then a quick trip through the garage, but when we get to the garage we'll have to be quiet. There's opening to the sky in there and we don't want to attract nothin'."

"I think you could leave me at the end of the stairs in that case."

"That sounds like a good idea."

As Jesse led the blind Dr. Rafei down the winding staircase to the garage level, they spoke of the researchers who'd staffed the building before the end of the world, their initial efforts to survive it, their dwindling numbers, and isolation limiting their previously presumed research capability. As they approached the lower levels, Dr. Rafei held up a hand, signaling Jesse to halt his line of questioning. As they listened to the silence, the sound of an idling diesel engine could just be made out coming from below.

~

Day 55

A little more than 30 miles north of Krasnoyarsk, and twenty feet under the ground, in a bunker lined with concrete and steel, wired to an antennae farm on the surface, Timor idly chewed a piece of jerky as he watched the counter click down until George came back on. A small piece of jerky flecked off and got caught in his beard. He'd get it out later. Just like he'd shower later. and cut his hair later. He had time now, time for everything. For all the books, movies, video games...

"Timor! Timor are you there?"

He threw himself forward in his chair, crumbs and caked debris falling to the floor off his growing belly in his rush to key his mic.

"Yes, yes, hello George, did you have a good rest? You've been off the air for nearly eight hours; I was beginning to get worried."

"Yes, Timor I'm here, of course. Where else would I be?"

"Of course, of course, sorry..."

"It's alright. Um... we have a bit of news from the Japanese."

"Yes?"

"They've had a bit of an earthquake. No warning. Tokyo is a wreck. There's no contact from the government anymore, just the engineers at the tracking station. They... they think... they think the entire metro system collapsed."

"So... that's it then? Do we consider the Japanese government gone? Is that it? Our last official link gone?"

"I'm afraid so Timor. And, you know what today is."

"I do."

"This is our last communique."

"Have the Americans calculated a landing site?"

"They think so. They've calculated a trajectory that'll put me off the coast of France in the channel. The French are going to try and pick our escape capsule up, but it's going to be a long shot. They've been making their way to the coast for a few days now, but they're not sure if they'll find a ship, much less figure out how to get her running or find us."

"So how long?"

"We've already fired the retrorockets. This is the ISS' last manned orbit, friend."

"And my last contact with anyone on the outside."

"You'll survive. You'll be found or make your way outside eventually. I believe in you, Timor."

"I wish I had your courage, friend."

"We're about to get ourselves into the escape capsule. Not too long now before we have to separate from the station."

"I understand. Fly safe, my friend. I hope you have clear skies and a soft landing."

"Ha-ha! Clear skies would indeed be a welcome sight! Goodbye, Timor."

"Goodbye, George."

~

Day 55

A middle aged man peered over his glasses at his much younger compatriot, a half-gone cigarette smoldering between his fingers as he carefully nuanced his speech with the proper inflections.

"Are we *sure* they've accepted our explanation?"

The younger man switched off the satellite radio he'd been using and leaned back in his chair, pulling his own cigarettes from his shirt pocket and lighting one. He responded with the first exhalation of smoke billowing into his elders face.

"They have no reason to doubt our word. All civilian communication lines were severed per procedure. We're the only voices out of Nipon they're getting."

"But do they believe us?"

"They show all signs they do. I'm not psychic; I can't tell you what they're thinking, only what they say."

"And they will not come to investigate?"

"I highly doubt they'd mount the effort. I told them exactly what we agreed: earthquake, metro system collapse, government cut off, cannibalism, all of it. If they have any fantasies about coming here, they involve waiting until this crisis has passed and claiming Nipon for the West, with no natives to account for."

"That *will not* happen."

"No, no it won't, but they do not know that."

"I will signal the Prime Minister then. It is time to begin."

The older man picked up a phone on the desk and punched a serious of numbers in. After a short delay as the line was transferred, he spoke briefly with the man on the other end. As they finished their cigarettes in silence, a voice began chattering through the intercom, addressing the residents en masse. As the speech concluded, they stood in salute.

~

Day 56

George had one thought running endlessly through his mind.

Gravity is a bitch.

He'd had forgotten how heavy his hands were. It was a funny thing, coming back from a long-term stay in orbit. One he felt wonder at each time. And this, now, was likely to be the last time, and all he could marvel at was the weight of his own damn hands. He manipulated the controls of the Soyuz capsule in slow, heavy precision, pressing each key, flipping each toggle methodically.

Again, he settled back into the seat. For the third time, there were no signals the Soyuz' radio could pick up. No civilian bands, no EAS messages, nothing. Of course, he couldn't remember which frequencies were within the set's range, and his Russian was too rusty to make any sense of the manuals.

But, his own beacon was functioning, that much he knew. So he waited, and hoped. At least he could open up the vents to breath the fresh air. He dared not look out the porthole though. He'd used gum to stick a few pages of the useless manual to the glass, just in case.

The ride was pleasant enough on the way in. Bumpy as usual, but not overly so. He tried not to think too much about the future. About the people coming for him, and whether they'd managed to make it to the coast or not. About what his life was going to be like on Earth. He didn't speak any French, after all. Thankfully, he'd never married or had children. He couldn't imagine if he had. One of the men on the American west coast that had been in communication with the ISS had a newborn, somewhere, he hoped.

He preferred not to think of the other distinct possibility. That the French hadn't made it to the coast, or hadn't found a ship that they could use, and no-one was coming. That he'd sit here, in the capsule, until either he starved or it sank.

He pondered what kind of future he could have if he was rescued. He was a physicist by trade. He couldn't think of much he could do as a member of a post-apocalyptic community. Unless France had a nuclear reactor that was still operable. Or, he'd always enjoyed metallurgy; maybe he could take up blacksmithing. That would be a proper survival skill in the new world, wouldn't it? His train of thought was interrupted by a sudden clanking as the capsule impacted something, or rather, something clanked into the capsule.

~

Four years prior to the end of the world.

Doctor Rodriguez was at a loss for words. Confronted with this new evidence, he was forced to alter his position as to the Project's efficacy, but his ethical opposition still stood. If not for the procedures in place, for which he'd argued, that curtailed the dangers of permanent damage, he would never have agreed to this.

As it stood, those procedures had been cut to the bone, and still they had very nearly violated them on countless occasions. But, all things considered, he'd do it again. The scientific applications of the findings were beyond reproach, and the applications of the findings would surely have far-reaching consequences.

... Not that he'd ever be able to publish his findings openly. The subjects would go on, forever connected by their experiences and training. Each were specially educated and trained based upon their unique characteristics and strengths.

He doubted they knew what they were getting into when they signed up for the program. They'd been recruited from all walks of life — military, trades, academia, white collar, blue collar. Each from somewhere different, all twenty-six of them.

They each had names before, but he knew them only by their designated numbers. Subject 12 was his favorite, but he wasn't about to show it. She had too much ego already, too likely to go to extremes at times; attention and praise only exacerbated her worst qualities. Better to keep her seeking approval. She performed best under pressure.

Now that the project was over, he was tasked with delivering their new identities, new names, assigned places of work. Subject 12 was next. He looked through the one way mirrored window into the room. It was sparse, just a twelve by twelve by eight foot space with two rolling chairs and a small round table. The walls were a dull slate grey, unmarked except for the two cameras in opposite corners that allowed for Security to view the entire room without blind spots. The carpet was a darker grey and the light fixture was a simple dome diffusing a soft 40-watt bulb and concealing the rooms microphone.

He sighed, and opened the door. She was sitting ramrod straight at the table, like always, hands folded in front, dark eyes following his every move as he sat across from her, like twin pools of ink.

"Good Afternoon, sir."

"Hello, 12. How are you?"

"I'm fine, sir."

"I suppose you know why I'm here."

"Yes sir, we're supposed to get our orders today."

"I wouldn't phrase it that way 12. It's not orders, they're assignments. You can request changes or even a discharge."

He knew she wouldn't, of course. None of them would. Ambition, loyalty, and desire to do great things were high on all their personality tests. They'd see things through to whatever end came.

"No sir, I'll accept whatever assignment is given me."

"Alright then, let's have a look at what's been chosen for you..."

He opened the manila envelope marked 12, and slid the leaf of papers out on the desk. A small plastic bag filled with identification cards, a passport, credit cards, and licenses spilled out along with them.

"Looks like... well, 12, your new name is Lucinda Alvarez. Oh, excuse me, *Doctor* Lucinda Alvarez."

CHAPTER 10

Day 56

· Commander Hawkins shook his head and rubbed his temples.

"It's a damn long shot, sir."

"That's the understatement of the century, Commander. This is a damn near impossible shot."

"Surely a boat in the Atlantic is closer?"

"COMSUBLANT has been out of contact since the day after this shit hit. It hit the East Coast first, they got the worst of it; their entire CoC is in tatters. Some subs reported in, some haven't. None of the ones that did have the shallow draft or bunk room to do it; they're all deep-water boomers."

"So who are we losing?"

"Perkins, Smoot, Winthorpe, a few others from the forward torpedo room, SONAR, weapons control. This isn't a combat op, and no combat ops are forecasted for the foreseeable future, so they're getting off here. Australia's converting the *HMAS Success* to operate in the blind by GPS nav and IR. She'll put out to get our boys home as soon as she's able. Hopefully we'll have got things in the US back in hand by then."

"Is it that bad, sir?"

"From what I've been told, we don't even want to ask how bad it really is, but what they've had to tell me is enough to make me think nobody on this boat may have any good news waiting for them when we get home."

"What should we tell the men? I mean..."

"We tell them the truth. We've got a long cruise ahead of us, plenty of time for the men to get their heads in the game."

"Aye sir, should I...?"

"No, I'll handle it. That's the problem with being the Captain, sometimes it has to come down on my shoulders. This is a textbook example of when that is."

He stood from table in the officer's mess to access to the communications panel, unclipping the handset he set it to broadcast ship wide.

"Can I have your attention please; this is the Captain. I'm sure a lot of you have noticed some odd goings-on of late. This cruise hasn't exactly gone as we'd expected. It's been left up to me to decide if you could be told just why that is. I have full confidence in the professionalism and maturity of my crew, so I don't see any reason not to tell you, because I know you'll all still do your jobs to the best of your ability.

To put it succinctly, two weeks into our cruise, the world ended. It wasn't any kind of war, or plague. Some kind of foreign object or entity entered the earth's atmosphere and broke up, spreading around the planet. It's up there right now, flying like a giant swarm all over the place, and, it's completely lethal to touch or to look at it in anything but infrared or ultraviolet, and those are safe only because the things are invisible in IR and UV. And gentleman, it is decidedly hostile. It'll fly down and cocoon anything generating noise, heat, or moving under the sky.

Even as it was still just over the east coast of the US, the President and FEMA took action to send out warnings to all civilian and military personnel to take shelter and avoid looking at the sky or attracting its attention. But in spite of that, estimates are that 85% of the civilian population died on Day 1. I don't like breaking this news to you but I respect you all too damn much to hide it from you. That percentage has only gone up since then. I can't say for sure who has survived and who hasn't. Communications are basically only still possible via satellite as most land based power grids have gone down.

I know this is a kick in the guts, gents, and I know we're all going to need time to process this, so for the next two days while we're still hooked to the pen I'm ordering double rations, Hollywood showers for all, and we're going to move from our normal three shift rotation to a four shift so everyone gets extra rack time. But, as soon as we put back to sea I expect everything to go back to normal, for all of us to have our heads in the game, and for us to do our duty as we always have. Godspeed, gentlemen; out."

~

The sounds of metal screeching together allayed George's fears that the impact was some inane and accidental contact with a buoy. He could hear voices, muffled, dim, and distant, though he couldn't make out what they were saying. He was sorely tempted to uncover the porthole and take a peek outside, but before he could even begin to reach for it the pod shifted and rolled onto its side, pushed, seemingly, from outside. A few panicked seconds and the craft begin righting itself, only to jerk to a halt at a 45° angle to the sound of yet another impact.

Moments later, he heard an electrical winch begin whirring as the pod was lifted, it's balance returning as she was pulled from the water. The voices were closer now, louder, though still tinny, as if coming through a long pipe. They were telling him (in English no less!) to remain calm, not to look outside, and welcome home.

A few minutes more than he'd liked of hanging in the air like a yoyo, and then he felt the pod thump and settle onto a hard surface. The glow of sunlight, filtered through the paper stuck against the porthole, suddenly dimmed as he heard large hydraulics humming above him. The voices were distinct now, telling him he was aboard a Royal Navy supply ship, and that after a waiting period of some few hours to let the event clear the decks, they'd seal the forward cargo bay he'd been lifted into, and then go about getting him out of the pod. Just a few more hours, a few moments really. A nap wouldn't hurt him one bit. After all the excitement of reentry and splashdown, he very easily let himself relax into a deep and thankfully dreamless sleep.

George was rudely interrupted by the chattering of his own teeth. It was freezing; he could see his breath fog the air. He looked at his watch and saw he'd been asleep nearly six hours. Far longer than he expected. They'd said it would be about three or four hours, not six... and they hadn't come. Something was wrong. He supposed, his exit this long delayed, that it was a reasonable choice to take a peek outside. He scooted over nearer to the porthole, and grabbed at the edge of the manual page keeping him from seeing outside, and with one quick yank ripped it off the window, the hard gum coming with it in on solid chunk.

Lot of good that it did. The outside of the window was completely frosted over. He couldn't make out anything beyond it.

George slumped back into the seat, disappointed and yet relieved that the porthole was iced over and dark. He felt like they'd had enough time, and he was through waiting for the Royal Navy to open things up and let him out.

Fuck it.

He grabbed the hatch and turned the handle, throwing his weight against it... and it didn't budge.

Of course. The outside is frozen, just like the window. Winter in the channel.

He turned away, shielded his eyes, and pulled the cord affixed to the inner hatch frame to blow the explosive bolts. With a sudden muted thump, they blew apart, simultaneously shattering the ice coating the pod and severing the hatch from the craft. It hung, balanced on the frame for a brief moment before falling to the deck outside, clanging loudly against the metal plating.

Do not make noise.

George suddenly remembered the cardinal rules of how to live on the surface. He'd been in space. He hadn't had to worry about these things until now, not really. His breath caught in his throat, he squeezed his eyes closed, and he strained to hear anything coming from outside... two seconds, three... nothing. Silence. Dead silent. *Too silent...*

He slowly turned, opening his eyes, petting out of the pod, breathing in the cold air. And saw nothing. The bay outside was empty. Cold steel flooring, and a cold steel wall with a lone lightbulb sitting high up in a wire cage. All seemed coated with a fine layer of white frost. He crept out onto the deck, his soft slippers doing little to protect his feet from the chill. He kept hold of the edges of the pod as he stood upright for the first time since landing. Feeling his weight settle and his back groan for the first time in month. He looked around, seeing the rest of the bay. Large crates stood piled against a far wall, obviously shoved aside to make room for the pod.

The ceiling was mostly taken up by four large doors with hydraulic pistons attached, the doors overhead slightly ajar, the gap between them only an inch wide and iced over, a cable leading from their center down to a hook looped through one of the grapple rings on the exterior of the pod. On the other side of the room, opposite of where the pod opened, a hatchway stood, the door within cracked a scant few inches.

George was beginning to think something was very, *very* wrong.

George's feet were starting to lose feeling. The decks were freezing.

The bulkheads were freezing. The whole damn ship was frozen. He made his way through the narrow corridors, the various markings and codes printed on various pipes and hatches a complete mystery to him. He just knew he had to find the berths. If he didn't find some thicker clothing soon and some boots he was going to start worrying about losing toes. Finally, he found something he could understand, a handmade sign, in plain English, warning him not to open the hatch above as it opened to the exterior.

Best not go that way, then.

He made his way, best he could figure, towards the center of the ship, the keel line, where the ship was most stable. He'd heard that's where most ships put their crew quarters. Two or three compartments in he found what he was looking for. He crawled under the blankets of the first berth he came to. Let his body warmth return. A brief foray into the nearest lockers for clothes and a scramble through another few cabins for a pair of boots that fit, and then back under the covers to thaw them before he put them on. Properly outfitted, he began to wonder just where the crew had gotten to. All his wanderings he hadn't found a trace of them.

He made his way up every ladder he could find. Most ships, he knew, had their control centers in a superstructure amidships. Even with precautions taken against the event, they had to use the bridge, and it would be manned. He passed through what looked to be the mess hall, meals frozen on plates with glasses of frozen coffee or tea next to them, forks and knives still neatly placed on napkins next to each plate. At last he began to figure out the stenciled codes, A for aft, F for Fore, P for Port, S for Starboard, deck number, then compartment. He followed them until he was amidships and then started moving upwards, finding the narrow, near vertical stairs to be worrisome.

At last a simple sign, "Bridge" with an arrow. As he opened the hatch to the bridge, he knew instantly that he'd made a mistake. The sound of howling wind and its bite against his face told him that a window was broken or an outer hatch was opened. He kept his eyes on the deck as he moved slowly into the room. The consoles were all smashed. There was nobody in the room. As he approached the forward view ports, he could see the ragged edges of the shatter resistant materials - not glass, certainly - and how they'd been painted over with black paint. Glancing out at the deck, and the channel beyond the railing, his already short breaths turned ragged with panic. Clothing was strewn about the deck. Haphazard and scattered. As if cast off in orgiastic dancing. But that, that was just unusual. The channel, the channel was frozen. Salt water. Frozen solid.

Well, at least if worse comes to worse I can walk to shore.

George was sure he couldn't be more than a few miles from shore. The channel was only 20-30 miles wide, and he could be certain the chances he landed in the exact middle were slim. If he were to make his way west northwest he'd hit the UK sooner than later. That had to be why he'd been picked up by a Royal Navy ship; he'd landed closer to England than France, that's all. With the fog, the things from the sky wouldn't see him direct, and with the frost that would cover his clothing and beard he was sure he'd be nearly invisible in infrared. A few miles to shore then finding shelter somewhere with a radio, police, fire station, hospital. It was a good plan, a solid plan... and he was scared shitless.

No use delaying things.

He climbed the ladder to the upper deck, keeping his eyes on the ladder. He wondered why he couldn't hear them. He'd always imagined that the "things" would make noise like a flock of birds. And shadows, there should be shadows, shouldn't there? He pulled his way along the deck railing to the point lowest and closest to the ice. There he tied up the rope ladder he'd found below decks. As he swung first one leg then the other over the side, he listened warily to the creaking and groaning of the ship, squeezed as it was in the ice...

One misstep was all it took.

His foot missed the rein below, his other slipped, and his grip couldn't hold him alone with the weight of his layers and supplies... It wasn't a long fall, only seven or eight feet. But, it was enough. The wind knocked out of him, his head cracked against the ice. And his eyes snapped open turned upwards towards the foul grey sky. There were shadows moving in the clouds above, hanging low like fruit on an overburdened tree. He rolled over, squeezing his eyes closed and curling into a ball on his stomach, his arms wrapped around his head, his hands and gloves in his sleeves, his face pressed to the ice.

One deep, ragged breath, two... and then they were on him. The first impacted square in the middle of his pack, it's impact a slight thump and muffled sound of cloth compressed. Others followed, five, ten, then too many to count all over. They were hard, and cold, and he could feel them shifting and pushing into his layers upon layers of clothing all over his legs, sides, arms. Even the back of his hooded head. They were squeezing him, pulling tighter and tighter together, and the pressure was unbearable. He screamed. It just drove them to push harder. An edge, a sharp edge pressing against his left cut through. He felt it pierce his skin, then a flash of understanding, knowledge imparted, a vision of elsewhere and strange shapes with too many angles and too few sides... a prayer to being without a name...

~

Day 57

Professor Walthers was 49 years old, and he couldn't remember a single time in his lifetime that he had been more terrified. His hands shook as he opened closet after closet, searching for wherever Susan had stashed the medical supplies. As their resident third year student in a medical field, she'd taken over as their medic in chief, assisted by two first year pre-med students, Phillip & Joyce, who served as nurses or aides as needed. They were all busy with his wife, who was in labor, and so the other tasks fell to everyone else. He'd been told to fetch the alcohol for them to sterilize everything.

Of course, they'd known that Evelyn was pregnant when they came into the bunker. They should've had all the supplies set aside and wrapped up as a kit since day one, but nobody had thought of it. They'd all sort of gone along under the impression that the all-clear would come through the Professor's computer any day, and thought that Evelyn would just deliver in a hospital topside, but the all-clear hadn't come. In fact, almost no messages had come. Professor Walthers checked each and every day, in the morning, in the afternoon, and in the evening, and besides cryptic messages for him to stand by and await instructions coming in once a day at noon, he never got any new messages at all.

Cell service was non-existent in the bunker, even right up to the outer door, which was as far as any of them dared to venture, so they hadn't received any news, trusting his assurances that if the outside were safe again, somebody would let him know. He himself was beginning to doubt whether or not that would ever happen. He could imagine at least three scenarios where they never left the bunker:

1. If the outside was permanently unsafe, and the all-clear never comes within any of their lifetimes.

2. If the messages to him to stand-by were automated and nobody remembered them down there to send the all-clear.

3. If the messages were automated and nobody was left alive to discontinue them.

He did have some small semblance of hope, however. At the bottom of each message was a small script that declared what number the message was of how many messages in the system that day, and that number, thankfully, varied day to day, meaning that there were people elsewhere in the system sending messages back and forth an any given day. He himself kept his reports updated, as per the Standard Operating Procedure (SOP) that came in a thick binder that he'd kept in the bunker. It was also filled with "what if" scenarios and instructions for what to do in case of fire, flood, earthquake, or other disaster scenarios. It had no section on delivering a baby, though; he'd checked.

He came to his senses just as he opened the last cabinet, filled to the brim with the medical supplies he'd scrounged from the various kitchens of the culinary building nearly two months previous. An entire shelf was a foot deep with rubbing alcohol and high-proof liquors. He grabbed four bottles of the rubbing alcohol and ran out of the storage wing, with its racks and racks of supplies and closets, and down the hall, past the bedroom, bathroom, and kitchen, to the living room, where they'd moved the kitchen table and Evelyn to have room for the birthing process. Half his students were crammed into the next room beyond, the alcove, originally intended for an entertainment room but now converted with pallets and all the spare blankets into the dormitory for the student body.

In the living room itself were only Evelyn, Liza, and Joyce. Phillip was nowhere to be seen. Evelyn was laying down on the table, a thin layer of blankets cushioning her repose as Liza was up under the blanket between Evelyn's legs once more. Joyce was by Evelyn's head brushing her hair and talking to her in a low voice.

"Where the hell is Phillip!?"

Liza answered very calmly, a counterpoint to the shrill panic edging into Professor Walthers voice.

"Professor, Phillip is in the archives, reviewing and printing the texts on home delivery. I asked him to since we're rather limited in materials and tools here. Please, try to keep calm; if Evelyn is relaxed and calm, this should be a great deal easier than if she were frightened out of her wits."

Evelyn spoke up from the head of the table.

"Henry, please try to stay calm; you're scaring the women folk."

Joyce and Liza chuckled as Professor Walthers shoulders slumped. Here he was in a panic as the woman actually giving birth made jokes!

"Well, fine. I got the rubbing alcohol, like you said. Where should I put it?"

Liza's answer was slightly muffled, as she was under the blanket checking Evelyn's dilation once more.

"Just throw it in the easy chair. She's not broke her water yet, and contractions are still a good ten to fifteen minutes apart."

"How much fluid will there be?"

"Lots, why?"

"I'll go get a tarp to put under the table, that way we don't have it sloshing around our shoes when everything gets into full swing."

~

Nearly two hours later, Professor Walthers sat next to his wife's head as she screamed through gritted teeth. Liza and Phillip stood side by side between her legs quietly consulting a few papers Phillip had brought back printed from the archive. Evelyn finally relaxed, her head falling back on the sweat-soaked pillows as the contraction subsided. Joyce had retreated, completely useless ever since Evelyn's water had broken ten minutes before. Suddenly, Evelyn's head snapped up as she let out a roaring combination of a grunt and a scream. The students between her legs immediately threw the papers aside as they crowded in to his wife's groin. Just as suddenly as it had begun, Evelyn rolled her head back and the students stepped back, a wriggling pink mass in their hands — it was a boy.

They beckoned the Professor over and handed him a small pair of steel surgical scissors and a long pale rope connecting Evelyn and the baby, now well swathed in warm, clean blankets. The Professor took the scissors, gulped down a lungful of air, and fainted dead in a heap.

His next memory was of being woken up on a bed, his child on his chest, Evelyn snuggled up to his side. For the moment, he forgot where they were and felt at peace.

~

Day 57

Sharon was not at all at ease. It was far, far quieter than she was comfortable with. It was eerie. New York city on a... hell, what day was it now? It didn't matter. It was afternoon in the Big Apple, and there was no traffic. There were no horns blaring. There were no crowds. And Sharon was alone. She was moving quietly and carefully car to car in the middle of the structure. The concrete edifice of a multistory parking garage echoed her every scrape and step. Eyes down, sunglasses dark, crouched, almost crawling. Quiet and slow from space to space, only looking up at the number on the wall.

Her bug-out car was parked in space B19, odd cars on the exterior spaces evens on the interior. She was on B12. Three more spaces then across. It was a silver bumper with a Semper Fi plate border. She wouldn't have to look up. B14, red Ford by the looks of it. It had a flat tire and was coated in dust; it had probably been here months before the Phenomenon. B16, a yellow Camaro, might make for a nice midlife crisis car if she ever got to live to have a midlife crisis. B18, green Range Rover, could definitely use that if she had to leave the city.

Across, by the bumper, down low, stay away from the opening in the garage that leads to sky. She could feel the warmth of the light on the top of her head, but she didn't look up. Key in, turn... damn. It's stuck. It hadn't been opened in a while. She gently pushed upwards but it didn't move. She sighed, squeezed her eyes shut, and stood up, putting both her hands into a strong heave on the trunk. It sprung open with an uncomfortably loud clang, the keys flying through the air overhead and landing behind her on the ground.

She peeked out of her right eye looking down into the trunk. It was all there, the duffel bags, the arms cases, the boxes of ammunition, the cardboard box full of MREs, the road bag with its blankets and flares and various emergency tools. The spare gallon of gasoline. This would all help. A little spray-paint, a stop by one of those spy shops to pick up a pair of IR goggles. It would work, she could do this.

Thump. Something hit the roof of the trunk, felt like inches from her hand.

Without hesitation she closed her eyes, threw herself in, and pulled the trunk lid down and closed.

As she lay in the dark, the stink of gasoline choking her, she heard, and felt, as innumerable things thumped into the outside of the car, she could tell they were covering it, cocooning it. And then they started moving, shifting, maybe vibrating, it was hard to tell, but they were tapping all over the car.

Shit.

The fumes were enough to make Sharon's eyes water. With nothing to look at anyway she closed them. The rustling and chittering of the things on the outside of the car was disconcerting, but only mildly so. In fact, it was rather soothing. Like a fan or rain on a roof, white noise. Despite that, there was no way she was taking a nap. No way she could sleep through that smell. Plus, she knew from the EAS that so long as she was still and quiet they'd leave her alone eventually. She had to find a way to bide her time quietly.

She figured if she made noise in the initial few minutes of her captivity it wouldn't be so bad. She began by rolling over on her side to face the bug-out bag and find her Gas Mask and flashlight. The Mask was easy, and she slipped it on, cleared it, and opened her eyes. The moonbeam was strapped to the pack itself rather than inside, and she found it right away. She clicked it on and began rifling through the pack for something to read. Survival manuals, hunting guides from various game reserves, game cookbooks, Everyday Chemistry, maps, guidebooks, reference manuals for various firearms... aha!

I can always reread The Art of War...

Rolling back, her left elbow and funny bone slammed into the roof of the trunk, sending lightning bolts of pain shooting up her arm. It was oddly quiet, the things had ceased their wriggling, their chittering. Whatever the hell they'd been doing, they weren't doing it now.

Thump.

Either one of the things had just thumped the car or a mass of them had coordinated to do so. Annoyed, Sharon slapped the roof intentionally this time, telling them under her breath to be quiet.

Thump.

Again they thumped right back at her. Angry now Sharon punched the roof of her confinement, rapid fire, three strikes, left-right-left.

Thump-thump-thump!

Sharon gave them one last slap before angrily grabbing for the book from where it had settled beside her.

Thump!

Thump!

Thump-thump-thump!

Despite the terror of knowing death itself was tapping on the metal inches from her, Sharon resigned herself to wait it out.

~

Day 57

Sharon was running. Something pursuing, something behind, something dark. She knew she had to get away. No way to fight back, nowhere to hide, escape was the only option. If she turned she would die, and she knew it. But the voices kept demanding she look. Or maybe they wanted something else. Her acquiescence, her surrender. As she focused her attention back on her path, she realized there was a precipice ahead. It was too dark to see the other side or the bottom. It had to be a leap of faith...

With a sudden jerk, she awoke, banging her elbow yet again against the hard metal of the trunk floor. She froze, straining her ears to listen for any indication the things had heard her. It was silent outside, until she heard someone fumbling with keys outside, heard one key after another pushed into the trunk.

She fumbled around trying to get at her weapon, but that hand was numb and the bug-out bag was in the way of the draw. Suddenly the trunk lid opened and a blinding light flooded in.

93

"Sharon!"

Emil was a welcome sight, even if unnecessary; all she had to do was hit the internal trunk release and she'd have been out.

"Sharon! Thank goodness I found you, I came looking after so many hours... found these keys right next to the drain grate... I was worried you'd, well..."

"I'm fine, but you shouldn't be here, Emil. What did I tell you!? What's the protocol?"

"One person..."

"One Person Out At A Time. OPAAT. One person out, everyone else waits, that way if one person does something stupid it doesn't put the others at risk. Where is Sarya? What would happen if you came looking for me and we both died? What would she do?"

"Yes yes, you're right... but I'm naturally an impatient person. I couldn't help myself."

"Well, help yourself next time, stick to the protocol. Stay home. I didn't need your help."

I'm sorry, I just...

"Enough, let's get back indoors. Even in the middle of the day, it's not safe out here."

Yes, yes of course, need any help carrying any of that?

"Well, you're here; might as well make yourself useful..."

CHAPTER 11

Day 77

Aboard the *Oregon*, nearly everyone in the Command Center was sweating bullets, even the Captain.

"Easy does it, Thompson; you don't want to oversteer here. There's no room for correction."

"Aye, sir, easy as I can..."

"You're doing a good job, just don't get nervous."

"Heh, too late for that sir...

"Wentworth, what's our depth sounding?"

A voice from an aft station pronounced, "We've got 12 meters under the keel, sir".

"You hear that, Thompson? You've got some wiggle room; relax."

"Aye, sir..."

"Nav!"

A twin pair of voices responded immediately "Yes sir?"

"What's our current position, how far have we gotten?"

The Navigator, a wiry redheaded Ensign, responded "We are approximately 6 miles upriver in the East River, west of Roosevelt Island. We're about to go under the Queensboro Bridge connecting Manhattan and Queens."

"And how much further until our destination?"

"Two and a half miles until we're sitting pretty off the coast of East 97th and FDR Drive."

"XO!"

"Aye, sir?"

"Are our accommodations ready for our passengers?"

"Absolutely, sir."

"Good, let's hope they're there waiting for us. I'd hate to have come all this way for nothing."

"Now that we're almost here sir, can I ask who, exactly, we're picking up?"

"No idea. All I know is they're Government Agency VIPs, people in the know who are important to the efforts to understand this whole thing."

"What if there are others waiting for us?"

"I somehow doubt the Chinese or North Koreans are waiting for us in the East River..."

"No sir, I mean, other survivors. New York's a city of a couple million, sir; there's bound to be survivors other than our VIPs."

"We only take the VIPs. It's a tough deal, but this boat doesn't have room for civilians. We're only here for the VIPs."

"How will we know them?"

"They've an authorization level and pass-phrases which were relayed to me. I've got them written down in the notebook in my left breast pocket. Wentworth, sounding?"

"Fifteen meters, sir!"

"Nav, position?"

"Only a few hundred yards, sir..."

"Good, time to hit the surface. Blow tanks, set planes at 15 degrees upwards bubble, rudder amidships, all stop on the engines, raise the AN/BVS and hit the Infrared. Let's see if there's somebody waiting."

~

Day 77

A man in a rumpled and grease stained black suit sat under an awning along the waterline of the East River. He was cold, tired, and the weight of the infrared goggles was beginning to make his neck hurt. He was dying for a cigarette, but even sitting still under cover from the sky, the heat of a lighter and then the slow burn of a smoke could still run the possibility of attracting the damn things from the sky.

As he shivered and wished for the thousandth time he had brought a blanket or something, he suddenly saw something he never expected in a million lifetimes to see so up close and in person. Through the various multihued rainbows that the goggles made of the world, he could see a sleek, cold, metal, rounded hump rise from the water, quickly taking a more recognizable form. He slowly reached into his inside vest pocket and keyed the radio tucked within.

"The ride's here, and it's a bloody submarine."

A crackling voice from the radio started speaking and then was drowned out in static.

~

Day 77

Lucinda hated flying, especially in a stripped down helicopter. The hard metal seat was cold, and the way it was bouncing up and down in the wind and banged against her rump wasn't helping. She was sure that when they got to their destination she'd have bruises all over from the rough treatment she'd received during her evacuation.

Omega Protocol, immediate recall of all $\phi 1$ Clearance to the Safe house.

That had been hammered into their heads over and over again at the Project. For years.

The Safe house, that was what they called it. When she got back out into the world and was able to look up what the coordinates actually meant she was taken aback, just as she was sure most of the world would if they knew. But it was the last stand. The final place where the best and brightest and most important were to take shelter if all else was lost. Every member of the Project was a part of it. Every member was aware. She didn't expect to see them all. Their contingency plans were all based around nuclear exchange, or biological or chemical attack. This... Phenomenon... was something else.

If she had followed her plan to the letter she'd have been dead multiple times over, stuck in a resort cabin in the Appalachians with no escape, too few supplies, and too many windows. Still, she expected to see most of them there, reunited after nearly six years. She wondered if any of them had gotten used to their new identities? Had they had families? Gone rogue? There was no way to know.

The choppers engine sounds changed, they were winding down. It was a subtle change, but with sound as her only real way to know what was going on it couldn't be helped. The pilot and copilot as well as the men who'd pulled her out, they all had IR goggles. She was blindfolded to keep her safe. Still, in the meantime she'd learned new information that might fit into the wider puzzle. The pilots had been very talkative about the things they'd discovered with regards to mid-Phenomenon flight.

The Phenomenon cocooned aircraft like they did cars or ships, but only while the aircraft was on the ground, and they avoided the engines. Once the plane was at speed or in the air, they peeled off and resumed their normal activities. So as long as you could board the plane and fly her in UV or IR, you could fly reliably. Air Force One was still in the air, moving from controlled landing site to controlled landing site.

The President, well, the old president, had died in the initial event, looked right out the window of the White House. The Vice President had as well. The new President, the old Speaker, was not the best person for the job (Lucinda thought) but he wasn't overreacting or going overboard. He was a cautious politician, and a cautious Chief Executive.

A sudden bump told her they'd landed. Now was the worst part, waiting. A couple of hours of being still and quiet. As the rotors wound down above them, she started hearing thumps all over the body of the helicopter. The... *things*... finding the chopper hot and on the ground, were suddenly interested again.

The pilots whispered that the best thing to do was take a nap, unless you snored — if you snored, it was *just* loud enough to keep them interested. A couple of hours, a quick run from the pad inside, and she'd be reunited with the Project. The only people she'd ever truly related to her entire life.

CHAPTER 12

Day 77

Timor was running for his life.

He couldn't remember how he got into this situation. All he knew was that he had to escape. He was moving through the tunnels of the station, dodging hanging pipes and debris left over from a cold war long ago. The sounds of his pursuer behind him were subtle. His own footfalls nearly drowned it out. The shadows of his pursuers stretched ahead of him. The cloud that chased him was a wall of broken glass, black and sharp, whirling and surging. As it moved through the station the world around it changed, he knew... but he didn't know how he knew. The voices from the dark were the damnedest thing. A constant cacophony of whispers and hushed commands. *Obey... bow... worship... sacrifice...*

They were getting louder; it was getting closer. The hall was twisting under his feet, his shoes sinking through the cold concrete as the angles went wrong and what was flat became curved and solid became pliable. An errant pipe snaked out of nowhere and caught the cuff of his pant leg, sending him flying onto his hands and knees. That was all it took; the void was upon him.

With a start, flailing against his attacker, Timor awoke in a cold sweat, wrapped too tightly in his blankets... again. He had to start taking a sedative before bed. He couldn't keep moving so much in his sleep. He swiveled his body to the side, throwing his legs off the side of the cot. His knees ached, his feet were swollen, and his breathing was ragged.

Unlike in his dreams, the real-life halls of the station were too cramped and narrow for running, and with no open space large enough for anything but tight circles of six or seven feet, the lack of activity and exercise, the wealth of processed foods, and complete boredom were taking their tolls on his health. His waistline was testing the limits of the biggest pants he had on hand. Pretty soon, he'd have to go nude and just bump up the thermostat.

As he made his way into the Communications Center on his way to the privy, he kept an ear out for an alert notifying him of active comm traffic, but as usual there was nothing. Timor was sure there were still satellites in operation, but the systems here were hardwired to certain frequencies, and none of them were military, commercial, or civilian. Unless somebody started making uses of the ISS bands or the NASA shuttle bands, he might as well be the last soul on earth.

As he sat on the cold steel rim of the privy, he contemplated what he was to do. The same options kept cycling through his head, the same ones he'd had since the ISS went silent two weeks before. He could try to live out the rest of his life in the station, or, he could take a walk outside and sky gaze. He was starting to think the latter was better than ending up obese and dying of a heart attack alone in a concrete cave.

His reverie was broken by a shrill tone coming from the Communications Center.

~

Day 65

"What do you mean it might be an infection?"

The Professor and Evelyn stood side by side as Liza used a flashlight and magnifying glass to look down their baby's throat.

"I think we're all aware I'm no MD, I can't speak with full authority, and without any way to culture a swab or blood sample I just have to go by signs and symptoms. Redness, swelling, sensitivity, pain... I think it just might be something simple, something a shot of Penicillin might fix."

Evelyn scooted forward in her chair.

"What if it isn't? We don't have all the immunizations down here..."

Liza removed her tools from the infant's mouth and handed the swaddled bundle back to his mother.

"Herd immunity is a wonderful thing. I already asked everyone down here what common childhood illnesses they've had or been exposed to. The only ones that we might be carrying are non-lethal so long as we make sure he's well hydrated and we keep him fairly sanitary we shouldn't lose him. Now, I hate to say this, but some of them used to, back in the day, sometimes lead to disfigurements and disabilities."

"What kinds of disabilities?"

"Some mental, some physical, depends on the specific disease and circumstances. Most of the mental issues are consequence of extended high fever, and we're well stocked with fever reducers, so those are very unlikely."

"What kinds of physical disabilities?"

"Lame limbs mostly, sometimes tics or tremors..."

"How soon will you know if a shot is all he needs?"

"About twelve hours I should think. If symptoms don't start to subside after that, we may have to give him more, possibly as part of an IV, mostly just to make sure dehydration isn't a major component."

"Okay... Evelyn, would you please stay with Liza and keep watch over Rowan? I'm going to see to something in the archives."

"Hurry back."

Professor Walthers got up from the chairs in what they'd come to think of as their medical room and went down the hall, through the common rooms, and to the reinforced door to the Master Control Computer for the vault. There, he sat down at the terminal. What the rest of the students didn't know, what even his wife didn't know, was that the computer also had access to the rooftop sensor and communications package. He'd used it to keep track of the EAS alerts and to communicate with the ISS and its sole surviving occupant, even had two of the physics majors calculate the astronaut's landing site as a part of their attempts to keep busy. But George was likely already picked up by the French now, and so his source of news about Japan was gone as well.

As he queued up its feed he noticed that the package was registering the temperature at a chilly 20F. He double checked the sensor with a quick self-diagnostic command. It wasn't malfunctioning. He knew not to use the high definition camera, but there was an infrared feed he could use, and the transmission the week before had said that it was safe, so he punched it up. It came up quickly and showed a rather odd sight. There were a series of sharp intersections all over the screen, and a slowly shifting pattern of swirling color behind. At first he was confused, but then he realized the camera was pointed directly upwards, the default position, and the camera must be seeing something on the top of the globe of clear plastic that contained and protected the camera, and the sky behind. What he was seeing, he realized, was likely the frost on the globe and the shifting weather above.

He engaged the directional controls and slowly panned the camera downwards to look over the edge of the building and down into the University grounds. He stopped the camera there and stared at the screen. He took his hands off the keyboard. He took a moment to consider what he was seeing. On the screen, the grounds of the University could be clearly seen. Lamp-posts, benches, and statuary dotted the grounds between buildings and they stood out clear as day, their materials showing clearly a few degrees colder even than the banks of snow that piled against them. Streaks of snow could be seen making their way down in flurries and gusts, their bright white streaks clearly visible against the black distance where he cameras sensitivity fell off.

Figures could be seen moving through the snow.

Judging by the way they came just over the lamp-posts, each one must be easily 9 feet tall, at least. Their precise details were hard to make out, but they were clearly non-human.

All their proportions were wrong. For one, their shoulders were far too wide, and the head seemed to rise from that plateau like a mountain before leveling off rather abruptly. The arms were long, almost down to the knees, and thin, like spiders legs almost. The legs were the same though they seemed to flare out a bit at the knees.

Professor Walthers sat back in his chair and reached up with a shaking hand to pull off his glasses. He closed and reopened his eyes several times, used the bottom of his t-shirt to clean his glasses then put them back on and leaned forward once more.

The figures were moving around the quad. Each seemed to be moving independently of the others, but at the same time, the ones he could see seemed to invoke some memory, some pattern he'd seen before somewhere. He tried recalling it, but came up empty. He slowly panned the camera right and left, finding the whole of the grounds within his view to be utterly infested with the things.

Then he saw something he did not expect to see. Crouched behind one of the benches along the nearest walkway was a figure, blazing with heat. A person, a human being. He was covered in what looked to be some kind of a blanket, and there was snow and ice piled onto it, but the infrared could clearly see his body heat through the thin veneer of the material. Walthers hurriedly pulled the camera back, to get a grander view, and saw one of the things, one of the tall things, walking slowly right towards the hiding person.

His eyes were glued to the screen, frozen by his complete impotence.

He watched as the creature took first one step, then another towards the man. Silently imploring him to move, to run, to escape, to fight, anything. And the creature kept coming.

Step by step, meter by meter, it was almost on top of the man behind the bench... and then it kept going.

The creature walked directly past the man without even a hitch in its step. Walthers suddenly remembered he was watching this whole scene in infrared, and the monster likely couldn't see the man's heat like he could. He let out the breath he hadn't realized he was holding. Then he gasped in right back in again as the man started moving.

As calmly as can be, he stood up and started walking towards the culinary arts building. He panned the camera to track him but it was only moments before the edge of the building itself obscured his view. The man had to have passed nearly a dozen other buildings with everything from weapons grade lasers to concentrated acids to nuclear materials, and he was coming here. He had to know about the bunker, it was the only explanation. Then a horrifying thought came to him. The baby —herd immunity — and whoever, *whatever,* that man was, he was threat to them all, but most especially to his little Rowan.

He ran from the archives at a dead sprint.

As he hurried through the living quarters he shouted instructions to the students to secure themselves in wherever they could get, to arm themselves if necessary, and for Evelyn and the bay to lock themselves into their bedroom with the flare gun from the emergency kit — the most potent weapon they had. By the time he got to the front door of the vault it was already cycling its action. He slid to a stop on the slick polished concrete, sweat dripping from his hair and down his face as he caught his breath. The door slowly opened into the vault.

Dear god, he had the access codes.

The thought came unbidden, but the implications exploded into his consciousness like a sledgehammer into a marshmallow.

He must be from the Project.

As the door came fully open he could see a poorly disguised ghost. Your typical white sheet with eyelets.

"Who are you and what do you want?"

The figure adjusted its sheet, then realized the silliness of it before pulling it off completely. Walthers' face lit up in an unexpected smile as he recognized the man standing before him, even swathed in the layers of white winter clothing. The black skin surrounding the silver smile was enough by itself to provide identification.

"Viktor! What in the world? How? I mean. Japan?"

"I'm very glad to see you welcoming me rather casually, Professor. Last time I dropped in on someone like this, I was met with automatic weapons fire."

The Professor became suddenly very aware of how inappropriate he had become in the last few months of isolation. He was wearing an off-white t-shirt emblazoned with the Berkeley logo and a pair of red and white striped running shorts with bare feet.

"Well, down here it tends to stay rather warm... But Viktor, what the hell?"

"What do you mean?"

"The sheet? Those things out there? For Christ's sakes, there's a lot of fucking questions I could throw at you, and a few pieces of furniture as well."

"Yes yes yes... all in good time. I'll be happy to address your concerns, but first, I am here with a purpose beyond a pleasant social visit."

"And that is?"

"The archives, of course. Are they here, are they intact?"

"Viktor..."

106

"It's important, Henry."

"Yes. Yes, they're still here. Why do you need them?"

"Two reasons. First off, I'm supposed to initiate an off-site backup. Second, there's a critical how-to manual I need to look up."

"Off-site backup? Viktor, that's nonsense; the amount of data alone..."

"...Is not going to be an issue; I come well prepared."

"I didn't see any tractor trailers pulled up outside with extra servers."

Viktor let out a deep rumbling chuckle.

"Nevertheless, old friend, I can do as I've said."

"And for the rest?"

"You mean the Tall Ones?"

"Is that what they're called?"

"In some circles, yes."

"In some circles...? Just how many circles are you in communication with?"

"Quite a few, but I don't think I'm really at liberty to get into all that, not at this time anyway. Never mind; it's an in-joke."

"This is bizarre, Viktor, even for you."

Yes, it is. May I actually come in, or should I just camp on your doorstep?

"Oh, yes, of course. Please come in."

With that, Viktor stepped in from the hall leading up to the door and down the steps on the other side, careful with his footing as the ice and snow all over him had melted and created quite a puddle in the blast of heat from the vault. As they made their way into the living area, Professor Walthers called out the all clear and introduced him to the student body, as well as Evelyn and little Rowan.

"Now, I'm sure you all have a great deal of questions but I hope you understand that while I trust all of you, and you certainly deserve answers, the very nature of the Project requires I get a few answers from Viktor myself in private before any kind of mass interrogation. So, if you'll excuse us, I'll be taking our guest back to the archives for now."

Ignoring the mass protests and appreciating the subtle nod of understanding from Evelyn, he kissed Rowan's forehead before escorting Viktor back to the archives. Once there they each pulled chairs out from under the MCP and sat down. Viktor shrugged off his heavy overcoat as well as the lighter one underneath, revealing he wore a set of thermal pants held up by suspenders, which he also removed after taking his boots off. Standing there in a simple set of black jeans and a white muscle shirt, he pulled a small black box, about the size of a pack of cigarettes, as well as a small cord from his pocket and set it on the desk. Walthers looked at it and back to Viktor.

"Am I supposed to believe that has the necessary capability to back up all this?"

Walthers punctuated his sentence by waving his hand at all the servers in the rest of the room.

"Yes."

"Viktor, I'm not crazy."

"No, but you are ignorant, or uninformed, if you prefer the term."

"If you expect me to believe..."

"I do. You see, the Project is divided into tiers. You, me, the other 24 of us, we're the lowest tier. We're the Ensigns, the Privates in this little organization, lowest level. Through necessity, I've been promoted, and so I have access to things most couldn't imagine. This

108

little device is one such example."

"What does it do?"

"Lots of things. It's first and primary purpose is pretty standard — data storage, only significantly denser than was ever allowed to be suspected by the public. This could hold fifty of your archives."

"Fifty!?"

"At least. You are looking at a quantum storage medium."

The blank look on Walthers face said enough.

"Okay, so. Normal files are written in magnetism, little bits of material that can be magnetized and demagnetized so that you can store binary, ones and zeros, that represent letters, numbers, anything you need, okay?"

"Sure."

"Well, that requires at least a whole atom of a magnetizable material, iron or something, right?"

"Logically."

"So now imagine if you don't need a whole atom, or even a whole electron, proton, or neutron, but only a much smaller component piece. Suddenly you open up the ability to store a lot more information in a much smaller package, right?"

"And that's what this does?"

"Essentially, except instead of using magnetism, which is limited to binary storage, this uses quarks, particles which can be in six different 'flavors': up, down, strange, charm, top, and bottom."

"So the information can be stored in hexadecimal?"

"You catch on quickly."

"So this little magic box of yours is going to copy down my entire archives?"

"Yes."

"How long will this take?"

"This little baby is remarkably efficient. The limiting factor, I think, will be how fast your servers are."

"Fastest commercially available as of the building of the vault, as I understand it."

"That's not as fast as I'd hoped, but it'll have to do."

Viktor connected the wire to the box and then, at Walthers direction, to one of the computers USB ports. Walthers logged into the computer and was surprised to find the copy already in progress. In fact, the first server was already done and the next was being started.

"And as for my questions about the outside?"

"I have some good news, and some bad news. But first, have you been keeping up with the EAS?"

"Yes, I know the current estimate, 97%."

"97% is the optimistic number. From dwindling signatures of human activity observed by satellite, we think that there's essentially five main pockets of any notable population still active. Tokyo, Moscow, Sydney, New York, and Washington DC. We think Tokyo & NYC took advantage of their subway system, while DC and Moscow still had massive shelters left over from the Cold War. There's other indicators of survivors in most major cities, but they're nowhere near the requisite population to ensure the survival of humanity."

"And Japan recently suffered an Earthquake, did it not?"

"And just how would you know that?"

"The package on the roof of this building includes satellite communications. I patched into the ISS, who were still in communication with both Tokyo and some small station in Russia, but not DC."

"Fascinating. I wonder how they're doing up there. Can they look out the windows?"

"They stopped transmitting nearly three weeks ago. They were initiating a landing in the English Channel, supposedly going to be picked up by the French."

"That's too bad. The Channel isn't a nice place to be these days."

"What do you mean?"

"Well, I presume you saw the weather outside? Yes? Well, that's here in subtropical Southern California. In temperate Europe, things are much, much worse."

"You said the things out there are called 'Tall Ones'. Where did that name originate?"

"East coast, group of surviving military affiliated with the Project out of the Secondary Facility."

"So the Project endures?"

"Yes, and it goes essentially as planned. I mean, not exactly as planned of course; most of the twenty-six are MIA or confirmed dead, but there's a few survivors, the most important ones at any rate. Most of mankind's pure academic knowledge is preserved, and quite a few practical skills. As I understand it, there's even a machinist making his way around the American south with a truckload of exobiological theory from Dr. Rafei in the back of his truck."

"That's an odd combination."

"To be sure. The point is, we're rather successful in our venture."

"And these 'Tall Ones', what are they? Aliens?"

"What makes you say that?"

"Well the things in the sky —"

"Shards, their nickname is 'Shards'."

"— the Shards, they originate from space, yes?"

"Yes."

"And so it follows these other things —"

"Are unrelated. The Shards and the Tall Ones coming about at the same time is related, but they themselves are not. Think of opening a door and letting a bit of wind in as you come in. You do not cause the wind, nor did the wind cause you, but you're both coming in at the same time, and to someone completely unfamiliar with either you or anything like you or the wind, they would seem very much connected."

"How do you know?"

"That, I can't tell you. All I can say is that the Tall Ones are the greater worry, the greater threat."

"And what are we to do?"

"Resist, survive, and it starts here."

"How?"

"With this."

Viktor grabbed up his coat and reached into one of the inner pockets, coming out with long wooden box, covered in black lacquer and tied shut with a red ribbon. Untying the ribbon, Viktor opened the box, inside, set down in fitted foam, was a copper knife, covered in deeply etched figures, symbols, and inscriptions.

"What is that?"

"It's a knife, of course."

"Yes, but how is that of any use?"

"Anything can be the right weapon in the right hands."

"And your hands are the right ones?"

"No, yours are."

"And what am I supposed to do with it?"

"I haven't the foggiest, to be honest."

"What?"

"I'm serious."

A tone from the computer indicated it was finished, the screen showed all servers had been backed up and verified by the little box. Walthers couldn't imagine what it meant by verified.

"And with that, I'm afraid I'm also done here."

Viktor started gathering his things as Walthers stuttered protests and questions, each coming and faltering as he thought of something more important. By the time he had his train of thought together,

Viktor was walking out of the archive, pushing past Alex who stood in the doorway with a frown on his face. As he walked, Viktor was putting back on his pants, coats, and other winter gear. Walthers followed, protesting the whole way. By the time, Viktor got halfway through the bunker proper, the students had caught onto what was happened and formed a wall barring Viktor from further progress. As he stopped, they crossed their arms like an impromptu student protest, which in many ways it was.

"So, you think you're going to keep me here against my will? The lot of you against me?"

Evelyn stood off to the side, cradling Rowan.

"You know my husband Henry?"

"Yes, ma'am I do."

"You're a part of the Project?"

"I'm afraid I don't know what you're talking about."

"They all know about it. I mean, *we* all do. Henry didn't feel right, keeping us in the dark."

"So you know. So what? That's not going to keep me here."

"Do you think you're stronger than the rest of us? Even the biggest running back in the NFL can't hold or drag more than maybe two or three people at once. We could dogpile on you and keep you down until we can tie you up..."

"I'm sure you could, all things being equal, in a fair fight, muscle vs muscle. I, however, do *not* fight fair, and I am *not* equal."

As quick as a flash, Viktor whipped a hand out of the pocket of his overcoat and turned around, a P08 9mm Luger with a 7.8" barrel pointed directly at the chest of Professor Walthers, who had finally caught up and been slowly moving up behind him.

"Professor, I admire your dedication, and while I would normally be more than happy to take the time to explain exactly how and why I have to be on my way, I simply *do not have the time!*"

These last words were shouted, and echoed off the concrete walls with remarkable ferocity. Rowan began crying as the students slowly eased apart to give Viktor a clear path to the exit. Professor Walthers put up his hands in defeat and indicated the path.

"Fine, go. Just go. Don't hurt anyone here, we are unarmed."

And with that, Viktor began walking sideways to the exit, one arm cradling his pack, the other whipping the Luger back and forth from the Professor to the students. As he closed the door, the Professor indicated that someone should go make sure it's secured. Then he looked around at everyone assembled and took a brief headcount.

"Where's Alex?"

Alex was in the Archives, a world away in his mind, using the MCP to search for anything relating to the copper knife that still sat on the desk to his immediate right. Something about it pulled strings in the back of his mind, something he'd read long ago. On the screen a list came up. Several entries were nonsense, of course, but one... he highlighted it and began the process of bringing up the book it was from.

1. Coppers of the Northwest Indians - Paulinski

2. The Wisconsin Archeologist, - Volume 6

3. Letter Knives of Hammered Copper - June 1955

4. **The Copper Blade of Inana/Summoning - Simon**

5. Religion and Society in Middle Bronze Age Greece - Artoro

1. Native American Weapons - Collins

As it came up on the second screen, his eyes widened in recognition as he recognized the work, something he'd been obsessed with as a teen. Spurred by a goth phase, he'd studied everything from the occult as well as everything macabre from Poe, Lovecraft, King, Rice and others. The knife was mentioned in one of those collections he'd loved so much. Fiction, but sitting not even a foot from his hand. He queued up the chapter and started reading. It spoke of using the knife in a ritual of calling, summoning.

CHAPTER 13

Day 77

The storefront was still decorated for *alla helgons dag*, or All Saints Day, Swedish Halloween. They did things a bit differently. There were no costumes, or trick or treating. For them, it was a quiet and solemn remembrance of those passed on. Lycksele celebrated with public decorations, little white bows on street poles and dioramas of the saints.

That had been nearly three months ago. Now, all that could be seen outside was snow. She'd taken refuge in this little shop when the warning came out. It was the only place still open, and the shopkeeper had run the other way. As she sought shelter, he rushed home, perhaps to a wife, or children. Regardless, they passed each other without words, and he'd left the place unlocked. She entered and, finding the keys in the office, locked the doors. Each day since, she'd used a display model of a little charcoal grill to boil water, cook food, and everything else, safely in the rear of the store where there were no windows to the outside. After a month though, she'd gotten fed up, and looked at the front. The view that morning was a crisp, sunny fall day. If not for the shriveled corpse of the shopkeeper she saw in his car, she almost might've convinced herself

115

it was safe.

The next day, the snows came, and they didn't stop. When Angela was a little girl, snow had always seemed magical. It was a rarity in Alabama, where she grew up, but the few times in her life it had come, it had come at Christmastime, bringing a little girl a wondrous few days of sledding and snowball fights. The smell of snow on the air used to bring to mind her mother's fresh baked cookies and hot chocolate, always waiting after a day in the cold.

Now, the swirling blizzard outside brought nothing but fear. There was no comfort to be found in its chill. Bizarre shapes moved in the darkness just beyond her vision, trees perhaps, maybe elk. She'd seen elk moving outside before, keeping their heads down and their eyes low, moving slowly, one hoof at a time. It was probably elk. It was hopefully just elk. This part of the country wasn't exactly foreign to them.

She shouldn't even have been looking outside, she knew, but she'd hoped, prayed even, that the snow would bring her some kind of respite from the loneliness, some shred of happiness. It was a hope she felt anew each day, yet each day a little bit less. Just howling wind, snow, and darkness beyond the glow of her flashlight.

But then, just there, in the trees, something... no, probably just a snow covered tree branch moving in the wind. As she turned to go back into the depths of the store, she heard the things from the sky impact the glass behind her, attracted by the glow of her brief search for happiness. She squeezed her eyes shut. They'd occasionally wrapped the building before, but never gotten in. She knew what to do, so she began walking as she heard them start their infernal noise. Despite her experience telling her she was safe, she quickened her pace.

Suddenly, the sound of shattering glass and the feel of a cold and biting wind struck her from behind. A quiet kind of dreadful panic swept through her gut.

They killed on sight, they killed on contact, too many corpses in those first few days. She ran, counting paces, keeping her stride even, she estimated distance travelled and time to get to the door to the back area of the store. She could hear something giving chase. Sledgehammers impacted the floor behind her, feeling as if they were on her heels. She opened her eyes in just enough time to see the door, slightly off to her right. She'd misjudged her steps, or her angles, and had drifted from her course.

She threw herself at the door, sliding into the employee break room on her side as her feet found no purchase. The door, on swing hinges, closed behind her as she scrambled up on her hands and feet. She moved to the nearest shelter, a storage cabinet behind the door, and crawled in as quickly as she could.

She wasn't in there more than a half second before she heard the break room door slam back open, it's impact into the cabinet making her ears ring. Once more, she wished they'd had some warning, some hint of things to come. That way she could've been retrieved and evacuated with the rest of the Project members.

She could hear whatever it was that had been chasing her stalking around outside. Its footfalls were strange. Definitely bipedal, but the floors here weren't made of glass, and the storm definitely couldn't penetrate this far indoors, certainly not this quickly, and yet... its every step crackled like it was crunching through icy puddles. If it had been an elk, or a moose, or a bear, it would have made other noises, but other than its footfalls it was silent. Eerily so. She couldn't even hear any breathing. Suddenly, she heard it rush off, heard the door slam open and wind howling as it rushed back out into the blizzard. She waited, listening, not even breathing, straining to hear anything and everything going on outside her hiding spot.

Three heartbeats, six... nothing. Nothing at all.

She gently pressed on the door of the cabinet and found it was freezing, the metal so cold it burned to the touch. It didn't move. She pressed harder, and still it stayed closed. She thought she might have jammed the latch when she slammed it closed, or maybe been damaged somehow when the door hit it as... whatever it was... came barreling into the room. She braced herself against the rear of the cabinet and heaved against the door. After an agonizing second where she was terrified she might be trapped, it broke open with a sharp crack. Peering around the break room she was astounded to find everything, *everything*, coated in ice. She'd been frozen in.

Nearly a quarter inch of ice covered every square inch of the floor, walls, and ceilings, every stick of furniture, even the grill, with its load of smoldering coals, was encased in rapidly thawing ice. The footprints of the creature were clearly outlined. The tiles underneath were shattered like glass. The shape of the footprints was odd in and of itself. Neither hooves nor pads nor feet. Just oblong ovals.

She'd only just hidden from the creature when it came in, and it had only stomped around the room a few seconds before leaving. She looked around, the shattered tiles, the layer of ice. Whatever it was, it was freezing by its very presence.

As she piled things in front of the door and started clearing up the puddles as the ice melted, she started to notice new details. The chair legs, the tables, the door frame itself were all slightly off. Bent, warped, as if they'd been exposed to heat instead of chill. Already her mind was working, running through scenarios and hypotheses. She was a physicist by trade; it was in her nature to wonder at seemingly conflicting data.

Heat was out of the question; there wouldn't have been ice. Acid, well, it would've left distinctive traces, smells, bubbling patterns, runs of dissolved materials, plus she wouldn't have been able to touch any of it so quickly and easily after exposure. Perhaps some kind of high level radiation, but even that was unlikely; at that high a dose, she wouldn't have survived and things would've continued to degrade instead of freezing in place. She was going to have to find some way to get out and make contact, get some kind of research team, or at the very least report this so it went up the chain and could be investigated later. She had no choice about it now.

~

Day 77

Doctor Rodriguez poured through his notes, looking again and again

118

at locations, assignments, addresses, drop sites. He had records of the eventual destinations of all twenty-six of the subjects, spread worldwide. He knew there had to be at least one of them posted near to where he'd taken shelter in St. Louis. It was a sort of bizarre irony that he, who had laid out the proper criteria for where to send the project membership, was now left searching for the nearest member. He'd ensured there were members in most major cities, taking care of critical infrastructure or safeguarding critical knowledge for after.

Now that he knew travel across the surface was possible, it was only a matter of getting the right materials and having a destination. All the subjects were well trained, and most were well equipped, with cover stories, drop sites, bug out locations, safe-houses. If he could find one of them, any of them, they would help him. He knew it, he was the one who'd argued for them, for their conditions, for their comfort and their treatment.

Still, there was the distinct possibility that they'd want nothing to do with him or the Project at this point, regardless of their previous orders. The nature of this... event, it changed everything. If this was a traditional WMD apocalyptic situation, a specialized command system would have been activated and each of them would've been picked up and gathered into a specialized facility in the Rockies. But the sudden and devastating nature of the event had been uniquely unlike anything they'd prepared for. They never considered the possibility of being totally blinded above ground in the initial stage, much less requiring specific precautions other than preserving environmental integrity from disease or radiation.

Twenty-six subjects, thirteen men and thirteen women, each with their own unique traits and specialties. Spread all over the world, to minimize causalities in the event of total thermonuclear war or an airborne plague with a rapid onset and kill-time. The last resort. There had to be one within reasonable range of the St. Louis area. And he was right, there was.

Subject 26, art historian, Zoe. Sweet, gentle little Zoe. The Art Institute of Chicago. It was a little far, but according to this her safe-house was optimal, underground, independent water & power, serious stores. Not that that was the deciding factor. The next likely candidates were Subject 23 in Atlanta or Subject 10 in New Mexico, and he knew 10 was dead, burned with his lab.

The Project was never intended for this kind of survival scenario, but, it could be adapted, even with their known losses. But, first things first, he had to get to one of them. His own access to the Project satellite had been cut off. It was one of those little complications one couldn't have predicted — a driver killed by contact with the event, their out of control vehicle slammed right into Rodriguez' own shelter facility in the initial hour, destroying his satellite uplink. He should've had a backup at a nearby secondary location. He'd argued for it, pleaded for it, but it simply hadn't been in the budget.

~

Day 2

In retrospect, whoever designed the CDC with one entire side of the building as floor to ceiling windows was an idiot. NASA had much better sense when it came to architecture. Large buildings, surprisingly few windows. As it stood, the CDC was in piss poor shape. Fully a third of the labs were inaccessible. The natives, as he thought of them, were getting restless. The people who worked regularly here at the CDC were still strangers to him, and he the outsider to them. They acknowledged that his expertise and the mandate of the Surgeon General were enough to put him in charge, even as half of them had better qualifications and many had decades in experience, his was the relevant field.

Even so, things were going quickly south. Many of them were completely irrelevant to the work at hand. And in survival situations as this, feelings of powerlessness and isolation could be a potent recipe for trouble. Not to mention the lack of supplies. The facility mess was well stocked, but perishables were going at a prodigious rate. The vending machines had already been raided and collected, though goodness knows what several weeks' worth of Juicy Fruit would do for them once the real food had gone. Fortunately, the underground facilities were untouched, but with travel impossible none of the proper staff were going to be coming in. He had no choice. He opened up his desk and punched the four-digit code into the pin pad there.

Day 16

Dr. Rafei finally gave up hope. Help wasn't coming. Food stores were gone. He was going to have to show them the subbasements. They'd be angry, they'd been working like dogs with little food and almost no sleep for over two weeks, and he'd been holding out on them. Angry... was probably optimistic, actually. Still, they would have to understand. He'd have to tell them about the Project, or at least his part in it, and the purpose of the subbasements.

Day 37

They were going to abandon their posts, and he couldn't do anything about it. He couldn't help but admire their courage. They had no way of seeing in the IR or UV spectrums, no definite guarantee of effective shelter at any stage of their journey, and little hope of finding food or help awaiting them at the end of their journey, and yet still they were going.

At least they'd used a gap to restock all they'd taken from his stores.

Day 55

Dr. Rafei winced as he pulled the bandages off. Each and every time the gauze liked to stick to his skin, sometimes *in* his skin as it healed. He braced himself, then leaned his head back over the washroom sink and poured the isopropyl alcohol over his face. The burn was intense, but he had no choice. It was the only wound disinfectant he could rely on, as it was the bottle in the med kit. Any number of other bottles throughout the labs could be any number of things that could be deadly to pour on his face or even smell.

Day 77

Dr. Rafei listened carefully to the men who'd finally exited the vehicle in the garage. Their hushed conversation was too quiet for him to follow, but he could hear a singular word here and there. Suddenly, he realized who the men were. He quickly pulled at the arm of the neanderthal Jesse to encourage him to lead them both back up the stairway towards the elevator lobby.

~

Sharon and Emil made their way quickly and quietly through a series of tunnels, headed towards their latest shelter in a warehouse along the waterline, lugging several large sea bags of gear and supplies.

"So do you think we'll make it?"

"Under normal circumstances, no. Way too much traffic on the river and in the bay. But with things the way they are, so long as we stay in the center of the current, we should easily be able to pass through to the Atlantic."

And what then? You still haven't told me where we're going.

"The way I figure it, there's bound to be more civilized survivors out there, and the best bet for where they'll be is Washington DC. Congress, the President, the Supreme Court, they're all high priority in situations like this. There'll be survivors there. All we'll have to do is get into an important building and wait. The White House, the Capitol Building, the Library of Congress. After that, we just trade services, my combat training and survival skills, your lingual skills, for food and shelter."

"Sounds like a good plan, but how will we navigate? We can't exactly navigate by the stars...

"My phone GPS still works. So long as the boat has an outlet, I'll be able to charge my phone."

"And if it doesn't? If we can't find a suitable boat?"

Sharon rolled her eyes in the dark. At each stage, as they moved from shelter to shelter, checking buildings both aboveground and below, Emil had shown his stripes. He sounded cowardly, but Sharon had realized he wasn't so much afraid as he was cautious, expressing every doubt and worry, even the stupid or silly ones, just to be sure they had every eventuality covered and planned for.

122

"Emil, we have the choice of every floating vessel on the New York waterfront. There's going to be at least one decent boat we can use."

"And if there are no suitable ships? If, say, someone stowed in each and every hull and they're all scuttled to the bottom of the harbor? What then?"

"Then we find one with a steel hull, a Coast Guard patrol craft maybe, or a tugboat; lord knows there are enough of them in New York..."

"I'm asking if there's an alternate plan if this one ends up fouled."

"Emil, you remember, about four weeks ago, we were up near the surface near Rutgers Park?"

"Of course. We heard a helicopter."

"That's right, and if there's a chopper in the air that must mean that IR and UV are safe, like they said. So if this goes foul, if we can't sail by IR and UV, then we'll drive."

"Are you crazy? You're going to drive wearing IR goggles while Sarya and I what, sit in the back blindfolded?"

"That's the plan."

"Sharon..."

"Shh! Do you hear that?"

As they stood still, listening, they could see a beam of light from a ventilation shaft ahead suddenly go dark.

~

Day 77

Jesse spooned out some soup from the pan for Dr. Rafei. Cheddar broccoli, not his favorite, but as far as pre-made powdered mixes went, it wasn't too bad. The simple fact that Jesse could cook without fear of burning down the building was a welcome relief. Dr. Rafei was sick and tired of playing guessing games with prepackaged food. Too many times he'd been hopeful he was opening a box of cereal only to find himself eating Cheez-Its or with hands full of pancake mix.

As Dr. Rafei brought the spoon to his mouth, he inhaled the rich aroma of the watery mixture. Suddenly though, he heard a tone coming from the secondary control room down the hall. The primary control room was uninhabitable; it took up several thousand square feet of the top floor of the building and had floor to ceiling windows along two walls. It was a shame, as the primary control room had the only controls for the buildings shutter system, which by all rights should've been deployed the instant the initial alert went out. Why they hadn't was a mystery. Jesse heard the tone as well, and placed his own soup down on the table before standing and walking down the hall to discover what was the matter.

Dr. Rafei carefully stood, reaching around for the furniture he knew was there, using it to guide him as he slowly followed. Along the way he listened for his new assistant's report. As they'd gotten to know each other over the past few weeks, he'd gradually reassured and allayed his companion's fears, explained his place as a part of the Project, and dissuaded him of his initial plans to evacuate them back to his bunker. They may have to retreat there eventually, but no time soon, thanks to his eyesight.

"Hey Doc, there's a little light flashing back here, has some letters next to it... E T S, what's that mean?"

"I'm not sure; it could mean several things. Which panel is it on?"

"Uh... says here it's "External Environmental Indicators", whatever that means."

"That would be the panel that lets us know when something has changed outside, whether it's raining, or if it's a blizzard or hurricane. Ah... ETS should mean "Extreme Temperature Shift". Tell me, is there a readout somewhere nearby it? It should show either a positive or negative number, uh, red or blue, what does it say?"

"Uh, er... It's blue... 8? What's it mean?"

"It means that the temperature sensor on the roof detected a temperature drop of 8 degrees in the interval since the last reading, there should be a small dial nearby with some numbers around it, thirty seconds, five minutes, half an hour, an hour, etcetera... What does it say? Oh! And check the display that reads "WD&S", what does that say?"

"Uh, hold on a second, lemme find'er... Uh, looks like the first one says 'Thirty S' and the other one... Uh, 'W2'."

"That means the temperature dropped 8 degrees in thirty seconds and the wind is headed west at two miles per hour, so it's not a sudden gust of cold wind, not fast enough to drive temperatures down that fast. It must be an errant sensor; nothing could drive it down that fast..."

"Doc, that readout's changing again..."

"Which one?"

"Uh, that there first one, the one that beeped, it's now blue 14."

"Definitely a glitch then, that's impossible."

"I don't think so, Doc..."

"What is it?"

"There's a camera here, out front, by that big fountain, y'know? It's uh, it's pointed at the ground, thank goodness, and, well, it's like noonish, right?"

"You'd know better than I."

"Well, it is, and it's pitch black out there. Only thing is, the fountain..."

"What about it, Jesse?"

"It's like, froze in mid-spray."

CHAPTER 14

Day 77

Commander Hawkins Flipped the handles up on the AN/BVS, what civilians would've called a periscope. Of course, this was no simple collection of pipes and mirrors, but a multimillion dollar assembly of fiber optics, fully equipped with infrared, rangefinders, and a built in signal processing system that ensured even the worst surface conditions were rendered in crystal-clear high-definition. He'd been scanning the shoreline in infrared.

"Everything looks clear, Captain. We're getting some funny readings on the temperature sensors, but we figure it's just a bad sensor."

"Funny, what do you mean?"

"Well, it's January, and its New York, so we expected cold, but the sensor's reading 20 below, and there's just no way it's that cold. Last reading when we were off the coast in the Atlantic had us at 35 above. Chilly, but not freezing. And that was just a 12 hours ago. Unless there's a major front come in, the sensor's got to be bad."

"And we certainly didn't crack through ice on our way up, so it's got to be the sensor."

"Exactly, sir."

"Alright, well, get the shore party ready. Make sure they bundle up. Even 35 degrees can be dangerous if they're wet going ashore."

"Aye sir... Should they be armed?"

The Captain let out a deep sigh as he considered it.

"Yeah... better safe than sorry. Have the Master at Arms issue out sidearms and longarms to the party, them as can use 'em."

"Shotguns or rifles sir?"

"Let Chief Petty Officer Cox use his discretion; he's sat in on the briefings, he knows what's up."

"Aye, sir. Who should lead the party?

"I will, XO."

"Sir, regulations..."

"More than 97% of the world is dead, Commander. We're picking up VIPs for the survival of the human race from the greatest city on earth, which it so happens I've never been to. I'd like to see New York, even as she is now, and this is likely to be my last chance."

"Sir, all due respect, I can't let you go. I just can't."

"Are you going to have Cox hold me here at gunpoint?"

Eyes all over the bridge of the submarine were locked on Captain Longmire and Commander Hawkins. This was the first time they'd ever disagreed in the view of the crew before, their normally smooth partnership suddenly in rough waters. Regulations were clear, and in normal circumstances the XO would be indeed well within his rights to have the senior Master at Arms, the previously mentioned CPO named Cox, keep the captain on the boat regardless of the situation, but even Cox himself at this point, standing at the aft hatch with his hand on his holstered weapon, didn't look too sure about what could or should be done under these circumstances. It's not like there was likely to be any kind of legal review in whatever port they ended up putting into.

After a tense number of seconds which felt like minutes, the XO turned his gaze to the Master at Arms and spoke.

"You heard the Captain, get the shore party armed and dressed for the cold, yourself too. If the Captain's going, you're going with him, and you're not going to let him out of your sight or out of arms reach, understood?"

The Master at Arms stood at attention, locked eyes with the XO and belted out a sincere "*Aye, sir!*" before turning and heading towards the arms locker.

Commander Hawkins turned to the Captain once more, a hard look on his face.

"This is the compromise: I don't presume to give you orders, but I'd rather not hear anything from Cox when you get back about you trying to get away from him."

"XO, that will work, that will work. It's your boat; I'm going to go get changed."

"Aye sir, my boat."

~

Day 77

Lucinda was shocked into silence. She felt her legs wobble and buckle, and was thankful she'd been going to sit anyway. At no point had she thought there'd be so few of them. The run in from the helicopter had been carried out with military precision, and she'd been debriefed for several hours before being let loose into the cavernous motor pool area of the Secondary Facility. Here, they were fully enclosed by massive solid hangar doors camouflaged to the outside world. There was no danger of exposure here, so things

128

were quite noisy.

Workers scrambled to and fro around the behemoth *Constitution* as they worked to convert her to operate in the event. She was told they were going to clear its aft deck and make it a landing pad for the chopper, which people had nicknamed the *Blind Ghost* based off it's completely enclosed cockpit and white skin. It was a surplus MI-26 Helicopter bought specifically for the Project. A Russian chopper bought off the international black market with black budget funds to serve the needs of the guardians of human civilization at the end of the world. It was being fitted for operation in the event long term, with extra fuel tanks, food stores, beds for hot swapping the crew, and 360 degree IR camera mounts. When it was finished it'd be very useful, especially with the *Constitution* as a launching point. The *Constitution* was a *Freedom*-class Littoral Combat Ship, especially built here, in the Secondary Facility, specifically for Project use. Of course, she had to be modified to carry the *Blind Ghost*, as she was never intended to carry the MI-26, but instead to carry a MH-60 Seahawk, a much smaller chopper.

Despite the noise of machinery and men, Lucinda was riveted to the single sheet of paper that was the list of confirmed status' amongst Project personnel. Dr. Ferguson had died in the Lantern, that she'd already known, but he wasn't so much of a loss as he was a bit of a pretentious windbag and his area of study had obviously dead-ended. However, Daniel, Gretchen, Patricia, and Quentin were going to be sorely missed. The few who were confirmed living but inaccessible were no better; Warren Rafei would be useful but he was out of reach at the CDC, Henry Walthers was alive and well at Berkley, Zoe was in Chicago, Nikki, Xenia, & Yosef were safe but with dwindling resources in London. There was talk of a mission to rescue them later, but their supplies might not last long enough.

The list of those missing and presumed dead was the longest, naturally, and read like a laundry list: Angela, Elaine, Kelly, Terrance, Viktor.

She'd been pressed into service in the infirmary. Even though the facility had the proper outfitting for her to continue her research, caring for the other, non-Project VIPs had taken priority she was told. She disagreed, but here she was just another cog in the wheel rather than the person in charge. She hoped that if the results came back positive from Robert's experiment they could re-prioritize, but contact had been lost. Hopefully just an equipment failure because the other possibilities were less than positive.

As she ruminated on the possibilities for future research in this environment, her charge reached out and grasped her sleeve, the famous (or infamous) former Vice President was having yet another heart attack.

She hit the intercom and called for her team.

~

Damn these concrete floors... my feet freeze every time I get out of bed, the shower...

As Timor made his way from his quarters to the storerooms near the bunker entrance, he ruminated and mourned his lack of adequate footwear. He'd worn through his sneakers in the first few weeks when he'd still pace for exercise. Cheap black market Nike rip-offs simply weren't up to par. As he approached the storerooms he wheezed and gasped and grasped at his side.

I've got to start shifting stores around the bunker, get a big empty space opened up... make myself a gym.

As he came round the last narrow corner into the bunker entrance, still crowded high with the crates and pallets of the last delivery before things had gone to hell, he caught sight of the massive steel doors that had seemed to superfluous on his first arrival. Now, knowing what last beyond, he was grateful for their weight. But... something was wrong. The doors seemed pale. As he approached, he saw what was the matter: the massive steel doors were covered with a fine layer of frost. Russian winters were notoriously cold, but, the doors were three feet thick. They'd never frosted before, no matter how cold it got.

Curious, Timor approached the guard post nearest the doors. Long unmanned, it still held readouts and screens for the suite of sensors

130

and cameras outside the bunker. He'd covered the camera screens when things first went to shit, but the other readouts were intact. The temperature gauge shocked him, and he guessed the readout was wrong, or perhaps in the wrong scale. He pulled out the binder that held the operator's manuals and quickly double checked the scale temperature was displayed in. -196 Celsius.

What the hell is going on?

Almost in answer, the door reverberated with a deep impact from outside.

~

Day 0

Viktor stepped out, off the platform from the high speed train. Looking around, he saw the crowd this afternoon wasn't as thick as normal. As he made his way away from the platform he saw many of them staring at him openly. It wasn't particularly unusual, his 6'4" frame and naturally white hair were unusual enough, but the dramatic violet contacts he wore, the silver caps on all his teeth, and the flamboyancy of his personal style — albino alligator boots with white leather pants, white silk shirt and a white cotton dress coat, all in contrast to his ebony skin — were always enough to draw an eye or two. It felt good to be noticed, to stand out.

In the Project they always told him he needed to dial it back, to try to blend in, better to insert himself wherever he would be going. They didn't count on his assignment being as outrageous as he liked to be. The Tokyo Fetish Underground wasn't where most people would assign a poli-sci expert, but then, they weren't as informed about the private habits of the upper ranges of the Japanese Government as the Project was. They knew where to place their agents.

Japan had been a tough nut to crack. Attempts to infiltrate through normal means and the government bureaucracy had been successful, but yielded no useful information. Officially, everything looked to be on the up and up. Unofficially, government works projects for the last two decades had been running through cash and materials about

5% faster than they should have. Not much, but enough that over time it was a significant gap between what was visibly being done, and what the government was budgeted for.

Seeing as how Japan's elite had recused themselves from the Project, the leadership was rightly concerned what other steps might've been taken that could be at cross purposes. So, Viktor was on assignment, getting close to Japan's elite in order to discover, if possible, just where those resources were being used. He was on his way to a discrete rendezvous with the spokesperson of the LDP.

He was meeting her at a rather unassuming hotel, the kind a lower middle class family might use while vacationing. Too cheap and it was likely they'd run into tabloid reporters cruising for lower-end politicians with escorts; too rich and she could be seen by the paparazzi as they looked for celebrities. A middle-class hotel for a high-profile tryst. Of course, the black town car with the driver in the tailored black suit and Ray-Bans not eating at the takeout place across the street was a little bit of a giveaway, but most people didn't look for such things.

He walked to the check-in desk and gave his name. As per the usual arrangement, a keycard was waiting for him. It told him the room number, even though the keycard wouldn't work — another precaution. He made his way up a set of stairs badly in need of a new coat of paint and then along the bare concrete walkway to the room directly above the one on the keycard, and knocked. A few tiny footsteps could be heard from inside the room and there was a pause as the occupant checked the peephole in the door.

Moments later he could hear the chain being withdrawn from the door and the doorknob rattle as they keyed the lock. The door opened and before him stood Mrs. Yuriko Koike. It was rare that his services were called on by a woman, but he didn't mind; he liked women as much as most men, he figured. He flashed his most charming smile and asked if he could enter. She smiled and welcomed him into the room where her toy collection was already waiting, clean and organized by color and size, on the bed.

~

Viktor straightened the collar of his shirt as Mrs. Koike emerged from the bathroom after her shower. Her mid-length black hair hung straight down around her face and she was without make-up, her exhaustion giving her the look of someone who'd just barely survived some tragedy at sea. One hand clutched the wall for support as the other clutched her fluffy white towel. Her knees still weak and her voice quivering, she asked if she was still his favorite. Always worried he'd find someone younger, someone prettier, someone more interesting. She could never know it wasn't her he was interested in, but her knowledge of the inner workings of Japan's Government.

"Of course. You know that nobody else gets such prompt and personal attention..."

...a common lie in his profession. He specializes in making them feel special, wanted, needed. To that end, he dropped his hands to his sides and gazed at her, his eyes half closed and his jaw slacked. A well-practiced pose he'd perfected before a mirror years ago. When she noticed him she was halfway into her blouse. She froze, asking what he was staring at, worried that he might have left a mark where it could be seen by a member of the public. Her husband never touched her, and they slept in separate rooms, so she wasn't worried about the marks he *always* left on her.

"It's just... you're so beautiful... and I'm so lucky to be at your service."

She blushed and turned away to hide her face and the smile that forced its way there. They dressed the rest of the way sneaking flirtatious glances at each other. Even in the wake of the act the Japanese attitudes towards intimacy made themselves fully known. A knock at the door came mere moments before Mrs. Koike would've opened it to depart. It was her driver, after a quick and urgently whispered conversation she turned to Viktor.

"You must come with me."

"But I normally leave an hour after you, in case the press..."

"That is no longer a concern, we must go, now."

It was a short and quick run downstairs to the waiting car. As they rode, Mrs. Koike read over an email that had been delivered to her phone while they had been finishing up. Once finished, she made a single phone call, of which Viktor could only hear her half.

"Yes, this is Mrs. Yuriko Koike, LDP Spokesperson..."

"Yes."

"I have one civilian along with me."

"No, it's not my husband. His name is Viktor Reitmeyer."

"He's an American."

"Not that I'm aware of."

"Implicitly."

"Yes."

"It's registered, and I'll turn it on as soon as we're off the line."

"Understood."

After she hung up, she did something with one of the menus on her phone before setting it back in her handbag. Not even ten minutes later a motorcade of police surrounded the car and escorted them through town. Viktor saw this as a signal to start asking questions.

"Yuriko, I know I've been curious about your job before, and you've been very accommodating to my inquiries, so I hope I'm not being too forward, but, may I ask, just what exactly is going on here?"

"There's an emergency, and we're being evacuated to a secure location."

"Is it a tsunami?"

Yuriko laughed, a soulless, mirthless kind of dark humor.

"If only it were, Viktor. A tsunami is something we'd be somewhat

134

prepared for."

"Terrorist attack?"

"Something like that. Most of the important people in government know a little, nobody knows the whole story, but there's something coming. Everyone's been on high alert for months., waiting for something to happen, and I guess it finally did."

Viktor didn't know what to say. He worried that if he were subjected to too much intensive research into his background or identity the falsified documents he carried might be exposed as frauds, and he might fail in his mission. Mrs. Koike continued speaking, however.

"Viktor, where we're going... they might not like that I've brought an American. So, for both our sakes, please, do not speak unless spoken to, and if anyone asks what you're doing there, just tell them that you're my Option. I can't tell you what that fully means, but it'll keep you out of trouble, I think."

With shock, Victor realized there were tears in her eyes. She was genuinely afraid of whatever was happening. That was an alarming realization. With a bump, Viktor realized where they were, one of the many construction projects on the outskirts of Tokyo that were the subject of his assignment here. It had gone on for years, sucking up funding and manpower, with no visible or appreciable results. A six-week observation of the site had shown that they were digging in one area and shifting its soil to another area, only for a few weeks later to reverse it, digging in the area they moved the soil and sending it to fill in the hole they'd dug before, all the while dump trucks took soil out of the site and concrete trucks brought loads in, and for nothing visibly to change over the course of months. It was damn peculiar.

Their convey moved through the site and down into one of the excavations, there to enter the mouth of a drainage tunnel large enough to move in a tractor trailer. Of course, vertical steel bars as thick as his thigh barred the way further in. One of the drivers of the lead vehicle got out and went over to one of the bars, where he placed his hand up against its rounded surface. There was a brief glow around his fingertips, and the bars started retracting, half of them upwards, half of them downwards. The man got back in the lead vehicle and they all drove through the tunnel one by one.

Around the first bend there was a sheet of black plastic strips, the kind you see at the entrances to walk in freezers in grocery stores, keeping the light from beyond from spilling back towards the entrance. There, the tunnel widened and the ceiling rose until he could swear he was in a closed down football stadium. Everyone parked off to the side and a number of armored men came forward from a set of double doors in the side of the cavern. They were escorted back into the double doors which led to a long hallway, with the walls covered in blown up photographs. Each photo seemed to include the same four scientists and some politician or another. As they progressed, the politicians became more and more recent, while the scientists aged, and eventually one was missing, then two, then three, until just the one aged scientist was there, smiling as he shook the current Prime Ministers hand.

At the end of the hallway, the men funneled them onto a large metal platform surrounded by guard rails, on the edge of a steep tunnel lined with pipes, wires, and some kind of track. Suddenly, the platform began to move down the tunnel. Viktor marveled at the engineering displayed before him. The elevator whisked through the tunnel at a steep angle, carrying himself, Mrs. Koike, a half dozen other government VIPs, their aides or wives or husbands, and a full platoon of a military Japan wasn't really supposed to have. These weren't JSDF regulars. These men were far, far more dangerous and better equipped. Viktor would've tried to memorize the symbols on their uniforms, their weapons, their nametapes... but they were all custom made. No markings on anything, and the weapons were unlike anything he'd ever seen.

After too long, Viktor estimated perhaps as much as three-quarters of a mile, he felt the platform slow, and ahead he could see a light. When things came to a halt he saw they were to be received by another dozen of the strange soldiers.

They were divided. The politicians were herded through one door, civilians through another, escorted by the soldiers. The room ahead

136

held showers, individual, with curtains and lockers. They were instructed to undress and place all their affects in the lockers and to close their eyes as the chemical solution contained a delousing agent. Viktor complied, wondering what sort of clean facility this was. What came out of the shower spigot wasn't fluid, and with his first breath he felt the vertigo wash over him and his legs grow weak. His last thought after crashing to the floor was that the floor tiles were like ice.

CHAPTER 15

Day 77

Doctor Rodriguez squinted through the IR goggles, confused as to what he was seeing. His progress has been simple for the most part. He managed to find an auto dealer and scrounge up a vehicle far superior to his own old broken down Hyundai. In fact, it was probably the nicest car he'd ever even ridden in. Even with his salary there was no way he'd have ever afforded a Lamborghini. He regretted the damage the things from the sky was doing to the paint job, but he supposed that wasn't important since nobody would be looking at it without IR goggles.

But all that aside, he was growing concerned. Temperatures had plummeted as he'd gotten further north, as expected, but not like this. Even as he made his way up the highway, the heat was on full blast and barely keeping up and the engine temperature gauge was barely registering, almost like the sports car had just been started rather than driven for nearly six hours.

The road was covered in a light layer of frost or snow — no telling which — and the only indication he had of the road ahead was the smoothness of the highway and the occasional mile marker, road sign, or wrecked vehicle, mostly large tractor trailers. But things were getting thicker, a haze in the air was beginning to make things difficult to see.

He reduced his speed further, now down to 30mph. He lifted the goggles to check his gauges yet again, temperature nil, RPMs holding steady, fuel... down to a quarter tank. He'd have to stop soon. A garage was his best bet. Closed interior, a few cars nobody would miss, easily siphoned from.

Pulling the goggles back down, he looked back to the road, just catching a glimpse of someone standing in the middle of the road on stilts just before he hit them. The Lamborghini was brought to a stop instantly as the front end crumpled around the figures legs. Broken glass peppered the Doctor's face, arms and chest as he stifled for breath against the pressure of the seatbelt. Looking up, his goggles lost somewhere in the maelstrom, the Doctor was eye to eye with something inhuman. Before he could so much as find and put on his glasses it struck forward with an and like a tree trunk, ripping Rodriguez out of the vehicle, bones snapping like toothpicks as the seatbelt held.

Shock kept the pain at bay just long enough for the doctor to realize he'd been ripped in half, and that his blood was crawling of its own accord up his torso before being absorbed by the creature's porcelain flesh. Then the pain and the darkness swallowed him.

~

Day 77

Sharon, Emil, and Sarya moved cautiously through the warehouse, passing rows and rows of shipping containers as they made their way towards the waterfront. Sarya and Emil kept their heads low, eyes shut as Sharon guided them between the containers and the wall with the only set of goggles they had, always cautious as they approached a door or window opening to the outside. There had been a bait stand at the entrance to these docks so she knew there had to be a civilian marina or tie up somewhere along the waterline here, though she had yet to see it.

She took the opportunity of another doorway to look out and see if they were any closer to escaping from New York when she saw something that didn't make any sense. She turned and told Sarya & Emil to keep low and their eyes on the ground. Looking down, Sharon removed the IR goggles and placed her hand across her forehead as a makeshift visor. Slowly she lifted her head and hand together making sure her hand blocked all of the sky.

There, in the bay, something was walking, and as it did the bay ahead and to the sides would freeze. The thing was tall, even at this distance that was clear. With alabaster skin and limbs that were longer than any man's, the legs ending in surprisingly narrow feet, the arms with long nimble hands. The eyes at this distance nothing more than small amber points of light. To the left of it she saw another, also making its way across the bay... and another, even more distant. A line of these... things... moving across the bay. The bay freezing around them as they go. Further out, the working winds kicking up snow and frozen fog obscured how many there might be.

She pulled the door gently closed and tugged Emil & Sarya down to the floor.

"We're going to have to consider a new strategy."

Emil's voice dripped with rising panic even in whisper.

"Why, what is wrong? Are there no boats?"

"No, there's something else. Things. Creatures, they're freezing the bay."

"How could beasts be freezing the bay?"

"I don't know, they just are. We've got to get back inland, back underground. Someplace that won't freeze, near a steam vent maybe."

"Whatever you say, we trust you."

"Let's hope it's well founded."

~

Day 77

Longmire took in a deep lungful of fresh air as he tried to keep his balance in the rubber zodiac.

"Keep your eyes down boys. Those goggles the Aussies gave us are supposed to protect us from seeing the things, but we're not paid nearly enough to risk it."

One of his crewmen, Seaman Homme, cocked his head to the side even as he pulled at the oar in his hand in conjunction with Kellogg to his side.

"Begging your pardon sir, but, uh, are we being paid? I mean... it's not like there's many stores left... or banks... or a Federal Reserve. I mean..."

"Well, Mr. Homme, if you feel three hots and a cot in the most secure vehicle in the world isn't good enough recompense for your paltry services, I suppose I'll have to take your arms, your uniform, and allow you to put about on a more permanent basis on our return to the *Oregon*. Is that along the lines you were thinking?"

"Uh, er... no, sir."

"I didn't think so. Cox, correct me if I'm wrong, but does that look something like a man waiting on shore ahead of us under that overhang?"

Cox leaned a few degrees port to clear his line of sight, peering through his goggles ahead of the boat.

"It would appear so, sir, but can we be cautious? We don't exactly know who else might have survived..."

"Cool it, Cox. Most of humanity is dead; I'm not about to make enemies of every last remainder we run across. In fact, while we can't take any with us except our assigned VIPs, I'm sure as hell going to tell any groups we encounter to head for shelters we've been informed are still operable."

"Aye, sir; just saying, having Forsythe keep a rifle trained on him from the bow on our way in might not be an unreasonable precaution."

"Is this you fulfilling your promise to the XO?"

"Partly so, sir. Partly, the other part being I'm making sure to cover my own ass. And, I'll admit I've just got a damned bad feeling about this whole venture."

"Don't be so paranoid."

As the zodiac approached the river wall, Forsythe kept his rifle trained on the figure standing against the building above, never moving. As they tied up to the boardwalk above, the Captain, Forsythe, and the Master at Arms Cox made their way up to meet the man on the shore. Approaching cautiously, they waited until they were a mere ten feet from the man before speaking.

"Captain Longmire, USS Oregon. I believe the passphrase is, 'Oh Say Can You See'."

The man finally looked up, responding "God save our gracious King."

"Yep, that's it. So, how are we doing this?"

"I've cleared a smallish corner of this little building here. Let's get you and your men inside and then we'll discuss things."

Longmire sent Forsythe back to get the others from the zodiac as he and Cox followed the figure into the building on the waterfront. What used to be a small bodega had been turned into a makeshift camp. There was a kerosene lamp and stove, sleeping bag, and most of the shelves had been cleared of food. There was also trash in the corners and the floors were filthy.

"Don't mind the mess, lads; the former resident didn't keep house too well."

"So what's the game plan? You've got one VIP inland that needs evacuation, we've got one very good way to get them where they need to go. We were told to be here, now. We are. Now as I understand it, you're supposed to bring your VIP to us; is that what's happening?"

The man from the sea wall warmed his hands over a kerosene lantern on the counter.

"Aye. But with a complication. Our VIP is a couple blocks away. We were going to bring 'em here by sewer..."

"Ugh..."

"Better than you'd think, you've got to remember this city's been a corpse for nearly three months. Rains in the first few weeks did wonders to clear out every drainage system she had, and now, without millions of people flushing warmth down the drains, even the sewers are frozen over."

"Right... so what's the hang-up?"

"The city's been dead for three fuggin' months, that's what. Sewer froze, pipes that weren't never supposed to freeze froze, burst, then froze over again. Half the sewers are blocked by big frozen sprays. The route we'd planned is gone. Our hope was that you fine folks might have means to bring 'em out. Frankly, we were thinking you'd arrive by whirly. Submarine, though... that complicates things."

"Hold on just a damn second. We didn't exactly plan for much of an inland excursion here. I mean... we're sailors, not Marines. Our Master at Arms here, Cox, has the most experience and training, but I don't think..."

"Oh, no, I know, I know. But, though you might not be Marines, I am, y'see. Second Lieutenant Hardy, His Majesty's Royal Marines, at your service."

"Good to meet you, Lieutenant. Now... what did you have in mind?"

"I thought I'd borrow two of your men and make a little jaunt inland, get my VIP, and get back here as quick as we can."

"That simple, eh? Where is he?"

"Just a few blocks in, shouldn't take too long at all."

"How long do you figure?"

"The cold's been kind, brought fog and haze in. The buggers up above seem to have just as much trouble seeing or sensing us through it as we would them, were we looking. Frankly, I think that's why you managed to survive on the trip ashore. If it holds... I'd say we could get there and back in two hours, maybe three if we have to detour around anything."

"Three hours it is. Homme, Forsythe, go with Lt. Hardy. Cox, get on the horn, tell the XO we're going to camp here and wait. When they get back, we'll all get aboard the *Oregon* together."

~

Day 77

Sharon took off her IR Goggles and hung them on the flashlight strapped to her vest just over her left breast. She wiped sweat from her forehead and pulled out her canteen, taking a few sips. Emil watched her, his expression incredulous as he spoke.

"There's got to be a way through... or under...?"

Sharon swallowed before she answered, the plastic taste of the canteen still on her tongue.

"Not that I can see. Sewers underneath are blocked. Building inside is... burnt out. Some fire sometime after things went to shit. Looks like the automated suppressors killed it but... there's no way through that's safe."

"So, around?"

Sharon nodded.

"Around."

"In the open?"

"In the open."

"Have you seen... I mean... have there been signs...?"

"No bodies. But that's no guarantee. I mean... I don't know. Slow and low and quiet, like before."

"Before, we had cover. Walkways, the streets themselves, heck, even that one crashed plane... This is *open* open... they'll be right above us."

"Emil... would it be better for us to..."

Sharon stopped mid-sentence, sensing something amiss. The very air had taken on an even more bitter chill. Its currents accelerated, the howling outside taking a high shrill tone. Motioning for Emil and Sarya to take cover, Sharon lowered her IR goggles down over her eyes and moved forward towards the storefront, stepping high to avoid tripping on anything that'd fallen off the shelves over the past eleven weeks. When she got to the door she paused. Pulling her sidearm from its holster on her hip, she gently pulled back the slide to put a round in the chamber.

Moving slowly at a crouch, she moved from behind the counter to the door. Reaching out, she gently pressed her off hand to it, and quickly withdrew. The door was cold, freezing in point of fact. She put her weapon on safe and holstered it for a moment, pulling out and putting on a pair of thin leather gloves. She then unholstered her weapon once again. She put her off hand back out and gently eased the door open a few inches, moved to look, and came face to face with three raised rifles.

For a moment, nobody moved. Sharon froze, but recognizing two official uniforms and a dress suit, she slowly lowered her weapon towards its holster. Three rifles followed suit until a loud noise

145

altered fate. A piece of office furniture on the fourth floor of the building they stood under, pushed by the quickening wind, rolled out a window and fell four stories, crashing to the street not twenty feet from where four very nervous armed individuals stood. Petty Officer Homme panicked. A single twitch on an improperly placed trigger finger and a weapon that wasn't on safe, and three times in rapid succession his rifle spit rounds that never should have flown.

The first tore through Sharon's thigh, grazing bone and splitting muscle.

The second flew through empty air through the door Sharon had just opened, ricocheted off the linoleum covered concrete inside the store, then lodged itself in the bottom of the top shelf that held bags of moldy popcorn.

The third blew through Sharon's left wrist, severing the ulnar vein.

Without a sound, Sharon pushed back with her right leg, falling back inside the store she was exiting. Emil, shocked into action by the sound of gunfire, grasped Sarya and pulled her into the back office of the store. Lieutenant Hardy, Seaman Forsythe & Petty Officer Homme stood shocked. Homme, at the rear, stood mute as Seaman Forsythe turned to him in anger and confusion before falling over like a puppet with its strings cut. Moments later Homme felt the impact as the first thing from the sky slammed into his back.

Hardy knew what was happening. And he knew not to look. He dove for the store entrance, trying to follow the unknown woman, but he wasn't fast enough and the opening simply wasn't wide enough. He impacted the door with one shoulder and rebounded to the ground. He felt small impacts as sharp indistinct shapes impacted all over his legs, cutting immediately through the thin material of his suit. Visions of beings moving among the stars like dust motes in a sunbeam, god-like beings no man ever before beheld twisting gravity and time like old women knit mittens filled his head as his body slumped to the floor.

CHAPTER 16

Day 77

Captain Longmire leaned back on the stool behind the counter of the bodega, his thick navy issue parka insulating his shoulder from the chill of the wall behind him. His Master at Arms, Cox, stood against the far wall. It was reinforced glass, but it was plastered over with adverts long ago. The remaining members of the shore party had taken up on the second floor, better view of the river, the zodiac, and the *Oregon*.

Their momentary reverie was ended by the sound of distant gunfire. Longmire and Cox were on the radio in seconds calling the *Oregon* and the retrieval party on the radios. The *Oregon* confirmed no shots fired aboard; the retrieval party answered only in static. Just as Longmire was about to speak, a flash of light from the stairwell told him his observers had something to report. Climbing the stairs two at a time, he came out in the paisley pink nursery that held the observers and their post. Without a word they, indicated he look for himself.

Looking through the IR scope they'd set up in a window gap, he looked down on the East River. It was frozen solid, the *Oregon* a solitary break in the otherwise smooth surface of the ice. Walking along the *Oregon* was a solitary figure, easily twice again as tall as a man. As it walked the IR scope registered everything around it drop in temperature, quickly and severely. Even so, he knew he had other priorities — his men unaccounted for, the English VIP they were supposed to be fetching.

Things were getting complicated, fast.

~

Emil shoved Sarya under the desk in the office. Putting one finger to his lips to indicate she should be quiet, he turned and quietly opened the door to the shop, peeking through the crack. The aisles of various consumer slop kept him from directly seeing Sharon or the front of the shop. He knew he could probably make his way back to the riverside with Sarya, but without Sharon he knew his chances, *their* chances, were slim. A couple of hours wait, he takes the goggles off of Sharon's body and then...? Then what?

As he pondered his course, he suddenly heard something which terrified him. Slow ragged breathing. Sharon had told them about the giants on the bay. If one of them were in the store...

A mere twenty feet away, Sharon used her one good leg to push herself further from the door. Her right hand gripping tight to her left wrist to slow the bleeding, her left leg dragging behind her. She took it slow, making sure she had solid purchase with her boot at each push. She could hear the things doing their damnable chittering on the bodies of the three just outside. One squeak, one loud kick against something, and they'd be on her too.

She regretted packing so much now. Her harness was loaded down with probably twenty pounds of shit that was only serving to slow her down and possibly hang her up. Slow breath in, lift her right leg, place the right foot down solid, exhale and push. In. Lift. Place. Exhale and push. Six inches. A foot every other time. Ten seconds a push. Three feet a minute, twenty feet to the office, five and a half minutes.

At least the cold was beginning to numb her leg.

~

Longmire was in crisis mode. His mind quick and sharp, making decisions and absorbing information at light speed.

"Cox, get on the radio with the *Oregon*. They know they're in ice; the sonar acoustics will have told them that. Tell them to adjust trim on the ballast tanks fore and aft, port and starboard, whatever they've got to do to get free. Let them know not to submerge just yet, just rock her loose. In the meantime, we're going to go after the rest of our shore party and the VIP."

"Sir, what about the XO's orders? I'm not supposed to let you get within a stones throw of danger, and charging off inland after some Brit VIP isn't exactly a low risk endeavor..."

"Let me worry about the XO; you just let him know what we're doing."

"Aye, sir."

The room was suddenly a flurry of angry whispering and repeated slaps as one of the seaman charged with keeping watch harshly berated the other. Their Captain strode over quickly, crouching and putting a hand on a shoulder of each.

"What's all this, then?"

The junior Seaman Apprentice responded before his colleague.

"Watkins here looked out at the thing on the river."

"So? That's what you're supposed to be doing."

"*Without the scope,* sir. Naked eyed it. He could've gotten himself killed if I hadn't pulled his silly ass back... sir."

"Is this true, Seaman?"

The other man looked up sheepishly at his Captain.

150

"Yeah, I guess it is... I was just curious, sir."

"About what?"

"Whether or not we could see them, sir."

"Explain."

"Well I figured if we can't see the flying things in infrared, but we can see the giants, maybe we can't see the giants in normal spectrum... sir."

Captain Longmire rocked back on his heels and stood up, looking down at the two Seamen.

"Watkins, that was kind of stupid. What if there were even one of the things out there? You'd be a dried up corpse right now. You're lucky Seaman's Apprentice..."

"Kellogg, Sir."

"Seaman's Apprentice Kellogg cared enough to bother saving your dumb ass. Kellogg, do you have time in rank yet?"

"No, sir; still have a month left."

"Well, I suppose circumstances being what they are, we can overlook that. When we get back to the *Oregon,* talk to laundry and see if you can rustle up all the proper accoutrements for a full Seaman."

Longmire then strode across the room. Grabbing a chair, he carried it back to where his two Seamen sat on the floor by the window. Setting it down and sitting on it, he looked at Watkins and began.

"Now, Watkins, you're the first person to get a good look at these things in full color, so tell me, what'd you see?"

"Well, sir, the things are white, like ghost white, snow white, chalk white, whitest damn things I've ever seen. Like they're made of porcelain or something."

"They're made of porcelain?"

"No sir, just white like that. Their skin is bumpy, like a crocodile's, rough, scaled, with bumps and nodules. And their proportions are all wrong. Like, their legs are thinnest just before the hip, and get wider as they go down until just before the knee, when they narrow again until their feet are just round pegs of what look like horn, or bone, emerging from the skin. Their arms do the same, except instead of narrowing to pegs they have hands. Long thin fingers, too many joints. Like Spiders legs. The heads are wide at the bottom, domed at the top. Like a tree stump that's been weathered and worn down. They don't seem to have no noses. But they have mouths, wide, thin, lipless, like, it's just a slit running the full width of their head. The eyes though... they're sort of... solid amber, or gold... yellow-orange like that, and they glow. Seriously, they emit light of their own."

"Did it look like it was wearing anything, clothing, equipment of some kind? Were there any seams in it, like it could've been a suit or something like that?"

"No sir, nothing like that. Just lumpy flesh all the way."

"Any sex organs?"

"Nothing I could see, sir; looked like a Ken doll down there."

"What was it doing?"

"Just walking, sir. It wandered back and forth on the river, around the *Oregon*."

"What do you mean, around the *Oregon*?"

"Ever since it walked here it's just been checking the *Oregon*, from the stern to the bow and back again."

The Captain leaned forward in the chair, taking hold of the IR Scope and peering through. He watched for a solid minute before leaving back and beckoning his Master at Arms over.

"Cox, tell the XO that once he's loose of the ice I want him to dive down beneath, get under the surface and let the giants freeze it over, I don't want them to be able to touch the hull, understand? They're pacing her off like they've got plans for her and I want her out of reach."

"Aye, sir."

With that, Cox disappeared down the stairs to the bodega where they'd left the radios. Moments later he came back, radios in each hand. As he sat down to contact Commander Hawkins, Longmire pulled out a couple maps of New York they'd gotten from the store downstairs. As Cox got off the radio, he came over to his captain and enquired as to the plan.

"Well, the way I see it, the mission is still a go. All that's happened is that Hardy, Forsythe, and Homme didn't make it, which means getting the VIP is now up to us."

"Sir, we're only supposed to just barely come ashore. I really don't think the XO would approve of us gallivanting around the island."

"I guess we'll just have to be really, really careful then, Cox. I'm not looking for your approval here. I've made my decision. We go a couple blocks inland and we get the VIP and we bring him back. That's it. I'm not exactly planning on taking a tour of Yankee Stadium or trying to climb Freedom Tower."

Cox thought a moment, then quietly nodded before speaking.

"Alright, sir, but if you try and put yourself in any unnecessary danger, I'm not going to hesitate to drag you back to the *Oregon* kicking and screaming.

The Captain silently noted the differences between himself, 5'10", 135 pounds, and his Master at Arms, a decidedly more imposing 6'1" and 180 pounds, before simply nodding his head in acceptance.

~

Captain Longmire, his Master at Arms Jim Cox, and the two Seamen Watkins & Kellogg, stood in the ruins of a frozen department store

153

four blocks from their former basecamp in the Bodega, peering over the checkout with IR Goggles, whispering back and forth.

"What's wrong with them, sir?"

"They're dead, Jim."

"Well, uh, yes sir, but... uh... why are they moving like that still?"

"The things got 'em. They're covered in 'em. When they cover a person or a vehicle, they vibrate like that. You just can't see them in the infrared... son of a bitch!"

"So they're covered right now? Right now as we're looking at them...? That's frankly terrifying, sir. Wait, how'd you know that?"

"It was part of the larger briefing materials we got from the Aussies. Good reason not to look outside without IR, huh? Shit... if that's Hardy, Homme, and Forsythe then we've failed."

"Sir?"

Hardy never told us where the VIP was, nor who they were. Shit, I shouldn't have been so trusting. Goddamnit!

Cox moved over between his Captain and Seaman Watkins, fiddling with a dial on his IR Goggles. He pointed through the doorway in front of the bodies of their shipmates and the Brit, Hardy.

"Sir? There's something on the ground in the shop there."

The Captain peered through his own goggles, then, giving up, he took them off, squeezing his eyes closed. Putting the IR Scope up to one eye and opening it, he used its higher magnification to look deeper into the store.

"There's someone in there on the floor. They're still warm, so they've still got blood in 'em, but they aren't moving. I'm seeing exhalations... son of a bitch... they're still alive. That may be our VIP."

"Sir, we can't go out there. The... the things are right there."

154

"We can't just leave 'em there."

"So what's the play, sir?"

"We backtrack. Find a way around with cover. Then we come in from the back."

"Sir, all due respect, they could be dead by then. They're lying on exposed ground in freezing weather. Even if they're just lying there to avoid making noise for the things to follow, they'll die of hypothermia if we don't get to them soon."

"You're right. That's why Watkins and Kellogg are going to stay here and keep watch on the bodies of Forsythe, Hardy, and Homme. When they stop twitching, when the things lose interest, if we haven't got over there yet, they'll wait five minutes then they cross the street quick and quiet."

"Sir, that's too risky, I can't let you be part of the scout around and I can't leave your side, so I'm going to have to insist Watkins & Kellogg do the scouting and you and I hope here and wait out the things."

"You going to shoot me, Cox?"

Cox tilted his head towards the still quivering bodies across the street.

"That'd kind of defeat the point a number of ways sir, but I would choke you out."

Longmire conceded the point with a slight tilt of his head before indicating Watkins and Kellogg move out.

"You know, Cox, if things keep going this way I may just have to start calling you sir. Either that or shoot you for mutiny."

"All things considered, sir, I'd prefer the former."

~

Watkins and Kellogg moved silently through the halls of what once

155

was an advertising company, passing room after room of drawing boards, focus group meeting rooms, and office storerooms and breakdowns. A successful one, judging by the bodies here and there, who'd been working long into the morning hours to be caught at their labor when the things from the sky came.

They moved carefully, stepping high to avoid obstacles and hang-ups. As they approached the rear emergency exit, they took cover at one side before gently pressing on the bar to open it. It stood resolute against their efforts, disuse and the freezing cold holding it in place.

With an exasperated sigh, Watkins stood back, preparing to shove against the door with his shoulder as he pressed the bar. Kellogg silently raised his hand with three fingers turned out, one by one they fell into a fist, as the last finger fell Watkins threw himself against the door, pushing the bar as he did so. With a crack like a shot the door flew open, both men froze where they stood, their goggled eyes immediately flying to the sky as if to choose their doom of their own accord before they could be ensconced. But their eyes met only the ceiling of the access hallway they'd entered.

Deep sighs of relief escaped both men as they more easily walked into the barren hall. As they took their bearings to decide which way to continue, they heard a curious and unexpected sound emanate from a set of double steel doors at the far end of the hall, *knocking*. Knocking, like, an invited guest or some such thing was politely waiting outside to be greeted. This did not last long, as moments later the sailors' bizarre and confused reverie was shattered as those same doors exploded into the hall, ripped from their hinges and frames simultaneously by a violent impact from the other side. On the other side, framed by the doorway midway up to the chest, was one of the giants they'd seen pacing the *Oregon*.

Kellogg reacted first, shouldering his rifle, taking aim center mass and squeezing the trigger... to no effect.

With horror he realized his weapon was still on safe, and without a round in the chamber to boot. He had no opportunity to correct his mistake as moments later the giant crouched, and faster than seemed possible, closed the distance between them, it's amber eyes fading to

156

black as it split open its wide maw revealing a swirling blood red chasm of light that became all he could conceive of. Watkins and Kellogg stood frozen, their will and motivation gone as the light filled their vision, transfixed until the sounds of their own bodies snapping and breaking joined as a grotesque soundtrack to the light.

~

A few blocks behind, Longmire and Cox heard the distant echo of a crashing sound, and quickly dismissed it as the city settling into its disrepair. Longmire went to check his watch, only to realize that it was fully covered by his gloves and coat sleeve.

"How long has it been?"

Cox shifted his goggles to his forehead looked down at his watch.

"Eight minutes, sir."

"You think that's a reasonable window?"

"I'll leave that up to you, sir. I'm just along for the ride."

"Real helpful, Chief..."

"I aspire to be an asset, sir."

"Shit... alright, let's go. Watkins and Kellogg are late; they can meet us there after we make sure whoever that is is okay."

"Aye sir, now, uh... how do you want to get across?"

"Fast is probably better than slow... get over there quick and quiet. Straight line, here to there."

"Er... sir? Isn't that rather, uh, blunt?"

"You're the one who insisted on us being the ones to sit here and wait; why the sudden apprehension?"

"I didn't actually think we'd be the ones jumping this particular creek, sir..."

The Captain chuckled.

"I don't blame you; neither did I. Best get it over with..."

"One way or the other, sir?"

"I was going to leave that part unsaid."

Quietly, the two stood. Cox slung his rifle before they both went over themselves, tightening straps, buttoning flaps, and generally making sure that nothing would dislodge on their short jaunt across the streets. A few moments later they crept forward to the edge of the storefront, moving as quietly as they could.

At the doorway they paused, staring intently through their goggles at the three bodies just across the street. When no movement could be seen, Cox switched to the scope to check on the exhalations of the person in the building across the way.

With a final nod, Cox put the scope back, secured his goggles, and they set out. Moving at a brisk pace and in a half crouch they moved in a direct line. It went quickly. A mere ten seconds and they were across the street and standing over the woman whose breath they'd seen.

"Jesus Christ... look at this... she's been shot!"

"I don't think this is our VIP, sir. She's armed and geared for war. If this was the VIP, she could've accompanied Hardy to the riverfront. This has got to be a civilian."

"I agree. Question is, are Hardy and them shot?"

"...I'll look."

"Be careful, there might be —"

The Captain was interrupted by the sound of a scraping footfall followed by the appearance of four dark eyes peering around the corner of a set of shelves deeper within the store.

~

Day 77

Evelyn set down her fork and looked imploringly at her husband.

"Baby, I love you, but there's something off about breakfast today."

Professor Walthers looked up as he was feeding little Rowan his bottle, the chef's apron still dangling from around his neck.

"I know honey, I know. I did the best I could under the circumstances. For some reason all the salt in the pantry is gone. So I had to try and make do with seasoning salt and other substitutes. Still, I know the eggs suffered for the loss."

"All the salt is gone? But when Phillip and I made dinner last night we just opened a brand new canister, and there were, like, eight left when we pulled it out."

"Well, I don't know then. I just know that shelf was bare when I went looking this morning."

"That's odd."

"And worrisome. Salt is an essential nutrient."

"I'm sure we'll figure it out. Maybe Mel and Ash rearranged things again. Ever since you put them in charge of keeping stock of our stores they've been constantly moving things here and there trying to find a good organizational system."

"You're right, they're the most likely culprits. I'll have a talk with them after breakfast, but definitely before lunch. I hear Don's planning on making chicken & dumplings again and he'll definitely need it."

"Chicken and dumplings again? Ugh. Jen's going to have a conniption fit. She hates chicken & dumplings."

"She'll either get over it or start taking her turn cooking. So long as she refuses to cook, Don's determined to punish her."

"We're going to have to have another 'Come to Jesus' meeting about

159

the petty dramas in the vault, aren't we?"

"Tonight, if not this afternoon."

"I know most of them are still children in their own minds but you'd think circumstances being what they are..."

"Very few people grow of their own accord via circumstance. People have to choose it, decide that they'll be better than pettiness, and put aside their feelings to do what's right."

"Do you think humanity will ever grow out of it?"

"Pettiness?"

"Yeah."

"I don't know. I hope so."

At that moment a stirring in Henry's arms led him to start shifting the baby up onto his shoulder, and he began gently rocking and cooing as he patted his young sons back, hoping to ease out a burp.

~

"Has anyone seen Alex?"

Professor Walthers poked his head into the main common room-come-bunkroom for the majority of the vault's inhabitants. He was met by confused stares and shrugged shoulders, as well as a few verbal responses stating none had seen him recently. He then made his way down the hall to the kitchen and dining area, where Don was now tending three large pots of boiling chicken while Evelyn, Karen, and Phillip were waiting with bowls and forks to debone the chicken being prepped.

"Have any of you seen Alex?"

Karen nodded as she responded.

"Yeah, he said he had some research to do in the archive earlier. I think he borrowed your laptop charger, too. Is that why you're

160

looking for him?"

"I don't have a laptop; what do you mean?"

"I saw him coming out of your room with a small black box. I thought that it was a laptop charger, you know how they have that black box thing on most of them?"

"I don't have anything like that, I don't even have a laptop, all I have that's like that is... hold that thought, you said he's in the archive?"

"He said that's where he was headed."

Walthers thanked her before making his way down the hall to the back of the vault, where the archive was. Ever since Rowans birth he'd left it unlocked as a way of allowing the student body access. Many of them had taken the opportunity to use it as a library of sorts, copying book PDFs into their phones and reading them as entertainment. As he entered the archive he could hear a low kind of throbbing noise, almost like a well-maintained car motor gently revving and then gently easing back on the other side of a wall. It was just loud enough to make out, but not loud enough to be worrisome.

A few steps into the server farm, with its rows of gleaming black cases reflecting the dim lighting from the wire conduit racks hanging from the ceiling, and he encountered the first canister. It held a few grains of salt still, but was otherwise empty. Ahead of him, strewn through the aisles, were more, almost half a dozen. In the center of the farm, kneeling over a large smooth spread out layer of salt on the floor, was Alex. He was shirtless, and his chest was crisscrossed with blood. He had the copper knife in his hand and was using it to draw shapes in the salt. As Walthers watched, Alex took the knife from the salt and very deliberately drew the blade across his abdomen hard enough to leave a cut. As he went back to drawing in the salt with the bloodied blade the line he drew erupted with a faint greenish glow and the humming sound permeated the air once again. He repeated the act, again drawing the blade across his flesh, this time from his left collarbone down across to his right nipple, before once more drawing in the salt.

Walthers let loose his anger, sharpened by the fear, confusion, and disbelief boiling up within him.

"Just what in the hell are you doing!?"

Alex paid him no mind, in fact seemed not to hear him at all, and instead drew the last line in the salt.

Suddenly the salt swirled and boiled with flashes of green, purple, and golden light. Specks of it flew into the air to fall like rainbow sparks against the servers. A concussion slammed into the air and blew Alex and Professor Walthers back several feet, and the servers surrounding them cracked out of their mounts and leaned away from the center of the room. As electrical connections severed here and there, more run of the mill sparks eked out from connections all over the room. There was a sound as if a giant bedsheet were tearing down the middle, only deeper, reverberating through the air in waves that were almost palpable.

A long white peg came into being in the middle of the air above the circle, as if it were simply emerging from behind some invisible curtain, and the rest of a Tall One followed, it's head finding itself nested within the racks hanging from the ceiling. As Walthers straightened his glasses, he watched as the creature bent lower, surveying the archive. Alex scrambled to his feet and began shouting at the giant, holding the knife up in front of him like a talisman as his mouth formed unfamiliar words shouted in defiance and alarm.

"Hid'ug! Ka'n'pa-ah-na! Sek-temoth het Ril-yeh!"

That was as far as he got before the behemoth opened its own mouth in a cacophonous roar, a crimson light spilling out from within its baleful maw. Walthers found himself completely immobilized. His muscles ceased responding to his will, remaining frozen in the position he was in. Alex seemed similarly affected. With a rapidity that belied expression, the creature reached out with a long spindly arm, snatched Alex from where he stood, and threw him clear across the archives in a straight shot between the sparking servers and into a sheer concrete wall nearly forty feet away, where he impacted with a sickening thud and slid down to the floor, leaving an ugly smear of blood down the wall. Walthers knew beyond the shadow of a doubt that he was dead before he ever hit the floor.

There was a commotion behind him but he couldn't turn to look. He could hear the voices of the rest of the vaults residents behind him. The behemoth did as well. It turned and the bizarre paralysis left Walthers. He was able to turn and see them, most of them, now frozen as he had been as the creature faced them. It ducked its head low and began moving towards them, it's long legs pumping underneath it, the arms reaching forward and grabbing at servers, shoving them aside, tearing them from their mountings to make room for its bulk. Walthers picked himself up off the floor and ran after it, hopelessly slower and too far behind at the start. He perceived the next moments almost in slow motion. As the giant cleared the servers it reached out with one spindly arm at the right side of the huddled group, braced it's peg like feet and drew it's arm sharply leftwards, bowling over the assembled mass like so many blades of grass. The sickening sounds of breaking limbs could be heard over the sounds of their bodies hitting the floor. Walthers reached the creature just then, and it barely looked at him before slamming him with the back of its left hand almost playfully. Walthers careened through the air down the side of the archive, first impacting the wall, then the racks in the ceiling before blacking out.

CHAPTER 17

Day 77

Cox went for his weapon, but his Captain's outstretched hand stayed him.

"Who's there? You there in the dark back there, come out, we won't hurt you. We're not here to hurt anyone..."

A voice emerged from the darkness, quiet, hesitant.

"Did you kill her?"

"We weren't the shooters; we know them but we don't know why they shot her. She's alive. We came looking for our comrades — they're dead outside — and we saw your friend here was alive. We came for someone specific but we're no threat to you. Can you take care of your friend?"

"No... she took care of us."

"You can come out and come get her. We won't hurt you."

Longmire and Cox watched carefully, still ready to draw, as a middle aged Middle Eastern man emerged, one hand clutching a worn coat closed and the other pulling behind him a young girl wearing a much better coat emblazoned with a cartoon character, mittens, and a hat.

Cox visibly relaxed. Longmire muttered a quiet curse, giving Cox a meaningful look as he did so. Emil broke the sudden silence, concern dripping from his voice.

"How did she survive? She was shot some time ago."

Longmire crouched over the woman unconscious on the floor.

"Well... looks like the thigh shot was a through and through. Soft tissue only, no major arteries or veins hit... clotted up on its own. The wrist... Jesus, that's lucky... looks like she held it until she passed out... long enough for the blood to freeze and keep her hand in place."

"Her hand is frozen in place?"

"Well, the glove. She got very very lucky, I think."

"So she'll live?"

"Looks like it. She might lose that left hand, depending on how much blood flow is getting through..."

"What can we do?"

"You? Almost nothing. I, on the other hand, can get her to a halfway decent doctor with halfway decent supplies."

"...and what of us?"

"Well, shit... I don't suppose I can leave you behind... you'll have to come with."

"Thank you, that's very generous, Mister...?"

"Longmire, Captain Longmire, US Navy. This here is Chief Petty Officer Jim Cox, my Master at Arms."

"My name is Emil, this is my daughter Sarya, and her name is

Sharon."

"Wish we'd met in better circumstances. Cox, her blood has dripped down and frozen her to the floor in a couple of spots, could you find something to melt or pry her off?"

Cox's head snapped up from where he was examining Sharon's thigh wound and he began scanning the shelves as he stood.

"Yes sir."

"Is there somewhere in back we can put her down? A bed, or desk? Anything flat that can be made comfortable?"

Emil looked up from Sharon to the strange man who was suddenly in charge.

"Uh, er, yes, I, I think so, a couch."

"Good, take your kid and go set it up, find blankets or something. She's frostbitten in the extremities and her core temp is borderline hypothermic at best. Cox, you find anything?"

Coming back from around the shelves Cox kneeled and showed two options, a bottle of rubbing alcohol and a barbecue spatula.

"Stone knives and bear skins, Jesus..."

"Sir?"

"Never mind, both. Use the alcohol to melt the edges then pry her up with the spatula, then you and Emil get her to the back. Then break out a med kit and bandage her wounds, make sure that once she thaws she doesn't bleed out. Pack her wrist especially; if that starts bleeding she'll bleed out fast."

"Aye, sir."

"Once she's taken care of, get on the horn with the *Oregon*, let them know we're bunking down here for the night."

"Aye, sir."

As they went about their work, Longmire searched the shop for edibles, finding plenty of frozen canned goods and bottled drinks, a few of which hadn't burst. Gathering them in a cloth bag, he took them into the back just as Cox got off the radio.

"Sir, the XO is all kinds of worried. He doesn't like that we've lost Hardy, and that we've no idea who the VIP is. He's especially unhappy we're staying ashore overnight."

Emil looked up from where he sat on the arm of the couch.

"VIP? What VIP?"

"We came here looking for someone, someone we know has survived, a Brit, someone the American and Australian governments hold to be very valuable. Problem is, we don't know who they are or where they are. The powers that be are paranoid to a fault, and so was our contact, Hardy."

"Hardy?"

"Unfortunately, he's one of the three outside."

"Oh, oh I'm sorry. But, uh... there was a bit of a hubbub here about a visiting bunch of Brits before things went badly."

"Really? What kind?"

"I'm not sure, something about the Metropolitan Museum of Art, and a new display, I don't know, it was in the paper."

"When was it in the paper?"

"The day before the things came."

"I was hoping you'd say something like that."

The Captain got up and went back out to the store, looking around, he grabbed a still-folded copy of each newspaper, still in the racks by the door, and took them back to the office.

"Here, which one do you read?"

"The Times and the Post, but the story you're looking for is in the Times."

"Yeah, page two, here it is: A British anthropologist is here to showcase the finds of a recent dig in Northern Europe. Alongside a number of other art experts, something about new theories about early European religious beliefs.

Shit, look at this: Terrance Opperthorne, Professor of Anthropology, Oxford, is a proponent of a radical new theory about early European religious beliefs, putting forth that rather than the primitive animalistic deities, that they worshipped symbols of animals that possessed characteristics which allows them to survive an ancient cataclysm, depicted in cave paintings, a deadly sky accompanied by winter hunters. That sound familiar to anyone else? Jesus Christ, no wonder we're here to get him."

~

Day 78

The Captain of the *Oregon* sat in the midst of his Master at Arms and the three civilians. After a brief breakfast of lukewarm soup and dry saltines, he spoke up.

"Alright, here's the plan. We're going to call the Oregon and have them send out another shore party with a litter. They'll make their way here with a GPS and get you three civvies to the boat. Cox and I will make our way to the museum, get Dr. Opperthorne, any materials he might need, and then we'll get back to the boat. Then we all get back down the river and to our next rendezvous.

We've had a lot more trouble and too many goddamn losses on this trip and I'm about tired of it. I want to get this done and get back under the water. Cox, get on the horn, make it happen."

As he concluded and Cox left the room, sudden movement from the figure on the couch drew everyone's attention. Emil went to the couch immediately followed by Sarya. Longmire and Cox held back, knowing a strange face wouldn't be a welcome sight to wake up to.

168

Sharon blinked her eyes until her vision cleared, recognizing Emil even through the haze and dim light.

"Where are we? Did you get me from the store? I tried to push myself to the back but I guess I had bled too much..."

Sarya spoke first, before her father could so much as catch a breath.

"Daddy, the Captain-Man, and Mr. Cox scraped you of the floor with a spatula!"

An alarmed and confused look came over her face before Emil jumped in to explain.

"What she means is, two gentlemen from the United States Navy came looking for the unfortunate fellows outside and found you, with your blood freezing you to the ground, and we, all three, worked together to gently unfreeze you and move you here before packing and bandaging your wounds."

Sharon moved her right arm to her head.

"And... how long has it been, how long have I been out?"

Emil looked at his watch.

"About sixteen hours. You're lucky it's gotten so cold outside. If your glove hadn't frozen in place over your wrist, you'd have died."

"The important part is, you're going to get to someplace with people with actual medical training and tools."

Sharon strained to sit up but a sudden wave of dizziness and nausea convinced her it was a bad idea.

"That's the Captain, I presume?"

Emil nodded.

"You're very very lucky. You lost a lot of blood. Much more, you'd have needed a transfusion for sure. Hell, I still think you need one just to be safe, but at least you're out of the woods."

169

"What about the men outside? What were they doing, why'd they shoot me?"

"They were on the way to the Metropolitan Museum of Art to pick up another survivor. We think your appearance, that you were armed and unexpected... one of the lesser experienced of the three panicked, shot you, and drew the attention of the things in the sky. They didn't get into the store like you did, not fast enough."

"I'm sorry."

"It wasn't your fault. Unless you intentionally provoked them into shooting you — doubtful — then the whole thing was one fucked up accident."

"I certainly didn't. Hell, my first thought when I saw them was rescue... I was going to holster, but then..."

"It's alright. Rescue is what you're getting, maybe a bit delayed but..."

Cox came back into the room.

"Sir, there's a problem with the *Oregon*."

"What kind of a problem, Mr. Cox?"

"When the XO surfaced the ship through the ice of the East River, she made one hell of a loud crack coming up. The giants took notice, sir. They hammered on the hull for a bit. No damage they could ascertain, but... something they did put the XO in a coma. He was observing the giants through the periscope when suddenly he just... well, they say he just collapsed."

"So the XO is out of commission. *Damn*. Tell me they've shelved the periscope for now."

"Oh yes sir, absolutely. Lieutenant Thompson is in charge there now. He's put the crew on standing orders not to observe the outside by any means, even infrared."

"Good. Where does that leave us so far as the second shore party?"

"They're waiting until the giants have stopped hammering at the hull, then they're going to wait a few hours before they'll chance going outside and making their way ashore and onto here."

"So we're on our own until then. Alright then. Here's the altered plan: Cox and I are going to go on to the Museum and get the good Doctor. Emil, Sarya, and Sharon, you stay here and wait for the shore party or, failing that, our own return."

Cox shifted uneasily from one for to the other before speaking again.

"Sir... splitting up hasn't exactly been a winning strategy here as of late. And quite frankly... these are civilians — no offense intended — and the one of them with any kind of real training is wounded and in need of a transfusion or plenty of recovery time. I don't think it's wise, or conscionable, to leave them behind."

Longmire appraised the CPO for a long moment before speaking.

"You know, Chief, there are times a man in command, especially an officer, forgets for a moment how capable the men under him are, and sometimes he intends or plans something damn foolish and needs a reminder. New plan. We'll wait here for the shore party and then we'll *all* head for the museum. Then we'll all had back to the *Oregon* —"

The Captain was interrupted by a cacophony of sound. Steel rending, concrete and glass shattering, a fury of noise coming from not too far away. Cox, Emil, and Longmire rushed to the storefront only to see that the streets were eerily empty, with nothing but a fierce chill wind blowing dust and snow equally at a gale force. Emil looked out, momentarily frozen, before racing back to the office where he tore open pocket after pocket on their bags to find his phone. Cox and Longmire followed behind, quietly awaiting some explanation. Emil looked up at them as he waited for the phone to power on.

"I was here on 9/11. I was here a few months ago when other buildings came down as well... I took some down myself on the orders of the government through the Emergency Broadcast System.

171

If there's new orders I must know."

The Captain pointedly put a hand on his sidearm before responding in a chilling tone.

"You didn't think to inform us that you've been going around New York demolishing buildings?"

"It didn't seem relevant; after the last broadcast my commitment seemed over, my duties fulfilled."

At that moment the phone finished its litany of startup services and error messages, only to begin flashing and emitting a familiar series of tones as an Alert message came through.

A new variety of sentient life has been encountered. It is extremely hostile and deadly. Survivor activity on the surface of any kind is highly discouraged. This new organism is accompanied by a marked drop in ambient temperature.

All survivors should be aware that these new beings seem highly intelligent. They seem capable of planning, adapting, and predicting the actions of others. They have been seen to work in groups, cooperate, and utilize readily available tools. They cannot be killed by any known means.

Do not look outside. Do not look at the sky. Do not make any more heart or light than is necessary for your survival. You are not abandoned. You are not forgotten.

Emil read the alert aloud to the assembled company, afterwards cursing and sitting the phone down. He began a tirade, getting louder as his anger and panic rose with each passing second.

"That tells me nothing! Why are there buildings coming down — again!? What are these things? Where did they come from? I'm sick and tired of having no answers! Of being afraid for my life and the life of my daughter..."

Longmire grabbed Emil by the chin forcing him into eye contact before putting a single finger up to his lips signaling quiet, but Emil continued, although in a desperate whisper.

"Captain, please, I beg you, abandon this foolish errand to find this man, take us on your submarine and let us leave this place. Take us to safety. Buildings are coming down, giants are swarming over the city and the temperature is steadily dropping every hour. There is no real chance we will get to this Opperthorne, much less that he will be alive."

Longmire and Cox shared a look before the Captain responded.

"I appreciate your point of view, but we have our orders."

"Surely, Captain, there's room for reasonable exception? I mean, buildings are coming down, you've lost two crewmen already. Another two missing presumed dead. How much is Opperthorne really worth compared to all our lives?"

"You've never served in any kind of military or law enforcement capacity, have you?"

"Not as such, no, not really. I was a translator for the Department of Homeland Security."

"But not an agent."

"No... no, I was never an agent for the DHS..."

"Well, then, I wouldn't expect you to understand. Those who put on a uniform in those fields know already that their life might be sacrificed in order to save others. You accept it, deal with it, and you hope that *if* the time comes, that the end goal is worth it. Today my end goal is the safe rescue of someone who may have key information on this, these phenomena. And I believe *that* is worth Watkins, Kellogg, Forsythe, and Homme, and I believe it might even be worth my life, Cox's, and yes, even yours."

"How comforting it must be to exculpated of all ethical responsibility for your decisions. You are following orders, orders which come from imperfect men making decisions with incomplete data. Your 'end-goal' may be a complete sham, did you ever think about that?"

"Every time I think about any member of my crew, here or on the *Oregon*. But I have my orders and I took an oath to follow those orders through."

"Well *I* never took any oaths..."

"And you're perfectly free to go off on your merry way! I'm not about to force you, but if you want to come along with us you're going to have to accept that we have things to do here before we head back to the boat!"

Emil opened his mouth to protest but Sharon cleared her throat to get their attention.

"Emil, the Captain is as dedicated to his duty as you are to Sarya. No amount of verbal sparring is going to budge him. So *sit down and shut up* before we lose the privilege of his help."

Emil looked as if he'd been struck. His face sank and he slowly turned and walked back to the front of the store where Sarya was playing with some of the cheap toys that were on the shelves there. Longmire waited until he was out of earshot before he spoke, this time to Sharon.

"I get the feeling he's going to be trouble at some point."

Sharon took a deep breath before responding.

"He's just at his wits' end. He wants his daughter to be safe, and soon. Any delay is going to ruffle his feathers."

"Well, he needs to understand that my intent is to get us *all* safe."

"He knows; he just wants it to happen now. Later might be too late. Things are strange, this isn't something anybody ever prepared us for."

"You're right. This is unprecedented, so any edge, any advantage we can get, including Opperthorne, has to take priority."

"I don't disagree on any particular point, but like you said, those who've worn the uniform see things differently."

Cox entered the room holding one of the maps.

"Ah, good! Cox! Let's see just how much further we've got to go."

~

The Captain and the Master at Arms took point ahead of the others. Sharon hobbled along, one wrist wrapped so well her entire hand was one large ball of gauze. Her leg was similarly bandaged, but a scrap of wood functioned well as a brace to keep it stiff and help it support her weight. Still, she had an arm each draped around the shoulders of Emil and Sarya. Progress was slow, what the Captain and Cox could've covered on their own in half an hour took the five of them two. Each crossroads was terrifying. They got lucky at one spot, with two entrances to the Subway a few blocks apart leading them direct.

There were signs that there were still those roving the subways, but they didn't encounter anyone, sticking to the service tunnels alongside. It took the better part of the morning, but at long last, the five of them stood across the street from the New York Metropolitan Museum of Art, and Central Park.

"Looks like someone took great care to button her up. Her windows are boarded, looks like chains on the doors... Cox, do you have any ideas?"

"Seems this calls for the direct approach, sir. We get up to the door and we knock."

"Knock?"

"Yes sir. The only one in there is supposed to be Opperthorne, right? We knock, we talk to him through the door, let him know who we are, what our intentions are, and hopefully he'll have a way to come out with his research."

"Seems reasonable."

175

Sharon spoke up behind them.

"The delivery dock."

"Pardon?"

"All major museums have delivery docks for moving in large exhibits. I'm sure the Met is no different. Due to the nature of most exhibitions, I'm sure it's covered from the sky to protect from rain. Likely underground, out of sight of the public. We find the delivery dock, that's where we get in. Inside, we just look for him, find him, and we take him and his notes with us back to the *Oregon*."

Cox and Longmire shared an impressed look. Cox continued.

"Good idea Sharon. Any idea where it might be?"

Sharon tilted her head to indicate the sign barely sticking above the snow on the museum side of the street. It read, 'Deliveries taken through E 84th St. Garage Entrance'.

Longmire whistled as he read, a low, quick show of admiration.

"Motherfucker. How'd I miss that. Alright, that's what, a block north?"

Cox was already looking at the map.

"Should be."

"Alright, let's get moving."

It was nearly noon before they got around to the garage entrance, where its appearance was less than promising. Longmire stared as his eyes grew dark and his countenance fell.

"What the fuck do you suppose happened here?"

They looked across the road at the large steel shutters that once held the garage closed, their center now a jagged hole. Cox spoke first in response.

"Sir, it could be something from the first days of the things in the sky. Or the giants. They hammered on the *Oregon*. It's easy enough to imagine they could do that. Or it could be something Hardy did at some point to ease access..."

"Regardless, I'm not one to believe in luck. It's an opening we can use, but I don't like the looks of it. We'll leave the civvies here and scout this alone."

"No argument here, sir."

Cox turned to Sharon, Emil, and Sarya.

"Any issues with you guys?"

Sharon raised her middle finger on her uninjured hand draped over Saryas shoulder. Longmire frowned.

"If you guys die in there, we won't have any way of knowing. You both have radios. Leave one with us. That way, if you don't answer in a couple hours, we can make our way to the *Oregon* without you."

Longmire pulled his radio from his belt and handed it to Emil without argument.

"No point delaying things. You three find cover, we'll be back as soon as we can with Opperthorne. Hope to god he's worth it."

CHAPTER 18

Day 78

Sharon, Emil, & Sarya huddled under a blanket on a couch in a spacious and well adorned cabin with a roaring fireplace. Or, they would've been, had the walls, fireplace, and fire been real, rather than matte painted pieces set out to display the furniture in a pleasing setting. As it was, the temperature was hovering around ten degrees. Sarya sat between the adults, getting the most of the body heat.

Emil was nearly asleep, his consciousness hovering between the waking world and... somewhere else. Shadows of people long dead flitted past the edges of his awareness like motes of dust in a flashlight beam. Some cried out to him, seeking his help, his guidance. Others cursed him for his faith, his tolerance. But they all reached for him, their fingers made of smoke freezing as they brushed his sleeves. Then they were gone. Stars wheeled past as he sped through the darkness into strange regions where things slid into and out of his perception like oil down a raging river.

He wasn't alone. There was something watching from above, beyond, there but not, elsewhere, distant. Beyond the walls of sleep it watched... waited... hungered. He felt its gaze focused on him, it's attention rapt. It shrieked at him, a shrill klaxon blazing into his ear.

With a jolt, Emil awoke, the radio in his hand buzzing intermittently a low tone. He brought it to his face and keyed it briefly, ending the alert tone. Captain Longmire's tinny voice came through the small speaker.

"Hello? Hello? Sharon? Emil? You still with us out there?"

"Yes, yes! We're here. Is everything alright there?"

"Absolutely. There's been... uh... a few complications, but we're about ready to get out of here. We've got, uh... well, we've got a ride."

"A ride? What do you mean a ride?"

"Something it looked like Hardy was saving. Get yourselves over here into the garage, you'll see."

"Alright, yes, we'll come, of course. Is Opperthorne there? What did he say?"

"...just get over here."

Emil looked over to Sharon, who seemed to have fallen to the sandman's charms as well. He gently stood, pulling the thin display comforter off his daughter and their savior. He was glad to see that Sharon's bandages were still tight and clean. Gently, he reached over and shook her shoulder.

"Sharon... Sharon, please wake up. We have to get ready..."

Sharon suddenly awoke, from unconscious to fight or flight in barely half a second. Her good arm snapped forward and grabbed Emil's arm at the wrist and started to twist before she realized just where she was and what was going on. She relaxed and released his wrist just as quickly as she'd snatched it to begin with.

"I'm sorry Emil, I was... I was having a bad dream..."

179

Emil rubbed his wrist. Despite her releasing it so quickly, he still felt like it would bruise soon. She had quite the grip.

"It's okay. I should've known better... Longmire says they've found something."

"Good or bad?"

"He didn't say."

"Well, you and Sarya should get over there and see what's up."

"Okay, um... aren't you going, too?"

"Yes, just I thought it would be quicker and safer if you went over there on your own at first. I'd slow you down. Then, after you're safe, Longmire and Cox can man up and come help a lady cross the street."

"I'm not sure that's such a good idea..."

"Look, before, with Longmire and Cox scouting ahead, we could afford for you and Sarya to stick with me and carry my butt around slowly. Now, you've got to get across the street quick and quiet. I hinder that, so it makes sense I stay behind. I'll be fine, you'll see."

"I really don't like it."

"I'm not asking you to like it."

With quiet resignation, Emil abandoned his instinct to keep Sharon by his side and gently woke Sarya. Wrapping them both in a comforter from one of the beds, they slowly made their way through the destroyed storefront and across the street. Sharon watched them go before taking stock of her position.

"Let's see, water, pack, sidearm... damn. He took the fucking radio..."

Sharons frustration was short lived, as peering out at the museum across the way, looking for some sign of the inhabitants within, she noticed a figure in the fog moving out from around what appeared to be a comically undersized tractor-trailer parked by the side of the road half a block down. Then she realized the truck and its trailer were in fact normally sized, and the figure, of which she could only see the outline, had to stand at least twelve feet tall.

"Oh... *shit.*"

Sharon moved as quietly as she could off the couch, taking the blanket with her and grabbing the pack as she half crawled, half dragged herself behind the display, keeping low and watching the figure from a gap between a fake potted plant and one of the scenery backdrops. The figure was walking closer, and as the fog became thinner between her and the figure, she could see that it was proportioned all wrong.

Its shoulders were at least five feet wide, but its waist, if you could call it that, couldn't have been much wider than a foot. The arms were long, and spindly, while the thighs were humongous, easily as big around as Sharons entire body, before tapering down to a knee that looked like it was stuffed with half a cinder block, as it was almost a perfect equilateral diamond shape, the feet were... never mind, it didn't have feet. Roughly half a foot below the knee the skin ended and what looked like a long peg of bone struck out at the pavement. The skin itself looked to be ridged all over, almost like corduroy, and it was pale as the swirling snow around it. Here and there, there were bumps, like pimples almost, rising from in between the ridges. The heads of these mounds were a mottled grey and sickly green. And there was a definitive ring of them around the shoulders, near what should've been a neck. Instead, the head rose smoothly from the shoulders like a single mountain rising from a plain, the top rounded and domed almost like a weathered down tree stump. The mouth was lipless, a slit that ran easily a foot across the width of the head at the midline. The eyes were glowing, and at this distance they seemed to be a golden amber color.

~

Day 78

The sound of metal scraping on concrete was not a pleasant one, but it couldn't be helped.

Timor dragged the heavy barrel assembly through the corridor, scratching up its smooth exterior on the rough concrete floor. He was moving an emplacement piece by piece from storage into the entry area, and assembling it bit by bit according to the manual with which it had been packed. After looking through the monitors at the exterior doors, and seeing the bald yetis outside, he was going to be prepared if they came knocking again. He knew he wasn't much of a warrior. In fact, if he had been, he'd have been able to lift the barrel he was dragging, but he could set the gun someplace solid, sit behind it, and press the paddle triggers as well as the next man.

He felt lightheaded. He slowly let the barrel fall to the floor before sitting down beside it. He looked down at the bulging gut he'd developed, listened to his own ragged breathing — far too shallow — and felt his pounding heart. His isolation had kept him safe, but his diet of junk food and near total lack of exercise had taken their toll. He was grossly obese and completely out of shape. He felt a wheezing deep in his chest; it hurt. He coughed. Something came up. He spit. It was a pale green... infection.

He sat another few minutes until the sweat of exertion was gone, then rolled to his side and got his legs under him. Standing, he went to the supply closet with his medical supplies and pulled out a bottle of antibiotics. They were old, and the label was mostly faded, but he could make out the directions and uses well enough. Plenty of fluids, he could manage. Bed rest would have to wait. He took the first dose of two pills, washed it down with a bottle of water, and then went back to the barrel assembly.

He took his seat again, once more exhausted, sweating, and out of breath. Just from the walk. Timor did a quick inventory in his head, calculating four more trips from the armory to the entrance, taking roughly 45 minutes each. It was just past midnight... he should definitely be done before dawn. At dawn, he planned on bundling up behind his weapon emplacement and going to sleep. If anything came while he slept, they could be assured of his response. He needed to do this because he couldn't lie to himself, if something tried to break in while he slept anywhere else, he didn't have the courage to run for his weaponry; he'd hide instead. He couldn't afford to hide. For all he knew, he might be the last human being on earth. He owed it to every man that'd ever lived to survive as best he could.

~

Day 78, ten kilometers south-east of Lycksele, Sweden

The tall things were all over the place. Seems they liked the cold and the quiet of the woods. She'd heard them roar more than once, found evidence of their work on other survivors — or hopefully just elk — the remains were so scattered and shattered it was hard to know which... except when there were clothes in the mix. She hated those, especially since they weren't always just adult clothes.

The store had yielded a surprising bounty when she actually got to looking. The seasonal storage, stock they'd have tried to sell come spring, stoves, tents, snowshoes. Not the best quality, cheap imitation junk. But better than nothing.

She'd been moving at night, sleeping in a tent covered in branches and snow during daylight, always set up under the boughs of a tree, never in the open. The tall things didn't go walking amongst the limbs of a tree if they could help it, much like people. Kept her from getting stepped on. The tall things didn't seem to have any sense of smell, nor the infrared sense of the flying things in the sky. She was making her way slowly but surely towards Umeå nearly 135 kilometers to the southeast. Luckily the E13 was pretty much a direct shot, and mid-morning commercial traffic meant there were cars and trucks — few and far between — but enough that scavenging and her non-perishables should get her there. From there she hoped to find a decent transceiver and make contact with one of the Project satellites.

She was talking detailed notes on her observations of giants as she went. Their heights and builds seemed uniform, no scars or other injuries had been seen this far, but the patterns of nodules seemed unique per individual. No gender traits could be seen either, nor waste excretions. She had seen very little interaction between them; they seemed to lack any uniform social structure, but on the rare occasion they did interact, there was definitely some kind of hierarchy at play. Vocalizations and movements indicated deference towards some, but the recipient seemed to shift at each new interaction. Their effects on the environment were pronounced, both in the obvious absorption of ambient heat energy, and also in the subtle ways the dimensions and angles of the world around them were shifted and twisted in their immediate proximity if they remained still for any length of time.

No evidence of their origin or intent seemed forthcoming. She hoped that by the time she reached Umeå she might have some testable hypothesis as to their role in the ongoing cataclysm, but for now, she was still. The Project needed their xenobiologist, and a snowball's chance in hell was better than no chance at all.

CHAPTER 19

Day 78

Dr. Rafei gestured vaguely with his hand towards the control panel, impatient.

"What are they doing?"

"I can't tell, Doc. They're just... standing around."

"Yes, but what are they *doing?* Are they communicating with each other? Are they moving at all? Are they eating? Dancing? Have they joined hands and starting singing Kumbaya?"

"Oh c'mon, Doc, don't be that way. I know you're frusterbated but you don't gotta be taking it out on me..."

"I'm sorry, it's just... I would prefer more thorough descriptions, if you don't mind."

"Alright Doc, alright... they're standin' in a circle around my truck, six of 'em. They're about equal distance from each other, hands at their sides, but they're swaying back and forth..."

"Swaying? Uh... there should be a small silver switch underneath the screen; flick it over."

Suddenly the speakers began emitting the static of a windblown microphone. But in it, and occasionally over it, was a deep hum, rising and falling in a discordant thread that switched pitches in an unnatural and inhuman manner from moment to moment. Doctor Rafei sat silent, listening to it for a few moments before speaking.

"Jesse, turn the volume down for a moment. There's another switch in this panel in front of us. I don't know where. It's a recording button. It'll record this camera and microphone to a digital file format. But before we use it, we need to find a thumb drive and put it in the USB slot so that it's recorded to something."

"Aw hell, Doc, I've got a thumb drive hanging off my dang keys!"

"Excellent! Put it in the slot and press the record button!"

"No problem, Doc. Just gimme a sec to find it, I gotta find it..."

"You *just* said it was on your keys."

"Yeah, along with a can opener, bottle opener, Swiss army knife, mini flashlight, mini marker, laser light, half a dozen little tabs with funny sayin's on 'em... Ah! Here we go. Alright, Doc, we're plugged in and... now we're recording."

"Good, good... any change in their behavior?"

"Not that I can tell."

"Turn the volume back up, please."

Jesse reached forward, giving a knob a spin and turning the volume back up. The room was again filled with static and... the hum had changed. The discordance had given way to a series of rising and falling tones, different notes from each creature surrounding the vehicle. Some went painfully high through the spectrum to abysmally low while others merely wobbled between two alternating tones, both at opposite ends. Some seemed to be pitched at multiple

187

tones simultaneously, as impossible as that seemed.

Suddenly, the image on the screen changed. Pinpricks of multihued light began emerging from the various nodules all over the bodies of the assembled contingent, the motes of light swirling gently around the circle of giants before tightening around Jesse's truck.

~

Day 78

Dr. Lucinda Alvarez scrubbed her hands slowly and methodically under the steaming water/antimicrobial/antiseptic mix they used in the Clean Wing of the facility. Traces of blood and detritus rinsed off of her hands in flecks and streams. This was the third emergency surgery she'd been part of since the emergence of the H-Type Phenomena. Of course, that classification was an intermediate one, since during the initial arrival of the Phenomena what they now were calling the C-Type had simply been *the* Phenomena. Now that there were two distinct, and presumably connected, entities the higher ups had started brainstorming and debating what to call them in addition to what should be done.

Personally, Lucinda thought the unofficial nicknames the troops had come up with, the Shards and the Tall Ones, seemed a lot better than any official classification or terminology assigned by some self-important spoon doctor. The new Tall Ones were aggressive, violent, and so far, invincible. Bullets and shrapnel just bounced off their skin like they were children's toys thrown at a trampoline. This had unfortunate consequences in that trying any form of conventional weaponry against them attracted the Shards from overhead in nearly all cases so far.

In the field, the scout groups had been suffering serious casualties in every encounter with the Tall Ones. Again, this was the third emergency surgery since they'd appeared. She was getting very tired and fed up with the incompetent focus of the higher ups. As she mindlessly pondered and scrubbed an idea began to form. A way to

188

redirect their priorities and redirect their focus. She'd have to be careful, and if she was found out the consequences would be... limiting, to say the least. But history would vindicate her. She was sure. She began by digging out the manuals for the various wings of the medical bays.

~

The cracks were growing larger. It was stupid. He should've known better. All the warnings, all the warnings had said it very specifically; 'Do not make noise'. But he'd just had to test it. He'd assembled it, checked it, rechecked it, loaded it, worked the action and the ejection system. He knew everything would work when the time came. So why'd he have to fire off a round?

Stupidity, plain old normal human stupidity. Now they were hammering at the door. The big steel door they'd been mulling around since they showed up a day and a half ago... and it was cracking. They were coming through. Timor sat behind his makeshift fortifications, piles of crates, metal and wood both, filled with various non-essentials like spare uniforms, obsolete radio equipment, dishes, and foodstuffs long, long past their expiration dates Looking out over them, the single bullet hole in the side of the watchman's shed stared back, taunting him.

Another resounding impact sent a booming ring through the bunker as the things on the other side hammered again at the door, the cracks expanding further. Timor took a moment to reflect on his life — a simple childhood in Minsk, his pursuit of Helena Mischkin throughout his teenaged years, his education in England for Astrophysics... his time as part of Russia's ISS participation program... entirely too much time spent playing video games... it didn't amount to much. He regretted never getting married, or having children, never traveling to America or the Orient. Too late, much too late...

Another boom. The cracks covered the whole of the door now. Not long...

He wondered if he was the only survivor. His earlier fantasies of going out fighting, symbolic of mankind's ancient struggles and defiance, seemed so petty now. He knew he couldn't be the last man on Earth. Some bloody group of government VIPs was probably in a bunker somewhere even more well equipped than this, totally free from worry or care, capable and in the process of going about a nearly normal life. In fact, he was sure of it. He remembered watching American programs in England, on the satellite, of American companies that built bomb shelters. They even had dance halls, some of them. He wasn't the last man. He was just a man... and the door was starting to crumble.

A loud ripping sound came through the door as a large chunk fell out. Through the hole he could see an unnaturally pale face with glowing amber eyes peer through at him. He could feel the palpable hate of its gaze. Timor spit out his most heartfelt sentiment at that face.

"Fuck you too!"

Timor opened fire.

~

Day 78

Sharon watched as the creature marched down the road, it's long strides making it deceptively quick despite such relatively slow movements. As she watched, it passed the store she hid in and continued down the road, seemingly oblivious to her observation. Just as it passed out of her sight, she caught movement coming from the truck it had passed. Around it came a man carrying a rifle, his head and face obscured by a balaclava and a heavy pair of goggles with extended lenses — infrared, no doubt. He moved at a crouch, his booted feet making barely a scrape over the frost and snow. As he moved towards the store, he slowed, his head on a swivel as he looked around and even up. The rifle followed, moving from a 45-degree angle down to the ready position forward, then horizontal to the ground. He was looking and aiming directly at Sharon. His right forefinger moved a scant inch and there was an audible click as he switched off the safety of his rifle — she could see now it was an

190

L85A2. As he entered and approached, he moved his left hand from the forward pistol grip to his mouth, where he raised one gloved finger in the universal shushing sign. He came within ten feet of her under cover of the store's roof before speaking.

"Oi there! Get up slowly and come out from 'ahind there, and stay quiet."

"I'd love to, but I'm wounded. Why are you following that, that thing?"

"Stay where you are and keep your hands empty. I'm going to come 'round."

As Sharon watched, the man navigated between the couches and love seat, made his way around the screen and the plastic plants, all the way keeping the barrel of his rifle aimed more or less at her location. As he came into full view of her, with her splint, bandages, and complete lack of weapons, he visibly relaxed. Clicking his weapon back to safe and lowering it, he spoke again.

"What the hell's got you out here now?"

"Well, that's a bit of a story..."

"Did you come with Longmire?"

"How did you... never mind. No. But, I know him and the guys who did."

"So you know Hardy?"

"Not really; he's dead."

"How?"

"The things from the sky. Attracted by excessive noise."

"Blasted buggers... Hardy was a good man."

"I didn't get to know. One of the guys he was with shot me, which as you can imagine..."

"...is what made the excessive noise, yeah."

"Bingo"

"Shit. Well, I'm awfully sorry to hear about that. I'm going to get on with it then, I've got to catch up to that thing."

"Uh... and why is that, again...?"

"Somebody or something has been bringing down buildings all around the city here, and those things have been crawling all over the wreckage almost as soon as they're down. I'm out to find out why. Now, let's go."

"I'm not going anywhere with you."

"I'm sorry, miss, but yes, you are. These things move like they're on a mission, including scouts ahead of the main body. I was five minutes ahead of them, just behind the scout. Now we've got to move before there's a dozen of them all over us. I've seen what they do to folks they don't expect; we don't want that."

With that, he hoisted Sharon to her feet, and, supporting her bad side, he set off, her right boot scraping the frost as they went.

CHAPTER 20

Day 78

Angela couldn't feel her face. The wind was biting and blowing any loose snow directly into her eyes. She ignored both. The tall things were digging. Three of them were moving in circles, each using their wide hands and spindly fingers as shovels, clawing up clods of dirt, ice, and snow. They'd been part of the larger herd marching through the woods that she'd been following until they came across this clearing. These three had detached from the larger line and begun digging in their peculiar way.

Angela was talking shelter halfway up the side of a pine tree, using its height and its uphill placement to get a better vantage point into their excavations. They'd been digging for nearly an hour and the hole was nearly as deep as they were tall, and nearly twenty feet across and getting wider. They seemed to be digging out a shallow bowl shape in the earth, making it wider as they went deeper. She desperately wished she had a camera or a camcorder of some kind, anything to get a visual record of this activity. It would be dark soon and her eyes would be insufficient to make out significant details. She'd have to move closer if she wanted to see, and that was out of the question.

193

She couldn't stay in the tree all night, either. She'd freeze to death. She began moving carefully down the tree, branch by branch, as slowly as she could, always aware of how much noise she was making and whether they'd stopped their work. Fortunately, they seemed completely oblivious. Once at the bottom she went about setting up her tent under the tree's protection, same as she had the night previous at another tree many kilometers behind.

Once inside and with her chemical heater activated by snow, she pulled out a number of small notebooks and began sketching out the patterns of movement and recording her notes on her observations. As she finished, she packed the notebooks into resealable plastic bags and carefully ordered them by contents and date with her other observations in her pack. Then she pulled out a can of condensed soup and let it and a cup of melted snow warm up nestled between her and the heater. She ate, cleaned her cup out with snow, then curled up to drift to sleep, idly wondering just what the tall things were digging for.

~

Day 78

As Jesse and Dr. Rafei watched the monitor, the swirling motes of light coalesced from a loose cloud around the truck into a spinning circle of multi-hued light. The circle widened into a disc, briefly resembling a set of planetary rings before it suddenly collapsed, impacting and rocking the truck before all the lights, the monitor, and the panel went dark.

"Uh... Doc?"

"Why did you turn off the sound?"

"I didn't. Everything just sorta shut down on its own..."

"EMP...?"

"Looks like it."

"Well...? What did you see? Don't spare any detail!"

Jesse began going over what he'd seen, describing all the minutiae of what the monitor had shown in the minute before everything went dark. Dr. Rafei listened intently, asking questions occasionally for clarification, before he spoke.

"Jesse, is there any light, of any kind, anywhere in this room?"

"Not that I can see, nah."

"Alright. I want you to listen very carefully to my instructions. Behind where we're sitting, on the wall, there should be a series of lockers. They're the lockers that held the various arms and gear for agents of the FBI who would've come here to protect us if this facility had been activated by some kind of plague.

Now, these lockers should be locked very securely, but the keys for them are in a desk just down the hall. I have been operating in the dark for long enough now that I feel comfortable retrieving the keys; however, once we've got them open I am far from familiar with the kinds of things inside.

I do not want to go blundering through them like a fool and set off some kind of grenade or something. I want you to feel around very carefully, very gently, and find a flare, or a glow stick, or a flashlight, or some other kind of light."

"Uh, Doc?"

"Yes, Jesse?"

"I already done got a glow stick and a flashlight on my belt."

"Why didn't you say so?"

"Well y'seemed to have yer britches in a bunch tryin' to gimme all kinds of specific instructions and I didn't wanna interrupt, Doc. My mama didn't raise me to be rude like that, that's all."

"Jesse, I appreciate your manners, but in a life or death situation such as the one we're faced with I think you can relax a bit and speak what's on your mind, even if it's rude."

"If you say so, Doc. Well... If that's the case, I gotta couple o' questions."

"Alright, ask away."

"Well, first, what the hell is this place? I mean, you take me through the CDC, into the lobby, and then take a special hidden elevator down to a secret subbasement that's got all the comforts of home and the very best security system government money can buy, but no labs, no scientists, nothing you'd expect from a super-secret hidey home under a government building, so... what's up with that, huh?"

~

Day 79

Professor Henry Walthers came to with a start. He looked around and he could see he was in his own bed, in his own room. Rowan was dozing peacefully in a little nest of pillows to his right. He was in a rather considerable amount of pain, he realized. His back, his head, but most especially his right leg was in agony. He tried to call out gently, as to not wake the baby, but he his throat was so dry he couldn't make a sound beyond a raspy creak. He turned to look around and had a moment of spinning dizziness. He noticed a small bell beside his bed, like the kind used at cheap gas stations or one stop shops to summon the sole employee after hours. He tried to reach out to it only to feel a sharp pain in the back of his left hand. Looking down, that's when he noticed the IV line taped to his hand, the tubing leading behind him, where, with some difficulty, he was able to see a small bag had been hung. Without his glasses he couldn't see exactly what it was.

More carefully this time, he reached out and tapped on the bell. It's silvery peal ringing out like a shot in the otherwise silent room. Evelyn appeared at the doorway a few moments later, her eyes red and puffy, obviously from crying.

"Oh thank god you're awake."

That was all she got out before she ran to him, bending over and delivering a passionate kiss, which, while enjoyable, threw him into a new wave of dizziness. As she moved to set her hip on the bed after breaking their embrace, Walthers felt his leg explode in agony. He swallowed the cry that struggled to come out for fear of waking Rowan, but the look on his face spoke well enough for Evelyn to immediately reverse course and stand.

She apologized and Walthers tried to reassure her, but only croaking emerged. He pantomimed drinking a glass of water and Evelyn understood, quickly leaving the room and filling a glass. She brought it back to him, where he greedily gulped all but the last sip down. That part, he gargled to moisten his throat and swallowed last.

Finally able to speak, he poured out questions. Knowing her husband, she indulged him, updating as best as she could.

"The students?"

"Half of them are gone."

"And the giant?"

"It seems contained in the tunnel to the culinary building."

"How?"

"After it went through the ones in the doorway, it rampaged through the common area and the kitchen. I was in the pantry and I guess it didn't see me. After it passed I went into the archives to see what had happened. I saw Alex, Liza, Jen, and the others scattered about near the door, and you were hanging, literally hanging from the racks above the servers on the right walkway. Your leg was caught in them and broken in, at least we think about four places, maybe more."

"How was it contained?"

"After I pulled you down and dragged you out of the archives, I hid you in the pantry and closed the door. I could hear it moving back and forth through the bunker. Once I heard it go out into the access tunnel to the culinary building I left the pantry and secured the door."

197

"It hasn't tried to escape?"

"Not as far as I can tell."

"It's a good thing that door is reinforced. How many are left?"

"Out of our original twenty-three there's only ten of us left, including we three here in this room."

"Jesus... who else made it?"

"Don, Phillip, Susan, Karen, Jerry, Seth, & Colleen."

"Hell..."

"What are we going to do?"

"I don't know... I have to see what's going on."

"Your leg is broken in at least four places. You can't go anywhere."

"There's a wheelchair in the storage room, the extraneous one we've been using for garbage."

"Oh no..."

"I'm sorry to say."

"Okay... you know if it was anyone else you'd be trapped here."

"I love you too."

Evelyn stood and walked out of the room, headed to the right. Moments later she passed the doorway again headed left, this time with a face-mask, rubber gloves, and carrying a basket heaped with cleaning supplies and rags.

Nearly an hour later she re-entered the room in different clothes pushing a folding wheelchair, its aluminum frame, wheels, and blue leather seat shining and clean. She then called in Phillip who assisted her in transferring the Professor from their bed to the chair and get his leg comfortably situated on a board to keep it straight. Walthers couldn't help but notice Phillip looked ashen and didn't speak any more than was necessary. Once he was set, Phillip left without a word.

"They're all taking things hard, aren't they?"

"We lost a lot of people, but Phillip is especially devastated. He and Seth have been the ones cleaning up the remains of the others in the archives. I thought since they were both men and Phillip was pre-med he'd have at least some idea of how to match up the various... and Seth, well, he's in criminology and forensics, so he's done some field exercises with bodies before... my mistake was in forgetting that he and Liza had a thing going."

"Oh... I didn't know that..."

"Nobody else did."

"Take me to the archive."

"Baby, you don't want to go in there."

"I need to, I need to access the MCP and see how much was lost. I also need to see exactly what Alex had been accessing."

"Is there some other access in the archive you think he might have accidentally opened?"

"No. While there is a walled off tunnel that was used to initially install the server farm, the giant didn't come in through that route."

"Then how did it get in?"

"That's what Alex did. He was doing some kind of... some kind of ritual, with the knife Viktor gave me."

"A ritual, really? Henry I know you hit your head but that seems a little..."

"I know how it sounds, but I saw the last part of it myself. He completed what he was doing, and then the giant came through into the archive. Almost like it stepped through some kind of invisible doorway. I think that he may have been attempting something different than what he accomplished, but the fact that what he was doing did anything means I have to take things into account I never would have before."

"Such as?"

"Such as the occult, such as dead religions and cults, such as ancient beliefs and practices."

"And you think that finding out where Alex learned the things he did may help you to eventually understand what's happening out there?"

"Maybe. It depends on just how much damage was done. Please, just take me there."

"As you wish. But I swear, if you turn into some kind of whacko I'm leaving you."

"No worries there, dear. I'm an academic; I have no desire to practice anything."

With that, Evelyn wheeled the injured professor out of their room, briefly stopping to ask Colleen to step into their room and sit with the baby. As they made their way through the halls they couldn't help but be disquieted by how empty the bunker felt. Everyone was quiet, and everyone wasn't nearly as many as they'd gotten used to. As they approached the archive, they came into the heavy scent of bleach. Seth was sitting outside the archive, staring blankly ahead as he drank a bottle of water. Sweat soaked his clothing and his dark brown hair. Next to him was a series of fourteen plastic totes, each spray painted black all over the outside to prevent anyone from seeing what was in them. Each had a single strip of silver duct tape with initials on it. Through the doorway they could see Phillip slowly dragging a mop back and forth across the concrete floor.

"Seth, Henry would like to access the MCP for something very important. Is it safe to go in there?"

Seth looked at her with eyes glazed over. It was obvious that, though he'd heard her, his mind was miles away from her or her query. Slowly though, his head nodded the affirmative.

"Okay, thank you."

Evelyn pushed her wheelchair-bound husband into the archives, having only a moment's difficulty in getting the chair up and over the raised threshold. Phillip didn't acknowledge them as she wheeled him over to the MCP. Through the aisles of servers, Walthers could see that there were strange lines seemingly burned into the floor where Alex had brought the monster to them. He made a mental note to investigate and compare it to anything he might find in the computer. Once he was stationed in front of the operating MCP, he turned to Evelyn.

"Love, I know you want to keep tabs on me, but I may be here for a while. Would you go and relieve Colleen and take care of Rowan? I can ask Phillip or call Seth if I need help."

Evelyn bent down and kissed his forehead, quietly nodding her assent. As she walked away, Henry reached over to wake the MCP from its standby mode and typed in his password. The initial screen after login showed the status of the system. Out of fifty servers, thirty-six were intact and running as expected. Eight were showing errors, but at least seemed to be responding in some way, and the last six were completely dark. With luck, some of the ones showing errors were simply in need of some kind of maintenance, and if he was really lucky then the six that were dark were simply disconnected and could be plugged back in, though that seemed naively optimistic.

Next, he punched up the MCPs access records, and sorted them by log in. As a precaution, he'd given each resident of the vault their own login credentials as well as the guest account intended for access by anyone who should find the archive should something befall all the residents of the vault. He couldn't rule out that Alex had used the guest account so he looked through both of them for what they'd accessed from the archive. Over the last two weeks Alex had accessed nearly two hundred volumes on archaeology, ancient religions, the occult, chemistry, physics, astronomy. He was going to have to go about this another way. He punched up the time logs for when and how long he accessed each entry. Most volumes he'd accessed he only searched through briefly; others, he seemed to read in their entirety. A small few, though, he referenced repeatedly throughout his research.

For those four, he punched up their locations, hoping against hope that they weren't on the damaged servers. Three of them were on undamaged servers, the last was stored on a server showing an error. He queued the MCP to download the three that were still accessible; *Early Ritualistic Worship* by Catherine Zhan, *On Totemic Gods and other Spiritualties* by Howard Phillips, and *The Astronomical Omnibus* from Swan Point Publishing. The fourth, *Peculiarities of the Aurignacian Animism* by Sonia Greenelove, was stored on the damaged server. Unfortunately, it appeared that last tome was the one most often accessed. All of this was extremely disconcerting to Walthers. He looked at the download status of the books. All three were ready to be punched up.

First, however, he realized he should have some idea of exactly what he was looking for in the volumes he accessed. Records didn't go quite so far as to log exactly what pages he'd looked at or for how long, so once within the books he was lost. He pulled up the keylogger and sorted through until he found Alex's searches. He first searched for something relating to the knife Viktor had delivered, it seemed. Then his searches expanded to prehistoric religions, then focusing down to the period around forty thousand years BCE. Then he seemed to jump to astronomical texts, star charts, then back and forth between rituals and Paleolithic cultures.

He was interrupted by a flashing notice from the computer that there was something amiss in the access corridor. Of course! How could he have forgotten? The creature was still here, just trapped outside! He quickly punched up the security system that controlled access to the vault and the archive. As he'd hoped, the front door still showed secured. But the door to the Culinary Arts building was reading as open. He clicked on the video surveillance of the tunnel and gasped at what he saw. The entirety of the hidden doorway to the Culinary Arts building was ripped from its frame, the entire corridor open to the pantry room with the decoy microwave he'd used to open the vault nearly three months ago. Standing in the corridor were three of the abominable things, seemingly idle.

No... wait... as one, they each started taking bounding steps from the corridor and out through the pantry. They moved through the tunnel with an odd manner of using both their legs and their arms, their legs taking enormous strides while their arms reached out and braced against the walls and pushed them along as well, all of it faster than he thought possible for the things to move. They reminded him, oddly enough, of spiders as they did so, the same kind of rapid three dimensional coordination. As the last limb disappeared from the screen, he could see on the floor where they'd been standing was some kind of black speck. The camera didn't have the resolution for him to ascertain exactly what it was.

He called to Phillip, who was still pushing the mop back and forth. Walthers realized that he did so with a dry mop on a dry floor. He seemed to be almost in a trance. He had to call twice more before Phillip seemed to notice and stop. As he walked over, Walthers undid the breaks on his chair and started pushing himself away from the table with the two MCP computers.

"Quickly Phillip, I need you to take me to the front door! They've gone but they left something, I need to see what it is!"

Phillip immediately sensed the urgency in the Professor's voice, and without further urging took the handles of the chair in his hands and started pushing the professor towards the door, over the threshold, and through the vault at a jog. As they made their way through, various residents came out of their isolated reveries to inquire what was the matter, each given the same answer by the Professor as they flew past.

"Find some place to hide! We're opening the door again!"

Shocked exclamations of surprise and fear were the only responses. As Walthers and Phillip made it to the door Henry looked back just in time to see Evelyn rushing down the hall with Rowan on her shoulder, making her way to the pantry, to her hiding place. Phillip began opening the door to the corridor as soon as the Professor was stopped in front of it. As the door opened, Walthers could just barely see up above the level of the stairs to the floor level of the corridor. In the center of it, halfway down was some kind of smoky black ball covered in glass-like spikes. Phillip looked down the corridor briefly before looking to the Professor.

"I'm going to go find some crutches."

The professor kept his eyes glued to the object in the corridor, He felt like he didn't even blink as he focused all his attention on it. It felt like only a second before Phillip returned with a pair of adjustable aluminum crutches and went to assist the Professor in getting to his feet with them. It took a solid minute to get him up on his good leg and get the crutches adjusted properly for his height. His broken leg screamed at him and grated in a way that felt like fire smoldering in his flesh, but he grit his teeth and bore the pain in his feverish desire to get into the corridor and examine the object.

Phillip stood by as he mounted the stairs one at a time, hopping with his good leg up the stair as the crutches supported his weight on the one below. It was only three steps but by the time he was at the top he was soaked through with sweat and his glasses were sliding down his nose. He took a moment to breathe before he started making his way down the corridor, only stopping some two feet from the mysterious orb. Phillip stood by his side looking down at it.

"So... what is it?"

"I haven't the foggiest notion, but I want to examine it."

"Is that safe?"

"I don't know. But there's only one way to find out. Would you be so kind as to go get us some kind of lidded container and a pair of tongs from the kitchen? The big ones, with the gripping edge, please."

Phillip nodded and headed back into the vault for the requested items, reappearing a few moments later with a slow-cooker and the tongs. Walthers looked at him, his face contorted in confusion. Phillip handed the Professor the tongs and then held up the pressure cooker, indicating the latches that could lock the lid in place.

"I figured we'd want something that locks, not just something that closes. Everything else was Tupperware."

"Not a bad idea. Go ahead and set the cooker down, open it up, and then we'll use the tongs to put it in there."

Phillip did as instructed, only hesitating when he tried to reach for the object with the tongs. After taking a deep breath and holding it, he grasped the object with the tongs closing down on one point of one spike near the very top. Then he lifted it slowly from where it sat on the floor and placed it carefully into the slow-cooker. The entire operation took less than a minute but it felt like an hour. As Phillip placed the lid and locked it into place, he let out his breath. Walthers let out the breath he hadn't realized he'd been holding as well. Phillip gently picked up the slow-cooker and looked at the Professor.

"What now?"

"We'll put it in the spare store room, the empty one we cleared out for if we filled the first one with trash, then we'll lock it until I can figure out what to do with it."

"I still don't understand how or why the government didn't supply this place with like a furnace or something for trash disposal."

"It was never meant for long term habitation. It was believed that the archives would warrant evacuation after the immediate threat had passed, a few weeks for a nuclear strike, a few months for a plague or other calamity. It was also assumed that only Evelyn and myself would be down here, and the extra store-rooms would be used for trash storage as we're doing, but fill much slower. It was never anticipated that the catastrophe would keep us off the surface for much longer. In fact, I don't think we will be."

"What do you mean?"

"Look down the corridor, what do you see?"

"The Culinary Arts building."

"And?"

"And... I don't know."

"Exactly. Whatever is out there, the giants can survive. If they can, I have to think we might be able to as well. Tomorrow I'm planning on taking Jerry and Don out with me to scout the surface."

"But Professor, your leg..."

"I'm aware of my limitations. I don't plan on going far, and if need be I intend that Don and Jerry may have to leave me to save themselves. I'm okay with that. Just don't tell my wife."

~

Day 78

Lucinda made her way on her hands and knees through the maintenance crawlspace, stopping occasionally to consult the blueprints she'd brought along.

... Another left, then two rights...

She moved as cautiously and as quietly as she could while dragging the two compressed gas canisters she'd 'borrowed' from supply while the Sergeant was preoccupied with his dinner and the buxom Lance Corporal who'd brought it.

In the absence of a civilian population and in light of the effective end of the world, a hookup culture was flourishing in the ranks, especially between officers and the Project personnel, but rates and nonrated were going at it like rabbits as well. It was degrading, and uncivilized, but with less than a third of their number made up of women it made a cold kind of sense that so many had thrown morals, ethics, and regulations to the wind.

Lucinda herself had already had to fend off two or three blatant propositions and ignore countless other subtler flirtations. Survival was survival, but there's be time for that one more pressing threats were dealt with.

... A right...

Not that she wasn't flattered. The officers and NCOs chosen for these kinds of assignments were always in peak shape, and most of them were decently handsome as well, but they were without exception good little toy soldiers following orders. Mindless, unthinking, blind... nothing she'd ever been taken with.

... Last right...

Ahead, she could see her goal, the supplemental oxygen routing for the hardened shelters. She dragged the canisters behind her and disconnected the lines for the ranking officers, Project leaders, and the VIP medical quarters, leaving the medical staff quarters, support staff, NCO, and nonrated lines alone.

She connected the canisters and turned their valves. Setting her watch, she sat for half an hour, then closed the valves and put all the lines back where they belonged before starting back to the maintenance access hatch with the now empty canisters.

She put the canisters into the nearest disposal chute. The incinerator would eliminate any evidence she might've left behind. She then

207

changed quickly in the nearest bathroom before calmly and quickly making her way to the medical staff quarters and bedding down in her dorm.

Things would be much better in the morning. In the absence of the project leadership, the military officers, and the VIPs, the head of Project Research was in charge... her.

She slept without trouble.

~

Day 78

Angela made her way back up the tree as she'd done the evening previous. Slowly, carefully, quietly. As she got to her observation spot, she gently pushed the branches apart to get a view of the hole the tall things had been digging. She gasped at what she saw.

They'd dug up a bowl roughly 70 feet wide and 30 feet deep. And at the bottom... Jesus Christ... was some kind of stone dome. Ancient, hand carved, with a rotten wooden plug at the cap torn aside and asunder, apparently at the hands of the tall things. There was no trace of them anywhere. Angela made her way back down the tree and towards the bowl. Slowly, she scouted the area around it, finding their strange round tracks moved on to the southeast.

Back at her camp under the tree, she pulled out all the rope and climbing gear she'd scrounged from a car ten kilometers back and set out back to the bowl. Near the edge she found a sturdy spruce and anchored her ropes there.

At the edge of the hole she looked over. It seemed to go down a further 40 or 50 feet before ending at a circular floor with four doorways leading off in the cardinal directions. Three of the doors were intact. The northernmost door was smashed through.

She threw down her ropes, put on the climbing rig over her winter clothes, tightened the straps, rigged the carabineers, and set herself up for the descent. As she held herself over the edge, she felt butterflies of fear and trepidation quiver in her gut.

With a final deep breath of the freezing air, she kicked off and swung over into the abyss. Her descent was quick; she squeezed to slow down her fall just so much to avoid injury. At the bottom she paused only long enough to shine a flashlight around the room and at the northern passage. Seeing nothing, she freed herself from the harness.

The doorways were of uniform design, each easily five feet wide and eight feet tall. Tall enough for the tall things, but obviously built by men, with their handle at waist height. She made her way north.

The passage seemed to slope down gently for about 60 feet before hitting a cross pattern in the stone. Inch-wide holes acted as a drain before the slope leveled off. There the passage split into three directions, with no indication as to which direction the tall things had taken.

The passage was damp here. Unknown years had let moisture through the gaps in the stone, through the rotted timbers of the plug in the dome. The smell of mold lay thick in the air as well as the actual mold on the walls, floor, and ceiling.

In the distance, she could barely make out the sounds of screams.

CHAPTER 21

Day 78

Zoe paced between the kitchen and the pantry, each way carrying single items back and forth. She'd gained weight in her initial months in sanctuary, and it was her way of exercising without feeling like she was exercising.

After that, she sat down with a bowl of plain unbuttered popcorn and popped in a Mel Brooks DVD. Tonight was Young Frankenstein for maybe the 19th or 20th time since the event began. It was one of her favorites but she bemoaned her limited film selection since the internet had gone down. If she'd really taken all this Project bunker stuff seriously she'd have stocked more of her personal belongings — including her film collection — into storage just in case. As it was, she was limited to the preselected, pre-approved, sanitized, and selected films put together by some bureaucratic flunky who was probably long dead now.

But, still, at least she had all the time she could want for her own projects, her paintings, sketches, and murals. She'd run out of materials eventually, and have to make her way up to the Institute proper and be careful of the windows. She'd made two trips before, for stupid things she should've remembered to stock, both times without incident, once for her portfolio — her own works deserved no less than the others — the second time for personal hygiene products. The bunker had been packed by men, unfortunately.

Inspiration was her biggest issue. All the films she had, the books, the catalogs of reprints and photos of all the classics. She wondered how many had been lost to fire without man to protect them? That was, as she saw it, her real duty, Project or no, to protect the world's artistic heritage.

But, without interaction, without drama, without other minds to stimulate her own, her works had all turned dark and morose. She couldn't help it. She was alone, surrounded by a city filled with millions of dried out corpses. Morbidity was a natural consequence of the age she lived in.

She supposed she should be worried about why she hadn't had any communiques from the outside since a week into things, but as far as she was concerned that was for the best. After all, what use was art and art history likely to be to a bunch of military officers and doctors in the post-apocalypse?

~

Day 78

Jesse scratched at his goatee with puzzlement.

"So, lemme see if I've got this straight now that I've had a bit to think it over. You *ain't* part of the CDC proper, you're just on loan. Well, you were on loan, from NASA, but through the whole thing, both at NASA and here, you're *actually* part of a secret project to collate, collect, and preserve mankind's sum total knowledge in the face of the apocalypse, as well as to investigate and deal with the cause of said apocalypse whether it's plague, nuclear war, asteroid impact, solar flare, or any other such nonsense?"

"That would be the very, very basic summation of the critical points, yes."

211

"And as a part of this, there's secret hidey-holes like this one in, under, or near every major government research facility and the homes and places of work of all the relevant Project persons?"

"Yes... as I said, this is the most basic summation. The Project has numerous goals and responsibilities. It was a public-private partnership between half a dozen major corporations, all branches of the US military, all branches of the US Government, half a dozen major research firms, as well as a number of wealthy and connected individuals and families. It is the last ditch effort to preserve mankind's leadership, knowledge, technology, and social order."

"And what did you do?"

"I'm an exobiologist, also sometimes called an astrobiologist, I worked for NASA looking for signs or indications of life beyond Earth. My expertise is the indications of life, its telltale traces, and the ways it may show itself. My work with the Project was in case mankind was killed by some disease from outer space. Did you ever see *The Andromeda Strain*?"

"Nah, but I read the book, so I get what you're saying, Doc."

Rafei's expression went blank.

"What? Michael Creighton was a helluva good author. *Jurassic Park, Sphere, Congo, Andromeda Strain*? Country don't mean stupid, Doc."

"No no, it wasn't that... I just... I suddenly realized I'll never read again, and it... gave me pause. I'm sorry..."

"Aw Doc, don't be like that. Your hands and fingers still work don't they? You can learn Braille."

"I suppose I could..."

"So uh... Doc, these things, these things up in the sky. They came from outer space, right?"

"Their arrival coincided with an object entering Earth's atmosphere. That's all I know. My true value, the work I can do, requires very different facilities than the CDC has or had at any rate. It's imperative that I reach the main Project facility. They have the communication equipment I need to access NASA's satellites, as well as the laboratories and personnel I need to investigate this thing.

They should've come for me by now, long ago. I can only assume my proof of life signal was interfered with somehow, some glitch in the system that's let them incorrectly continue in the belief that I am dead, that the whole of the CDC is dead."

"But Doc, the CDC *is* dead. We're the only ones here..."

"That's not... entirely accurate..."

"Well who the hell else is here? 'Cause all I seen is you and me..."

"First, Jesse, you have to understand, the Project goes beyond survival of a bunch of VIPs. There were certain selections made, individuals gathered..."

"No, hold on a minute, you said there were others here, now I wanna know who they are and where they're at! I done showed you all kinds of courtesies and kindness Doc but with everything that's going on I'm getting a bit fed up with secret after secret here..."

"You're right! Yes, of course, Jesse. The others, the other men and women who were here in the CDC when everything happened... most of them died. They were on the side of the building with floor to ceiling windows, and scientists are by their very nature a curious breed. But those that didn't... well... they fell to bickering, to conflict. Research was pointless, there was no disease to control. The people here were... argumentative, unstable. Something had to be done. So I did. I put them in the isolation levels and simulated a Class 5 Breach of Upper Containment."

"Uh... okay? What the hell does that mean?"

"I locked them in the deepest subbasements, the emergency shelter in case of catastrophic incurable plague. Designed to keep them safe

213

until such time as the remote instruments detected a safe environment for them to leave."

"What's that simulated whosawhatsits you was talking about?"

"I sabotaged the testing apparatus they'd use to open up the locks."

"So you trapped them in there."

"More than trapped, sealed. With a Class 5 Breach of the Upper Containment of the testing apparatus, the system presumes that the pathogen has a caustic, highly dangerous chemical makeup. It seals them in on a time for a period of time predetermined to guarantee that any such pathogen would've broken down."

"And how long is that?"

"Six years."

"*Six years!?*"

"Yes. They're quite safe; I'm not a monster. They have food, water, entertainment. They just can't leave short of the possibility that they figure out how to drill through 6 feet of steel."

"Doc... you trapped a bunch of well-meaning Doctors in an underground prison for six years for disagreeing with ya?"

"It was, and remains to be for the foreseeable future, for the greater good."

"And we can't get 'em out, no way no how?"

"None at all, it's completely automated."

"What about the EMP? What'll that do to it?"

"... Jesse, we need to leave."

~

Day 79

Dr. Lucinda Alvarez awoke refreshed and energized, eager to start her day. She was a bit surprised, though. She'd expected to be awoken by MPs escorting her to take charge in the wake of the night's development, not her own alarm. There must have been some delay in the machinery of the bureaucracy. She'd simply have to go about her business until the wheels turned and she was called upon.

Morning reports and breakfast it was, then. The medical personnel had their own quarters, support staff, recreation room, and mess hall. She made her way there, grabbing the overnight reports from her box on the way. Normally, she'd have looked over them immediately as she walked, but knowing what they'd contain, she could wait 'til she had witnesses in the mess hall to see her reaction when she read the news.

Today was French toast with bacon, coffee and cranberry juice. She sat alone, as was her habit. Taking a few bites of the French toast, she was disappointed. There was a bitter aftertaste to the syrup. They'd obviously used the low sugar, low calorie syrup. She might not be the fittest person here but she didn't think she needed to be on dietary restriction. She'd consult with the nutritionist tomorrow after spending the day realigning the priorities here.

Her hunger sated for the moment, she picked up the stack of reports and flipped back the cover sheet and looked at the current status of her VIP charges. But she couldn't. They were... blurry. Something was wrong. She wiped at her eyes and blinked a few times. She looked again. The paper was still blurry. She looked up, the room itself was blurry and spinning. She felt herself off balance, rocking in her seat as she attempted to remain upright. She could just make out two figures approaching her table. They were wearing blue pants, khaki shirts, and armbands... Marine MPs.

Oh no...

The darkness swelled up from the edges of her vision and swallowed the world as she felt herself fall out of the chair.

~

Lucinda could hear voices. They were talking about her. The fogginess and weakness was slipping away, her mind becoming clearer. She stayed still, kept her breathing slow, concentrated on staying still. She listened.

"...how could this happen, and why!? All our personnel were cleared. Nobody got in without strict safeguards. We're sitting here on top of thirty bodies, the President is on his way to the primary facility and wants a report on this shitstack ASAP, and we're on the verge of wholesale transfer and no idea what the fuck happened."

"It might've been an accident. Those quarters all share ductwork for their primary circulation. There are filters — best in the world besides the primary — but it's conceivable..."

"No, no it's not. We've checked the whole system. Nothing tripped the sensors in the primaries, secondaries are a closed system just for the delivery of supplemental oxygen and gaseous medicines to the bedrooms in case of outbreak — which hasn't happened. The rest of the Project personnel are completely fine."

Lucinda felt the time was right to find out what was happening. Familiar with how unconscious figures awake from surgery, she began by faking a minor shiver and a deeper breath, followed by a whole body shift and a low groan.

"Looks like she's coming to. Get one of the nurses in here; they said there was a slight possibility of side effects and we need her healthy..."

Lucinda fluttered her eyes open, kept them unfocused, looked at the ceiling. Wood paneling — one of the bureaucrat's offices, they were all paneled. She was reclined in a chair. It was comfortably soft, but hot. She'd been in it awhile. Felt like leather. She turned her head. One of the bureaucrats, an undersecretary of the interior or some such nonsense, sat behind a desk looking at her. Sitting on the desk, resting on a hip, sat a naval officer of some kind, though she didn't know ranks. *The sub; she'd forgotten about that damn fucking sub.* He must've been staying in his berth on the sub rather than in the officers' quarters in the facility. She spoke for the first time.

216

"What... what happened...?"

"There's been an... an incident."

"What was it? A poison, something in the syrup, it didn't taste right... Why me? Why aren't I in the medical wing?"

"Not that kind of incident. You weren't the target. Every other leader was. Every member of the Council, every military officer — with the exception of Lieutenant McGuire here, who was on night watch on the *Nautilus* last night. All the VIP patients in the medical wing too. We're still trying to figure out exactly how, but they're all dead or dying as of this morning."

"And me, what happened to me?"

"We couldn't be sure that you were spared intentionally. You're the only one in the chain of command whose housing was unaffected. I'm told you asked to be housed with the medical personnel rather than the council section on your own. That probably saved your life.

We felt that a quiet extradition from the general population, making it look like a medical issue, a stroke or heart attack, would take you off the radar of whoever or whatever elements did this. So, we drugged your breakfast. Had the MPs on hand to whisk you out in a big hustle."

"You faked my death to keep me safe?"

"Essentially, yes."

"Why am I that important?"

"You don't know? Doctor, according to the chain of command, you and Lieutenant McGuire are now the Project heads, cooperatively. Civilian/Government and Military, working together as intended."

CHAPTER 22

Day 78

Angela made her way carefully along the center passage, still headed north. The floor was smooth, slippery with mold and slime. Her flashlight could barely distinguish between black stone, black mold, and the black darkness of the seemingly endless tunnel sloping gently downwards for as far ahead as she could see. The screams were getting louder.

Each breath was getting more labored, ragged, the thick air heavy and difficult to draw. She was starting to sweat. It was warmer here. That didn't make any sense. She unzipped her coat and fanned it a few quick times, the light of her flashlight splaying back and forth as she did so, illuminating motes of dust and spores and god only knew what else drifting in the beam.

The path continued down. She estimated she'd been moving steadily northward for nearly a kilometer now, possibly as much as a kilometer and a quarter, and downwards nearly a hundred meters if the slope was consistent, which she felt it was, though it was difficult to tell.

The screaming was nearly deafening now, the sound reverberating off the walls, echoing back on itself, doubling and redoubling. She couldn't tell if it was one person screaming or all the denizens of hell — easily enough to believe the latter in light of recent events. A few steps more and she could see the tunnel widening, The floor leveled off, but the walls and ceiling spread out, leaving a slick bridge through the dark to traverse without a railing of any kind.

Suspicious, she edged forward to the very last point where the wall was reachable and shined her light down into the void. There she saw figures, beings... men and women, bound, chained, pale, hairless, and naked, secured to the walls by chains red with rust and blood. There was something wrong here. The faces... these were people she knew!

~

Day 78

Zoe hated computers. Always had. The impersonal nature of them, the sanitary and inhuman logic of their language. She preferred the natural feel of ink on paper; fountain pens and papyrus weren't unknown to her. Oils on canvas, hell, finger paints on construction paper. But, she was supposed to document her time in the bunker on a daily basis. A diary of sorts. So she sat down at the clunky government computer in the hard plastic chair they'd provided and started topping her brief and dreary listing of her activities.

Finishing up, she exited the program and went back to the home screen. Her pointer maneuvered over the shutdown icon before she noticed a little red check that hadn't been there before on the mail icon. Someone, or something, had gotten a message through. Hardly believing it, she moved the pointer over and double clicked.

A new window opened to show her the same three messages she'd gotten in the first week, a listing of known resources in her area (useless since she couldn't leave), a reminder of the Project command structure (useless since she was alone) and a reminder specifically to her about her duties (which at this point she considered fulfilled). Nothing new.

Then she saw it, a small line at the bottom of the window, a progress bar, "New Mail Downloading". It stood at 3% and seemed frozen. She stared at it, wondering if it has been there before and she simply hasn't noticed. It had been long enough she knew the effects of isolation and stress could've been getting to her.

4%

It wasn't frozen, just ridiculously slow. She didn't know anything about how the communication system worked or how the message was being delivered; quite frankly she'd zoned out during that briefing, but at least she wasn't totally cut off. She wondered what the message would be. She powered off the screen but left the machine itself on, that way it would continue to work.

The new event, the first she hasn't invented herself in months, was like a lit fuse in her mind, a bright burning spot that would lead to... something extraordinary. She pulled out canvas and paints. It was time to be creative.

~

Day 78

Jesse wiped his face with his hands, feeling his oily skin and unkempt goatee grate along his rough palms... He needed a shower.

"Alright Doc, we've just got to get to the garage then."

"But why? The things are in there, and surely the EMP has left your truck useless."

Jesse laughed. "Doc, I built that truck to take me through a post-atomic wasteland, with extra paneling and lead paint for radiation shielding and hardening of all the electronics. One switch under the dash and she'll be good to go."

"Jesse, I'm impressed."

"Hell, Doc... I just do what I gotta do."

"Well, what are we waiting for? We need to pack, we need to get to the staircase, we need to scope out the garage, get things loaded!"

"Hold your horses... I got some more questions."

"Jesse, we don't have the time. If they come out, if they find us here... they'll be very, very angry."

"Yeah yeah, I know, you trapped 'em in there for what would have been years and now they're gonna get out and they're gonna be angry and we're gonna get yelled at by a bunch of bespectacled scientists."

"Oh no, no Jesse... no... they're liable to do far, far more than yell at us. They blinded me in their attempt to get past me the first time. This time, I have no doubt in my mind they'll try to kill me and anyone helping me."

"Uh... so... what do we do?"

"We get moving!"

With that, Jesse cracked a chemlight, grabbed a number of duffel bags from a drawer, and made his way to the storeroom where he began packing foodstuffs into them. Dr. Rafei felt his way down the hall to his quarters. There, he searched drawer after drawer of clothing and junk until he found what he was looking for, a small revolver. Hammerless, with a rubber coated grip. He opened it, felt to ensure it was fully loaded, then closed it, placing it in his lab coat pocket.

Two subbasements down, inside the isolation levels, three men began the painstaking process of manually working the gears to unseal a large steel door.

~

Day 79

Lucinda had a headache, either from the aftereffects of the drug or from the stress of dealing with all this bullshit. Lt. McGuire was remarkably efficient and professional, the consummate Naval

221

officer. Naturally, this meant he was completely useless. Lucinda looked over the desk they'd given her in the council chambers. With no council left, it was just her, McGuire, and a horde of minor functionaries, bureaucrats, and busybodies, none of whom seemed to have anything important to do or say — and yet none of them could shut up.

She flipped through the guide one of them had given her on council procedure. Earlier, she'd ignored it; now it was her only hope for a respite. She fell on a page that looked promising. She read over it, then tapped her microphone to get everyone's attention.

"While I'm sure many of you have pressing issues that need the urgent attentions of this council, if I may, I'm going to call for an hour's recess so that we can all collect our thoughts and present them in a more orderly fashion. Thank you."

It seemed to have worked. They were clearing out of the room. When they were all gone she looked over at the lieutenant, sitting serenely in a high backed leather chair with his folded hands sitting on the desk in front of him.

"There's a term for this kind of thing, kind of ubiquitous throughout the military."

"And what's that?"

"Clusterfuck."

She couldn't help but laugh at the aptness of the description.

"I guess everyone's getting screwed but nobody's happy?"

"That's the long and the short of it."

"Nice... very, very nice. Any idea what the hell we're going to do about this mess?"

"Not a clue. It all seems so, so..."

"Petty?"

"Yes, exactly. You hit the nail on the head."

"It is, all of it. We should set up a subcommittee to deal with it. Say, the heads of all the different departments?"

"With a military representative and someone from accounting."

"Accounting? Seriously, we're keeping track of costs?"

"Well no, accounting is what a lot of folks have taken to calling the supply folk, since they're the ones worried about budgets and sustainability now."

"Ah... see that, that's clever. I wish I'd thought of that myself."

A knock on the chamber door was shortly followed by a Naval ensign and an Air Force first sergeant.

"Sir, madam, I'm afraid we've received some disturbing information. It appears Air Force One has gone down a few miles outside Boulder Colorado. There doesn't appear to be any sign of survivors."

~

Day 78

Angela looked down on the faces, so familiar, and yet none of them had so much as a single hair. Suddenly, she noticed their features shifting. Jaws lengthened and shrank, noses grew wider, or thinner. One by one their eyes darkened to black. These were not people. People don't shift and change like this. Her father became her first grade teacher. Her first boyfriend became her first boss. And they all beckoned to her, their hands pleading, even in chains.

They're lures...

She pushed herself off the wall and back to the center of the path. Once her light came off the... whatever they were... they stopped screaming. The silence echoed worse than the screams. She peered back over the edge, shielding her light. No one, no figures, no chains. But where they'd been she now saw a number of skeletons.

223

Some in rags, some in furs, some in what looked to be chainmail armor. One looked to be still leathery, and was that a Nazi uniform?

She continued on the path. The walls and ceiling of the chamber pulling away to the sides and above. Only the narrow path of uneven stone, without railings or handholds, continued forward in the dark. After another few hundred meters she began to see a pulsing light. Blue or purple. As she moved forward she could see that it was illuminating the floor of the chamber far below her. Ahead, the path came to a stop at a circular staircase, down the inside of a tower of stone, headed down.

The stairs were steep and slippery. Her way was slow and cautious. The flickering light from below was occluded here, and she had to rely on her flashlight. Her foot slipped on a particularly slimy patch of mold, her leg flying out ahead of her. Her rear hit the stone hard, sending jolts of pain up her back. She slid down the stairs, rolling, tumbling, gear flying every which way, stones kissing her arms, her knees, her face. One planted a particularly affectionate peck to the back of her head, and the world went black.

~

Day 78

Zoe absentmindedly chased the last bit of her slice of cheesecake around her plate as she watched the screen. She'd put off her other normal activities for the day, watching the progress bar grow incrementally over the course of the day as she sketched and painted. She was still in her pajamas even, but she had penned rather detailed sketches of... nothing. All her drawings... there was something about them she couldn't quite place. They were different enough; the first was of a family walking down a road, with the ruins of a city distantly behind them across fields of golden grassland. The second was of some kind of farm scene, with two spruce trees hanging over a half-collapsed barn. The third was of a set of distorted skyscrapers, like they were melted by extreme heat, very much a Dali-inspired work. And the final was of a family of beached dolphins, mother, father, and pup, set against a beach with an uncommon number of seashells mixed up in the sand. The progress bar on the computer sat now at 97%.

She scooped up the last bite and downed it before standing and making her way to the kitchen. The plate and fork went in the dishwasher, the cheesecake itself — a no bake version made with powdered milk — went into the fridge. She pulled out a can of Yoo-Hoo and shook it back and forth, twisting her wrist one way then the other as she made her way back to the seat in front of the computer. The bar said 98%. Frustrated, she spun around in the chair, letting her head fall back and her hair fly out due to centripetal force. When she came to a stop she faced away from the computer. She sat up, halfway popped the tab on her Yoo-Hoo and quickly sucked at the top of the can to avoid the Yoo-Hoo spray. Her sketches were set on easels around the living room space, she looked at them from left to right and back again, still feeling odd, like she was missing something.

When she turned back to the computer it was just in time to see it change over from 99% to 100% before reloading the incoming email page. One unread. It was titled "Prof. Opperthorne's cave paintings, Subject Expert Consultation". She clicked on it, the screen immediately filling with paragraphs and images. She read over the first few pages intently, her curiosity gone cold with recognition and her dread driving her forward.

The summary of the professor's findings were chilling, but the images irrelevant — they were pictures some ignorant had collected to try and show similarities, but the examples were poor and misinterpreted. None of the professor's findings were down in picture form. Apparently, they were trying to find him and his works in New York even now. She finished reading the email and printed it. Taking the warm papers from the tray she slipped her feet into her slippers and began the long walk through the underground to the archives. She had some comparisons to make.

~

Day 78

Jesse looked over The lists he'd written out at the Doctors direction, the light of his flashlight indirect as it sat on a table pointed at the ceiling.

"Are you sure ya didn't forget anything Doc?"

"If you got everything on the first list I made out to you then we have the important things. After that, the food, which I left to you, and we may have some luck scrounging on the way."

"Well, I got everything on the list, I made damn sure of that. So long as you made the lists up right then we're about finished."

"So, what's the next step?"

"Well, I've got everything packed up in cases and staged at the stairwell entrance to the garage. Next up, I get in the truck, open up the back doors and latch 'em open, reset her electrical systems, then pull her around and back it up tight to the stairwell. Then I'll climb in back and into the stairwell and start loading. With even the tiniest bit of luck the things wouldn't get all over the truck until we're packed and ready, then we can put all the stuff in back in webbing, close off the cab, and go on our merry way without too much concern."

"Excellent, and you have fuel?"

"Yep, fueled her up before I got here. Thought there was a possibility I might be needing a quick getaway, you know."

"Good, good. We'll be headed north at first, and towards the coast."

"Where, exactly, are we headed? I've got a good GPS in the cab, and the satellites still work. I can just punch it in and we'll hit the road. I gotta warn ya though, it ain't a pretty sight, I lived in that cab for a couple of weeks, with infrequent stops. And none of those were at a wash or detailing joint."

"I can't see it anyway, so long as it doesn't smell too badly, I think I'll live. But we're headed for Beaufort, South Carolina. There's a facility on Harbor Island there—"

226

Dr. Rafei was interrupted by a loud noise from down the corridor. A number of individuals were approaching, flipping tables and screaming out for Rafei.

~

Day 79

Alvarez walked into the council chamber with her coffee and briefing folder, finding Lt. McGuire already sat down in his preferred chair looking through a thick binder of printouts. As Lucinda moved around the semicircular stand to her own seat at the center, she didn't waste any time.

"Any news on Air Force One?"

"None. Infrared satellites show that most of the fires are out but they're not picking up any indication of survivors. And the closest group that could possibly assess the site is still sixty miles away and moving slowly up mountain roads clogged with snow."

"I understand. Well, Lieutenant, now that we're freed from the burden of pointless frivolities by our new subcommittee, I think it's time we had a frank discussion about the future of the Project. In fact, considering we're now essentially the leaders of what remains of the human race, I'd say we had better get down to brass tacks, don't you agree?"

"I don't disagree on any particular point, but there is something else that we need to discuss first."

"Oh?"

"This morning, I got a memo from the records department. Apparently we're supposed to use the mics and cameras in the council chamber to record our proceedings. Yesterday, we didn't do that."

"Well, that's no issue, all those yes-men must be good for something, right? Records can interview them."

"Oh, absolutely, but, it gave me the idea of having Records pull the transcripts from the last few days of the council's meetings and the relevant files on the subjects discussed therein. That way we can see what direction they were headed in and get some idea of exactly what we should be doing."

"Quite frankly, I think our direction should be our own, don't you think?"

"Maybe, but, these transcripts... they're considered top secret. They discussed, openly and without reservation, all the little side projects and directives and far flung operations associated with the project. In fact, Records was loath to give up the matching files until I pulled rank.

Apparently there's a few things in here the general project membership were kept completely in the dark about. Things that we're going to need to know if we're going to run things."

"Really? Well... call down to Records and order me up my own copy of the transcripts and files. We'll go over them separately, and then meet later to discuss what we find. You look at it from the military angle, and I'll look at it from the civilian and governing angles, like we're supposed to, and then we'll hammer out our differences."

The Lieutenant smiled and smugly pulled a second binder out of the seat next to him before pushing it along the table to Lucinda.

"I had a feeling you might propose something along those lines, so I had them send two copies initially."

"You must've gotten up very early, Lieutenant. I'll get right on this and we'll get back together, say, this afternoon?"

"Sounds more than fair. But I've had a little time to look through it this morning already. I'd recommend you skip to page 12. They discuss something about tomb excavations that looks interesting. And after that page 45, Operation Monument."

"Really? Nothing about Shards or Tall Ones?"

"Both. Just... just read them."

Lucinda grabbed up the binder and folded it under her arm. She didn't want to be disturbed while reading this and figured McGuire could handle any minor details that might come up in the meantime.

Once she found a nice spot in the recreational greenhouse, she started going through the council minutes and cross checking with the files. Tomb excavations were nothing; the Tall Ones liked to dig up old ruins, satellites found them digging into places in Egypt, France, Mounds in the Midwest, Cliffs in Arizona, all along the Great Wall of China and a massive hole in downtown Beijing. It was curious behavior but nothing indicated how to fight them.

Operation Monument was more promising. Some doddering old English fart had found cave paintings of previous Shard phenomena during the Stone Age... and the paintings might also give clues as to how to deal with them...? And a US Sub crew was in New York right now recovering the professor and his records. That would definitely qualify as useful.

She kept reading. A few pointless discussions about finding other groups of survivors. Hypothesizing about conditions in Tokyo. An operation here, a supply cache there that needed retrieval. Then something new. She read and reread the file twice before gathering everything up and racing to the council chamber. When she burst through the door the Lieutenant looked up at her before saying:

"The Schmitt discovery in the Taurus-Littrow valley?"

"Yes!"

"And they didn't do anything."

"We've got to get somebody to Washington."

"Agreed. I've already issued orders to divert the *Oregon* on her return trip."

~

Day 79

Angela awoke in agony, her initial breath a gasp as she felt her body and the numerous injuries she'd sustained. Without even looking she could feel that her left arm was broken at the wrist and her right at the shoulder, possibly dislocated. She tried to open her eyes but could only open one; the other was painful to try. She was laying on a roughhewn stone floor, surrounded by items torn from her as she fell. Canteens, her binoculars, flares, pitons, notebooks, pens.

She went to lift her head up and felt a grinding in her neck and back that nearly put her out again, but she pressed through, rolling onto her back before pulling herself to a sitting position. Her legs were battered and bruised but the heavy winter pants seemed to have protected them. Taking off the jacket, in retrospect, may have been a mistake. As she went to stand a sharp pain in her right ankle and a rapid fall back on her ass told her that getting back up the stairs was going to be next to impossible. Rolling over to her knees and crawling to the base of the stairs, she used them as leverage to stand on her left leg. Twisting, she looked around the chamber at the base of the stairs for the first time. Standing not twenty feet away was a circle of the tall things.

Six of them, standing still as statues. In the middle of them, floating above a polished silver depression in the floor, was a human figure, seemingly made of smooth glass. The light came from her. Shining from the center of her belly, blue light distorted purple as it passed through her curves and limbs as she slowly rotated in midair. Her features were exaggerated, grossly so, like some Polynesian fertility figure, her breasts and buttocks easily each twice as large as her head. Her arms were thrown behind her, her hands meeting several feet behind her back. He legs splayed open, her knees bent, as if giving birth. Her face was turned to the sky, her expression a scream unending.

Around the chamber, the walls stood festooned with bodies like she'd seen earlier, skeletons in furs, armor, and decorative uniforms, mummies in uniforms more recent, Nazi, Soviet, even a few American Army doughboys. Civilians too, here, unlike above. She recognized styles going back perhaps some three hundred years. And there were many she didn't who might well have been older. She imagined there must be other entrances explored by other peoples somewhere else for this many to have found their way here. But these bodies were different. They weren't thrown haphazardly atop one another, as the ones above. These were... poised, posed, put on display. Starkly upright, at attention, hands at their sides, faces forward, eyes open, where applicable.

Angela decided she'd had quite enough. Her curiosity wasn't *that* powerful. She'd had her limit. This was too much. She turned to head up the stairs, on one elbow and her knees if need be, but she was done.

A tall thing blocked her way. She looked up at it. It looked down at her.

Goddammit.

~

Day 78

"...just get over here."

Captain Longmire switched the radio off before turning to his Master at Arms, Cox. Looking around the loading dock, they were surrounded by crates labeled for Professor Opperthorne containing large prints of the various photos he'd taken in the caves south of Norsjö, Sweden, according to the labeling.

"Cox, are all these going to fit in the, uh, in the vehicle?"

"It's designed to carry eight in the passenger compartment, sir. Somebody's got to drive, and after that we're only taking four, so it'll be a tight fit, but we should be able to haul it in one trip."

"Good. Have you been able to make heads or tails out of his notebook yet?"

"No sir, seems the late professor was rather fond of taking his notes in French. I remember a bit from a single year in High School, but not enough to make heads or tails of this."

"Alright, well, Emil, Sarya, and Sharon are going to be on their way over in a few minutes. When they get here, you and Emil get to work loading up these crates. In the meanwhile, I'm going to see if I can find where the professor and Lieutenant Hardy holed up here in the museum. There might be more they didn't get down here to the loading dock."

"I'm not supposed to let you out of my sight, sir."

"Would you give it a rest, Cox? Opperthorne and Hardy were here for months. I'm sure so long as I keep to the back halls and offices and don't venture into the museum proper, I'll be fine. Besides, I've got my IR goggles. Even if I accidentally walk into a greenhouse or something, I'll be fine."

Cox looked at his Captain, and then at the stacked crates around the loading dock, then back at his Captain.

"These things are the reason we came?"

"All the way from the Pacific."

Cox looked again at the crates.

"I... I guess these things shouldn't be left alone then."

"That's how I think of it. Relax, nothing's gonna happen."

"Funny thing sir, I have a feeling Hardy told him the same thing."

Cox jerked his head in the direction of the loading dock doors, where Professor Opperthorne's desiccated husk was curled on the floor.

"Cox, I'm not a fucking civvie!"

"No sir! Wasn't insinuating you are, sir. Just... neither was Hardy, sir. Be careful."

Waving off Cox's concerns, Captain Longmire strode off down the storage area, past crates and shelves of art, some mundane, others priceless, now doomed to rot. After about twenty meters or so he turned, going through a pair of double doors, and began following a wide hallway flanked by offices. Each office was opened, peered into, and, seeing no signs of habitation, left open.

At the end of the hall he came to a large open workspace, ostensibly used for art restoration. It had been converted almost totally into living quarters. A refrigerator, microwave, a pair of beds made from office furniture pads and drop cloths, lamps, boxes of canned goods, likely looted during a gap. The captain excitedly began looking for something, anything that might not have made it to the loading dock.

CHAPTER 23

Day 78

Zoe read and reread the descriptive paragraph except in the email from the professor's submitted papers, comparing what it depicted to picture after picture of cave paintings in the archives. Twenty years ago they would've been microfiche, but now it was a dedicated laptop with biometrics chained to the server. She flicked the trackpad every few seconds, occasionally giving one a little extra scrutiny or switching to another file if the set was exhausted.

They were organized by era and region. To save time she was limiting herself to only the oldest caves of northern Europe. So far she hadn't had any success. The professor's findings appeared to be unique.

Three hours of searching and the search proceed fruitless. Nothing in the oldest caves paintings in Northern Europe. She sat defeated, slumped, starting at the screen before standing up and stretching, arching her back and throwing her arms above her head as she stood up on her toes. A cramp shot through her left calf sending her falling back into the chair, her arms falling down and impacting the table on both sides of the laptop.

234

As she moved her hands down to massage her aching calf she briefly looked back at the screen, now displaying a selection from the Kamchatka Peninsula in eastern Russia. There were only four images, but one of them... she clicked on it to get it at full resolution. Zoomed in. And reread the paragraph from the professor.

She got up and hobbled her way as quickly as she could through the warehouse, to the living quarters, and to the government PC. Flopping into the chair, she swung round twice before she scooted forward and began typing up an addendum to her daily report. When she finished, she hit send and sat back. She stared at the screen. Its plain interface was not revealing where the report was being sent, or if, or how fast. She hoped the upload was faster than the download had been.

After rubbing her calf a bit more, she went to the fridge, got herself another slice of cheesecake and another Yoo-Hoo before heading back to the archives. Holding herself to northern Europe had been a mistake. She was going to have to look everywhere. Southern Europe, west Asia, the Middle East... it was going to be a long night.

~

Day 79

Six hours later Zoe had a pile of notes made out freehand on printer paper. Suspicious commonalities between paintings from every continent, roughly around the same time. Depictions of the sky as aflame, or as a rain of spears, or as predatory animals. One with a sky full of plants that she was betting would turn out to be some kind of local poison. In their own unique ways, a half dozen ancient cave dwellers had expressed in their art a profound fear of the skies. Many also had pieces dedicated to odd pillars, mountains, or mesas from which strange tall hunters, beings that hunted man like men hunted deer, came pouring forth, though these were rarer, found on two continents only.

There were also other images. Worship of icons, figures, animals and people. Always colored blue or purple or some combination of the two. The tall hunters were shown worshipping them too. Almost like, on worshipping the blue idols, the tall hunters were made allies. Zoe had no idea what use any of this might be. Whatever idols were depicted, they were eons lost and of no use to anyone.

~

Zoe finished typing up her second addendum to her report, including all the information and image files of all the various cave paintings. As she hit send she leaned back in her chair. She wondered what other service she could possibly perform besides keeping the archives. Probably nothing. She shut down the monitor and walked back to the bedroom. It wasn't much, a full size mattress and box spring on a plain metal frame. A closet. A nightstand that looked like it came surplus from a no-tell motel.

She decided that she was going to start a mural for that room first thing the next morning, and next time there was a gap she'd go find some better linens. The plain government white with green wool was hideous. At her apartment, which was sadly too far to risk, she'd had numerous sets she'd kept on rotation. Astronomical views, abstract mathematical patterns, Día de los Muertos Sugar Skulls.

As she settled under the sheets, she pulled off her jewelry, setting it in a small bowl she kept by the bed specifically for that purpose. Once down and covered up, she thought she heard an odd buzzing. She ignored it; probably a scrap of paper caught in a ventilation duct somewhere. She started taking deep breaths and holding them in timed patterns, part of an exercise she'd learned years ago to get the body primed for sleep.

But something was wrong. The buzzing... there were patterns there, too. It wasn't constant... *Bzzzzzzzz Bzzzzzzzz Bzzzzzzzzz Bzzz Bzzz Bzzz* ...a long pause... *Bzzz Bzzz Bzzz Bzzzzzzzz Bzzzzzzzz Bzzzzzzzz Bzzz Bzzz Bzzz* ...another pause... Dear God! Was that an SOS!?

She jumped out of bed, racing as well she could towards the computer... but it was silent. That's when she saw it, in the living room, the monitor panel for the bunker, red flashing light. Hopping, hobbling, falling over the couch, she closed on the panel as the buzzing, much louder here near the source, began again.

236

"Exterior Controlled Access Delivery Port", read the indicator. She had to rack her brains for a moment to remember just what that was, the loading door to the warehouse, the food, the pantry... where they had brought it all in.

She ran. The delivery doors were an airlock system. The outer doors could only open if the inner ones were closed, the inner doors could only open from the inside and if the outer doors were closed.

The inner doors had portholes in them so that delivery personnel could be seen and recognized before opening the door. As she approached the doors, she could see a figure, one hand on the porthole, leaned over pressing the buzzer relay in the SOS pattern.

~

Day 78

Jesse's left hand grabbed Dr. Rafei by the shoulder while his right unholstered his sidearm. He said one word before he began shoving him down the hall towards the stairwell.

"Move!"

They ran, the Doctor slightly wavering left and right as Jesse's hand moved slightly back and forth with each step. Jesse turned his head over his shoulder to see if their pursuers had passed the lanterns he'd set up yet. They were already close enough to occlude them. Jesse would give directions under his breath for the doctor as they went.

"Left!"

"Right!"

Jesse pulled Rafei to a stop just before he ran headlong into the door to the stairs. Turning, he saw shadows in the candles he'd left lit along the way. He opened the site to the stairs and guided his blind charge through. He pulled a spare glow rod out of his vest and chucked it down the hall, past the stairwell, before quickly and quietly closing the door. He could hear the racket the glow stick made as it clattered down the hall, and the footsteps as their pursuers raced past the stairwell after it.

Jesse and Rafei then carefully and quietly made their way up the stairs to the hidden access to the first floor elevator lobby. From there they made their way to the western stairwell and the ground level garage access. Once in the stairwell, they could hear steps coming from below. Apparently their pursuers had found a different way out.

"We have to grab the boxes! They're critical to my work!"

Jesse responded in a harsh whisper as he struggled to pull his IR goggles up from around his neck and fit them over his eyes.

"Doc, we ain't got time to do our loading thing we was talking about. Pick one and we'll haul ass with it."

"Uh... hmm... I can't decide!"

The sounds of the footsteps were getting louder; the faint glow of candlelight could be seen coming from below.

"Doc, we're out of time!"

"The one with the papers, whichever that was..."

"I've got it; now let's go!"

With that Jesse threw the relevant box over his shoulder and opened the door to the parking garage. The sudden chill as they were confronted with the subzero temperature outside did little to stem their hurry. He grabbed Rafei by the shoulder, and ran for his truck. Hearing the door open, the footsteps below turned into a stampede and voices arose, calling for blood. Jesse ran around the passenger side first, opening the door and throwing the box in, then pushing Rafei towards it. Then he ran around the front end to the driver's side door to climb in himself.

Reaching under the dash, he flipped two switches before he closed the door. Looking and seeing Rafei just pulling his door closed as well, he turned the key to start the truck, and... nothing.

CHAPTER 24

Day 79

Dr. Alvarez angrily waved the papers at McGuire.

"Why wasn't this disseminated the second everything went to shit?"

"According to the minutes, they felt that widespread knowledge of the Schmitt discovery would serve no useful purpose. We can't send anyone to the moon, and as far as they were concerned at the time, Project Monument was the best chance for discovering a weakness or weapon to use against the Shards."

"But we have some. Dead ones. Ones we could autopsy or scan or..."

"I'm on your side. Admittedly, they've done everything to it they could over the last few decades to them. X-Ray, CT scans; hell, according to the file, DARPA developed Affinity Chromatography specifically to examine the damn things, just letting some engineers named Cuatrecasas and Wilchek take the credit and take it public after their work for the Project was done."

"What all does the file say they found?"

"You've got your own copy..."

"Yes yes yes, but you've read ahead; give me the highlights."

He laughed dryly. "Okay. The Shards are Euhedral Amorphous Solids, composed of roughly equal parts carbon, silicon, and calcium."

"And?"

"And... that's it. In thirty plus years, that's all they ever managed to determine."

"That's ridiculous! You're telling me they've had a couple dozen Shards to poke and prod and subject to all sorts of..."

The Lieutenant put his hands up in mock surrender.

"Hey, I'm just the messenger, doc."

"Any ideas as to how they made the connection between the Shards and the Schmitt discovery?"

"Yes... Dr. Jocobi's experiment."

"I thought that was a failure. No communication had been received since they signaled they were ready."

"Apparently, a follow up team went and retrieved their records. Including some foam insulation that had distinct impressions from the attempt to contain one. One of the Council members was also in the know on the Schmitt discovery and brought out the records to compare. While not exact, he felt that they were close enough to bring it up for debate."

"And that's the minutes we've got, when they decided against doing anything."

"Precisely."

"So what's the latest from the *Oregon*?"

~

Day 79

Angela stood transfixed, precariously balanced on one leg, blood oozing from her head, arms, and back from various cuts and scrapes. The tall thing stood not two feet from her looking down at her. It was... shocking... to see one so close. She noted details she couldn't have seen from a distance. The nodules that covered them were more like large nipples than anything else, the flesh going from an alabaster white to a sickly grey-green around the openings. Their skin wasn't smooth like she thought, but ridged, almost like corduroy. The eyes, mere amber dots of light at distance, were far more detailed. Streaks of gold shot chaotically through the ebony orbs, the light breaking from within like fire through cracked iron. The creature had no neck to speak of, the shoulders smoothly rising like the slopes of a mountain to the rather featureless head. There were no ears or nose, merely the odd eyes and a wide slit for a mouth. A mouth which now opened, a baleful crimson light escaping as those thin lips formed words.

"Why this form?"

The voice that issued forth was deep, melodious, like a rolling peal of thunder.

"What?"

"Why this form? It is flawed."

Angela was at a loss for words. The sudden development of a conversational giant had momentarily shocked her right out of her wits. Flabbergasted, one might say. The tall one, however, suffered no such difficulty.

"This form is flawed... Take another."

"I... I can't."

At this the tall thing recoiled, briefly, as if struck, before splitting its maw in a cacophonous roar that vibrated in Angela's very bones.

242

Under the circumstances, with her injuries, it was a decidedly unpleasant sensation.

Her initial flinch gave way to a deadpan expression. The blood light filled her gaze and her being. The world faded away, her aches and pains deadened, her fatigue and worries faded and disappeared.

~

Day 78

Captain Longmire was flipping through yet another stack of useless papers, travel documents, looked like. He collapsed into the desk chair the professor must've appropriated from one of the offices and exhaled deeply in frustration. As he sat there, he heard footsteps echoed from the hall. He turned his head to see who it was, only to see Cox peering in. Annoyed, Captain Longmire waxed sarcastic.

"Didn't I just order you to wait for Emil and Sharon at the loading dock? I could've sworn I did. Oh, but then, silly me, I'm just your Captain and superior officer; why would I have any authority?"

"Sir, you did, it's just, Emil and Sarya came over. Emil says Sharon stayed behind."

"Son of a bitch. Are you fucking kidding me!?"

"I wish I was, sir..."

"Goddammit. Well when is she supposed to join us, and how!?"

"According to Emil she said it was the smarter option for he and Sarya to cross by themselves, unburdened by her, and for us to come and get her when we're able."

"Well, shit, she's gonna have to wait."

"The crates, sir? You think that they're more important than Sharon's life? I mean, what if something happens while she's over there?"

"I know I know I know. But the contents of these crates might give us the clues we need to clear the skies, defeat the giants and regain

243

control of the surface again. I can't prioritize any one person over that."

"Personally, sir? If it means this generations children and grandchildren live on the surface, I think my life would be a fair cost. I can't imagine Sharon or anyone else could feel much different."

"I don't think any of us quite anticipated the end of the world on our watch."

"Maybe not. But the end of us? All of us, even? Yeah. We knew the *Oregon* could go down in wartime. Sharon is a former Marine. And we both know how Jarheads are..."

"Maybe, but if we get Emil or Sarya killed? Where's the justice there? Innocent civvies endangered by tagging along with us."

"Or more so by being left to fend for themselves."

The captain looked at his Master at Arms for a long second before speaking again.

"You know, being a pain in my ass isn't quite a court martial offense, but I can still make life aboard the *Oregon* hell for you."

"Oh, no doubt. But one must have their hobbies, sir."

"Alright, alright... let's go see to getting those crates packed, then we'll get across the street and grab up Sharon."

"Yes sir... oh! One more thing. Emil pointed out that we should heat up the APC's fuel tank and make sure her batteries charged before we get loaded."

"What? Oh, yeah, the cold, diesel and batteries don't go well with cold. Good thinking. Pick out a few ugly ones and break them up."

"Ugly ones sir?"

"Paintings, Cox, ugly paintings. Preferably oils; they'll burn better to uncongeal the diesel."

244

"Oh... aye sir, and the batteries?"

The Captain pointed out a series of large car batteries wired up and attached to a converter that were powering the floodlights in the room.

"Hardy and the professor did us the favor of procuring what we need. Either they're spares or they'll jump the ones in the APC as it stands."

~

Day 78

Dr. Rafei listened to the unexpected silence a moment before commenting.

"I take it there's a hiccup?"

"Oh goddamn it... it wasn't freezing out here when I parked. The fucking fuel must've congealed!"

"Well, is there anything you can do?"

"Uh... not really, Doc. Well, I can at least keep us safe for a bit."

"How do you purpose to do that?"

"Like this."

Jesse pressed his palm against the center of the steering wheel. The horn of the truck sounded impossibly loud in the concrete box of a garage. Within seconds, thumps and thuds sounded out from all over the body of the truck. Rafei was incredulous.

"You attracted the phenomena to the truck."

"Yeah."

And this keeps us safe?

"Well, yeah. The folks chasing us can't get us, can they?"

"Well, no..."

"And neither can the phenom-ila, uh, phenominyuh, er, the things. C'mon back wit' me Doc; the back of the truck is set up for travel."

"Jesse, what is your plan? What are we going to do?"

"Well, we'll sit tight in here for a few hours, then I'll go load up the rest of the boxes, and set up a couple road flares under the tanks then climb inside real quick. When the truck starts we let her idle a bit to make sure the battery is charged and the fuel is warmed, then we set off for Beaufort."

"And the giants? What plan have you for dealing with them, since that horn trick just as surely called them?"

"Well, I figure if we sit still and quiet, just like with the sky things, the giant things'll have no reason to be overly curious as to what's in the truck. I mean, it's not like any of 'em saw us climb in."

"And if they did?"

"Don't mean to patronize ya, Doc, but... you can't see the arsenal that is locked up in cages all over the walls of the can back there. I've got a good selection of heavy hitters. Things that'll punch through two or maybe even three feet of wood, six inches of concrete. No way they won't kill the giants."

"The alert said they weren't vulnerable to mundane weapons."

"And I'd put dollars to pesos that was just so a bunch of ill prepared scrubby survivalists with .22s wouldn't get themselves killed."

"Maybe. I hope you're right."

~

Day 78

Sharon's eyes blazed with indignation and petulant stubbornness as the strange figure carried her over his shoulder away from the ruined storefront where they'd met. Every bouncing step his shoulder was

246

driven into her belly, causing arcs of fiery pain to shoot through her leg and arm. Facing downward, she could see the snow and frosty concrete over which they travelled in between buildings as her captor followed the giants through the city.

Suddenly, he stopped for a moment, and before Sharon could draw breath to speak with, he made a shushing noise under his balaclava and then wheeled to his left, cutting into an alleyway and pushing open a set of swinging doors. They were in the kitchen of some kind of restaurant, apparently one open 24 hours, as there were traces of meals halfway completed and abandoned all over the counters and stoves. He set Sharon down on an errant stool that was leaning in one corner near the doors, pulling his sidearm from its holster as he did so. Once she was set, he came face to face with her, once again shushing her, this time with a finger to where his mouth would be under the mask and a nod to his sidearm.

"Listen here and listen well girly, you keep quiet now. The building two blocks ahead was apparently their destination, but they're flustered a bit gathered around it, as it's been right properly buggered up, just as expected."

Keeping her voice low and calm, Sharon responded.

"And just what the hell does that mean? Any idea what building?"

"Oh yeah, I've got a GPS here been running, let me see..."

He pulled a small black square device out of a breast pocket before flipping up his goggles, his brown eyes piercing the darkness and gaining their own shine from the screen of the device.

"What did you mean by 'buggered up'?"

"It's gone, totally smashed, destroyed, demolished like."

"Yeah... we've heard buildings coming down occasionally as time's gone by. You said they've been searching others? What building was this one, or the others?"

"Hold on, hold on... Signals pretty weak and things are slow, must be the coverage overhead from all these bloody skyscrapers..."

"I don't doubt it."

"Here we go here we go; things are loading up now. Looks like... some kind of municipal office building. I can't be sure exactly what offices, though; that info's only provided when the regular wireless network is up."

"And what were the others?"

"Some astronomy society HQ, a UN server farm, and the central library."

"Wait, *the* New York Public Library?"

"That's the one."

"Oh, now I'm pissed. Destroying books, what the hell? Are they goddamned Nazis or something?"

"I don't think it was them that's done it, Miss...?"

"Sharon Harvick, and yourself?"

"Sergeant Eldritch, Her Majesty's Royal Marines, ma'am, at your service."

"Former Sergeant of the US Marines myself. You know, we're descended from you guys, so far as traditions go."

"Is that right? Well, I suppose I should treat you a bit like family, then?"

"Certainly not as an enemy, if you don't mind."

"Eh?"

Sharon nodded at his unholstered weapon, as he seemed to have forgotten he was holding it.

"Oh, righty-oh."

He put the weapon on safe and holstered it before addressing her again.

"Look, I'm trying to figure out what's behind all these demolitions, and why the giants are crawling over them like ants on an apple core. Everything I've seen points towards them operating on some kind of instinct, so I want to know what it is about destroyed buildings that attracts them. You're wounded, but you're no threat to me, I reckon, so the choice is yours. I can wait until their attention is elsewhere and take you back where I found you, or if you can keep up, you can join up with me and maybe act as an advisor. Seeing as how you're from here and all, you might have some insights."

~

Day 78

Captain Longmire, Cox, Emil and Sarya sat around the loading dock in silence. The crates were loaded. The APCs batteries had been tested and found adequate, and a small fire of shredded oil paintings from the 30s was smoldering under the armored fuel tanks, warming and re-liquefying the diesel fuel inside. No sign indicated that the Shards had taken notice; apparently what little noise they'd made and what little heat they created weren't strong enough to exit the well-covered loading dock and alert them.

All that was left was for them to retrieve Sharon, then load up in the APC and make their way back to the *Oregon*. Captain Longmire broke the silence.

"I don't think we should delay much longer. It's almost dark."

Emil raised his head, his eyes dark and resolute.

"No, we shouldn't. She's been out there alone long enough. We should get her and get to the *Oregon* as soon as possible."

"Emil, get yourself and Sarya into the cabin of the APC so when we get back, we'll just load up and be ready to depart. Cox, you get set to cross the street with me and grab up Sharon."

Cox nodded before putting on his coat, hat, gloves, and IR goggles. Longmire followed suit as Emil took Sarya out to the APC. Scarcely a minute later they could hear the muted clank as he gently pulled the hatch closed behind him, sealing them in for the time being. The radio crackled briefly as he informed them there was still no trace of the phenomena in the loading dock.

The Captain and his Master at Arms then exited the loading dock for the final time, leaving behind only footprints in the dust and the shriveled remains of Dr. Opperthorne. They walked around the APC and to the opening to the street. From there, Cox reached out a hand to Longmire, before whispering that he couldn't see Sharons heat signature. Longmire turned up the sensitivity of his own goggles, peering through the swirling snow to see if he could catch any glimpse of Sharon, but there was nothing.

We should still go over there, just in case she's moved behind cover.

"Aye sir."

With no further conversation, the captain and his Master at Arms once more secured their gear and made sure that nothing would shake loose in the crossing. Then the captain raised three fingers for a countdown, dropping one, then two. On dropping the third he and Cox crossed the road at a light jog. It was only a few moments of searching before they had some idea of the story.

"Sir, look..."

Cox clicked on a small penlight and illuminated the tiled floor, revealing that there were scrapes and footprints in the frost that covered everything. The scrapes seemed to originate at the couch where they'd last seen Sharon, and went around to behind the scenery. Small droplets of blood marked the spot where she had apparently waited.

The footprints came from outside the store, moving in a semi-circle around Sharon's hiding place, before moving in, then, the footprints move off, one full set of prints, left and right, and one incomplete set, a scrape and a left foot print, only, moving off, out of the store and down the street.

Longmire indicated for Cox to switch off the penlight.

"What do you think, sir?"

"Well, isn't it obvious? Sharon saw someone coming, a stranger, and not being in any condition to fight, she hid. It wasn't enough, she was found out, and then taken, willingly or forced."

"What's the plan, sir?"

"Nothing we can do."

"Nothing we can...!?"

"What do you want me to do? Compromise our whole mission to go searching for one woman who isn't actually involved?"

"Well, not when you put it like that, but, I mean, it's kind of..."

"She's a tough one. I have no doubts she's planning an escape from her captor even now."

~

Day 78

Sharon looked through the small circular window of the restaurant and down the street at the ruin, crawling with the giants, their limbs unnaturally long and spindly. Looking around at the surrounding buildings, she suddenly had a realization.

"Hey, Eldritch, where are we?"

Sergeant Eldritch looked up from the MRE he was wolfing down at a table deeper in the dining room.

"Uh... I think Park Row?"

"You didn't spend much time in Manhattan before things went to shit, did you?"

251

"Er... no. I didn't come here until after."

"How the...? Never mind, that can wait. Do you have any idea what building that is?"

"No clue, love."

"It's One PP."

"Excuse you."

"No, goddamnit, One Police Plaza, NYPD HQ."

"So..."

"So? So Somebody demolished one of the most important government buildings in New York, for chrissakes! And shit, I was just here!"

"What's that then? What do you mean 'just here'?"

"After everything went to hell I made a tour, as best I could, of major government buildings, looking for some kind of surviving authority."

"And I take it from the way you're not involved with any of them that your search was fruitless?"

"Essentially. The FBI, NSA, and CIA substations were all vacant, all dead. One PP Still had survivors, but..."

"But...?"

"But the maniacs were running the asylum."

"The prisoners?"

"Right, the people who had been put in holding overnight outnumbered, overpowered, and took over from the police that were on duty overnight."

"So, exactly what would be the purpose in bringing it down?"

"I'm not sure. What now? I doubt you're itching to go join them in crawling the wreckage."

"Not a bit. But then, this isn't the last wreck I'm set to look over."

"So, where next?"

"I'm not right sure, miss; I've been following the Giants from ruin to ruin, followed them here. I suppose we'll be following them elsewhere. But, this is the first time I've been able to watch what they're doing about the wrecks, so I'd like to stay and see just what they're on about."

~

Day 78

Cox closed the hatch to the driver's seat of the APC as gently as he could. Hearing the gentle thud as the heavy door set into its mounting, the Captain clicked his radio twice, sending a signal to Cox, who turned the key of the APC to on, activating its electrical systems without starting the engine. Just enough for the captain to press the button to activate the hydraulics and lift the armored ramp and seal the rear compartment. This was the most dangerous part. The ramp was a noise making affair, and if there was a time that there was a chance that the things in the sky would take notice before the engine were cranked, it would be now.

Seconds after the hatch sealed with a deep metallic clang and the hiss of hydraulics, the armored exterior of the vehicle responded from the impacts of countless Shards. Without further signal, Cox pressed the ignition, the engine of the APC sputtering and coughing only twice before turning over and settling into a raucous growl. Cox eased the throttle forward as he released the brakes and the behemoth steel box began moving forward on its treads, heading directly towards the gaping hole in the rolling aluminum doors of the dock.

CHAPTER 25

Day 79

"Lost contact? What do you mean, lost contact?"

Dr. Lucinda Alvarez stood towering over her peer and erstwhile ally Lt. McGuire who, sitting with legs spread and arms draped over the arms of his chair, seemed singularly unperturbed at his declaration.

"We've sent a packet diverting the *Oregon*, but we've been unable to get an acknowledgement signal from them indicating they've received their altered orders. We've lost contact."

"Well, what does that mean? Do we send another op to DC? What about the Opperthorne research? What about..."

"Whoa whoa whoa... slow down. All it means is that we've lost contact. Now, it could be a glitch in the satellite, it could be a mechanical fault on the *Oregon* herself. We have thousands of different things that could muck up comms and we can only eliminate about a hundred of them with the resources we have."

"It was unforgivably stupid of us to put all our eggs in one basket.

How could we be that stupid!? Shit!"

"Calm down, Doctor; we haven't. At last report, the *Oregon* was in the Atlantic moving south on their way to DC. Now, if it's just a glitch, then no harm done. If they're gone, we'll have lost Opperthorne's work but we could still use alternate resources to retrieve the Shard. There's no real scenario where we're 100% up the creek."

"Over 95% of humanity is dead, we're completely incapable of living on the surface, the planet is experiencing a supernatural winter in both hemispheres, and we've just lost contact with the couriers of the one slim hope we have of finding an acceptable end to this. How exactly are we not up the creek and paddle-less?"

"You haven't read through the rest of the files, have you?"

"No, not all of them. I came as soon as I read about the Schmitt discovery."

"Well I, for one, am very curious about why the Tall Ones are excavating all over the world."

"That doesn't give us anything we can use; it's a dead end.

"You're thinking like a doctor. That these problems are like a disease, that we need to find some agent or method of fighting them wholesale. But I'm a submariner, I fight wars in ever-changing three dimensional environments. I can't operate on one track like that. If we can determine what the goals of the Tall Ones are, what they want, it may enlighten us as to the course of action to take."

"I see what you trying to say, and I get it, I do, it's just... that course of action might reveal something to do about the Tall Ones. What about the Shards?"

"Are you really of the opinion they're entirely unrelated? That one is unconnected to the other and we 'just happened' to end up encountering two distinctly unnatural and possibly supernatural types of life within weeks of each other, completely coincidentally?"

"Of course not. That would be naive and ridiculous. That's why we've continuously operated under the presumption they're connected."

"Then why suddenly worry if we lack progress in addressing one? Won't any line of research we take on either eventually converge and give us the solution for both?"

"Well, not any line of research, but... I see your point. It's just... we're responsible for the continued survival of the human race. It seems prudent to me to attack the problem from multiple angles."

"We are. Opperthorne, the Schmitt discovery, our continued observation of the Tall One's excavations, your research into the exact pathology of how the Shards kill has been continued and expanded upon to include those few remains we have from Tall One attacks..."

"And yet our primary tactic is still avoidance."

"Until we have actionable intelligence or some kind of new weapon, that's our best bet."

The door to the council chambers opened and a young Marine poked his head inside.

"Sir, Madam, there's a Naval ensign here that says he has an urgent matter to discuss with you."

"Send him in."

"Yes, ma'am."

A few moments later the same ensign that had delivered the news about Air Force One came in with a sheaf of papers tucked under his left arm. Two Marine MPs followed, taking position by the chamber doors.

"I'm sorry for the interruption but this couldn't wait. Sir, Madam Councilor, we've completed our initial investigation into the deaths

257

of the previous council membership."

"And what's your conclusion thus far?"

"I'm afraid we've completely ruled out accident or happenstance. There's a murderer in the facility targeting people of authority."

"Do you have any leads as to who it might be?"

"Yes ma'am, we do."

At that, the MPs stepped forward.

~

Day 79

The world came back slowly. Everything was in a haze, sounds echoed and reverberated unnaturally. All she could see was the pale blue purple shimmer of the otherworldly figure in the center of the giants.

There was no pain.

Her broken limbs, scrapes, and bruises seemed to have miraculously healed. She could hear a deep and bizarre hum. The rhythm and tonal pattern couldn't seem to make up its mind. It sounded like every form of wind instrument being played on random notes and switching from instrument to instrument with a maniacal fervency from a deaf orangutan.

It lasted only a few moments before changing into a symphony of singular tones, each just as bizarre as the whole of the last. Some were so high Angela wondered that her ears didn't hurt, while others sent deep vibrations shaking through the stones under her legs and back.

She began to see other colors, lights, poking through the haze, pinpricks of silver light with shades of every other color tainting the edges.

She strained to focus her eyes, to make out greater detail, but her eyes refused to cooperate.

"Don't bother, it's not going to get any better."

Angela struggled to turn her head to find the source of the voice, but her gaze remained fixed and pointed at the glowing figure in the center of the room.

"Shhh! They'll hear you!"

A cacophony of laughter sounded out in response. A new voice spoke up from the pack.

"Oh, mon chere... they do not hear us. They cannot hear us."

"Why not? Are they deaf!?"

Yet again a different voice answered, in a thick German accent

"Zere is leetle zey do not zee or hear, but vee are silent to zem."

"Why, why can't they hear us, why can't I turn my head, or focus my eyes, what's happening?"

"Oh you poor naïve girl, haven't you figured it out yet? You've joined the collection."

"What collection? I don't understand, I don't..."

"When you first came here, did you not see us, standing at attention round the chamber, staring at the center, just as you are now?"

Angela's scream did not echo, as her throat made no sound.

~

Day 78

The radio in Captain Longmire's pocket clicked, an indication that Cox, up in the drivers compartment, wanted to talk. Longmire pulled the radio out and, setting it a few inches from his mouth, spoke.

"Go ahead, Cox."

"So how do we do this, sir?"

"Well, I've been thinking about that. The river's frozen, so the dinghies are out, but the river's not *so* frozen we can take this APC down there direct.

I'm thinking we park right next to that little shop with the upstairs office Hardy used, wait a few hours 'til the things from the sky lose interest, then unload into the building. After that we do quick runs. Shore parties from the *Oregon* come ashore, we unload the crate's contents and take them aboard through the forward torpedo hatch.

Each shore party can escort one of us back aboard as well. Sarya first, Emil, then myself and you go last Cox; that way you lived up to your promise. Does anybody have any objections?"

Emil raised his fingers off his knee.

"I'd like to go first."

"Why?"

"If there's anything wrong, if anything goes wrong... I want it to happen to me, not Sarya."

"Fair enough. Cox, you have any objections?"

The radio crackled briefly before Cox's voice came through.

"Only that we've got to move these crates again, sir."

"Ah, quit your bitching."

"Well sir, we're about there."

"Good. Back us up to about eight feet from the bodega entrance, then shut everything down."

Emil stared at the captain.

"Where do we go after we're aboard your submarine?"

"Our orders were to make for a port in South Carolina to deliver the Professor and his materials. I'm presuming that's still true but once we're underway I intend to report in, give them an update, including the information about you."

"What if they tell you to leave us here? In a frozen, dead city?"

The captains smirk highlighted that he'd thought of this before Emil ever asked.

"Well I was going to wait 'til we hit the open Atlantic to report, that way it'll be a little too late to send you back ashore."

"I appreciate that, Captain."

"Think nothing of it."

At that, the APC shuddered to a halt, then kicked over into reverse and turned a full 90 degrees before stopping and shutting down. Suddenly, without the constant din of the diesel, they could make out clicks, scratches, and squeals on the outer skin of the vehicle. The occupants in the back each shifted nervously as the realization of the exact origin of the sounds set in.

~

Day 79

"You think they've lost interest?"

"Well. I can't hear them squirming no more..."

"Is there any way to check?"

"Not really, Doc. Everything's blacked out so far as the windows go."

"How long has it been?"

"...about... 2½ hours."

"That's not long enough, is it?"

"Three hours would be a safer bet."

"So after that, we're free, we get the crates inside the truck, we liquify the fuel, and then we head for South Carolina?"

"That's the plan."

"Do you have any more questions?"

"To be honest, Doc, I'm still kinda processing what you told me before. I mean... secret projects, hidden facilities, conspiracies of secrecy. It's kind of heavy."

"Very well, then... If I may, could I ask you about your past?"

"Aw heck, that ain't nothing interesting."

"Isn't that for me to judge? Come now, Jesse, surely you didn't simply spring into being inside this truck the day the event came."

"Aw heck no. Well... I guess you could say I had a normal childhood. I grew up in this little town up in the Florida panhandle called Wewahitchka, but as an adult I moved up to this place called Greenville in Alabama. That's where I built my bunker and prepared for the end of the world. World ended, I customized this truck and came here."

"No no no... I mean, what did you do? What was your job? Do you have family waiting anxiously in that bunker? Details! We have time to burn and I know next to nothing about my traveling companion. All of our conversation has been about the end of the world. A conversationalist yearns, on occasion, for lighter fare."

"Alright, Doc... geez... I was into metal fabrication. Ever since shop in middle school. Went to a trade school for it. Worked at a little place that manufactured precision pieces for military aircraft, C-130s mostly, but occasionally we got a special order for some pieces for B-52s. I worked a machine doing the rough cuts.

I never married, but I was seeing someone when everything went down. They didn't make it past the first morning though... but anyway, that suitable details for ya?"

"I'm detecting there's some sore spots there."

"Kinda."

"All right then, but just know when we get to the facility in South Carolina they'll want to fully debrief you, and they won't take kindly to lies or deflections."

"Just so long as they take me to dinner and a movie first. I ain't no hussy."

~

Day 79

Lucinda widened her eyes and let her jaw hang loose in faux surprise and indignation as one of the MPs produced a set of handcuffs and pulled her arms behind her. Lt. McGuire broke the shocked silence first as the cuffs clicked into place.

"I presume, Ensign, that you have some evidence to back this up?"

"Yes sir, we do."

He took the sheaf of papers from under his arm and handed them to McGuire.

"We have her fingerprints in several key locations, including on the supplementary oxygen feeds leading to the VIP Quarters and the VIP medical wing. We have the remains of two compressed gas canisters —we don't know what kind — pulled from the incinerator the day after. We have the sworn testimony of one of the supply sergeants that he saw Dr. Alvarez briefly the night before — he's on report for failing to carry out General Order 11 — and we've got them doing an intensive inventory now to find out just what agent was used."

Lucinda found her voice.

"This is ridiculous! Why aren't I being informed of my rights!?"

"Ma'am, with the current situation, martial law is in place. You're a civilian; at the moment you don't have any rights. Technically speaking, ma'am, you're a traitor in a time of war. I'd be within my full authority to summarily execute you. We're choosing to be a bit more humane."

Lucinda thought it would be wiser not to press the issue. McGuire began looking through the papers the Ensign had brought.

"Ensign... these arrest orders aren't signed; neither are the official charges."

264

"No, sir."

"And why not?"

"As the OIC, it's you who has to sign them, sir. Considering Doctor Alvarez's position, we couldn't have brought this to you without legally also having to inform her. It seemed best to simply carry out the arrest as we informed you of our results."

"So if I don't sign these..."

"You'd be considered an accessory after the fact. Lieutenant Hartzell would take over, and he'd sign them for both of you."

"Lieutenant Hartzell doesn't have time in rank or service, nor is in a command track. He's an engineer."

"Nevertheless, he'd be the ranking officer if you were to refuse and make yourself an accessory."

McGuire let a moment or two pass as he evaluated his choices.

"...I'll sign them. But I want five minutes alone with Doctor Alvarez first.

"Sir..."

"Call it a professional courtesy. I'd like to hear her side of things."

"Yes sir... five minutes, and she stays cuffed."

Of course.

With that, the MPs and the ensign retreated out the council chamber doors. McGuire followed and closed the doors behind them. Turning, his face took on a dark aspect Lucinda had never seen before. Walking towards her, he unsnapped the holster of his sidearm, drew it, pulled the slide to chamber a round and, clicking the safety off, aimed directly at Lucinda's head.

*"Give me *one good reason* not to."*

~

Day 78

Captain Longmire sat at the edge of his seat at the navigation table, having finally made it to the bridge after overseeing the onboarding of his passengers and the stowing of the Opperthorne materials. He'd issued orders to get underway just as soon as the outer hull was sealed, and now he wanted two things: a decent cup of coffee, and a progress report on their return to the Atlantic.

"What's our depth?"

"We're running with an even keel at... ten meters of water above the conning tower."

"How much water does that put beneath us?"

"Current sounding is 15 meters."

"Ugh... that's a very tight squeeze. Cox, any news on the XO?"

Cox dismissed the seaman who was handing him a report and turned to address the captain.

"No sir, he's still comatose."

"And our guests?"

"Emil is putting Sarya back to bed as we speak. She's having trouble, the ships too strange and the bunk too hard, she says."

Longmire chuckled. "Alright. Well, seeing as how it's 0330, I think I'll follow their example. Get Thompson up here to take command while I'm down."

"Captain, Lt. Thompson had been up nearly two days before you relieved him last night. With no other Command officers aboard, he refused to hand command over to an enlisted man."

"Stubborn... Alright, who's aboard who isn't dead on their feet but has some decent experience?"

266

"Colquitt?"

"Ensign Colquitt? The navigator?"

"Yes sir. He's at least an officer."

"How long has he been off duty?"

"About six hours. But before that he was only on duty three. He came on duty just before we came aboard and you sent him off as soon as we were out of the East River."

"Perfect, get him up here. After that, you going off duty?"

"With your leave, sir. To be honest I've been up just as long as you have and I'm just aching for a quick shower and a bunk."

"Make it a Hollywood shower; you've earned it."

"Aye, sir."

"And Cox?"

Cox turned back to his captain.

"I want you to know you'll be getting a citation for your performance ashore. You did a hell of a job, sailor."

"Thank you, sir."

As Cox disappeared astern to look for Ensign Colquitt, Longmire looked around the bridge. Assessing his crew, who performed so well in spite of such hardship. And he felt a quiet sort of pride.

"Now that we're not going to run aground, and we've got our mission materials... anything else anyone's failed to report, before I go sleep for a couple days straight?"

A seaman at the port trim console cleared his throat.

"Yes, Seaman Gomez, what is it?"

"I just thought you should know Kellogg and Watkins made it back safe sir."

~

Day 79

Zoe rushed to the inner door panel. She dialed up the floodlights and peered through the porthole to get a better look at her guest. The man was wrapped head to toe in rags of every color, his eyes obscured by a heavy pair of electronic goggles. As the lights came up, they must have made an audible noise because the figure in rags stopped mashing the buzzer and straightened up, obviously with difficulty.

The figure pulled his goggles off, peering through, and saw Zoe. He tiredly gestured for her to hurry and open the door before keeling over and slumping down against the door.

Zoe reached for the door control, then hesitated. She didn't know who this person was. Hell, she couldn't even be sure the person wasn't dangerous, out carrying some sort of disease. Why had they collapsed? Was it simple exhaustion like it seemed?

She pulled her hand back from the control, turned around, and began walking towards the aisles. She grabbed a tray and started picking items out as she went. After about twenty minutes, she'd gathered what she thought she needed. An MRE, two rolls of gauze, a bottle of rubbing alcohol, two boxes of bandages of various sizes, two bottles of water, four Aspirin, a toiletries kit, two erasable markers, two whiteboards, and from the emergency cabinet, a .45 pistol.

Returning to the airlock, she set a marker and whiteboard aside before racking the slide on the pistol. She checked on her guest — he didn't look to have moved — before triggering the door control halfway. Holding the .45 on the ragged figure, she slid the tray holding the rest of it through into the airlock before closing the door again.

Now she just had to wait. She pulled up a chair from the nearby post. Had the bunker been fully manned to capacity there would've been a guard on duty near the airlock. She sat down, feet propped up on the panel. She had just been about to go to bed... she figured she should be here when her visitor woke up.

~

A number of hours later Zoe awoke to a polite series of gentle knocks against the glass. Blinking the sleep from her eyes she looked up to see a familiar face smiling at her, violet eyes, silver teeth and ebony skin holding up a whiteboard with a message.

Hello Zoe. It's nice to see you again. May I come in now?

~

Day 79

"Do you think it's time yet, Jesse?"

"...Yeah. Yeah, I reckon so. We ain't heard no chittering and no scratching for awhile now so..."

"Should I get in the front?"

"Yeah, go ahead. Get yourself up there and I'll secure the door, then go outside through the rear and grab up the boxes with all the supplies. Get them in the back, then I'll set up a couple of road flares under the gas tanks and get back in."

"Jesse..."

"Yeah, Doc?"

"Good luck. I wish I could see and be of some use to you."

"Don't worry about it. Everything considered, we humans gotta stick together, y'know?"

"Yes, right... be careful."

Jesse gently closed the reinforced door to the cab of the truck before turning and grabbing his gear. It was already freezing in the truck and he had remained appropriately clothed, so all he needed to add were his body armor, balaclava, and IR Goggles.

He carefully opened the armored rear door of the truck, taking great care not to let it get slammed by the wind. He carefully hooked the door open before turning and surveying the 15 feet between the back of the truck and the stairwell door, which hung open, its entryway piled with some bizarre shape he couldn't identify through the filter of the goggles. As he approached he realized that they must be the piled and desiccated bodies of the rest of the CDC staff.

They were piled roughly waist high and the boxes he was after were strewn on the landing behind them. They'd have to be moved if he was going to get the boxes.

Jesse hesitated a moment. He didn't know these men or women. He didn't bear them any kind of ill will, and they'd been nothing less than scientists dedicated to fighting the forces of plague and malady that have tried for centuries to wipe man from the surface of the Earth. They deserved better than to be thrown aside like cordwood. And Doctor Rafei, as their tormentor and the one who wrongfully imprisoned them, should by all rights, blindness aside, be the one to do it.

As Jesse sat pondering these thoughts and felt his resolution growing firm, his goggles registered a differential between the bottom of the pile and the top. The bottom of the pile was warmer. Jesse reached up to adjust the sensitivity of the goggles, but as he did so there was a faint pop as some circuit within them shorted. Jesse was then plunged into darkness as he considered his next move. He could feel his way back to the truck, not even eight feet behind him, there to withdraw another set of goggles, or, he could take them off and investigate the pile with his own eyes. Within a covered garage, as long as he was careful...

"Help."

A voice, not his own nor Rafei's, eliminated all confusion. He stripped the goggles off his head and, blinking furiously, beheld daylight for the first time in months. The garage, the pile, everything was coated with the fine white hallmarks of frost.

A single hand, pale and slender, inched out from beneath the dried and shriveled remains of the CDC's last casualties. Jesse knelt by the hand and took it in his own. Giving it a squeeze he began speaking in a low voice.

"Shhh-shh-shhhh-shhhh... It's alright. Look, I'm not the Doc, ok? I just found him, alone and blinded wandering the halls. He didn't tell me anything about any of y'all until this morning. Now, I'm gonna get you out of there, and we're gonna take you with us, but you've got to stay quiet, and you've got to stay calm, 'cause any kind of undue ruckus is gonna bring them things back and then we'll all look just like your friends here, understand?"

A small voice, wavering with the cold, answered.

"I understand, please hurry..."

Jesse patted the hand from beneath the pile of corpses reassuringly.

"Now, I'm gonna move all these folk off of ya, and its gonna take a minute, and when we're done you're going to have to keep your eyes shut, y'understand?"

"Yes..."

"Alright then. Just hold on a tick."

As Jesse got to work carefully pulling the bodies apart and moving them aside, he stayed wary of how much noise he was making. His breath, the dry crackling of dehydrated flesh, and parched tendons creaking all seemed to boom out like gunshots and echo in the frozen garage, carried perfectly by the still and freezing air. Every loud scrape, every dull thud, set him on edge, poised to dive for the truck. He didn't know how fast the things were, but he could pray.

The job was difficult, as the bodies had settled and interlocked together as their flesh shrank and dried. As he got near to the middle of his task, he heard an odd rustling sound, like a piece of paper being gently crumpled and uncrumpled again and again. He paused, listening. It seemed to be coming from the pile. He crouched down and whispered into the dark space beneath those left.

271

"What the hell are you doin' under there!?"

"I'm not doing anything; I'm waiting until I can get up."

"Well, what's that crunching noise?"

"I thought that was you."

"Nah, it's definitely coming from the pile."

"Well, it's not me."

"Anybody else survived in there?"

"No, no... I wish but no."

"What the heck is it then...?"

"Oh god..."

"What?"

"What if one of the things got trapped?"

"Whatcha mean?"

"What if one of the things is stuck in between one of the bodies?"

"Like, got caught between 'em as they fell?"

"Yes!"

"Then we got a problem..."

CHAPTER 26

Day 78

Eldritch spat out the peppermint gum he'd been chewing and called out to Sharon.

"Hey, hey look! They're dragging something out of the wreckage!"

Sharon hobbled over from the counter she'd been leaning against while reading one of Eldritch's field manuals and took the offered infrared scope from his hand. Putting it up to her own eye she squinted for a moment at the unaccustomed brightness before her vision adjusted and she could make out details. The creatures had been swarming over One PP for nearly an hour, seemingly excavating its ruin. Now they were clearing out as a smaller number of them pulled something from the rubble. It looked to be a cylindrical vessel of some sort. It was covered in rivets and bent in numerous places, likely the result of having a building collapse on top of it.

As she watched, they set it down on the road in front of the wreckage, then a few of them went to it, gripping it on the edges and seams, pulling, tearing the metal like it was tissue paper. Almost as soon as they started they managed to tear one side of it completely off. It was just another second before she saw something that made her gasp.

"What, what is it?"

"Here, look for yourself."

Eldritch took the offered scope and put it to use. Peering through, he saw the bright white outline of the creatures as they stepped back from the tank. Exposed within it, a pinpoint of brilliant heat flickered and danced, almost as if there was some primal fire spirit floating within. Taking the scope down, he joined Sharon in looking down the street with his naked eyes. Without magnification, details were hard to see, but as the behemoths moved out of the way they could make out that what was within the cylinder was another one of the giants, folded and packed in on itself. Sharon and Eldritch shared a look of incredulous disbelief before turning back to the sight atop the wreckage of One PP.

Almost on cue, the giant within the cylinder opened its eyes, the brilliant gold lightning of its eyes visible as a yellow glow even at distance. As it unfolded its long limbs and pulled itself from its container, the rest of them began moving off like a colony of ants, in unison, moving with coordinated effortlessness. Something about the way they moved triggered something in Sharon, a quiet unease, like there was something familiar and troubling about their discipline. She shook herself. It didn't matter. What mattered was finding out what they were doing, not how they moved with precision.

"They rescued the bloody thing. Why would New York's Police HQ have a fuckin' 3-meter-tall albino spider monkey in a can?"

"Is that a joke?"

"I'm sure there's one somewhere but I'll be fucked if I can laugh at a time like this, darlin'."

"Should we follow them?"

"I think so. There's enough of them and the snow's deep enough we'll be able to follow their tracks for a goodly long while though. Might as well wait until the coast is clear."

Sharon nodded and slid herself sideways into one of the empty booths in the restaurant. Her heavy overcoat made it a bit of a squeeze. Eldritch walked over to the corner where they'd thrown their packs down and started rummaging through his own, coming back a few moments later with an MRE. Ripping it upon, he grabbed out the powdered coffee and tea bag and set them aside before setting up the chemical heating pouch between a set of napkin holders. Reaching behind him to the smaller pack attached to the back of his belt he pulled out his med kit and his canteen cup. Setting the kit on the table, he reached into his coat and retrieved a bottle of water. He filled the canteen cup and balanced it with most of its side up against the chemical heater before pouring the last few drops from the water bottle into the package. The air filled with fizzles and pops as the chemicals inside the heater reacted with the water. Vapors carrying the unique scent of the heating elements filled the air as the reaction accelerated, heating the canteen cup and the water within.

Nearly twenty minutes later Eldritch judged the water inside the canteen cup to be at least warm enough and poured the powdered coffee, sugar, and creamer into it before stirring it with a spoon and handing it to Sharon.

"You look like you could use this."

"I normally don't drink coffee, but I think I can make an exception under the circumstances."

"So what's your story?"

"What do you mean? I heeded the warning and survived, then ran into your man Hardy and ended up with a bullet through my leg and another destroying my wrist. Then I run into you."

"Well beggin' me pardon miss, but I already know ya weren't alone."

"No, I wasn't. I was with two other survivors, a father and daughter, and two men with the US Navy, a sub captain and his master at arms."

"Longmire? Captain Longmire?"

"That's the one."

"Hardy was supposed to go meet a Captain Longmire them and take them to some egghead. We thought he'd be an Air Force or Army captain though, not Navy."

"He came in a sub called the *Oregon*. And the egghead, would that be Professor Opperthorne?"

"Aye lass, that's the very one."

"Well, I think they made it without him."

"Eh? Hardy was under orders not to reveal where he was. He didn't even tell us."

"We found papers from before everything went to shit. They mentioned a visiting group of British anthropologists doing a presentation at the Metropolitan Museum of Art in Central Park."

"Jesus, that's right where I found you!"

"They'd just crossed the street to get into the museum when the things passed by and you came up on me."

"Fuck me!"

"Do you think we might be better off going back and meeting them?"

"Well, I mean... shit... no. Hardy was going to get Opperthorne to your man then come back and join back with us."

"You keep saying 'us'. Just how many Englishman are here?"

"Oi, now hold on a tick, love. Hardy and Wentworth are Brits, Jones is Welsh, and I'm Scottish and right proud of it so don't do me like that, all right?"

"Fair enough, you're all members of the UK, right?"

"Aye."

"So what's the right way to talk about you as a group? 'UK-ers" doesn't sound quite right."

"Well, we're all from Great Britain so 'British' would the right term yeah?"

"Fair enough, how many British are here?"

"Just we four."

"And where are the other two?"

"Holed up at the consulate."

"The British consulate on Third Avenue?"

"Aye, love, that's the one."

"Good. We can get there by heading straight up Bowery."

"Ma'am?"

"It doesn't make any sense for us two to be wandering around following these things as they go from ruin to ruin. We need to make a plan to either meet up with Longmire or get off this island ourselves."

"And just abandon finding out what they're up to?"

"Eldritch... I appreciate what you're trying to do, but right now the priority should be survival. What were you originally sent here for?"

"To get Opperthorne ourselves. When our method of extraction went tits up our government coordinated with yours to send your Captain Longmire up here to get him out."

"That gets Opperthorne out. What about your team?"

"We're supposed to go with Longmire if possible; if not, we were supposed to hole up and wait for this to blow over."

"So you were basically abandoned to fend for yourselves."

"Well, no, I mean yes, I mean, not quite. I mean, they said they'd send a retrieval when they were able."

"But to go with Longmire if possible."

"Aye."

"Well that seems to decide it then, we need to meet back up with Longmire, we need to get your men and then head for Central Park."

~

Day 79

Alvarez's eyes remained locked with the young Lieutenants.

"I can only tell you what I know."

"Don't play games with me!"

"Fine. Look, we both know that the majority of the council's time was spent wringing their hands and sending out parties to secure their relatives, and bullshit art pieces and..."

"Enough!"

"...they wasted time, resources, and —"

"I said *enough*!"

"*Lives*! Do you know how many men were lost in their bids to preserve their petty and selfish interests? Forty-two! We lost forty-two men. And if it weren't for me working in the trauma room after getting here it would've been more!"

Lieutenant McGuire slowly lowered his sidearm so that, rather than her head, it was centered on her solar plexus.

"And so..."

"Do you need to hear me say it?"

"Yes."

"So... I... removed the barriers to progress."

A shot sounded out, echoing off the linoleum and concrete.

Lucinda looked down at her chest, seeing her blouse turn dark from her blood as it began soaking through the material. It felt like a sledgehammer had impacted her. She couldn't breathe. She didn't feel any pain. Not at first. Then it hit her, but her legs were failing her. No breath. No feeling. She saw McGuire's finger turn dark, no longer squeezing the trigger. The world tilted. She saw the ceiling; the lights were dimming... why were they dimming?

McGuire looked down at Dr. Alvarez' body, the legs still twitching, the putrid smell of her death void filling his nose.

"Right decision, wrong time."

The Naval Ensign and the MPs entered the room in a rush, their weapons drawn, fanning out on a standard room clear for the first few impressive seconds before they realized what had happened and went about putting their weapons back in their holsters.

The ensign stepped forward, halting just to the left and rear of the lieutenant.

"Lieutenant? Did she...?"

"She didn't go for my weapon. I offered her a quick way out, without the shame or drama of a trial, without hours of torture and interrogation. She accepted."

"...I understand. But how will we know her reasons?"

"Do you really think they matter?"

The ensign stared hard at Lieutenant McGuire before shrugging his shoulders and indicating that the MPs should clear out and get the post mortician and his team up to retrieve Doctor Alvarez's body.

"You should get back to your post too. I can remain here and watch

280

the body."

The young ensign nodded and withdrew, leaving the papers and orders set on the council table. McGuire pulled up a chair and sat down next to Alvarez's body, her glassy eyes staring upwards at the ceiling.

If you'd just come to me with your concerns we could've worked together, could've fixed the Project together. Now I've got to do this alone... shit. I had so much I could've gone over with you, details you didn't know... I couldn't afford to let you go over things with anyone else on post. Damn it Doc, you should've come to me god damn you!

~

Day 79

"More coffee sir?"

"Yes, please. Thank you, Seaman. Ah! Thompson! Good, I was hoping you'd join me."

The young lieutenant stood awkwardly in the door of the officer's mess, barely moving aside as the seaman who'd delivered the three officers lunch left. Captain Longmire eagerly removed the cover from his plate and gestured for the young officer sit down.

"Colquitt's on duty still so one of those plates is his, but the other is yours. Dig in."

"Thank you Captain, it's, er... it's good to have you back."

"Good to be back. It's damn cold out there. Heard you had a time of it. You don't like long duty shifts?"

"That... was a bit more than a duty shift."

"Admittedly! I've been looking forward to a civilized breakfast somewhere warm. Well, to me it's breakfast. We'll get back on our standard rotation soon enough, I think. Now, I'd like to be briefed on just what turn of events led Watkins and Kellogg to disobey my direct orders. They showed up under your watch so I thought I'd get your impressions before reading any of the official reports or writing my own."

"You haven't reported yet sir?"

"Not as such, no. I had Colquitt send in a position and course report so they'd know we were back in the Atlantic and headed towards the next port of call, but I haven't sent in the full report of my activities ashore or of the goings on in the wider New York metropolitan area. I figured I should get all the reports of what happened here first and be a little more awake then I was this morning."

"Makes sense, sir."

"So anyway, what's your impressions of Watkins and Kellogg, why didn't they follow orders?"

"Well... according to them, they ran into an impassable barrier."

"Of what kind, exactly?"

"Debris and rubble. Some kind of purposeful demolition they said. A number of buildings on a specific city block were blown outwards, like it was made to block off all the streets around it."

"Were their reports recorded, transcribed, anything like that?"

"Not initially, but I had them each write up their reports separately to make sure they weren't slacking off or hadn't come back because of cowardice, but their stories matched up, except a few minor discrepancies."

"Any explanation of why they didn't report via radio?"

"Yes, when they got back to the boat they only had the one radio, and it had a fault in the transceiver, it could receive but not transmit."

"So, unable to move forward and no way to signal for further instructions... why didn't they try to get back to Cox and me?"

"That was the most difficult part to get out of them. They got lost."

"Lost?"

"Yes. They hated to admit it, but they couldn't find where you'd been waiting. So they went over their options and eventually settled on quietly making their way east to the river, then they'd go up and down the bank until they found the *Oregon*. They lucked out and hit the river within sight of us."

"They got lucky. Get me their reports as soon as we're done with breakfast, then, after I've reviewed everything and drafted a proper report, we'll head topside and send it in."

"Aye, sir."

~

Day 79

Zoe's eyes widened in recognition and surprise

"Holy crap! Viktor!? How'd you get here? What are you doing? Why are you dressed like that?"

On the other side of the reinforced glass Viktor took his whiteboard down, erased it, wrote on it, and held it up, displaying two question marks.

"Oh damn, right. You can't hear me."

Zoe leaned forward and looked over the control panel, her fingers wriggling and waving in the air as she searched. As she spotted the proper control she dramatically extended one finger and arced it overhead and into the button.

The sound of hissing hydraulics accompanied the raucous sound of Viktor's baritone laughter. Zoe hurled herself to her feet where she danced as she put her arms in the air and ran towards Viktor, throwing herself around him in a sincere bear hug of overwhelming and sincere joy... before recoiling in horror and disgust.

"...What?"

"You stink, Viktor!"

Viktor chortled. "Oh! No doubt! Not a lot of places to shower out there you know..."

"Yeah, but you smell like you've been bathing in urine and god knows what else..."

"Sometimes you've got to take shelter in less than ideal places."

"Like what, a port-o-potty!?"

"Well not to be blunt, but, yeah..."

"Oh... oh Jesus I'm sorry. C'mon, this way. I'll show you where you can shower."

"I'd be much obliged. I don't suppose you'd happen to have anything more fashionable than this improvised number, would you?"

"I'll see if I can scrounge something up."

"That's how I got in this mess!"

As they walked through the warehouse towards the residential compartment, Viktor unwound the various bits of torn and filthy clothing from his body, leaving only his grungy boxers and a tank top by the time they got to the unit. When Zoe turned around to direct Viktor down the proper hall to the showers he stood there, nude except for a pile of filthy and stinking rags in his left arm. Zoe immediately averted her eyes before speaking, a tremor in her voice.

"Oh! Um... showers are... uh, down the hall and to the left. Soap and... uh-hm... everything you might need are in a closet just inside there."

"Thanks, I think I can find my way from here."

Viktor ended his sentence with a wink before walking past Zoe, who immediately uncovered her eyes and shook her head before sneaking a peek at his retreating form. He paused briefly, holding out the pile of rags.

"What should I do with these?"

"There should be a buns — I mean a bin — inside there, too."

"Thanks."

~

Day 78

Sharon leaned heavily on Eldritch as they made their way down Bowery slowly and carefully as they could. Their breathing was the only sound they'd dared make, and even that came in hushed gasps. Luckily the street was lined on both sides with parking, and the shops and business' mostly had small awnings, so the sidewalk formed a kind of half covered tunnel through which they could avoid being out in the open completely. Occasionally they'd come across a vehicle stopped in the middle of the street, usually with the doors open, as the occupants had fled so long ago when the first alert had gone out. It was impossible for them to know now where they had gone or if they had survived. Rarer still, they found vehicles crashed into the parked cars or into a storefront always with the occupants still within. The swirling wind and fog kept visibility low and made every sound echo with a foreboding eeriness.

They passed storefronts hawking everything from dry cleaning to model and escort services. Every few blocks they'd find one that wasn't locked and rest inside for a few minutes before continuing. This one was some kind of karaoke bar. It had apparently been a halfway popular little place. There were quite a few people still inside. None of them were alive, but none of them looked to have died from whatever phenomenon dried you up into a husk either. The bodies — all fairly young men and women of Asian descent — were laid out in chairs or on tables with glasses in their hands. On the stage was a large punch bowl surrounded by bottles of liquor and more than a few bottles of pharmaceuticals. The board up by the stage was marked with hash-marks and tallies. From the looks of things, they'd survived nearly three weeks before all agreeing to take their own lives rather than starve to death or go outside.

Neither Eldritch nor Sharon said a word. The last two places they'd rested had been similar. Small businesses open in the early hours of the morning with the proprietors and the customers trapped within for too long. At least this one wasn't as grisly as the last, where one of those who were trapped had apparently gone violently insane and hacked everyone else to death with a meat cleaver before walking outside. Eldritch finished off a small pack of dehydrated cranberries and pulled his balaclava back on. That was usually their unspoken indicator that it was time to get going again. He paused before he opened the door and looked back at Sharon, who nodded. She hefted herself up out of the chair she was resting in and hobbled over to him, resting her arm over his shoulder and allowing him to get his arm around her lower back and get a grip on her web belt on the other side to help support her.

Nearly an hour later Eldritch broke the silence with a hushed whisper as he pointed out a pair of stiff flags hanging from a rather nondescript building with the large numbers 845 on the side of the building overhanging the entrance.

"There's our consulate. Wentworth and Jones should be inside."

A few minutes later they stood facing the entrance. Two large and imposing wooden doors inscribed with the emblem of the consulate, a lion and a unicorn flanking a shield topped with the British crown over a ribbon bearing a Latin motto. The doors were covered in frost and closed tight. Eldritch let Sharon lean against the side of the building while he went to pull the door on the right open. At first it seemed it wouldn't budge but as he heaved the door slowly began opening, with just the faintest crack as the frost broke and a puff of a breeze as the air inside eked and out equalized. As soon as he got it open fully he invited Sharon to make her way inside.

Sharon limped her way through the doorway and Eldritch followed, gently pulling the immense door closed behind them. The foyer was cavernous and imposing, a large, polished marble affair with a hardwood desk in the center. Everything looked set up almost for a photo shoot, every pen, every sign, every piece of paper in its place. Eldritch indicated a door off to the right of the receptionist's desk.

"There's a hallway and a flight of stairs. We're bunked up on the second floor; that's where the armory was and we thought we'd best be close as possible to that."

As he went ahead of her and opened the door he stopped in his tracks. Sharon caught up with him and peered over his should only to recoil in shock at the sight beyond the doorway. The building beyond had been utterly gutted. Walls were smashed through, the ceiling was gone. She could just make out the various support structures and columns left intact, but everything else that had been in the building looked like a tornado had ripped through it. They could see the alleyway behind the building clear across the piled rubble of what had once been the structure's innards.

Sticking up from one of the piles of debris was a human hand, clad in a black glove, identical to the ones Eldritch wore. Eldritch walked across the pile to the outstretched hand and grasped it before pulling. It came out of the rubble easily, attached to only another six or seven inches of arm before ending at a shredded stump. He dropped it as if it had burned him before turning to Sharon.

"What could have done this? This was no explosion or else all that glass making up the front of the building would've shattered..."

Sharon felt her throat dry out as her thoughts whirled. She managed a dry croak before clearing her throat and responding.

"I don't know what happened here. I can only offer my condolences..."

"Oh, bugger your condolences! I want to get these bastards and make them pay!"

"I don't think we can. I mean, if they could do this? This... this is precise. They didn't just destroy this building, they gutted it with engineered precision. I mean, it would take a human wrecking crew weeks to figure out how to do this. They did it in, what, how long since you've been here?"

"Roughly seventy-two hours. I made it a point of checking back, resupplying, getting a shower on the regular, keeping them informed and me sane, eh?"

"So seventy-two hours max to do this. That's not instinct, that's intelligence. Coordinated, complex problem solving. We need to come at this a different way."

"What are you suggesting?"

"I think we should meet back up with the group I was with."

"Longmire and them, yeah?"

"More importantly, Opperthorne. He's supposed to be the key to figuring out this whole mess."

"Well I suppose I'm not really in a position to object now am I? If we might, I'd like to take a look-see through the wreckage here. There were some things here I think might be useful."

"No problem, just make it quick."

~

Day 79

"Officer on the deck!"

The Master at Arms went to parade rest as Captain Longmire passed him after walking onto the bridge, the ring of the ship's bell announcing to the rest of the boat his arrival.

After relieving Ensign Colquitt and sending him to his rack, Longmire strode over to the navigators table, pulled out one of the chairs, and sat down. Leaning in, he propped his head up on one elbow as he looked over the chart. As he traced their path with one finger he idly wondered if their cargo was worth all the trouble, the distance, the lives. It wasn't the first time he'd thought this way and it wouldn't be the last.

He pulled a notepad and pen over in front of him and began drafting

288

his report to send in. The bustle and hum of the submarine and its crew around him faded into a dull noise in the back of his mind as he attempted to boil down the experiences of the previous few days into a succinct report capable of being understood by the civilian leadership of the Project.

His concentration was broken by the boat suddenly heaving forward and slightly aport. Coffee mugs flew from tables, men lost their feet, and the captain was thrown onto his side, since he was sitting facing starboard.

Moments later alarms started ringing, different alarms meaning different things. The collision alarm, the sonar, flooding alarm, fire alarm, & the depth warning intermixed as a warbling cacophony no Captain ever wants to hear.

Using the table to pull himself to his feet he shouted over the din.

"Shut that shit down!"

The crew scrambled to get back to their seats and posts. As Longmire righted and stood, he noticed a very slight list in the deck to starboard.

"Helmsman! What's our depth and speed?"

"Just passed 150 meters and going down! Screws turning at ten knots sir!"

"All planes full rise, increase speed to flank, and blow the tanks; emergency ascent now!"

"Aye, sir!"

"Get every bulkhead sealed and the bilge pumps started, people; move!"

The helmsman pulled back on the control column with his left hand even as his right pushed forward the throttle sending directions back to the engineering compartment before flipping banks of switches. Other members of the crew hurried to carry out their predesignated tasks.

"CO! Goddamnit motherfucker I forgot he's in a coma... *Cox!"*

"Yes sir!"

"Get on the horn with all compartments starting at the bow and working your way aft. Get me damage and casualty reports!"

"Aye sir!"

The helmsman turned and called to the Captain.

"Sir!"

"Yes, Helmsman?"

"We've leveled out but we're not rising very fast, sir!"

"Are we at full rise with the planes and tanks?"

"I'm not getting much positive trim, sir! We seem to barely be rising even with the tanks blown dry."

"Shit, just keep pulling for rise... Cox!"

"Aye, sir!"

"Where's those reports!?"

"Spotty sir, very spotty... everything aft is reporting shaken but solid, got one injury in the galley. Forward Torpedo is reporting flooding before we sealed bulkheads, now nothing. Forward berthing compartment isn't answering; that's where the flooding alarm is."

"Sonar! Anything in the water? Was this a torpedo?"

The redheaded sonarman popped out of his cubby, one earpiece in place and the other dangling by a wire.

"Er... no sir, absolutely not!"

"You're sure?"

"Absolutely nothing on passive, sir! But we're not getting any signal at all from the sail array. I think whatever hit us took it out, sir!"

"Damn. Go active! It's not like we're worried about hiding from anyone anymore."

"Aye, sir!"

The distinguished sound of an active sonar pulse rolled through the boat from the forward sonar sphere encased in the bow dome.

"Sir! Sonar contacts bearing one seven zero, range three miles!"

~

Day 79

Zoe rearranged herself for the fourth time. The living area of the bunker had a slightly sunken living room area where she watched her movies, and it had a love seat directly facing the entrance. Knowing Viktor would be coming through that door she had placed herself in the love seat to be the first thing he saw, but she couldn't decide on what position he should see her in.

Legs crossed, uncrossed, slightly leaned over with her feet on the seat, ankles crossed, fully reclined with her feet propped up. She thought her legs were her best feature; she should put them on display...

She heard soft footfalls coming down the hall and hurriedly decided — reclined, legs up and crossed.

Viktor came into view, barefoot. He wore the rather loose white linen pants and shirt she'd pulled from the warehouse for him while he showered. They were cinched tight by a drawstring at the waist but otherwise floated and followed over his body like robes on some kind of jungle monk. When he saw her, his eyes briefly and rapidly flitted from her eyes to her legs to her breasts and back to her face before he spoke first.

"Thank you, Zoe. You have no idea how good it feels to be clean after so long being filthy."

"I'll bet. So, are you going to tell me how you got here? Last time I saw you was... what, like a month and a half before things went screwy, right? You stopped by the Institute and told me you were headed for Japan for a while on assignment, I think?"

"Well, you're not wrong. I did go to Japan, and I was there when the shit hit the fan. Survived with the assistance of one of my contacts in the government. They knew, Zoe. They knew this was coming. They didn't know when, but somehow... they knew. They knew and they were prepared."

"How did they...?"

"Zoe, I didn't come here to catch up. Sad to say, I didn't even come here for you. I came here for that." He turned and nodded his head in the general direction of the bunker computer, the very same one that Zoe had used the day previous to send in her report on her findings from the archive.

"You came here for my computer?"

"For its link to the Project leadership."

"Didn't you have a satellite phone?"

"Everything I had, even the clothes on my back, were taken from me in the initial 24 hours of the situation. I haven't had any contact since before things went bad."

"They probably presumed you didn't make it."

"I'm sure they did. But I'm alive, and I know some things that they critically need to know. They've been led to believe Japan is a total loss. That is far, far from the truth."

~

Day 79

The little voice from inside the pile sounded small and frightened to

Jesse's ears, not that he blamed her.

"So... what do we do?

"Hold on a minute. I'm gonna go ask Dr. Rafei for a hand."

"No! Please... you don't know him. You don't know what he's done..."

"Now, he's told me plenty. You ain't got nothing to fear from him. He's blind and damn near helpless. But he can help me get the rest of these off of you all at once, maybe leave whatever's in there in there, y'know?"

"Don't trust him. For the love of God, don't trust him..."

"Lady, this is the only way; now, do you want to get out of there or not?"

"Just, just give me a minute..."

"Lady, the longer I'm out here, the greater the chances are one of them things is gonna spot me or come looking for their lost little one in there with ya and then you'll be up the creek with only the blind doc to help ya..."

"Okay, okay okay... I have an idea. You said you'd get Rafei to help you lift all these off me at once, right?"

"Yeah."

"Well, can't you just lift them a little bit, pull them up enough that I could maybe arc upwards and then crawl out?"

"You know, that just might work."

"Could we try that, please?"

"You got it. But uh... hold on just a minute, let me set something up."

Jesse walked quietly back to the rear door of the truck before gently unlatching the door so that if needed he could close it in a hurry. Then he went back to the pile of corpses under which the woman was trapped.

"Wait, just a moment... what's your name?"

"Jesse, ma'am."

"Linda... my name's Linda. I just thought... if things don't go well... if this doesn't work... we should at least have been properly introduced."

"You're right. Now, you ready?"

"One moment, I have to... yes. I'm ready."

"Okay, count of three. One... two... three!"

Jesse heaved at the shoulders of the bottommost body, throwing his shoulders back and keeping his spine straight as he pushed upwards with his legs. For a moment nothing happened, then with an uncomfortably loud crack the body separated from the frozen ground and the space between the bottom of the pile and the ground began widening. It was only a few moments before hands and a head of dark hair emerged and scrambled out.

Jesse wasted no time on pleasantries as he grabbed her under the arms, hauled her to her feet, and pushed her forward into the back of the truck, grabbing and slamming the door closed behind him after throwing himself in.

Moments later the truck reverberated with the sounds of dozens, then hundreds of impacts as the vehicle was once more cocooned by the things from the sky.

Linda rubbed at her shoulder where she'd landed on the textured metal floor of the truck before sitting up and diving onto Jesse in a sincere embrace.

"Thank you so much. You know you saved my life, don't you?"

"Aw hell, it wasn't nothing. Anybody would have."

A voice came from the door to the cab, where Dr. Rafei suddenly stood, a pistol in his hand pointed at the floor.

"I wouldn't have."

CHAPTER 27

Day 1

Viktor regained consciousness in waves, emerging from the darkness
a little more each time before receding back to the somnambulant
place where time passes without passing. Each time he'd have new
pieces of the puzzle, new understanding. But, at each flirtation with
consciousness, they faded from memory, stolen, destroyed by the
harsh solidity of conscious thought.

The wave crested and he emerged to something resembling a
wakeful state, the taste of stale plastic in his mouth. His eyelids
seemed heavy, his senses dulled. Whatever drug they'd given him
was still in his system, still affecting him.

He managed to open one eye enough to see he was in some sort of
hospital ward. Rows of cots, each contained within a clear plastic
sheet, all occupied, a nurse going from person to person drawing
blood before using an eye dropper to deposit some kind of fluid from
one of those ubiquitous olive green canteens every military in the
world seems to use. After each patient she'd throw the eye dropper
and needle into a bin before pulling a fresh one of each from boxes
atop her cart.

296

At least they're being sterile, he thought.

He tried to lift his arm to his face to rub at his eyes but found he was restrained at the wrist. With tortuous effort he raised his head to look. A cloth strap was secured around his arm with Velcro.

"Nurse! The black one is awake!" A voice called out in rapid Japanese.

He turned his head to see one of the soldiers he saw earlier standing guard at the door peering at him.

The nurse hurried over to him, readying a syringe.

"This is the sixth time since he was brought in. He's metabolizing things much more quickly than his size would indicate."

"Just jab him. If he breaches containment or infects others there'll be hell to pay."

"This one's healthy as a horse. It's the others infecting him that's the greater worry."

Viktor attempted to sit up, to struggle, to fight, but his muscles felt like Jell-O. His bonds, weak as they were, more than enough in his weakened state.

Six times... I can't remember six times... how long have I been here..? What infection..? What are they doing to me..?

He felt the brief sting of the needle in his thigh before the darkness at the edges of his vision grew.

Shadows of shadows faded and swirled through a crimson mist, the denizens within moving like behemoths in the deep, briefly emerging, partially exposed, their forms impossible and the cold intelligence of their too-many eyes all the more menacing for it.

~

Day 79

Captain Longmire stared hard at his sonarman.

"Are they surface or subsurface?"

"Seems... both, sir. I'm getting mixed echoes... wave impacts on metal hulls and surface chop. But there's definitely something subsurface, sir. Unless one of those things has a draft down to two hundred feet..."

"Any indications of life? Reactor noises, screws?"

"Still nothing on passive... but at three miles I might not be that good, sir."

"Helmsman?"

"We're gaining ascent speed, now at one-three-zero and rising, sir."

"Thank heaven for small favors... Cox!"

The Master at Arms put his hand over the handset before responding.

"Yes, sir?"

"Head forward to the aft bulkhead of the berthing compartment and hammer against it. See if there's anyone left in there."

"Aye, sir."

"Helmsman, depth?"

"Seven-six meters sir."

"Sonar, any activity from our neighbors to the south?"

"No sir, profile is unchanged."

At that moment Emil emerged hesitantly from the aft passageway.

"Emil, I'm rather busy at the moment..."

"Of that I've no doubt, Captain. I'm simply wondering if I might be of service in some way."

"Do you have any medical training?"

"First aid...?"

"Get back to the galley and see if you can be of some assistance to Doc Holmes. She's shorthanded — her nurse got off at Oz."

"Of course, Captain."

"Oh, and Emil, is Sarya alright?"

"Yes, she's just scared."

"Well, tell her we're not sinking."

"That's good news for all of us, I think."

With a nod, Emil disappeared back the way he'd come. The captain turned back to his helmsman. Peering over at the display board, he saw that they were just fourteen meters from surfacing. The boat was still on a mostly even keel. Everything he knew told him they should be at a significant angle, with the bow raised due to the weight of the ships reactor dragging down the stern. The only explanation for an even keel was that they were carrying a greater amount of weight forward them they were supposed to... like a flooded forward berthing compartment.

"Sonar, any changes?"

"Possibly..."

"What do you mean, possibly?"

"I don't know sir, I'm hearing... creaking, almost like pressure effects on the hull of a diving sub but there's nothing diving. And I'm hearing splashes."

"Depth charges? At this range?"

The helmsman broke in.

"We're surfaced sir."

"Thank you, helmsman; trim us out and get us steady."

"Aye, sir."

"Continue, Sonar."

"Well, no sir, not big enough to be depth charges, or surface launched torpedoes. More like... debris."

"How do you mean?"

"Remember when we did that live fire exercise off of Oahu last year, and we torpedoed that old decommissioned Perry Class to make that artificial reef? When the torpedo hit it snapped her spine in half and bits and pieces went flying everywhere when they splashed down... it's a similar noise, sir, like pieces are falling off the ships into the water."

"You said they were clustered, how close are they to one another?"

"They're right on top of each other, sir. I couldn't say how many there are. But unless someone had the really bad idea to get together two or three aircraft carriers, there's definitely quite a few ships."

"And they're unpowered?"

"No engine or screws I can make out, sir."

"Hmmm... Sonar, you ever been to the Sargasso Sea or the Northern Pacific Vortex?"

A look of dawning understanding came across the Seaman's face as he realized the import of the question.

"Yes sir. Saw the Pacific Vortex on a flight from Juneau to Pearl when I was a kid."

~

Day 79

Zoe's gaze darkened as she grew concerned.

300

"What do you mean, Viktor?"

"Japan knew this was coming."

"Define 'this'?"

"This. All of this. The Shards, the Tall Ones, the cold, the dreams, all of it."

"Viktor, I'm not sure where to begin. What are you taking about 'shards, tall ones the cold and dreams'?"

"...You've been isolated here, haven't you?"

"Oh no, I have tons of visitors. We did a classic film festival in here last week. Of *course* I've been isolated. You're the first person I've seen outside a mirror in months."

"Why don't you tell me what you are aware of then?"

"A little more than three months ago, I was working late putting together a piece for the Institute illustrating the early origins and notable figures of postmodernism. I was finishing up the Warhol panel when all hell broke loose. My phone went off with the Project alert first, then the Emergency Broadcast System message a few minutes later. By the time it was finished with the first alert and was doing its first repetition I was in the subbasement keying my access to this bunker. Once I was in here, that was it. Just the official Project all points communiques until the day before yesterday."

"And what happened the day before yesterday?"

Zoe turned her head slightly to the side, narrowed her eyes, and twisted her mouth into a frown.

"I'm not entirely sure how much I'm allowed to tell you. I mean, isn't there supposed to be some sort of official orders, written and signed by the Council heads involved in any kind of debrief?"

"We're both Project members, both been through the orientation courses, both been cleared to the same levels. Anything I can know, you'd be allowed to access and vice versa, don't you think?"

"I'm not sure..."

"Look, Zoe, I didn't trek nearly a hundred miles through the frozen wastes of the Midwest just to get you in trouble. But before I can tell you what I know I have to know what page to start on."

"I'm just not sure. I don't feel comfortable with this."

"Alright, how's this: I'll log into my own Project access through your computer. I haven't been able to check it since before this whole thing began. If there's anything in there you don't know, I'll consider it an information exchange for anything you know that I don't. It's not like either of us can accomplish anything from here, anyway."

"Deal, but I get to sit right there over your shoulder and watch you go through it."

"Agreed. Tell me, do you have anything to drink? I'm parched."

"Yeah, the fridge is right over there."

Viktor strode up into the kitchen as Zoe went to start up her computer. Viktor fumbled through the cabinets until he found a glass. Giving it a quick inspection, he nodded to himself before going to the fridge and opening it. There he paused and called over his shoulder.

"Anything in here you're particularly attached to you'd rather I not take the last of?"

"No, feel free, help yourself. Plenty more of everything in the warehouse."

Viktor pushed aside containers of leftovers and pitchers of juices from concentrate before pulling out a single-serve can of V8 Vegetable Juice. He popped the top and poured the contents into the glass before throwing the can into the wastebasket at the end of the counter. He made his way down to the computer where the login screen was just coming up and Zoe was getting out of the chair.

Viktor took a long swig of the thick red drink before setting the glass down to the side and sitting himself down in the chair. He typed in his full name, then his password before hitting enter. The screen froze for a moment before going black. Amber text scrolled from the bottom to the top of the screen too fast to read for a few seconds, then went back to black before the words 'Priority Access Granted' flashed in the center before returning to the log in screen. Viktor repeated his previous steps.

The screen went black one last time before going to a similar menu as the one Zoe was used to... but with far more options. He hit the Mail icon immediately, and as the page filled with correspondence Zoe couldn't help but notice the download bar, which had taken hours for her, seemed to fill multiple times per second for Viktor, who already had more mail backdated to the first week than Zoe had received in her entire hermitage.

"I think I'll be getting the most benefit from our little deal."

Viktor sat rooted to the chair, the glass of V8 suspended midway between the table and his mouth, wide-eyed at the still increasing volume of correspondence filling the screen.

"I think you're probably right."

~

Day 79

The muzzle of the small revolver shook as it waved first in one direction, then in the other, seemingly in sync with the breaths that Jesse and Linda took.

"Now Doc, this lady ain't done nothing to ya, and I sure as hell ain't neither. So why don't you just do us all a favor and put the gun down, okay?"

"Jesse, you've been of great help to me these past few weeks, but anybody who was down in those isolation levels either did me harm or intended to. The peaceful and reasonable ones took their chances and left. Those of them who didn't were dangerous, they threatened

303

me and the Project. I can't allow that threat to continue."

"Doc, for Christ's sakes, she's half froze to death and unarmed. You're armed, and I'm armed, I can cuff her —"

"Do it."

"Doc..."

"*Now*, Jesse, or I'll start pointing this anywhere I hear movement or breathing and pull the trigger!"

"Calm down, Doc! I'm gonna cuff her but you've got to let me know I'm not gonna get shot when I unsnap the holster."

"I'm not unreasonable."

"Well, to be fair, you ain't exactly broadcasting the picture of sanity right this second neither."

"Get her cuffed Jesse!"

"Alright alright... keep yer lab coat on..."

Jesse reached behind him and unsnapped the leather holster for his handcuffs, bringing them out he looked to Linda before raising a single finger to his lips. He then placed one handcuff against his own wrist and snapped it closed, then he put the other cuff against the same wrist and did the same.

"Okay, Doc, she's cuffed."

"Do you think I'm an idiot?"

"Uh, what?"

"They blinded me last time I tried to contain them, Jesse. Do you really think I'd believe she'd willingly submit without struggle or complaint? Cuff her, Jesse; for real this time."

Linda let slip a sob as she put out her hands in front of her to be cuffed. Jesse heaved a sigh as he reached into his pocket for his keys, then searched them until he found the handcuff key, then unlocked them from his wrist before handcuffing Linda.

"Now Jesse, remove the handcuff key from your keys and give it to me."

"Doc, you'd be able to hear if I was gonna —"

Dr. Rafei pointed the revolver in Jesse's direction.

"I'm not brooking any argument on this point! Take the key off and give it to me now, Jesse!"

"Alright, Doc... you win." Jesse removed the handcuff key from his keys and held it out to the doctor. "Here, take it."

Dr. Rafei put a hand out. As Jesse placed the handcuff key in his palm, Dr. Rafei reached forward and grabbed Jesse's sleeve before pulling Jesse closer and jamming the revolver against his chest.

"Do you really think I'm that stupid!? You've got spares even if you really did cuff her this time! Don't you understand the importance of my work!? Of what I can do to save humanity!? Do you understand what they did to me!? What they took!?"

"Doc, calm the fuck down! Ain't nobody here trying to hurt you!"

"No, I'm just surrounded by Judases who don't understand the depth of their betrayal! But I only need one of you to drive the truck!"

With that Dr. Rafei pulled the trigger on the pistol. Once, twice, three times. The report of the revolver firing into Jesse's chest at point blank range was deafening in the confines of the trucks rear.

As such, as Dr. Rafei released Jesse, who immediately fell to the side, he did not hear Linda as she picked up one of the ammunition boxes from its slot in the floor. Her first strike was aimed directly at his hand, knocking the pistol from his shattered fingers. The second blow was equally as accurate as it crushed his temple like wet cardboard hit by a bowling ball.

Linda stood shocked at herself. She dropped the ammo can and covered her mouth to stifle the sudden onslaught of fear, rage, relief, and sadness that threatened to pour out.

The ringing echoes of the gunshots and the ammo can impacting the floor of the truck had barely stopped when the rat-a-tat of impacts all over the truck awoke Linda's most pressing fear and instincts. She scrambled to stand on top of the askew ammo can and crouch away from the ceiling and walls. The ammo can, however, couldn't stay stable at the angle it was and shortly fell over, throwing her atop Jesse's prone form.

"Ugghhiiii..."

The high pitched squeal of the last of his air being squeezed out sounded like the dying hiss of some bizarre tropical lizard. Jesse's hands twitched and shook as he urgently motioned for her to get off of him. Once Linda had rolled off, Jesse began gasping in lungfuls of air, replacing the volume that had been pushed out of him first by the doctor's .38 and then by Linda's weight.

Linda looked on in confusion and amazement as Jesse unbuckled his vest and pulled it off, two smashed rounds dislodging from its weave. Jesse then reached inside his shirt and pulled out a small .38 of his own from an interior pocket, the wooden grip splintered and useless from the third slug embedded there. Placing it in his lap, he continued to strip, removing shirts until he was bare-chested, his left breast marred by a softball sized bruise roughly shaped like the state of Florida.

He moved back, leaning up against the wheel hump and the freezing metal of the lockers mounted above it. His chest still heaved as he then took his bearings. He motioned to Linda to pick up the doctor's .38 and hand it over. Once she'd retrieved it he unloaded his own, reloaded the doctor's, and threw his old one aside.

"Linda, right?"

"Yes?"

"Check the doc, would ya?"

306

"O-okay..."

Linda tentatively reached over and pressed her fingers against Rafei's neck, holding them there for several seconds.

"He's got a pulse. It's weak, but steady. He's still alive."

"What kind of doctor are ya?"

"Excuse me?"

"Are ya a surgeon, or a podiatrist, or what? What's your specialty?"

"I'm a Virologist."

"Bug Doctor."

"In a way. Little bugs, viruses, like HIV."

"Yeah... I get it."

"How about you? What do you do?"

"I'm a metal worker."

Linda looked blankly at Jesse, her mouth agape... She glanced at the body armor, the weapons, the gear in the wire cages lining the walls of the truck.

"A metal worker...?"

~

Day 79

Longmire took his replacement cup of coffee from a young seaman who was making the rounds since the disturbance.

"Helmsman, cut engines back to one quarter, rudder to one seven five."

"Aye, sir."

307

"Cox!"

"Yes sir?"

"Get a team topside, stay in the sail. Use IR goggles to do a purely visual inspection of the foredeck. But before you go up there, send another team to the forward torpedo room get me an updated report on that flooding."

"Aye, sir."

"Sonar!"

"Yes sir?"

"Distance to surface contacts?"

"Two point seven five miles, sir."

"Colquitt!"

"Yes sir?"

"What's our current position?"

"We are... five nine miles south southwest of Long Island."

At that point Seaman Watkins emerged from the forward hatch in wet coveralls.

"Sir?"

"Yes, Watkins?"

"Report from the forward torpedo room. We've got flooding coming in through the overhead from the forward berthing compartment. Pumps are keeping up for now but if it gets much worse we'll be in trouble."

"Get back forward and monitor those pumps, then. If they start falling behind, you report it immediately."

Watkins shouted an 'aye, sir' as he hurried from the bridge through the forward hatch. The flashing light and repetitive tone of the intra-ship telephone system alerted Captain Longmire to an incoming call. According to the readout next to the receiver cradle, it was coming from the sail. Longmire waved off the navigator who went to answer it and picked it up himself.

"Bridge, Captain speaking."

"Sir, this is Cox."

"Tell me something good, Cox."

"Sir, the foredeck is all torn to shreds. Missed the ballast tanks... no idea how. The forward berthing compartment looks to have been vented. I'm watching the Atlantic surge in and out with wave action and the motion of the boat. I'm not seeing any survivors in the water."

"Damn. Alright, what else?"

"The sail itself was hit sir. It looks like the sail mounted sonar array is wrecked. The antennae cluster housing is all kinds of bashed up too."

"And we traded in the towed array for those extra torpedo countermeasures back at Pearl... shit. We're incommunicado. Get back down here, Cox."

"Uh... sir?"

"Is there more?"

"We're in visual range of those surface contacts, sir."

"Okay, well what are they?"

"*Magic* and *Globe*, sir; can't make out the others."

"Say again, Cox. I must've misheard you."

"A cruise ship and a container ship, sir. *Disney Magic* and the *CSCL*

Globe, big bastards, both of 'em. Looks like they've smashed together with two or three smaller ships too... maybe yachts. I'm seeing one bow nearly vertical on the other side of 'em. Must be a ship found equilibrium instead of sinking somehow... can't tell what is yet."

~

Day 79

Viktor couldn't help but let out a low whistle as the screen finally settled, 251 unread messages.

Zoe's eyes were locked on the screen as well.

"So... you want to maybe illuminate why it is that you get emails from the Project multiple times a day while I get, like, four?"

"I'm not sure."

"Viktor..."

"I'm serious, Zoe. I've been on assignment for the duration. This is my first chance to get into contact with the Project."

"Well, let's check out what they've been sending you."

"Uh... looks like... mostly... general updates. Like, a daily newsletter from the North Carolina Facility. Shit, I think most of this is spam!"

"The world ends, most of humanity dies, and spam lives on. What an appropriate legacy for mankind."

"Yeah, yeah, yeah... there's still actual communiques in the mix."

"Let's see them."

"Do you think it might be just a tad easier if I just go through them and sum up? I'll let you keep access so you can confirm, but I don't think sitting over my shoulder is going to be very conducive to this, especially if you're going to ask questions every thirty seconds."

"Why would you think I'd ask questions like that?"

Viktor laughed. "Because we went through the Project orientation together. I remember you interrupting with questions every other sentence."

"Oh... yeah. I forgot about that..."

"So, if you don't mind?"

"Oh... yes, of course."

Two hours later.

"Zoe!"

Zoe grunted from the couch, her attention riveted to her sketchpad.

"*Zoe!*"

"Oh. Uh... yeah, you finished?"

"Indeed I am."

Zoe set aside her sketchpad and sashayed up the steps from the sunken living area to the computer cubby where Viktor sat reclined, his long legs crossed at the ankles and his arms crossed over his chest.

"Well?"

"You first, how much do you know about what's going on in the outside world."

"Just what the Project emails and the Emergency Alert System tells me."

"So you know about the things in the sky?"

"Don't look at them, don't attract their attention with heat, light, or movement, they cocoon vehicles and structures they know contain survivors, they can't be seen in infrared or ultraviolet and they get bored and leave after three or four hours without stimulation."

"Textbook. Now, what about the other things, the ones on the ground?"

"Uh... tall, about eleven feet, long limbed, intelligent, aggressive, tool-using, coordinated, hostile. They also somehow absorb heat from their environment, leading to unnaturally low temperatures everywhere they go."

"Good. That's about... well that's... that's what the public knows."

"But the Project knows more?"

"Oh yeah... I mean, not a lot more. And not as much as the Japanese, at least I don't think, but more than the public, what remains of them."

"So fill me in."

Viktor indicated a stool near the kitchen island, which Zoe immediately retrieved and seated herself on. Viktor leaned forward and began.

"Okay, from the beginning of everything or from the beginning of this ordeal?"

"From the beginning."

"Well... alright. But I've only got the barest understandings of some of it, and some sounds like more legend than history."

"That's okay."

"A long time ago in Japan there was a war. One of those old wars over territory and honor and some such thing. One Samurai of one side, after the barest victory, wounded, took refuge from the weather in a cave on the slopes of Mount Unebi. There, he was discovered by a hermit, the last in a long and once-noble line stretching back before the dawn of history.

"This hermit was childless, and so he showed the Samurai a secret

312

entrance deep in the back of a cave to a series of underground tunnels running through the mountain. The passages led miles down into the dark. After passing many fantastic sights, traps of the mind, temptations and horrors, at the bottom the hermit showed the Samurai his secret. An army of stone beings standing at attention in passages surrounding a central chamber. In the chamber was a glowing figure made of crystal.

"The hermit told the Samurai that his line had guarded the cave for generations beyond count. Passing from father to son and when necessary father to daughter to mother to son, the secret of their existence. They were sleeping, awaiting the conditions under which they could awake. According to the... well whatever it is, myth, legend, history... the army would awaken only when the skies are about to turn hostile."

"Okay..."

"Anyway... the Samurai honored the hermits request and took guardianship of the cave. His children did as well. And over time the successes of his family multiplied and their fortunes grew... culminating in their supplanting of the previous Imperial family, and taking control of Japan in the sixth century BC. This was done by the Samurai's descendant, who became known as Emperor Jimmu, the progenitor of the modern Imperial line."

"Bullshit."

"This is what they told me, okay? I might've left out some details, honorifics and whatnot... but this is what they believe. And I've got reason to think they're right about a goodly portion of it. If I might continue?"

"Yeah, sure, go on."

"That secret, the secret of Mount Unebi, has been passed down through the Imperial line ever since. After WWII, Emperor Shōwa, Hirohito, y'know... he decided it would be... prudent... to establish a series of subterranean shelters, unbeknownst to the Japanese people or the West, in case of nuclear war, to shelter himself, his family,

313

and those Japanese who were loyal to the Imperial Family only and not to the occupied interim government."

"Most governments did around that time. The atom bomb was a game changer."

"True, but these were different. At first they were just for the Imperial Family and their loyal entourage. Construction was begun amidst the rebuilding period immediately after the surrender. After their new constitution came about in '47 and the Emperor became a figurehead and Japan was deprived of anything but a paltry and ineffective defensive force, the idea expanded to include specific loyal members of the new government, their families, and an elite guard, a military force trained and equipped to carry out covert operations for the good of Japan. They've been essentially dormant for decades, the occasional intelligence foray against China, but nothing major until four months ago."

"What happened four months ago?"

"The army in Mount Unebi woke up."

CHAPTER 28

Day 79

Eldritch was kneeling, going through one of the duffel bags they'd been carrying since the consulate nearly two hours before. A slight grunt indicated he'd found what he was looking for. Standing, he pulled out a small foil wrapped package of granola bars before ripping it open and handing one to Sharon. Unwrapping his own, he took a large bite before speaking with a hushed voice between chews, flecks of granola erupting with each word he spit out.

"So you figure even if we missed them by hours we've got a bit of a chance that they may be waiting at the waterfront for a spell *just on the off chance* that you or other survivors may show up?"

Sharon looked up at the low hanging fog, barely 30 feet above their heads.

"We've been fortunate enough not to be too noisy, for the sounds we make to be dampened by distance and the weather. Whatever tracked vehicle they moved off in certainly wouldn't have been quiet, so they would've had to stop, sit, and wait for the things to lose interest. That wait may give us the time we need. Plus, they would've had to move from land to sea in shifts, and whatever Opperthorne had may have taken a good long while to get aboard."

"So we're still looking to meet up with Longmire and the US Navy, eh?"

"Yes. It's the safest way off this island, since you can't call for pickup."

"Ehh... bollocks! I might as well throw my lot in with the US of A. The Royal Marines've prolly writ me off as worm food by now. Lead the way, lass."

Without another word they picked up their gear and started slowly Making their way east along 84th street, they stayed always aware of how much noise they were making and the gentle rolling of the fog overhead, their only real protection against a rapid and unpleasant death.

After a block, Eldritch suddenly motioned for Sharon to halt before he made a slow purposeful walk across the street to a large white panel van parked along the road. Emblazoned across its side read *East Side Medical Supply* in large fluffy blue letters. After fiddling with the lock for a moment Eldritch retrieved a knife from his pouch and punched it through the rubber gasket running around the rear door. A moment later there was a gentle click as he broke the lock. Opening the door, he climbed inside for a moment, seemingly searching. He emerged a minute later with an odd sort of a bag containing a series of rods and straps. Coming back, he indicated the bag with a tilt of his head.

"Look-see what I've rummaged up, eh? It's an adjustable brace! As soon as we're aboard the *Oregon* we can set this up and adjust it and it'll fit to your leg and torso and help you to hirplin, eh?"

Sharon nodded, sweat dripping from her chin as she did so. Her skin was still too pale for Eldritchs liking.

"Good thinking, but it's only a mile and a half to the river. We can make it that far easy."

"Aye, I might, but you're not looking too well."

Sharon managed a half smile before taking a deep shaky breath and responding.

"I'll admit, I haven't felt too well since we left Chinatown. I worry

316

some kind of infection might be setting in. I was shot, you know, twice."

"Aye, lass, I know. I think we may need to make a stop at a chemist as soon as we can."

"Chemist?"

"Eh, pillsy? Drug store, ya know? Chemists?"

"Pharmacy?"

"Aye! There's a cannie lass! We stop by yer pharmacist and we grab an antibiotic, one of them that fights near e'rething and we give ya a loadin' dose and we take as many as we can carry to keep givin' ya o'er time."

"Okay, we'll do that, as soon as we get to the river. There's bound to be a pharmacy somewhere along the way."

"Aye."

~

Sharon and Eldritch looked over the East River from the East 90th Street Ferry Terminal. The ferry itself was not in attendance. The river itself was frozen a sheer white sheet from the shore of Manhattan all the way across to Brooklyn on the other side.

"I don't know which way they were from here. North or south?"

Eldritch chuffed a despondent groan before pointing upriver.

"North, but I think we're too late."

Following his gesture, squinting to make out details in the darkness and fog, Sharon looked upriver where they could just make out the shape of a submarine's conning tower slipping below the waves, a flurry of bubbles indicating the sub was in a dive as it disappeared, leaving nothing but a large hole in the ice to indicate it had ever been there.

"Aw hell... fuuuck..."

"Aye, lass, that's a fair sum up. What now, eh?"

"Motherf... I don't know. I don't fucking know. The only plan I really had was to escape this miserable island and get somewhere else."

"We could still walk across the bridges..."

"The bridges are all immense things set high over the water, and that means they're likely over the fog too. They're death traps. We can't use a car; it'll be too loud. Same for a chopper or a plane. They're supposedly sound if you've got IR or UV vision, but we only have one set of IR goggles and no UV. That's one failed battery away from a deadly wreck we don't walk away from."

"What about by sea?"

"The river is frozen."

"Aye, but she's cracking. Look southerly, lass."

Sharon followed his lead and looked downriver. In the distance, she could see that he was right. The ice was starting to fracture and crack, there were thin lines of open water already forming as the pieces slowly started flowing south with the current.

"That's it, then. We head south to the bay and take boat. There are supply warehouses all along the waterfront we may be able to use to supply us for a long trip, then we head to sea and go south to DC. If there's any authority that's survived, it'll be there."

~

Day 5

More Jell-O. Or, whatever Jell-O like substance the Japanese preferred. Today's flavor seemed to be green tea and... kiwi, perhaps? Honeydew, maybe...? It was hard to tell. He wondered sometimes if maybe the taste buds of the Japanese were different. His reverie was interrupted by his doctor's daily visit, his third since

318

waking up in this room rather than the big room with the patrolling guards and nurses.

"Good morning, Viktor. Still feeling very well today, yes?"

"Just like yesterday and the day before. How much longer am I to be kept here?"

"I couldn't tell you until today, but just one more day. You see, all optional companions brought in must undergo a thorough delousing and a battery of tests before we can let you rejoin your advocate. As of this morning, the primary cultures were ready, and you and those others who aren't carriers of a specific list of unacceptable diseases will be allowed out into the facility."

"If I'm free of them, why the days delay now?"

"We're very careful here. We have a backup panel we took the second day after you arrived. It's extremely unlikely, but there is a statistical chance the first panel missed something. With the primary passed, the secondary is mostly just a formality, but I'm confident you'll be reunited with your advocate tomorrow."

"And then what?"

"Then, Viktor, then you survive."

"Was that in doubt?"

"More than you'd think. We see the current situation as an opportunity. You see, if nobody with a disease carries it through this event, then that disease will be effectively wiped out. If we can eradicate it ourselves we will, but then there's the danger of a Typhoid Mary, an immune carrier that will infect others on the other side. That's too great a danger. But you seem fit as a fiddle, and the medical records provided by Madam Koike seem quite in order."

"Nobody's told me just what the hell is going on. What are we hiding from? What is this event? War? Solar flare?"

"Oh no, nothing like that, but... well, let's just leave that for tomorrow after that second panel, yes?"

"Doc, just, answer me this one question, who are these soldiers that are everywhere? They're not JSDF, the uniforms, the weapons... they're completely different."

"Yes... tomorrow, after the panel, don't worry, all your questions will be answered. Just, bear with us, yes?"

Viktor relaxed back into the bed in silent assent, his doctor smiling and giving one of those little half bows before turning and walking out the door. Viktor contemplated going back to sleep but decided he'd had enough for one day.

Viktor had been having periodic visits from nurses checking his vitals every few hours since he'd awoke here, but they had no monitors on him, just the handcuffs attached to his ankle and the bed railing. He reached for the remote, knowing as before that the TV would display only static on 99 of its channels and a test pattern on the last. But this time he wasn't going for the TV functions, or the bed controls. He decided to try something new, he hit the call button. It was barely three seconds before a scratchy but obviously feminine voice answered.

"Yes, Mr. Viktor? Is something the matter?"

"I'm thirsty. Would it be at all possible to get a cup of coffee or something?"

"We do not have a coffee machine on this floor. However, I can brew you a cup of tea if you like."

"Do you have anything other than green tea?"

"I think we may have a few other kinds in the break room. Would you like me to check?"

"Please. If it's no trouble."

"Not at all. I'll be in in a few minutes."

"Thank you."

As the remote clicked off Viktor pushed down his blankets and sheets to the foot of the bed, exposing his muscular calves. He pulled his gown down tighter around his body, exposing its outline more prominently. Then, he waited, like a spider awaiting its prey.

~

Day 79

Captain Longmire swirled his nearly drained cup of coffee in impatience.

"Sonar."

"Aye, sir?"

"Distance to target?"

"One point three miles, sir."

"Helmsman, full stop. Don't reverse us to, just shut 'em down and let us drift to a stop."

"Aye, sir."

Longmire moved from where he was leaned up against the port bulkhead and went to the center console. Looking over the board at the noted damaged sections and the most recent figures on the pumping out of the forward berthing compartment, he sat down and pulled out a notebook and pocket calculator.

Cox entered the bridge from the aft passageway, still wearing the all-weather coat he'd worn while in the sail.

"Sir..."

"Oh, good, Cox, sit down here a second, get that coat off. I need you to check my math here."

"Math?"

"Yeah, just go over these numbers really quick, make sure I got 'em right."

"Aye sir."

"Meanwhile, did you see anything unusual about the *Globe* and the *Magic* up there?"

"You mean more unusual than that they're parked alongside each other like they're meant to be that way?"

"Yeah, did you see any signs of life aboard?"

"Details are hard to make out at a distance in infrared, sir."

"I know, I know, but did anything stand out to you? Any exhaust from the stacks or anything? Any unusual heat sources?"

"Uh... your numbers are good, sir. But, uh, no, both of 'em are still, quiet, and cold so far as I can tell."

The redheaded sonarman once more stuck his head out of his cubby, one headphone still pressed in place, the other dangling.

"Now that we're closer, I'm getting some noise out of them, sir."

"What kind of noise?"

"Hard to tell, but this isn't wave action on the hull or pressure creaks... sounds like shipboard activity... but there's no engine noises running through and over it all like I'm used to. Footsteps on decks, muted and distorted voices, objects being scraped on tables, that sort of thing. It's all getting channeled through their hull and put out in the water... it's just real, real faint, sir."

"Can you tell which ship it's coming from?"

"No sir, they're way too close, and touching like they are they're echoing each other vibrations going back and forth like nobody's business."

"Alright. Cox, here's the plan. *Magic* would've had a helluva lot

322

more people aboard her, so if there's people I'm betting they're there. I want you to go ahead and get together a boarding party and get over there and find them. Take as many extra IR goggles as we can spare. Let them know that there are survivors elsewhere."

Cox looked genuinely confused as he responded.

"Sir, there's no way we can take survivors aboard. We don't have the room and we're already in dire straits because of whatever hit us!"

"Cox, settle down. We're not taking survivors aboard."

"Then what're we doing, sir?"

"Salvage. That ship was in good shape, you said?"

"Yes sir, but..."

"Then they, unlike us, have an undamaged communications suite over there we can use to report in. Furthermore, if we can get her detached from the *Globe* and whatever ship's on the other side of the *Globe*, we can give them enough IR goggles to pilot the ship themselves, get her engines started, get her moving. She can follow us down to North Carolina, get those civilians somewhere safe."

"And what if they can't, sir? What if she's out of fuel and her batteries are dead and she's a useless hulk, what then?"

"Then we try the *Globe*. Either way, there's likely to be useful salvage we can take from the *Globe*. Who knows what she was shipping, might even be foodstuffs we can haul back to the Project."

"And survivors?"

"You're right, we can't take 'em aboard. But one ship or the other, we might get them under power and ashore."

"And the other case?"

"What other case?"

"What if it's not people over there, but those Giants?"

~

Day 79

"Seriously? A metal worker...?"

"Well... yeah."

And you survived the apocalypse?

"I'm not sure we should call this 'the apocalypse' per se... I mean, just cuz most'a mankind's gone the way the dodo don't mean the world stops spinning."

"Semantics aside how did a metal worker — no offense — how did a metal worker survive a cataclysm like this?"

"Well, I was prepared for it, that's how."

"Prepared? How were you prepared for something nobody in their right mind could've seen coming?"

"Well, I wasn't prepared specifically for this scenario, no, but a sort of general 'end of the modern first world' situation... yeah. Canned goods, guns and ammo, heavy duty vehicle, couple'a thousand gallons of fuel stashed away. Weren't nothin' special about what I did. Hell, I was just fortunate to be at home and able to jump into m'bunker when the emergency alert system went off."

"So... so you were one of those doomsday prepper type folks...?"

"I don't think, considering the current state of things, anyone would say such preparations were unwise, would you?"

"No... no I suppose not... it's just surprising, that's all..."

"Survival of the fittest, ma'am."

"I certainly can't disagree at this point. Speaking of survival, what are we going to do with Doctor Rafei?"

"I don't know. I mean, part of me thinks he wasn't joking about how

324

important it was to get his materials to them Project folks — er... he did tell y'all about that, right?"

"Yes, he did."

"Okay, just making sure we're on the same page here. As I was sayin', part of me wants to get him and his notes there, just let them deal with him. I mean, looking at that head wound I don't think there'll be much chance he'll tattle on us—"

"No."

"—but at the same time, carting a half dead blind man all the way to North Carolina don't seem to make much sense."

"No."

"On the other hand, the folks at the Project ain't gonna be stupid, they'll examine us and interrogate us; hell, they might even drug us! There ain't no telling... but they might just find out we was involved with the good Doctor getting the way he is and they might not be too hap—"

Jesse was interrupted by sudden movement from Rafei, who rolled over onto his back, flailing his arms ahead of him at the roof of the truck as if swatting away a cloud of gnats. His voice was uncharacteristically heavy and slow as he cried out.

"Gods! Formless Gods! They're not meant for us! It's too soon! They must be recalled! We're not ready! The way is closed to us and the bridge must stay unbuilt!"

His flailing arms fell to the sides, one hitting the door to the cab of the truck, the other falling across Jesse's ankle as Rafei seemed to slip once more into unconsciousness.

Jesse broke the shocked silence first.

"Oh no, he definitely ain't—"

Rafei's hand suddenly grasped Jesse's ankle with a deceptive strength as his bandaged head rolled over and seemed to peer up at him where he sat before once more speaking:

"They're wrong, Jesse! They've made the wrong assumptions, dismissed the wrong possibilities! If you don't save them from themselves, they'll end any chance you have... oh... oh they're coming..."

Linda looked on in alarm as Rafei seemed to momentarily stiffen before relaxing, his hand falling off Jesse's leg as his last breath escaped him.

"Well. That solves that issue, I guess..."

"Yeah… but maybe it raises another."

"What do you mean?"

"You ever dream, ma'am?"

~

Day 79

Cox looked expectantly at his captain as he considered the possibility his question raised. The captain paused briefly before continuing.

"Tell you what. Since the Giants don't kill on sight, if you see one, high tail it back to the *Oregon* and we'll make best speed for North Carolina. It's one thing if there's people we can help, but according to the EAS broadcasts we don't have a chance in hell of fighting them, so if we run into them we don't even try."

"'We', sir? Don't tell me you're planning on coming along. Just a second ago it was me and a boarding party."

"Sorry, you're right... habit. I should stay here. But I want you on the radio constantly. Step by step reports. 'I have arrived at the ship, I am boarding the ship, I have boarded the ship'. Stupid-simple level of blunt and comprehensive reporting, got it?"

"Yes sir. Any recommendations as to who I should take with me?"

"Watkins and Kellogg have experience ashore in the current tactical situation, and they may be some kind of good luck charm. They found their way back once; it might help. Them and three others, leave two near wherever you board to make sure your means back is secure."

"Aye sir, anything else?"

"Yeah, when you get on deck keep quiet as you can but look around. I'd hate to think whatever hit us is lining up another shot."

"Aye, sir."

"Dismissed. Sonar!"

The sonarman, Colquitt, poked his fiery head out of his cubby once more.

"Yes, sir?"

"Any further info you can give me? Any more contacts? Clearer sounds coming from those ships?"

"No sir, nothing new making noise in the water."

"Well, at least that's some good news, I hope."

The handheld radio sitting in its charging cradle screwed to the bulkhead cracked to life. Longmire strode the three steps to it and clicked the volume up.

"Can you hear me, sir?"

"Well enough, Cox. Go ahead."

"Sir, I've got the party assembled by the ventral hatch, we're about to go above deck."

"Very well, proceed."

"Opening hatch... Watkins is ascending the ladder. He reports no unusual activity. I'm following..."

"Take your time, I don't want you getting sloppy."

"Aye, sir... the deck is clear, waters a bit choppy. There's probably a four knot wind coming out of the south southwest. Sir...?"

"Yes, what is it?"

I think I know what hit us sir. About a half mile astern there's a serious gathering of birds.

"Birds?"

"Yes sir. Birds feeding on what looks to be a whale carcass, sir."

"Say again, did you say a whale carcass?"

"Yes sir. It's too distant for me to see what kind, maybe a small white whale or a large humpback, sir..."

"Oh for god's sakes, seriously?"

"Yes sir."

"Well, at least we won't be hearing from the PETA folks on this one... Carry on, Cox; get the Zodiac inflated and boarded."

"Aye, sir."

~

Day 79

Zoe sat forward, on the edge of her seat, held enthralled by Viktor's deep baritone voice unfurling the tale.

"And then what?"

"It was an unmitigated disaster. Due to the depth of the army within the mountain, the pair of Imperial servants sent to monitor them

328

were done in week long shifts. When a pair went down to relieve the last and none came back up, a squad of the Emperors elite were sent down to investigate. Twelve men down after four, one came back. They sealed Mount Unebi immediately after. However, the Imperial Family and the larger Japanese government were only aware of one enclave further abroad, which they'd believe they preempted, and only just in the nick of time, in Beijing."

"Tell me about Beijing later, what about the army in Unebi?"

"The lone survivor reported the fates of the other 15, as well as one very important and heretofore unknown fact. The Giants absorb heat from the surrounding environment with remarkable efficiency. Using that, satellite thermal scans identified six other sites that were the geographical center of sudden marked temperature drops across the globe."

"Where?"

"One each in Australia, India, Russia, Germany, Libya, and America."

"Where here in America?"

"Utah."

"Huh."

"Yeah. Anyway, Japanese 'mineralogists' had discovered another set of catacombs in Beijing during the Japanese occupation during the second Sino-Japanese War that was a part of World War Two. The Imperial Family has been monitoring it ever since through a private shell company that's owned and maintained the entrance site. When the Unebi site went active they were ordered to destroy the tunnels leading into it and evacuate. They did so, and it was reported in the local news as an unexplained subsurface vibration as monitored by seismograph."

"So the army in Beijing is..."

"Buried beneath 400 meters of rock."

"Do we know who built these tunnels and catacombs? Or these armies?"

"Carbon dating puts the tunnels and catacombs at nearly 40,000 years old."

"How could tunnels that old survive?"

"They were extraordinarily well constructed. Stones were fitted together with a form of mortar rivaling modern industrial recipes, and layered. The tunnel walls were layers of these fitted stones five deep, each some being roughly the size of one's head. The mortar mixture was tested. It's anti-fungal, water repellant, airtight. The stones themselves are of uniform density and makeup, mostly granite with impurities of mica and marble... which is astounding."

"Umm... why?"

"Granite and marble are two different kinds of rock. They don't form together in nature. Whoever or whatever made these tunnels used primitive methods, but incredibly advanced materials that we can't replicate."

"So who—"

"Or what."

"—or what built them?"

"We don't know. The Army, the Giants, the Tall Ones... according to the EAS Alerts and the Project Emails they've been observed using simple tools, levers, clubs and the like, but no more advanced technology. Certainly nothing on the order to manufacture bizarre stone and advanced mortar. It's almost like they expected to be discovered and wanted to be mistaken for less advanced than they are."

"Is that good or bad?"

"Neither. It carries no moral weight to it. It's the purpose behind the action which gives it a moral value, and that purpose is unknown."

~

Day 79

Sharon reached down and adjusted the straps keeping the series of metal bars and joints attached tightly to her left leg. She felt the blood rushing to her head and her breath get short, dizziness set in and nausea. She straightened and took a deep breath. Too fast, the dizziness only intensified as she leaned against the doorway leading from the small office they occupied into the larger warehouse beyond.

Eldritch looked up from the desk he was sitting at with concern, a sheaf of papers in his hands as he tried to determine if there was anything useful in the aisles of boxes and pallets beyond.

"You alright?"

"I'm fine. Have you found anything?"

"Seems this is mostly textiles. Rugs, clothing, sheets... all coming in from someplace called Wuhan-Hubei in China."

"Damn. So no food?"

"Doesn't look like it."

"On to the next one."

"Maybe you should rest a bit. You look a little piqued."

"I'm fine."

"Look, I get the whole tough girl bit, but you've been shot and you've been pushing yourself bloody hard. You're no use to me, you, or anyone else if you're dead."

Sharon set her jaw, but said nothing.

"Just saying. We never did find a chemist. It might be best if you find a place to rest for a bit. You're showing classic signs of shock and you can't ignore that."

331

Sharon stared at him with hard eyes before looking away. She hobbled from the doorway to one of the chairs and settled herself into it, a defeated look coming onto her face.

"You're right. I can't keep pushing. The pain in my thigh is making me nauseous. I feel alternatively like I'm on fire or like I'm frozen. Would you be willing to scout inland for a pharmacy while I go from warehouse to warehouse along the waterline looking for anything useful?"

"So long as you take some time to rest at each building, aye."

"Sure."

"Alright. I'm'a go and find you some drugs."

And with that, Eldritch stood and went to the door. Pausing before the opening, he turned back to speak.

"Look, if you find everything we need, but I don't come back within a few hours... you just head out without me."

Sharon looked up at his face, meeting his gaze and seemingly memorizing his face.

"Fuck you, Eldritch. Come back on your own or I'm coming to get you."

Eldritch shook his head, opened the door, and walked out, muttering under his breath.

"Daft woman..."

Sharon let a half smile grace her features before she swiveled the chair and grabbed up one of the clipboards Eldritch was looking through.

~

Day 79

Linda looked at the ever more confusing Jesse with an expression of

332

pure bewilderment.

"Well of course, doesn't everybody?"

"I mean lately, have you dreamt lately?"

"More like nightmares."

Jesse chuckled. "That's right they would be... can't blame ya... but what kind?"

"Does it matter?"

"It might. Doc Rafei there... he said something that sounded a bit crazy there at the end—"

"Well, he did have a traumatic brain injury..."

"—I get that, I do, but... that bit about "formless gods" struck me as familiar. 'Cause, y'see, lately I've been having these dreams."

"...dreams about alien beings without distinct shape..."

"...impossible forms, voices echoing in a void, beckoning, entreating..."

"...a heavy sense of threat and impending horrific doom?"

"Yeah... yeah!"

"..."

"...wait a minute..."

"This is incredibly surreal..."

"That's one way to put it."

"Normally I don't remember my dreams at all but lately these have been..."

"...vivid. Like you can't forget 'em."

"Yeah... wait. Do you think this means something?"

"Well hell yes I think it means something!"

"Well, I mean I'm certain there's a reasonable explanation for it."

"What do you mean?"

"Human psychology is a science. Science depends on repeatable results. Statistics. Maybe there's something about this situation, the psychology of the apocalypse, of desperation and isolation, something that works to cause similar patterns of dreams."

"Ain't that overlooking the obvious?"

"What? Something supernatural?"

"Well, we're sitting in a truck cocooned in flying death that's invisible in infrared or ultraviolet, half froze because of some wicked magical giants that sing EMPs into existence. Supernatural ain't exactly far-fetched no more."

Linda's already perplexed expression darkened.

"...What giants?"

"Aw... shit. I done forgot you been locked up and isolated this whole damn time. It ain't just the sky things that we've got to worry about."

"There's giants?"

"Yeah."

"Like... fee fie fo fum? Beanstalks? Golden eggs?"

"Oh lord no ma'am, hell... these things are about 7 or 8 feet tall, pale as death, freaky shaped arms and legs, all kinds of funky little bumps all over 'em, with no noses, glowing eyes..."

"They sound horrifying."

"They are! And like I said, they get together and sing, and they make this swirling thing made up of lights and then it collapses and shuts down everything."

"And you've seen them? Dealt with them?"

"What'cha mean?"

"Linda looked and gestured pointedly at the various rifles in their cages along the walls."

"Oh, oh no, we watched 'em on the CCTV inside before they mucked everything up. Never run up against em myself. And I don't want to."

"Oh... okay. So... how do we deal with them?"

"I dunno. The EBS said they're about invincible. I ain't exactly looking forward to the opportunity to test that."

"So... any idea where they come from? How they connect with the sky things?"

"Strictly speaking, we don't know they do."

"Well, what are we doing then?"

"We're waiting until the things outside lose interest, then I'm gonna go load up Rafei's notes, set up a flare or two under the gas tanks, then make our way to that place in North Carolina, that place where there's survivors."

"Oh... right. Wait, why would we light a road flare under the gas tank!?"

"The cold's made the diesel fuel gel. We've gotta warm the fuel, make it liquid again, then we can drive on. I already reset the electrical systems, so that's all we're waiting on."

"Oh... well... okay. So we've just got to be quiet and still for a bit?"

"Yep."

"Okay then. I suppose we can always talk on the road."

"Sure can."

"Okay. Well then... I'm going to just wrap up then and try to get a nap."

"Hold on a sec."

Jesse turned and unlatched a hatch to the rear of the driver's side wheel well. Inside were a stack of plastic wrapped silver survival blankets. He pulled out two and handed them over to Linda.

"These should help."

"Thank you."

"You're welcome... and goodnight."

CHAPTER 29

Day 5

There was a slight knock at the door before a slim young nurse came in carrying a tray with a steaming pot of water, two cups, and an assortment of tea bags.

"Mr. Reitmeyer?"

Viktor ignored the sharp mispronunciation of his last name and slightly bowed his head to acknowledge her before indicating she pull over a chair and one of the small tables that could be positioned over his bed. Her eyes smiled at his face as it bowed before rapidly glancing down to his chest, then forearms, crotch, and legs on their way quickly down to the tray. As she went about getting things set Viktor made no effort to hide his own examination of her form in her scrubs, which only served to hide some features while accentuating others.

"So, Mr. Reitmeyer, I hope your processing hasn't been too uncomfortable...?"

"Oh, it has truly been an ordeal. I've been gassed, poked, prodded, interrogated as to my personal habits and history... and the meals have been entirely unsatisfactory. Your hospital food does very little to satisfy a man's... appetites..."

Her eyes grew wide.

~

Viktor adjusted the pillow back beneath his head as Nurse Oren slipped her feet back into her flats, picked up the tray, and with a slight wobble to her step went to the table and gathered up the cold pot of water and the cups — only half finished — back onto her tray before walking out without meeting Viktor's gaze.

Just moments after the door closed Viktor pulled the hairpin from where he'd hidden it under his tongue. Reaching down he pushed the sheets aside and went to work on the handcuffs keeping him attached to the bed. In less than twenty seconds his leg was free and he was furiously rubbing the place the cuff had been, the indented skin evidence of its ill fit on his generous frame.

As soon as he was sated, again, he replaced the cuff, though not as tight this time, and hid the hairpin in his armpit before settling in to take a nap until dinner.

~

Day 79

Cox raised the radio to his face and clicked the mic.

"She's the *Lyubov Orlova*, sir."

Back on the Oregon, sitting at the navigators table, Captain Benjamin Longmire picked up his radio and did the same.

"What is?"

"The ship on the far side with her bow facing sky, sir."

"…should I know that name?"

"She's a Russian passenger liner sir."

"You know her?"

"Yes sir, before I transferred to COMSUBPAC and shipped with the *Oregon* I was with COMSUBLANT, spotted her once before while earning my dolphins aboard the Missouri in 2014 out of Groton. She was actually a little bit of an oddity. She was undertow after being decommissioned and broke free in international waters. The cost of finding and recovering her would've been more than the proceeds of her scrap so she was left to drift, unmanned and unguided."

"So she's a derelict?"

"Has been for years, now she's bow to sky with... looks like her port anchor caught on one of the *Globe's* amidships cargo cranes."

"So she's already stripped of any useful gear?"

"Guaranteed, Captain."

"Then ignore her. Find your way aboard the *Disney Magic*."

"There was a boarding hatch on her port bow we saw on her first way round, looked like it had a recessed access handle. We'll make it around that way."

"Good. Get back to me with any further observations..."

"I have one already sir."

I'm sorry, go ahead then.

"The starboard bow cargo access on the *Globe* is hanging open, ramp extended down into the water. If need be, we could board her no problem."

"How many radios do you have with you?"

"Six, one for each of us."

"Alright, well, first priority is still the *Magic*. Continue headed around and board her; her survivors and communications suite are the only reason we've bothered stopping."

"Aye, sir."

~

"Sir, we're coming around the bow of the *Globe* to the stern of the *Magic* now. I'm seeing a couple of lifeboat davits extended from the port side of the *Magic*... sir! The port side amidships loading ramp of the *Globe* is extended directly onto the *Magic* through some windows on the... looks like the third or fourth deck."

"Is that how they've gotten stuck together?"

"No, sir. I'm also seeing two, no, three of the *Globe's* cargo cranes hooked onto the *Magic* at different points."

"Intentional?"

"Looks that way, sir."

"Interesting… anything else?"

"No, sir."

"Very well, proceed to that entry hatch you spotted."

~

Day 79

Zoe sat silently considering what she'd heard a moment before responding.

"So... what does this mean for us, for the Project, I mean?"

"That's not for you or I to decide. But I do know that the Project is dedicated to ensuring the survival of the human race on the best terms possible. What the Japanese are doing may cause them to butt heads once this whole ordeal is over with."

"Is that likely to happen? I mean, is this going to end?"

"All things do, it's just a matter of time."

"But that time could be years, decades, or even centuries. Mankind couldn't survive underground that long, no matter how well prepared."

"In the past that may have been true, but now? With our technology and a bit of centralized planning and authority?"

Zoe slowly shook her head.

"Absolutely impossible. Technology breaks down. Even if you have a hundred people trained to fix it you've got a limited supply of spare parts and materials to create spare parts. Diseases will evolve, social bonds and barriers will break. Over any significant length of time, no amount of preparedness or planning will be up to the task."

"That sounds like simple pessimism."

"Oh no, normally I'm very optimistic, but on this all you have to do is look at history. Lost colonies, exploratory parties, settlers traveling across continents, there's numerous examples of isolated groups in dangerous situations ending up devolving into desperation and anarchy no matter how well prepared or led they were."

"Things fall apart; the centre cannot hold; mere anarchy is loosed upon the world, the blood-dimmed tide is loosed, and everywhere the ceremony of innocence is drowned; the best lack all conviction, while the worst are full of passionate intensity."

"Shakespeare?"

"Yeats. But just as fatalistic as Shakespeare."

"Realistically, I think... I wonder... I'm the Projects answer to preserving the Art of the old world. Do you think there's another bunker out there with someone dedicated to preserving the literature?"

"I know there is. I met him, shared a flight with him, he's an associate professor in California, has a very similar cushy bunker somewhere in the Sierra Nevadas loaded down with essentially the entire Library of Congress backed up three times, just in case."

"How'd you meet?"

"Doctor Rodriguez introduced us before we went to our assignments. Then he happened be flying on the same plane I was headed for the West Coast, of course for me it was just the first leg."

"Huh. So anyway... what exactly are the Japanese doing?"

"They're—"

Viktor leaned forward to answer but was interrupted by a buzzer coming from the control panel set into the wall of the living room. Someone, or something, was asking for access through the secondary airlock, just as Viktor himself had earlier that day.

CHAPTER 30

Day 79

Cox grabbed onto the handle with both hands and heaved, his feet set
in the bow of the Zodiac forcing it forward and squashing the
inflatable side against the hull of the Magic. The handle remained
flat in its place within the recessed hatchway. Placing one booted
foot against the frame and trying again with greater leverage, he was
rewarded with a high pitched creak just before the rubber seal around
the door parted and allowed the atmosphere to equalize on both sides
with a hiss. Then the handle moved more easily to withdraw the
latch from the frame and the door began to open in earnest, swinging
inside the ship.

As Cox pushed the hatch, Watkins and Kellogg moved forward, their
sidearms out and pointed at sky before they moved past Cox and into
the *Magic*. Their initial sweep ensured the small entryway beyond
held no surprises. The inside was cheerfully painted in aquamarine
and yellows, with a deep burgundy industrial carpet underfoot.
Railings along the side were polished brass and the walls were
adorned with colorful vinyl stickers of the most popular Disney
Characters associated with maritime adventures. Captain Hook,
Nemo, Ariel, & the whole cast of Jake & the Neverland Pirates

looked down on the Navy boarders with looks of glee, seeming almost malevolent in the shadows cast by the flashlights. There were also a few signs mounted on the walls and hanging from the ceiling directing boarding passengers where to go.

"Clear!"

"Clear!"

Cox secured the hatch with a chain and hook inside before reaching back for the radio on his belt.

"Captain?"

"Go, Cox."

"Sir, according to the signs posted here, we're in the forward tender lobby. I can see on the forward bulkhead a line of four elevators. There are signs directing along a forward passageway to a health center... probably some kind of gym... and aft to passenger cabins and the amidships elevator lobby."

"Any signs of habitation so far?"

"Not really, no, sir. Everything's dark. She seems to be without power. There's detritus in the halls... trash, papers, brochures and maps, looks like."

"Grab one, we don't know the layout of the ship."

"Sir I've got one in my hand already. It looks like they're just maps of the public areas of the ship."

"Damn. Any idea where the bridge is? What about the galley? If there's survivors, I'd bet they're there."

"The bridge is... Deck 8. Galley is... best bet, deck 3, that seems like where most of the restaurants are."

"Say again, did you say the bridge is on Deck 8?"

"Yes sir. Apparently the decks here go from the keel up rather than from the superstructure down."

"So what deck are you on now?"

"Looks like Deck 1 sir."

"They don't count the decks below the waterline?"

"Apparently not, sir, not according to this map, anyway. Probably to avoid confusing the passengers."

"Great. Well, make your way to deck 3, keep away from any windows, don't take your goggles off, and see if you can locate a more accurate map in one of the crew only areas."

"Yes sir."

~

Day 79

Viktor turned his head and gazed down at the sunken living room area.

"What's that?"

Zoe's shoulders slumped.

"The doorbell."

"Pardon?"

"It's the buzzer from the secondary airlock. Same place you came in."

"So somebody else is here?"

"Two new visitors in as many days after months of nothing."

"You must be excited."

"Concerned, actually. I'm wondering what I did to get so popular."

The buzzing once more rang out from the panel across the way.

"You should probably go answer that."

"Yeah probab— wait, what? Me? What about us? Won't you go with me?"

"I'd like to but I don't think it's wise."

"Why not!?"

"I have more information. If the people or person at that door is hostile, if they appear innocuous and then become a danger, then my information will be lost before I can make a full report."

"Oh, so I'm expendable but you're too precious to risk answering a door!?"

"I didn't say that."

"But that's what you meant!"

"Not at all I just—"

The insistent buzzing interrupted them yet again.

"Whatever, you... you just do whatever you've got to do. I'm going to go see who it is."

With that Zoe rose and marched from the room. Her bare feet scraping against the concrete into the distance never faltering or slowing.

Viktor considered for a moment following, but quickly decided against it. Pulling a thumb drive from his armpit he took his momentary solitude as a blessing and inserted it into the USB on the front of the computer. Attaching its contents to an email he sent it to the Project server. After that he formatted the USB drive before copying over Zoe's reports and emails.

~

Zoe kicked aside yet another piece of Viktor's makeshift outfit as she stalked through the aisles of the warehouse on her way to the airlock. The entire warehouse was beginning to reek of their foul miasma. She made a mental note to go through with a pair of tongs and a garbage bag later and dispose of them.

Coming around the final corner her pace faltered as she saw what awaited her in the airlock.

Eight men in military uniform, each with IR Goggles, a rifle, and balaclava under their helmets.

~

Day 79

Linda awoke to an unfamiliar vibration running through her entire body. It made her teeth chatter, her insides quiver, and set off every aching joint she had. The freezing cold and the unearthly sounds that accompanied the vibration seemed to penetrate to her very bones, and the pulsing red light broke through her eyelids like an angry dawn. In an odd sort of way, it was... peaceful. It felt like giving up, like sinking into death. An abrupt and decidedly unpleasant bump that broke her reverie assured her that was not the case. Her eyes snapped open and she realized the interior of the truck was bathed in red light bleeding in from the taillight mounts.

Suddenly she recognized the vibrations and sounds that had plagued her as the sounds of the truck running and on the road. After months without being in a vehicle the once familiar sensations had felt alien to her.

She looked around the cargo area of the truck and realized she was alone. Jesse would surely be in the cab, but Rafei's corpse was nowhere to be found. Even the small drops of blood that had fallen to the deck after she'd killed him seemed to have been wiped up.

Raising herself up off her back into a sitting position was agonizing as every muscle and joint screamed in resistance, but she pushed through the pain and got herself there.

With another minute of effort, some stretching, and some challenges to her balance from the road and suspension, she got herself standing and facing the hatch leading to the cab.

Considering how long she'd known Jesse, she considered knocking, but in the end she dismissed that as misplaced sentiment and simply unlatched and pushed open the door.

On the other side, with all the windows blacked out, Jesse sat in the driver's seat facing a pair of small flat monitors, both displaying the road ahead, their odd glow and that of the dashboard the only light. One display showed the road in infrared, the other in ultraviolet. Linda stooped over and sat herself in the passenger seat, a light cloud of dust erupting from the seat as she did so.

"Uh… sorry about that... I didn't think to dust while you was sleepin'. T'be honest I didn't really think I'd need to. I mean…"

"It's okay. Just being in a moving vehicle again is..."

"Sorta almost makes ya feel like the world ain't so far gone?"

"Yes! Yes, that's it exactly."

"Yeah… don't get too comfy though, we're gonna have'ta make a stop to refuel before we get to North Carolina."

"What will that involve?"

"We'll find a fuel depot or a trucking company lot, something with aboveground diesel tanks or enough trucks with diesel we can siphon. Warm 'em up, suck 'em dry and keep rolling."

"Oh. Charming."

"Nah it ain't, but you gotta do what'cha gotta do."

They rode in silence for a few minutes before Linda simply couldn't stand it anymore. She turned to Jesse and asked the question that had been on her mind ever since sitting down.

"Jesse... what did you do with Rafei's body?"

348

"I put him back in the CDC. Back where we met, actually. I loaded up his notes and stuff though."

"Oh... okay. What about... what about my colleagues?"

"I put them in the stairwell. I didn't know where they worked and we was kind of pressed for time so... I figured they deserved a little better than the garage at least."

"I understand... thank you."

~

Day 6

The doctor and a younger man walked in just past 10 in the morning, if Viktor had timed the nurses correctly. The younger man had every hallmark of a military man, though he didn't wear a uniform. The close cropped hair, the quick brisk manner of movement, the way his eyes darted around the room and over Viktor... All indicated a man secure in his ability to handle himself.

Viktor put aside the mug of green tea he'd been nursing since breakfast and leaned back in the bed in order to give the doctor and his guest his full attention. The doctor began.

"Good morning, Mr. Reitmeyer. I'd like to introduce Mr. Itoh. I have personally examined your secondary panels, and approved you. Mr. Itoh here is a representative of the Emperor."

"The Emperor?"

"Yes. The Emperor of Japan."

"What exactly is going on here?"

"Mr. Reitmeyer... this will come as a shock, and there's no way to break this gently, so I won't patronize you. Within 24 hours of your entrance to this facility, the world was devastated by an event which has killed, at this point, more than 80% of the world's population."

Viktor sat silent in shock. Trying to absorb what he'd heard. He had no family, no close friends, no one to mourn... and for the first time, he felt the sadness of that. He should have people to mourn. People he cared about.

He shut that down quickly. His talent, his greatest tool was in reading people and giving them what they want. Looking at Mr. Itoh he saw immediately that he was watching him very carefully, gauging his reaction. He realized Mr. Itoh's purpose was to sit in judgement of him. So, Viktor rolled to his side and crossed his arms before responding, the classic body language of emotional distress.

"So... it's very likely everyone I know... with the exception of Yuriko... is dead?"

"Yes."

Viktor thought of his saddest memory, and let a small tear escape to add to the performance, as well as a heavy sigh before he continued.

"How, may I ask? Was it... was it us? Did we do it? I mean... did it finally happen? A nuclear holocaust?"

"Thankfully, no. This was an external event. Something mankind didn't do, and without certain precautions, couldn't have survived."

"What was it? Asteroid? Solar flare?"

"Nothing so... mundane. I'll let Mr. Itoh explain further."

~

"So these things, they just came out of nowhere from space?"

"Essentially, yes. We've calculated their trajectory and it showed them coming in from outside the solar system."

"But then how would the Army in Mt. Unebi... you know what, never mind, I know what you'll say: 'We don't know.'"

"You see our conundrum."

"Putting aside their violent reaction inside Unebi, you don't know

350

whether the Army is an enemy or an ally."

"Not only that, but the damage done by the extraterrestrial phenomena to the planet's population is already considerable. If this is a temporary event, the survivors will be unable to maintain the agricultural and technological basis of a modern first world economy. We estimate that the best and most efficient society we could hope for would be one akin to the Western Colonial period, albeit with modern arms and communications."

"I see what you're getting at. During that period of history, Japan was severely isolationist. It put them at a disadvantage during later eras. You don't intend to make the same mistake this time around."

"The Emperor is wise. He intends Japan to rise from the ashes and become the dominant power around the world."

"There will be other survivors."

"Of course. But they will more than likely be concentrating on agriculture to begin with. Food supplies will be low; fields will have lain fallow. Most survivors of government will have to relocate to places where they can live and grow food locally. They will not interfere with our plans for several decades, by which time it will be too late."

"And you've stored up enough food to make you the exception?"

"No, Japan has always been reliant on the seas for the bulk of our nourishment. In the aftermath of this event, that will remain true. But unlike farming or animal husbandry, fishing requires no large investment in time or manpower, especially when the fishing boats of Japan will be the only ones fishing the Pacific."

"We estimate that in the first few years, with no competition, no overfishing, that nearly every species of fish will bounce back to their pre-man levels. Our hauls will be overfull while their populations will be minimally affected. And best of all, Japan's shores are replete with thousands of fully equipped ships ready to go. We just have to go and get them once the skies are clear."

"Doesn't all this rest on the presumption that this will end, and shortly? What if this lasts years, or never ends?"

"We have an alternative plan if that becomes the case."

CHAPTER 31

Day 79

Cox leveraged the door open from the emergency stairs to the 3rd Deck of the *Disney Magic*. Looking around through his IR goggles, he could see a large staircase leading to the 4th Deck, a gift shop called "Sea Treasures", and a bank of windows on the port side.

Retreating back into the stairwell he pulled his radio from his belt and keyed it on.

"Sir, we've gotten to the third deck. We're visible to sky from the port side. According to the map I've got, we're quite a bit forward of the galley. We'll be rather exposed for a bit if we move aft from here sir."

It was a few moments before the radio crackled and Captain Longmire responded.

"What are you thinking?"

"Deck 2 has full coverage, sir; we could go down a deck and make our way to the aft elevator lobby without danger, then we just come back up and we'll be right by the galley. Of course, that'll mean we'll have to double back to search forward and aft of the lobby, rather than coming from forward and making one clean sweep. Then make our way forward once on Deck 8 for the bridge."

"Cox, you're afield. I expect you to report to me and follow my orders, but you're there, you've got the map and the men of your party. You're in charge of deciding how best to follow my orders and protect their lives."

"Aye sir. We'll make our way to Deck 2 then."

Cox holstered the radio once more before indicating to his men to retreat back down the stairwell. Emerging onto the second deck, they found themselves in a small lobby with gaily yellow painted walls and a rich carpet in aqua green. Signs indicating room numbers hung from the ceiling indicating the directions in which passengers would have found their cabins. As they moved aft they would briefly open any doors that were unlocked or ajar and look in on the rooms, but found each as immaculately kept as the last. No personal affects, no unmade beds, heck, even the TV remotes sat velcroed to the nightstands beside the beds.

It wasn't long before they arrived at the aft elevator lobby and the attendant stairwell. Moving up, they found themselves emerging directly across from a pair of polished silver double doors adorned with small portholes in the triple circle shape of one very familiar rodent's head. A quick jaunt across and Cox and his team were in the galley. As they fanned out searching, they each called out their findings, Cox following and checking them all before declaring their work satisfactory. Looking around, he shrugged and once more pulled the radio from his belt.

"Sir, the galley is clear and clean."

"What do you mean, clean?"

"It's... clean, sir. The rest of this ship has obviously gone a bit without cleaning. Dust, debris, things fallen over, trash scattered. The galley is pristine, sir. Every pot in place, every spoon polished.

Like she's never been used."

"No survivors, I take it?"

"None apparent. Also, no food."

"Food?"

"The freezers are as clean as the rest. It's like the ship sailed with no intention of feeding anyone."

"Cox, I don't like this. Get to the bridge as fast as you can."

"What about the survivors, sir?"

"We'll worry about them later. You get to the bridge, see about the communications, and get back home."

"Aye, sir."

~

Emil came forward out of the aft passage, his dark hair a mess and damp with sweat.

"Captain, can I have a moment of your time?"

"Sure Emil, what's up?"

"Well, it's just that Sarya and I are somewhat out of the loop back there. Have we been attacked? Why aren't we moving?"

"You're right, I've been remiss. Hold on."

Longmire reached up for the mic to the ship PA.

"This is the Captain. As some of you may or may not be aware, we have, in the proud and long tradition of the Navy, accidentally struck and killed what appears to be a North Atlantic white whale—"

"By Allah, are you kidding me?"

"—which damaged and disabled our sail sonar array, our

355

communications array, and vented the forward berthing compartment to sea. We do have some minor flooding in the forward compartments but our pumps are keeping up. Also, in the course of our investigation we've run across three ships adrift. The *Disney Magic* cruise liner, the *Globe* cargo ship, and the *Lyubov Orlova*, a defunct cruise liner that was a derelict before any of this which is already bow to sky and half sunk.

"We have heard through our sonar that either the *Globe* or the *Magic* seems to have survivors. Now, our Master at Arms and a boarding party are aboard the *Magic* making their way to the bridge to try and use the *Magic's* communications suite to send our reports in and update the remaining government on our status.

"After that, we intend to find the survivors, and if they're few in number, we take them with. If they're too many, well see about getting either the *Globe* or the *Magic* underway and have them follow us to a safe harbor.

"Now, as it stands, I do not believe we will be able to submerge the boat. So for the duration we will be operating on the surface. This will present certain changes in how we operate. Noise ordinances are temporarily rescinded, we will be cycling in outside air, and our speed will be reduced. This will not stop us from accomplishing our mission. That is all."

The captain hung the mic back up and turned back to Emil.

"Captain, I appreciate your taking the time to do that, but, I have a rather more pressing specific concern about Sarya."

~

Day 79

Zoe stared at the men in the airlock. The men in the airlock stared at Zoe. The man at the front, nearest the glass reached up and switched his goggles off before raising them on the helmet mount. Then the chin strap was unbuttoned, the helmet pulled off and the balaclava was lifted off.

356

The man's short cropped light brown hair glistened with sweat. His brown eyes took in Zoe, the warehouse behind her, and then flicked back inside the airlock to the rest of his party before coming to rest somewhere on the floor of the airlock.

Bending, he picked up the whiteboard and marker Viktor had left behind. He wrote on it for nearly a minute then turned it around for Zoe to see. His newest crisp handwriting was small but very orderly and easy to read.

"Hello, Ms. Zoe Wilson I presume? My name is Lt. McGuire. I'm from the Project, and I apologize for our unannounced visit. We received your report the other day and came post-haste when our records showed you here alone. No one should be left behind and alone. We're here to start packing you and your archives up for transfer to the secondary facility in NC."

Zoe remembered her briefings on the primary and secondary facilities, one in the Rockies, one on the coast of North Carolina. She'd never met this Lieutenant McGuire before but he didn't seem to be showing any signs of deception. Instead his awkward smile and easy stance said he was unused to being in charge.

Zoe walked forward the few paces to the control console where she'd sat and waited for Viktor to come around and picked up her own whiteboard, which had gone unused. She quickly wrote out her response and held it up for his inspection.

"Why now?"

His smile faltered for an almost imperceptible moment and he blinked before erasing his board with a sleeve then writing.

"I'm afraid you slipped through the cracks. Some reports had you alive, but the overall summary the leadership relied on listed you as MIA. This would be much easier verbally."

Zoe thought for a moment before hitting the switch to open the airlock then quickly cancelling the action. The door cracked open a scant half inch, the pressure differential whistling as air was sucked from the warehouse to the airlock before equalizing.

357

"Can you hear me?"

McGuire stepped up to the crack before he answered.

"Yes, barely. What's got you so skittish?"

"You're a strange man I've never met who offers no proof but shows up armed at my doorstep demanding entrance."

"Fair point. I did know your name though."

"So? I have no idea how important or unimportant I was to the Project. You could've found my name and location in some unlocked drawer in Washington, DC for all I know."

"True, but then I wouldn't have known about your recent report."

"Coincidence."

"Pardon?"

"Could've been a shot in the dark."

"Really? Ms. Wilson?"

"Yeah... you're right. That's a bit farfetched. Okay, I'll let you in, but, I want you and your men to leave your guns here, just inside the airlock. You don't come armed into my home."

"Agreed."

CHAPTER 32

Day 79

Jesse looked over at Linda. Sitting in the passenger seat, without so much as a view out of a window to distract her, she'd fallen asleep again.

He figured he'd let her sleep until they got to Charlotte. The first refuel had gone well just out of Atlanta, where a Ryder maintenance shop had had all the fuel they needed, some of it even in underground tanks which apparently were actually warmer than the surface tanks since they had still been fluid.

Jesse's belly started growling at him. He'd lost weight by force of circumstance in the last few months, but his old appetite was still an ever present reminder of his old habits and ways.

He decided a stop for lunch wasn't unwarranted. He had all kinds of MREs packed in the back and the water to heat them. He was thinking Jambalaya. Hopefully it came with that jalapeño cheese.

Looking at the monitors, he saw the distinct shape of a Shell Station sign. In infrared and ultraviolet he couldn't see much better than shapes, so things with writing were pretty much illegible unless he got within spitting distance, and even then only in the ultraviolet. If there was a Shell station, there may be a convenience store, which may present an opportunity for topping up the tanks and perhaps scrounging extra necessities.

He saw where the road dipped to join with the slight off ramp to the station, so he slowed and pulled the wheel slightly to the right to pull in. He could make out the shape of a car sitting at the pumps. Pulling up beside the store he shifted the truck to neutral and applied the parking brake to let the truck idle and keep the heat on.

Careful not to wake Linda, he unbuckled his seat belt and got up and made his way into the back. There, he pulled out two MREs and three bottles of water. He set each main meal and a few other chosen sundries into the heating pouches and poured half a bottle of water into each.

It wasn't long before the chemical stink of the heating packs started to make it unpleasant to breathe, so, very carefully, Jesse slid aside the panels closing off the exterior vents, allowing a sudden chilly draft of fresh air in from outside while still not allowing any views out.

With a few minutes to kill, Jesse began opening and closing cabinets and drawers, rustling through things until he found what he was looking for, a set of metal cutlery. Grabbing up the contents of the heating packs as well as the rest of the MRE contents he slid open the door to the cab and got into the driver's seat. Reaching over he gently shook Linda's shoulder.

"Hey... hey...! I got ya some lunch."

Linda stirred, inhaling deeply as she approached consciousness.

"Hmm... what...?"

"I hope ya like tortellini."

"I don't think I've ever had it..."

"It ain't too bad. I prefer it over the spaghetti anyway. I've got jambalaya with jalapeño cheese. Apologies in advance if it makes the ride unpleasant."

Jesse chuckled at his own joke as he pinched and pulled open the various packets of their meals, passing Linda hers first before getting to his.

Jesse reached forward and turned the key back, shutting down the engine. Suddenly, the sound of the Shards all over the exterior of the vehicle, their scratching and scraping at the metal and glass surfaces, could clearly be heard.

Linda visibly shuddered at the sudden reminder of their circumstances.

"Do you think they'll ever go away?"

"I don't know. I hope so. But, if they don't, I'm sure some government facility, somewhere, has underground farming. I'm about dying for a cigarette."

"Ha! I somehow doubt they'll grow tobacco, but at least you're staying optimistic."

"Hey if they don't they're sincerely stupid."

"You think so?"

"I doubt our government will be the only one to survive, and we'll need to have trade goods to deal with after everything. In my bunker down in 'Bama, I've got pallets of snuff, a humidor filled with Cubans I imported after the embargo ended, and all kinds of other stuff just for trade. Water pumps, solar panels... you name it. I highly doubt the government was so shortsighted to ignore the economics of the post-apocalypse."

"You really gave this a lot of thought, didn't you?"

"And it's all turned out to be well worth the time and effort too."

Linda finished eating in silence, wondering just what sort of person Jesse would've ended up if the world hadn't ended.

~

Day 6

Viktor look at the Mr. Itoh with shocked curiosity.

"What sort of 'alternative plan'?"

"I'm afraid that's above my authority. I don't know. I've just been reassured one exists. And so, I pass that reassurance along."

"Oh, that's bullshit."

"I'm sorry you feel that way."

"So is that it? I mean, the world ends and simply by virtue of being cared for by someone who is important I survive while billions don't?"

"Fate rarely indulges our sense of egalitarianism."

"Fate shmate. It's damn unfair."

"I'm sorry you feel that way."

"So what happens now?"

"Now that you've been medically cleared, we'll have to find you something to do. No one may be a part of Japan's new empire without earning their keep somehow."

"So what do you do? Past this, I mean. Once all the prospective persons like me are evaluated, what's your role? Do you become superfluous?"

"Actually, this is a break from my normal duties. Once this initial phase is over with, I'll return to them."

362

"So, more specifically, what happens to me now, today?"

"You'll be discharged from the medical wing and escorted to the quarters you'll share with Ms. Koike. Tomorrow you'll begin a battery of skills and aptitude testing alongside the other Companions who've been medically cleared."

Viktor's deadpan expression and tone expressed his lack of enthusiasm for the prospect.

"What fun."

"So, do you have any more questions?"

"Not offhand, not regarding what you're here for, anyway."

"Good."

Mr. Itoh and the Doctor stood and offered their hands. Viktor shook both of them before falling back into the bed. As they turned to leave Viktor called back the Doctor for a moment.

"Doctor, if I might ask, how soon will I be getting out of here, and will I be under guard or free?"

"Well, you've just passed the test that decided if you'd be under guard, so you don't have to worry about that. But as to the timetable, I'd say just as soon as we can get someone with a key up here to undo your cuffs you'll be free to go."

"How long does that normally take, though?"

"Usually no more than about twenty minutes."

"Alright. And then to my quarters."

"Right."

"Will I have the opportunity to thank the nursing staff for their attentiveness during my stay?"

"I suppose, when you're on your way out, you'll pass by the nurse's station. Most of them are on duty today, lots of discharges."

"Thank you."

The doctor gave a perfunctory nod before turning and leaving. Moments later, Mr. Itoh returned with a clipboard.

"I'm sorry for the further interruption Mr. Reitmeyer but I neglected to take care of one important detail."

"How can I help you?"

"All nonessential personnel are entered into a lottery system for certain things, miscellaneous work details, a weekly monetary award for morale, things like that. But you need to sign into it with your information to be registered."

Viktor's suspicions were immediately roused.

"What kinds of 'miscellaneous work details'?"

"Oh, nothing too bad, polishing signs, washing vehicles, stupid things like that that the regular maintenance people may not have the manpower to take care of, that's all."

"Uh-huh… I suppose I'm free to read this over and fill it out at my leisure?"

"No, actually. It needs to be done before we can release you, that's why I came back. I'd hate to delay your release."

"Alright, give it to me. I'll fill it out and leave it with the nurse's station on the way out."

"Excellent, thank you."

~

Day 79

Longmire looked at Emil for a second before responding.

"What's the matter with Sarya?"

"She's been having dreams... nightmares."

"This whole situation is a nightmare. I'm not surprised a little girl is having bad dreams because of it."

"No, Captain, you misunderstand. She's having nightmares, had been for weeks now, but... I only recently, here, in the security on the *Oregon*, bothered to ask her what her nightmares are about."

"So?"

"So... her nightmares are the same as mine. And taking an informal poll of your crew, quite a few others, two dozen and counting, have all had very similar nightmares."

"Are you saying they're related?"

"I'm asking if you've had nightmares lately, Captain, and if so what are they?"

"Well... I suppose I've had some nightmares, now and then, sure."

"Captain, have they featured voices? Or a red mist? Titanic creatures? Titanic beings?"

"I think we should take this conversation off the bridge—"

"I agree."

"—after my boarding party has made it safely back. I doubt our dreams are going to do us much harm anytime soon."

The captain turned away from his passenger and checked over the gauges at the helm. Emil followed the captain, stepping forward from the passageway into the bridge proper.

"Captain, this sort of thing is... unprecedented. We can't just brush this aside!"

The Captain continued forward feigning interest in the port trim display.

"Not only can I, Mister Emil, pending the safe return of my sailors, that is exactly what I intend to do."

"Sir!"

"*Enough,* Emil. Later."

At that the radio crackled.

"Captain?"

Longmire took a deep breath before returning to the navigation table and picking up the radio.

"Go ahead, Cox. Have you made it to the bridge yet?"

"Er... no sir. But I think we've found something you might be interested in."

"The survivors?"

"No, sir, the opposite. We've found that deck seven is littered with bodies... and something else. We're not sure what to say they are."

The giants?

"No sir. These aren't exactly beings. More like things. Small black spiky... Things. They're littered about the deck on and amidst the shriveled corpses of the crew."

CHAPTER 33

Day 79

The men inside the airlock stripped themselves of their weapons and body armor as Zoe watched through the bulletproof glass. When they were sufficiently disarmed, Zoe leaned forward and pressed the door control, allowing it to open the rest of the way.

"Thank you, Ms. Wilson."

"It's no problem. Could you tell me just how you got here? Last I heard, overland travel was rather difficult."

"We came by air. Helicopter, with a refueling stop at Nashville International."

"How's that possible?"

"You fly by infrared or ultraviolet. Black out the windows, wait for the Shards to lose interest after you land. We actually landed on your doorstep four hours ago."

"Do you expect to transport all my stores and the archives in one helicopter?"

"Not at all. There's a backup option, copies and transfers all data from the archives to the central database of the primary and secondary facilities via satellite. It's just that you need Administrator access to the system... and I brought those codes with, to initiate the backup."

"And my stores?"

"This is only the initial expedition. Once the backup is initiated and you're safely with the remaining Project personnel in North Carolina, we'll send a number of flights here with the sole purpose of collecting and transferring the bulk of your stores."

"All this for little old me?"

"Humanity mustn't lose out on its artistic heritage."

The officer gestured to his men to stay at the entrance.

"If you'd be so kind as to show me the way to the Archive retrieval station and your communications hub, I'll start the backup process so you can get to packing your personal belongings."

"And your men?"

"They're really just here to watch over me. There's been some unexpected complications and we've had to take some rather unfortunate precautions."

"Complications, precautions, backups... squads of soldiers... you make it sound like we're at war."

"Old habits. No, we're not at war, at least we don't think so. The difficulties we've encountered have purely been the results of human foibles and people unable to handle the stress of the situations we find ourselves in."

"Such as?"

"Dangerous mental breaks, delusional beliefs and behavior, even violent psychopathy I'm afraid."

"And yet you trust me?"

"To be frank, Ms. Wilson, I don't think you could take me."

The subtle humor and smile he affected seemed meant to show her he intended the remark in reassurance, but nevertheless Zoe felt something cold behind his words, saw the briefest flicker of danger pass behind his eyes. Zoe realized she may have made a terrible mistake in allowing this young Naval Lieutenant into her sanctuary. They made their way in silence to the Archive terminal, where the Lieutenant retrieved a small notebook from his inner breast pocket before using a keyboard command and typing a short series of directives into the resulting window. He replaced the notebook and stood back up straight before he spoke.

"Alright, the system is ready to send the backup. I just need to authorize the connection at your personal terminal in your quarters."

As they began the slow walk to that destination Zoe wondered what Viktor had to hide, where he had hidden, and what he'd do if they evacuated her to North Carolina as they indicated their desire to do. She didn't voice any of these concerns, however.

"What will become of the originals in storage here and above in the Institute?"

"There are plans, once the skies are clear and we can operate freely once again, to recover most Project resources and protected archives to Washington, DC. The Smithsonian Institute facilities there have all the resources for preservation and storage we may need, plus there's still an operating government, even though we're in a state of Martial Law."

"We are?"

"Of course. In fact, I wasn't going to mention this, but due to a series of unforeseen events, I'm technically the Commander in Chief at the moment."

Zoe stopped in her tracks.

"You're the *President*?"

"Oh, no, no election, no Executive Authority, but the Project has operational control of the military for the duration, the actual line of succession is in tatters, and I'm the head of the Project at the moment."

"What happened with the President?"

"Lost in the initial day, same with the Vice President. The Speaker was President for awhile but then Air Force One crashed and nobody in line after that can be located."

Viktor stepped forward into the light, his baritone voice revealing no trace of emotion as he addressed the surprised Lieutenant.

"I suppose that means you're the man to talk to then, doesn't it?"

~

Day 79

Linda crossed her third X, filling the grid. Jesse looked up from the board where he was staring intently for another space to hash out a grid for a rematch.

"Cats game."

"Yep."

"You wanna go again or do you wanna switch to something else? We ain't broke open the deck a'cards, we could play some Rummy."

"I'm about gamed out, honestly. How in the world did you figure on bringing so many travel games?"

"It wasn't my first thought. But on that first ride, after I got'er squared away? That first stop for gas? Hours and hours waitin' for it to be safe to get out? I grabbed hold'a a couple books. Then, later, when I figured on company, a stack of these here travel games."

"Well I'm glad you thought ahead. It's certainly made the wait more

370

bearable."

"Yeah... but I think the wait's about over. You hear anything?"

"...No. Why?"

"I don't hear nothing either."

"So?"

"So that means them things ain't all over us no more and we can get out if we play it quiet."

"Oh! Well alright then! Where are we, what are we doing?"

"Just a little gas & go, convenience store kind of thing. Figured we could grab up some more bottled water, some canned fruit or some cracklins... things we ain't got. Hell, I'm dying for a smoke."

"I could use a drink... with all that's happened..."

"Yeah, I getcha. Well, let's get going then, but remember, you wanna keep your eyes on the ground 'til we get inside, be quiet as possible, and if you see one of them Giants..."

"If I see one of the Giants... what?"

"Uh... I don't really know. I'm not sure there's anything you can do... so if you sees one, just lemme know, okay?"

"Will do."

"Alright, let's go."

Jesse flipped down his IR goggles and switched them on before gently pulling the latch to open his door. He slowly slid out of his seat, pushing the door closed but not latched as he landed.

Then he made his way around the front of the truck to the passenger side. Opening Linda's door, he reached up and took her waist in his hands, guiding her down to the ground before leading her to the door of the shop. Once inside he made a beeline for the counter where the cigarettes were. Stopping short at the entrance to the counter area, he flipped up his IR goggles then blinked away the odd coloration they lent the world and looked down.

Two of the stores former employees lay behind the counter, their dried bodies still wearing the brightly colored uniforms of Shell Oil. Jesse looked over at Linda, who was perusing the coolers, before he leaned over and grabbed three cartons of his preferred brand, tucking them under his arm before grabbing a zippo and two bottles of lighter fluid.

Across the store, Linda hopped up and down before opening the cooler case and grabbing at a 12-pack of fruity daiquiri-like drinks. It was only a moment before the smell of rot, mold, and mildew washed over her, causing her to gag. She hurried to close the airtight cooler door.

Jesse walked over to her, his goggles still perched on his forehead.

"What's wron— oh holy God what is that stench?"

"I don't know, something in these cases must be rotten but I don't know what..."

Jesse followed the cases as they moved down the side of the store, going from alcohol to sodas to the culprit.

"Ah, here we go, this explains it."

Jesse waved over Linda, as she approached she saw that the far end of the cooler was covered in the exploded remains of sandwiches. Prepackaged sandwiches which had rotted, the gasses expanding their packages until they'd burst, spraying muck all over the inside of the case.

Jesse indicated the shelves of bottled water in pallets behind them in the aisle and the stacks of canned sodas in 12 pack boxes the aisle over.

"We should definitely take a few pallets of water. And if you've got any preferences for sodas I'd grab as many as you can. In a few years

372

there won't be no more sodas, so get while the gettin's good, y'know what I mean?"

"Hard to imagine. No more Barqs, no more Fanta, or Mello Yellow, or Pibb, or Sprite... ooh! They have Fresca!"

"I've always been a fan of Cherry Coke m'self."

"I'll make sure to grab some. How are we going to carry all this out to the truck?"

"Very carefully, one load at a time. We can't overburden ourselves on any one trip, cause if we drop something we'll have to get inside either the store or the truck right quick. Best to just not drop nothin', y'know?"

~

Day 12

Viktor pulled out a handkerchief from his back pocket and wiped his brow. The already sweat soaked rag did little but move around the sheen of fluid that coated his face and dripped from his hair. He replaced the cloth and looked over the working party he'd found himself assigned to.

Julia, a Brit, Companion to one of the scientists, met at Oxford and married, who was just as confused as you would expect by this whole turn of events. Hibiki, who didn't have a single original thought in his head. Osamu, who never complained or questioned, always did just as he was told. Minoru, who couldn't tell a lie to save his life (or the rest of them work). They weren't bad people, or bad workers; still, he felt he shouldn't get too attached. He was a bit grateful to them as they provided just enough banter and distraction to cover his observations.

The facilities of the Emperor's chosen hadn't been properly prepared when the world went to shit. Tunnels needed cleaning, walls needed painting, and unfortunately, the compact nuclear reactor they'd bought from the Russians, intended to power the facility, wasn't yet active, so the generators needed constant tending. They were, after

373

all, nearly half a century old. Pipes leaked and needed to be patched, the ventilation clogged and needed to be blown out, fuel needed topping off. These were daily chores, and each day a new working party was needed to see to them. Today was his party's day.

He'd realized how things worked here. Supposedly, the Companions of the chosen and the chosen were equal, and only the Emperor was of greater value and importance. However, he'd noticed that the Companions were often, too often to be random, grouped together and given the shitty assignments. Still, dirty hard work meant he was assigned places and tasks which gave him a better picture of their activities than he'd have otherwise. His original assignment, to investigate the Japanese government and determine their intent with all their diverted resources, had been successful, though not in the way he'd ever expected.

They were very, very concerned with the reactor of course. Some of the engineers were starting to think Russia had sold them one that was already worn out. Other groups were concerned with the food stores, or water reclamation. But the most personnel were scientists of every persuasion. Physicists, biologists, meteorologists, chemists... and they all were heavily engaged each and every day in some kind of conclave. Each day they'd assemble in the rotunda, each group would update the rest on their findings, and then they'd separate and go back to their own research facilities up near the surface.

Julia had mentioned her husband, one of the meteorologists, was deeply concerned with the radar results they'd been getting over the Bering Strait. She'd mentioned it was almost like there was a typhoon there, but... not.

Viktor made a mental note to approach Yuriko on the subject.

CHAPTER 34

Day 79

"...They're littered about the deck on and amidst the shriveled corpses of the crew."

Longmire paused a moment to absorb the information before responding.

"Any idea what they are?"

"No sir, not at all. They kind of remind me of sea urchins, but they look to be made of glass. Black glass. Maybe volcanic glass... except the tips of the spikes. There they become slightly translucent, like tinted glass, gray-black. Gotta be honest, sir, I don't like this. Of all the times in the world to run across something unknown... this isn't exactly comforting."

"Well, that's understandable. You said you're on Deck 7?"

"Yes sir, but we've got to go up one more deck and then forward to get to the bridge."

"Well, get to it. The sooner you get that communications suite and

375

reestablish contact the sooner we can get you back aboard and then get us underway."

"Looking forward to it, sir. Been dreaming of a proper meal."

"Speaking of which, Emil says Sarya and a few members of the crew have been having 'odd dreams'. Anybody over there reporting any 'odd dreams'?"

"Heh... no sir. Well... actually, hold on, yes sir. Yes. I have had odd dreams. The rest of the party says they have as well."

"What kinds of dreams?"

"Hold on, sir; let us compare notes over here."

"Alright, don't take too long about it."

Aboard the *Disney Magic,* a spirited discussion ensued. Cox and his four companions sat in the stairwell to Deck 8 and compared their dreams. Although some had differing elements, where one would say 'red mist' the other would say 'a fog of blood', they quickly came to their conclusions and Cox shushed them in order to report their results. As he peered out through the window to Deck 7, he pulled the radio from his belt and held it up to his mouth and spoke.

"Sir?"

"Go ahead."

"Seems we've all been dreaming the same dreams. Damn spooky, sir."

"Er... alright. Add 'odd dreams and sleep disturbances' to the report you send in, then."

"Aye, sir."

"Alright Cox, I don't want to keep you. Get going, just remember—"

"...Sir...!"

"—not... What, what is it Cox?"

"They're moving sir... the little urchin things... they're sort of wobbling. They're not coordinated, some are wobbling left, some right... one... one of them seems to be bubbling or some—"

"...Cox? Cox are you there? Cox!? *Cox answer me! Hello!?*"

~

Day 79

"I suppose that means you're the man to talk to then, doesn't it?"

Lieutenant McGuire registered the barest hint of surprise before quickly regaining his composure. Zoe stood still, caught like a deer in the headlights, unsure of just what to do. Turning to Viktor, McGuire responded.

"I am. And you are?"

"Viktor Reitmeyer. I'm a part of the Project as well."

"...Riiight... that's right... I remember now. The investigator. The one of the twenty-six without an academic background. You were supposed to be in Japan, weren't you? Seeing about some kind of budgetary discrepancy?"

"That's right."

"The Project counts you as dead, Mr. Reitmeyer."

"I'm quite pleased to prove the Project wrong in this instance, then."

"I'm sure there'll be quite a few people who are glad you're still kicking. And I shouldn't have to tell you that you'll be fully debriefed when we get you to the Facility."

Zoe finally shook herself out of her reverie and spoke up.

377

"That'll be true for both of us, won't it?"

"Oh yes... I expect there'll be quite a few questions for everyone involved on both sides."

McGuire stared Viktor down as he continued.

"Most especially about how you managed to get from Tokyo to Chicago in the midst of all... this."

"Ah... yes. That."

Zoe spoke again.

"Yeah, Viktor… you never did explain that part."

"It's... complicated."

"Would you care to? Like, to both of us at once maybe?"

McGuire let Zoe's point hang in the air for a few heartbeats before he spoke again.

"So Mr. Reitmeyer... how did you get from Tokyo to Chicago...? In this situation?"

"Would you believe I flew commercial?"

"…bullshit."

"It's true. If we're going to get to the specifics, I flew here on a 727 with a big 'Japan Transoceanic Air' on the side."

"And…? Just how did you end up on a JTA 727?"

"I think it's best that wait until my debriefing... sir."

"And I frankly don't give a shit what you think."

"Well, alright then. I'm here for Zoe. Or, rather, I was sent for Zoe. Her and her information. The archives."

"Why?"

"Japan isn't dead as they've led the world to believe. They're just dormant. Intending to rebuild, regrow, expand. After this all passes. Like a seed through the winter. They want the archives and Zoe's data in order to facilitate their activities afterwards."

"And just what plans are those?"

"The same as yours, as ours, I imagine."

"And why you'd help them?"

"...whoever said I was? I'm something of a double agent in the favor of the US at the moment. I've gained the Empire's trust..."

"The Empire?"

"Yes, Japan has always been an Empire, headed by an Emperor."

"But I thought his position was largely ceremonial."

"Appeared that way, intentionally. Post World War II, they simply assumed a new tactic."

"And what do they want with Zoe's Archives? Hell, how do they even know about them?"

"Well, I presume they had a source deep within the US Government previous to this whole debacle."

"Fair enough, can't do anything about it now, can we?"

"Damage done."

"And their plans for Zoe's Archives?"

"...I can't tell you."

"Can't or won't?"

"Both, bizarrely enough."

"I don't like half answers, I don't like wise-asses, and I expect cooperation."

"This goes above your pay grade."

"Mr. Reitmeyer... I'm the current head of the Project. The President you know died in the initial event, as did the Vice President. The Speaker of the House was sworn in until he died when Air Force One bought it. After that there's nobody in the Chain of Command above me. In this situation, *I am* the highest paygrade, so *talk*."

"All due respect, but operational control isn't the same as actually being or having the authority you'd need."

"...Fine."

Lt. McGuire whistled three short notes and two of his men materialized from the shadows behind them, fully armed once more.

"Gentlemen..."

Zoe found her voice once more to protest.

"Hold on, you said...!"

"Quiet! Gentlemen, I want Mr. Reitmeyer bound, gagged, and strapped into the chopper as soon as possible. We'll continue this debriefing at the Facility."

"You agreed to disarm while here!"

"...And *I* did. You can get mad at the men if you'd like."

Zoe opened her mouth to complain further but a glance at the armed men now roughly manhandling Viktor into a set of plastic zip cuffs made her reconsider.

~

Day 79

Jesse set down the second set of water bottle pallets on the deck of the truck, careful to make as little noise as possible as he did so. The plastic wrapping around the bottles and the bottles themselves were already very noisy on their own. Rough treatment would only make them deafeningly loud. Linda watched from inside the store, a 12-pack box of Soda balanced on each of her hips. When Jesse started back she'd go out for her third trip, four boxes already sat beside the water inside the truck.

Jesse pushed his water a few inches back into the truck so that they sat within the truck proper and in a hurry the door could close. Sure of his work he turned from the truck and started his slow, measured walk back to the store, where Linda was already making her way to the truck, her head down, following the tracks they'd made in the frost in their previous trips.

As they passed each other Jesse took the opportunity to whisper.

"Next trip I'm'a grab some bags of chips, y'want anything in particular?"

"Yeah, make sure to get some salt & vinegar!"

Jesse got back under the cover of the stores awning and quickened his pace, grabbing a basket from the stack near the door before going to the snacks and chips aisle. He lifted his IR goggles before he started loading up the basket with jerky, chips, and crackers. Glancing occasionally back outside at Linda and his truck. He reached the end of the aisle near the coolers and was debating with himself if the individually packaged pickles in their little sleeves with the pickle juice would be safe at this point when he glanced back at the truck again.

Something in the corner of his eye caught his attention and he did a double take looking out at the road beyond his truck. A giant stood there, staring at them with glowing golden eyes. Jesse didn't move for two heartbeats. Then he slowly began stepping sideways to go back to the entrance, keeping his eyes locked on the giant. It stood there, slightly swaying, its arms moving from its sides first on one side then the other.

As Jesse reached the threshold of the store he risked a glance towards the truck, where Linda appeared to be taking a quick inventory of what they'd loaded so far. He could still see the upper half of the Giant over the hood of the truck, easily 5½ feet off the ground. He decided to risk warning her. None of the warnings had mentioned anything about whether or not the Giants' hearing was any good.

"…Psst!"

Jesse kept his eyes flicking back and forth from the Giant to Linda and back again.

"Psst! Hey! Hey Linda!"

Linda finally seemed to hear something, her head turned up to the interior of the truck and cocked to the side. Unfortunately, so had the Giant. The behemoth began taking slow and easy strides towards the front end of the truck.

~

Day 40

Viktor retrieved his undershirt from where it had fallen next to the bed, used it to wipe clean and dry his face. Julia had rolled over on her side in the fetal position, legs clamped tightly together and shaking. Viktor chuckled as she let out a little whimper from the aftershocks. She lashed out trying to seem mad but her own laughter ruined the effect.

"It's not funny Viktor!"

Viktor laughed. "Yes, it is."

"Is not! Goddamn!"

Viktor stood and picked up his underwear with the toes of his left foot, flipping them up into the air and catching them before bending over and stepping into them.

"...yes it is..."

~

Viktor shimmied through the pipe, the caustic smell of petroleum burning his eyes and nose as he disturbed the layers of oil sludge on the sides and floor. As he approached the next junction he started searching the tunnel for the bolts of the hatch. A few feet further on he found them, immediately knowing something was wrong since they were already loose. He had two heartbeats to consider his next move, but before he could act at all the hatch was lifted off and three men with rifles looked down at him, loudly barking orders in Japanese.

~

The bailiff checked Viktor's wrist and ankle cuffs for the third time as the other guards watched, weapons drawn. Having already escaped, twice, they were talking no chances this time. A tone from the intercom signaled that the sentencing commission was ready for him. With slow and methodical precision, two guards unstrapped Viktor from the chair and lifted him to his feet before slow-stepping him through the door into the next room. There, Viktor was set down in another chair facing a single man, the Emperor's Representative, who would decide his fate.

"Mr. Reitmeyer, I am very sorry our meeting had to be under these circumstances. A man as skilled and resourceful as yourself should have come to my attention in a very different way."

"Unfortunately your unwillingness to abide by our Emperor's law will have all but eliminated any room I may have had for mercy. You have one opportunity to save your life, Mr. Reitmeyer, but I must insist on total compliance. If you so much as breath a whisper that could be construed as disobedience, you will be abandoned to whatever fate destiny affords you. Do you understand?"

"I do."

"Very well. For the crimes of Conspiracy to Adultery, Accomplice to Adultery, Disturbing Societal Harmony, Resisting Arrest, Assault on an Imperial Agent, two counts of Escape from Lawful Confinement, and Espionage, I hereby sentence you to death."

"By His Majesty's grace and mercy, on the condition of your compliance with tasks to be assigned, I hereby commute your sentence from Death, to Exiled Service."

"And just what form will this service take?"

"You will be sent on an errand. Despite what you may have thought, His Majesty's Imperial Government has been well aware this entire time of your involvement in a certain American government program, one of their notorious 'Projects'?"

"Oh... Hell..."

"Oh, yes. The Project has several Archives which we are very interested in. Specifically, one of written materials, and one of art. You will infiltrate these Archives and upload a program of our design into their system."

"You realize that once I'm away from Japan you will lose me, correct?"

"You underestimate us. We have some leverage you may not be aware of."

"And just what do you think that is, some kind of microscopic bomb implanted in my neck? I'm not stupid. That's sci-fi movie bullshit. That kind of thing isn't real."

"Indeed, that kind of thing isn't real. The three fetal heartbeats from your children, however, are very real."

"I have no children."

"Oh, yes you do."

"I had a vasectomy before I ever left the US, and had the requisite testing done to ensure I was completely sterile."

"A situation we couldn't allow to remain. As you are aware, we have suffered a rather significant population drop, and during your initial check in it was a rather simple procedure to reverse it."

"You didn't..."

"We did. And between Ms. Aiko, Mrs. Koike, & Mrs. Dorsey, we have three children from your inhibitions."

"And you think that three fetal heartbeats, children I never wanted and certainly won't be a father to, will be your leverage?"

"No, six heartbeats will. If you fail to accomplish your assignment, we will execute all three mothers and the children."

CHAPTER 35

Day 79

Sharon fiddled with the doorknob to the next warehouse, finding it locked much like the last few. And just like the last few, she retrieved a thin slip of metal, a ruler she'd found in the first office, and placed it in the crack between the door and the doorway below the lock. Then she drove it upwards, forcing the bolt to separate from the strike plate ad withdraw within the door far enough for her to pull the door open. She pulled the door open an inch and set the ruler in the way to keep it open. She needed a moment to catch her breath. The fatigue and nausea was coming in waves, forcing her to rest far more frequently. To be honest, she was glad Eldritch had gone. She was only barely able to keep pace with him, even as he slowed to wait for her.

She took a deep breath pulled out a small flashlight, activated it, and opened the door. She stood in shock at what she saw within. Seven children and two adults, all wrapped in blankets, staring back at her in shock, gathered around a small Sterno-stove on which sat two steaming pans. Her mouth fell open and she looked for words to say but one of the adults, the man, spoke first.

"Are you going to kill us, or come in and close the door? Either way hurry up about it, you're letting in a draft."

Sharon moved in through the doorway, letting the door close behind her. The woman pointed out Sharon's leg and wrist to her companion before speaking.

"You're wounded and armed. Are you going to hurt us?"

Sharon raised her hands in mock surrender.

"Not at all. I'm just searching for supplies. These warehouses seemed promising."

"Well, they have sustained us. Of course there's no telling how much longer this whole thing may last..."

"Much less how long the supplies might. Everything has an expiration date, it's just a matter of when."

The man broke in, impatient.

"Are you alone? How many are with you? Are we to feed an army and starve ourselves? What—"

The woman placed a hand on his arm to quiet him before she continued.

"You'll have to excuse Wayne. We've survived here only because we were waiting to pick him up after work when things went bad. He was the overnight security guard for these warehouses. We were going to get on the road and take ourselves and our nieces and nephews on a road trip to my parent's place in Bethlehem. We haven't left this building in nearly two and a half months."

"So you haven't been outside at all?"

"Not at all."

"Good. You're safer in here."

"What is it? What exactly is out there? We had our phones but when

387

the power went out we couldn't charge them anymore so we... we haven't had any news. We thought that once things were clear that somebody would come, that somebody would find us. Is it over?"

"No. So far as I can tell it's gotten worse."

"What exactly is it that's going on?"

"That's a long story..."

"We have time."

"I don't. I'm not alone. I have a companion, a friend, he's Scottish, a Royal Marine from the UK. He's looking for some antibiotics for me."

"We have medicines. Come rest yourself."

Wayne made a disgusted sound and indicated for the children to move off as he tended to the Sterno-stove.

~

Sharon awoke confused. The last thing she remembered was taking an oral suspension of some kind of antibiotic and resting, dizzy. Now she was looking up at the wooden rafters of the building, the pale light of dawn glowing through the windows of the warehouse. Of course, they were mostly covered with a kind of pale blue film designed to make them impossible to see through, but on one she could see the film had peeled off and there was clear blue sky peering through at her.

She sat up like a rocket. A mistake, as she was immediately struck by a wave of nausea. She felt her stomach tighten and the bile rise in her throat as she doubled over. Heaving, she felt her stomach acid come up he throat. She had just enough time to make sure she aimed her head off whatever she'd been laying on and towards the floor before the deluge poured forth.

One of the children, a little girl who'd been introduced as Alannah, came over with a bottle of water. Sharon took it with a nodded thank you and proceeded to gulp it down. She could see the woman, Martha, watching her as she rocked the youngest of them.

"What happened?"

"Your thigh is horribly infected. Your fever was nearly 104F. We gave you antibiotics and you conked out."

"How long?"

"About twelve hours. Eldritch came looking. Found your tracks in the snow leading to us. Wayne and he are in the other room going over plans to leave. Find a boat that we can all get below-decks on to shield us from the sky, with a closed off pilothouse that one person can run with your goggles."

"We won't need it."

"What? We're not leaving?"

"Oh no, we are definitely leaving, but we won't need all those precautions. Follow me!"

With that Sharon stood, leaning heavily against the crates and shelving that made up their home. She made her way through the curtained partition to their 'living room' where she saw Wayne and Sgt. Eldritch deep in conversation, pouring over an old road atlas laid across a crate labeled as full of potato chips. She stormed past them and out the door, cries of terrified astonishment in her wake. She stood on the cold gravel outside the warehouse looking at the morning sky, the sun just barely up.

Eldritch cautiously peeked out from the doorway behind her, his eyes squinted against the unaccustomed brightness.

"Sharon, you damned crazy gash what the bloody hell!?"

"They're gone, Eldritch. The skies are clear. It's over!"

"Well yeah, I mean, looks like it... but what about the giants, eh?"

"They've got to be connected, don't you think? Once the skies are

clear don't you think they'll be gone too?"

"Begging your pardon, ma'am, but not really. There's no guarantee that's quite how it works..."

"I'm willing to risk it."

"Oh yeah, I can see that. Question is, what's the plan now?"

"Still DC. We should still head to DC, only now we can go by land. We need to find a truck or a van or something, something that can fit us all in."

~

Day 79

Captain Longmire held the microphone in a fist, his fingers white from his iron grip.

"...Cox? Cox are you there? Cox!? *Cox answer me! Hello!?"*

Emil's voice came from behind, suffused with concern and a rising note of panic.

"Captain, I may be speaking out of turn here but I'd highly recommend we submerge and start for South Carolina."

"We can't submerge the boat, not with this much damage, too risky. And we're not going anywhere until Cox and the others get back."

"Captain Longmire, I hate to be the one to state the obvious but... Cox and the others are very likely to be dead. With these... things... I don't think a rescue would be possible, much less likely to succeed. We should leave, and the sooner the better."

"I am not going to abandon half a dozen members of my crew on a derelict! End of discussion!"

Emil opened his mouth to speak again but a sharp look from the Captain made him reconsider, and he closed his jaw with an audible click.

"Does anybody else have any objections to us making absolutely sure we can save as many lives as possible!?"

The silence on the bridge was heavy. Nobody seemed intent to breath much less speak. The redheaded sonarman slowly leaned out of his cubby and raised his hand.

"Oh, you want to abandon them too, eh, Colquitt?"

"Uh, no sir, unrelated? I'm hearing a lot of splashes and clangs and groans out in the water sir. Hell if I know what it is though..."

"Understood. Well, good... at least the Navy is consistent in its value for lives."

A buzzing tone came from the intercom panel, a small green light indicated the call was coming from the sail. Longmire reached up and picked up the microphone before putting it to his mouth and responding.

"Bridge, Captain Longmire, go ahead."

"Sir, this is Seaman Causey up in the sail."

"Go ahead, Causey; what is it?"

"Well, sir I'm not quite sure how to describe it. It looks like the *Magic* is... uh... It looks like it's... popping... sir."

"What the hell does that mean?"

"Parts of her are flying off. Like as if she were filled with popcorn and it was popping and putting pressure on the inside and she's bursting from it."

"What about her superstructure? The antennae and radar, anything happening to them?"

"The bridge was the first part to start popping, sir; all that's popped off and flown all over her decks and the Atlantic sir."

"Well... great. Just... fucking great. If there's anything else that can

391

go wrong somebody tell me, please?"

Longmire leaned over the navigation table, the microphone making a solid thunk as it hit the plastic surface.

Emil stepped forward slowly, planting a hand on the Captain's shoulder.

"Captain..."

The Captain reacted quickly, turning and throwing his full weight behind a right handed uppercut that sent Emil flying one way and several of his teeth another.

"I'll be good and God damned before I'll let a civilian tell me how to run things on my own fucking boat! You say one more word and I swear I'll have you put in irons!"

Colquitt stood and went to Emil, helping him to his feet.

"I'll take him below sir, back to his berth, and let the guys on B Deck know he's not allowed up here anymore."

"Stay at your post! I'm sure Emil can behave himself in the future, can't you Emil?"

As Colquitt released him and went back to the sonar console, Emil looked on the verge of speaking but then resignedly shook his head.

~

Day 79

Jesse watched, horrified, as the giant slowly strode towards the front of the truck, it's peg like feet oddly having no trouble finding purchase on the frosted concrete. The quiet click-crunch of its step finally reached Linda's ears. A confused look passed over her face and she started to lean over and look under the door and down the side of the truck before she thought better. She squatted down on her heels, looking through the undercarriage of the truck. She saw the peg feet of the giant, and her confused look changed to pure bewilderment.

Jesse watched this unfold with one thought running through his head; *She's never seen the giants before, she doesn't know what she's looking at... I hope she's smart enough to think anything strange is dangerous...*

Linda stared at the giant's feet for nearly a five count before she stood and climbed into the back of the truck. The slight bounce of the truck on its suspension gave the giant pause, it stopped and reached out to the hood, opening its fist and extending its fingers in a splayed hand. It placed the hand down on the hood, it's width covering nearly half the hood before it pressed it down, then released it, watching it bounce back up.

It pushed down again, harder, and released. The truck bounced higher. It pressed harder still, the sharp ends of its long fingers beginning to pierce into the hoods metal, and the truck bottomed out its suspension before it released. This time it bounced hard enough the front wheels came off the ground slightly.

A muffled collection of thuds and clangs came from the back of the truck as various bits of gear were dislodged from racks and settings by the motion of the vehicle. Jesse acted quickly to duck down on his hands and knees between the aisles of the store, squeezing his eyes tightly shut. A second later he heard the back door of the truck slam closed as Linda took action herself.

Jesse started crawling deeper into the store, careful not to make any noise that might attract the giant. He could hear the distinctive click-crunch of the giant's footsteps as it moved towards the rear of the truck. In his own ears, the slow scrapes of his own crawling sounded like so much rolling thunder.

~

Day 79

"Professor, am I hallucinating?"

Walthers looked himself at the scene before them. The Berkeley

Quad, partially covered in melting snow, but otherwise seemingly normal under a clear blue sky and a blindingly bright early morning sun.

"No, Don, I don't think you are. Everything looks remarkably... normal. I mean, I see some broken windows here or there, but otherwise…"

"Where do you want to go first?"

"Let's look around a bit, peek in some buildings."

At that, the trio began moving cautiously away from the Culinary Arts building. Professor Walthers directed them at times to look in this building or that, open doors, or help him explore inside and upstairs in some places. Their initial survey took some four hours, with Henry occasionally sending either Don or Jerry as a runner to take news back to the vault to reassure them that they hadn't come to any unfortunate ends. Walthers' directions didn't seem to make sense to either of his assistants until they were headed back, at which point he explained his priorities.

"We all know Berkeley is a public research University. As such, we have departments doing everything from art to advanced theoretical physics. The reason I took us into the buildings I did is because the University holds some things, samples of diseases, radioactive materials, etc., which, if they had been taken, or their containment was damaged we might have to either reseal ourselves in the vault or evacuate the area entirely. I wanted to make sure what needed to be contained *is* contained before we risk anyone else outside."

Jerry stopped in his tracks and looked at the Professor.

"Wait, so, we were the guinea pigs?"

"More like canaries in the coal mine. If anything seemed out of sorts, we'd go back to the Culinary Arts building and shout down the corridor what they were to do, then we'd hotfoot it elsewhere away from them, well, so to speak."

"But everything's fine?"

"Yes, so far as I can tell. I'd say once we're back to the vault we have a sit-down and we all discuss what's next."

Jerry seemed satisfied with the answer and they continued on. As they made their way back to the vault, the Professors mind was occupied with his own next steps. He's have to report in to the Project of course, but what then? Suddenly he was struck by inspiration. He smiled as he started compiling a mental to do list. First would be to look up in the archives all the how-to manuals on repairing the model of servers the archives used, then, to see about repairing the servers with errors. He'd start with the one holding *Peculiarities of the Aurignacian Animism* and then on to the others. If he could determine exactly what Alex figured out he might be able to safely, less impulsively, unravel the mystery of just what ended the world. He'd also need equipment from around the university, maybe even setting up a laboratory of sorts in the Culinary Arts building in order to analyze the object he had sealed in the spare store-room.

~

Day 79

As Emil walked off the bridge Captain Longmire turned to his men.

"Gentlemen, I apologize for that display. We're in a combat situation. Whatever it is that's out there, the things that've taken over the sky, the giants... they are our enemy. They have taken, and I'm not exaggerating, billions of lives over the past few months.

"Whatever has happened to Cox and our boarding party, we're not going to leave them behind. We've lost enough good men to this. If we can bring back even one of them, we will not only have saved a member of this crew, but one of the last survivors of humanity.

"In the wake of all this, whether it ends by the hands of men or never ends, every last man, woman, and child will be of utmost value. I spoke harshly and without thinking in ordering Mr. Cox to give up on finding survivors on the *Magic* and the *Globe*.

"I need another boarding party to go over and search the *Globe* for survivors. Mr. Cox already searched half the *Magic* and didn't find anyone, but from the looks of things the *Globe* was tethered to the *Magic* with intent from aboard the tanker, so that's now our best bet for survivors.

"From what I understand, the Starboard forward loading ramp of the *Globe* is extended and in the water. The next party is to get over to the *Magic*, pick up what crewman Cox left at the Zodiac, and then continue around and board the *Globe*. After the *Globe* has either been cleared keel to above decks or its survivors found, you'll board the *Magic* and find the rest of Mr. Cox's boarding party. You will bring them, or their remains, back to the *Oregon*. We will assist the survivors in any way we can, food, medical supplies... if they're few in number, we may even have bunks for them here.

"Are there any volunteers?"

Before anyone could respond, the boat was filled with a cacophony of noise, like an endless stream of ball bearings being poured across a piece of corrugated tin roofing. Men clutched their ears in pain and the screams of the crew could be heard just above the din. The sonarman Colquitt collapsed to the deck, trickles of blood coming from both his ears. Captain Longmire fell into the navigator's chair, his balance gone, his head screaming. Just before his vision went black, he heard the noise stop as quickly as it had come.

CHAPTER 36

Day 79

Zoe stood silent as Viktor was dragged away. Lieutenant McGuire looked at Zoe with an expression of cautious curiosity.

"I don't suppose you'd like to explain why you didn't mention that you had company here?"

"I wasn't sure your intentions here. I'm still not. But, he acted as if he was being pursued, so I didn't want to put him in danger."

"And it didn't occur to you that his intentions might not be on the level?"

"I know him from the Project. I don't know you."

"Don't pretend you were trying to do the right thing here. You're lucky I'm not ordering you bound alongside him. I'm hoping you'll have more sense here."

"The one who isn't using their sense here is you. The world is on the raggedy edge and you're stomping around like a bully on a playground."

Lieutenant McGuire seemed for just a moment to be on the edge of striking her before the old serene stoicism of military bearing descended once more.

"Zoe... you're not fully aware of certain things, so I can let an awful lot slide on that basis alone. But, don't mistake my placidity for apathy. Your little contribution to this Project is appreciated, but it isn't license to passively disregard my authority, or to actively work against me. You're a very minor cog in a very big machine."

"Uh-huh... and is that what you tell yourself makes you different? That you're a big cog? I understand you've got 'authority', but what does that matter if the fucking world is ending around us? We're all just human beings trying to survive."

"Survival requires that order must be kept..."

"Whose order!? Yours? The United States? Look around! There isn't a 'United States' anymore! Just a bunch of people hiding in bunkers!"

Lieutenant McGuire's face turned to an almost sadistic smile.

"Not for very much longer."

"What do you mean — what are you talking about!?"

"Viktor's given me my next course of action, he just doesn't realize it yet."

~

Day 79

Linda sat sprawled on the various boxes of sodas and pallets of water she'd leapt atop of when she piled in. Their hard edges and corners pressing into her and making her uncomfortable. Numerous tools and pieces of gear she could only guess at lined the walls around her. She closed her eyes and took a deep breath of relief. The sudden violent bounce of the truck underneath her and their supplies shocked her but she stifled her instinct to cry out.

Another bounce, more energetic, slammed her elbow into the corner of the wheel well. Stars of pain danced in her eyes as she looked around at their groceries scattered around her. Another bounce, this time enough to throw her into the air and flip her over. She suddenly had a vision in her head of a spiraling flock of darkness twisting from sky to ground and pouring through the back of the truck. She scrambled to get to her feet, and grabbed at the strap affixed to the inside of the door. Squeezing her eyes shut lest she catch a glance of sky, she threw her weight back, dragging the door round on its hinges and slamming it closed.

She pulled in a deep breath of relief, feeling it freeze in her throat as she broke out in a cold sweat at the sound of hundreds of thuds, thunks, and screeching scratches as the truck was enveloped. She felt the rising bile of a panic attack clawing at the back of her throat as she realized Jesse was likely dead, and her soon to follow.

~

Jesse was very surprised he wasn't dead. Whether from the things currently flying through the store or the foul air of the rotted food in the cooler area he'd sought refuge in. Which, as he'd discovered, also contained another desiccated body; this one looked like a customer. There were nearly a dozen single serving cups of wine and two bottles of antihistamines by the body. It was pretty easy to see they'd chosen the easy way out. Didn't look nearly like they'd been dead long, maybe two days.

Jesse wondered who they were, how they'd gotten here. The store hadn't shown any signs of habitation. They must've just come here to die. Odd choice, but Jesse didn't have the particular presence of mind to think too deeply on it. He had other concerns. He was effectively blinded, for one. High windows, a skylight, and enough gaps in the shelving to provide views of the store meant he either had to keep his eyes on the ground, or closed. He didn't have his goggles. He'd set them on the back end of the truck his first trip.

He was also unarmed. The sidearm he'd worn before was in pieces in the back of the truck; he'd started cleaning it while they waited to leave the CDC but his attention had wandered and he'd never

399

reassembled it or brought it with him. At least he wouldn't starve. There were boxes of chips, candy, sodas. Of course there were also hordes of bugs, roaches mostly, a few beetles, ants too, forming neat and orderly lines from where they gained entrance by the service door to the bottom of the cooler racks and suicide Stu.

~

Linda watched a line of frost move down the passenger side of the truck, the condensation on the interior freezing solid before her eyes, moving from the cab to the rear of the truck.

A high pitched squeal began emanating from the center of the line, a series of cracks began forming in the ice behind the front as it moved, a series of pops and clinks like a glass toast began coming as something scratched and pressed in the metal on the outside, the things covering the outside being peeled and pried from the truck by its passing. As it reached a seam in the skin the joint popped and a bolt flew from the panels, bounced around the interior twice before embedding in the cardboard of a 12-pack of Cherry Coke.

A thin, bone-white spike poked through the gap made by the popped seam for a second before quickly withdrawing. A shaft of sunlight stabbed through in its place before being replaced by a strange black pool with golden cracks emanating from its center, it twisted to and fro, the golden cracks shifting, twisting, swirling, and reforming with different courses with each rapid reorientation until it finally settled on Linda's face.

~

Day 79

Ben Longmire woke up drenched in sweat, his mouth dry and his head throbbing. He cracked open one eye. All he could see was a shock of short orange-red hair.

His body felt strange, stiff, and he could tell he was positioned oddly, his feet were kicked up on top of something, his left arm under something else. He was hot. The air was sweltering. It was difficult to breath, there was something pressing down on his chest.

400

He could hear... something. He couldn't quite make it out. Some sort of tapping, each tap followed by a short, high-pitched hiss. There were also slow footsteps, like someone was slowly walking down a metal deck in combat boots.

He raised his head to see if he could make out just what was weighing him down. It was a leg clad in service khakis. Following the leg up to its owner he could just make out the profile of his XO. The head next to his own belonged to his Sonarman, and the tap-hiss was a set of pipes on the wall of the chamber they were in, one hot below, one with a minor leak above. A drop would fall from the one above and boil away nearly instantly on the pipe below.

There was a dim crimson light emanating from the hatch to the next chamber. Longmire raised himself up, shoving his crewman aside and off of him, pulling his arm out from under another. Each felt warm and pliable to the touch, it didn't appear any were dead. Standing, he was struck by a wave of nausea that nearly took him back down again; as it was, he stumbled and had to throw a hand down on Colquitt for balance. He groaned from the sudden impact. The sound came through hollow, as if from far away.

Shaking his head Longmire felt a stabbing pain and another wave of disorientation and nausea. Inner ear damage, seemed like. Looking around he could see that all his officers and warrant officers were here, none of the enlisted. It appeared the crew had been sorted. Taking his first shaky step over his XO to a space between him and his Engineer, Longmire again felt off, wrong. He wobbled, but steadied himself. Nearly a decade at sea meant he had some skill with balance even without the normal apparatus to do it by instinct, awareness of his body, it's position, and the distribution of his weight, all combined for him to remain upright when every part of his inner sense told him to throw himself in the wrong directions.

He took another step, and he was humbled when his skills proved insufficient and he found himself yet again on the deck, next to the pile of his men. He heard the heavy footsteps once more, turning his head to the hatch and fighting back the vomit threatening to rise in his throat, he saw a shadow form in the ruby light. A figure formed from the shadow, tall, pale, it ducked down, bending at the middle, its head and shoulders coming into view where it's chest filled the top of the hatch before. A long fingered hand with too many knuckles grasped the hatch border, golden pupils set in black pools scanned the room until they found Longmire.

A lipless slit of a mouth parted, a baleful light hypnotizing him.

Come, it said.

And then it turned and was gone.

~

Day 79

Lieutenant McGuire paced back and forth from the kitchen to the sunken living room. His steps sharp clipped impacts on the bare concrete. He nervously puffed on a cigarette, a habit he'd long disdained but decided perhaps held some merit as a superficial stress reliever.

"Are we connected yet?"

The young soldier wiped his brow and continued clicking through the settings on the computer.

"Sir, I don't think we'll be able to."

"And just why not? What did they do?"

"I don't think they've done anything here, sir; everything on this end is squared away. But we're not getting any real return from the Facility."

"Could the satellite be the problem?"

"No sir, this system isn't satellite based."

"What do you mean? I thought everything was routed through the satellites?"

"Most of it. There's still a few minor facilities that weren't yet

402

upgraded to the uplink. Chicago here was one of them still on landlines. The Archives were like that, they had too much data to effectively work through the uplink. They had to have land lines in order to efficiently do their jobs."

"Could it be a downed line between here and there then?"

"No sir, we're getting a ping. They're there, but other than acknowledging the connection, which is automatic, they're not responding."

"Could it be some other kind of mechanical fault?"

"Unlikely, sir."

"Okay... so what do you think is happening?"

"Well sir there's three things, in our current situation, that is, that stand out as possible causes. One, purely mechanical fault on their end, something crapped out and we happen to be trying to connect while the systems down. Not likely, million to one.

"Two, they're receiving but intentionally not answering. Some breakdown in C&C, orders got mixed up, they're responding as if it wasn't us but an unscheduled attempt from an unknown outside source. Possible, but unlikely; I'd say a couple thousand to one."

"And the third?"

"Sir, the world's gone to hell. We've lost thirty surviving groups in a little over two and a half months. Some to isolation and starvation, some to exposure, and some just went quiet. I have to think the Secondary Facility could have suffered a similar fate in our absence."

CHAPTER 37

Day 79

Zoe sat uncomfortably on the concrete floor of the airlock, still in her pajamas. The chill from outside was bleeding through the steel doors. She looked around at the men who had invaded what she'd begun to think of as her bunker. They were all stone faced and grim, men who'd seen combat and watched friends die, men who'd watched the world die. They didn't speak much, and when they did it was short and clipped orders. No manners whatsoever. She looked at Viktor. He was bound, gagged, and blindfolded on the floor opposite her, laying on his side.

One of the men's watches beeped. He looked at it briefly then looked at the others.

"It's been enough time; chopper should be clear. Let's get these two aboard."

~

Day 79

The golden lightning swirled and retraced itself across the ebony orb as the iris narrowed and focused in on her face. It withdrew, a momentary shaft of sunlight streaming through the hole before four sharp bone white spikes entered, extending into the gap and the joints bending, two splaying in each direction, forward and back. They began pulling, separating, the gap forcibly widening moment to moment, the screech of metal a horrifying din within the small enclosed space. She screamed.

~

Jesse could hear the giant tearing into his truck outside, and then a muted scream rang out, the cinder block walls rendering it brief and dull. He jumped to his feet from the ground, a few stray insects that had found their way to him flying off in every which way by his sudden movement. Jesse reached for the door to the store but he froze scant inches from the handle, fear and realization striking him to his core.

...I can't get to her, I can't save her, I can't fight that thing, or the things flying around in the store... I'm completely impotent in this here situation...

Jesse moved back from the door. Sitting down on a pallet of Coca-Cola, he put his head in his hands and tried to block out the world. The smell of his refuge-prison kept him from success. The scream echoed in his mind and blended with the sounds of his truck being ripped apart.

~

Linda watched the gap widen inches at a time. The sunlight and the strange profile of the creature filling the opening. She realized her mistake. Quickly and tightly closing her eyes, she rolled over onto her hands and knees, turning towards the cab of the truck she frantically pawed at the sliding door to the cab. Finding and grasping the handle she heaved her weight against it, sliding the door open and jumping into the cab.

A quick reorientation by touch, and she went to grab and close the door. She miscalculated, her momentum carrying her face first into the side of the door, the hard edge slamming into her left cheekbone and forehead. She recoiled, the pain causing stars to whirl in her head. Momentarily senseless, Linda's eyes snapped open. In a short second, she saw the giant, its upper torso leaning into the hole it had torn in the side of the truck. Over its shoulder she could see sky... blue sky! Clear blue sky!

And then she realized, and she shut her eyes tightly once again. Grabbing the door, she slammed it closed. It was a brief reprieve. Only moments later a series of ivory spikes pierced the door, then bent from invisible joints, grasping the door and pulling it from its track.

~

Day 79

Longmire stood fixed, confused and uncertain. The creature of nightmare he was quite sure had spoken, and yet, he was equally sure it didn't. He found himself questioning his wakefulness. He considered for a moment that he may in fact be dead. A footfall from behind broke him from such thoughts. He twisted in place, noticing for the first time the hatch behind him and the heap of his men. Sarya stood there, another creature like the one who'd spoken to him bent in the doorway, holding her hand in its own. It would've been absurd if it wasn't terrifying.

"Mr. Captain man, are you okay?"

"Yes, Sarya... I'm just fine."

"But you've got blood on you."

"Oh honey, it's okay... I just had a little bump on the head, but I'm alright now. Why don't you come here?"

Longmire crouched down to one knee, extending his arms in welcome.

406

Sarya looked up at the creature holding her hand.

"I'm gonna go with the Captain now. Bye..."

The creature looked down at Sarya a moment before turning its gaze on Longmire, a short roar was accompanied by a flash of the baleful light from its mouth which froze both Sarya and Longmire in place. At the conclusion Sarya withdrew her hand and calmly walked around the heap of officers on the deck.

Longmire gathered her in his arms and stood, the creatures gaze following him until he was fully vertical with Sarya perched on his hip, one arm locked around and underneath her. Then it turned and began making its way down the passageway. Longmire immediately turned to the girl in his arms.

"Sarya honey, are you okay? What happened?"

"I'm okay. There was a bunch of noise, and it woke me up, and then everyone fell down, and then the big white men came and gathered us all up and walked everyone across the ice outside the boat to another boat but because I wasn't asleep they let me walk myself so long as I promised to hold their hands."

Longmire was taken aback by the brevity and detail of the girl's descriptions, it certainly answered his question well enough. Still, he had others.

"Did you see what they did with the rest of the crew?"

"Yeah... they put most of them in a couple big rooms and a few here too. Daddy and I got a special room all to ourselves though, he's on a bed taking a nap but he looks like he fell really hard cause his mouth's hurt."

"Okay... did they do anything to anyone? Did they say anything?"

"One just said I should follow that other one and hold their hand. They don't talk much elsewise."

"Okay Sarya, is there anything else you can think of, anything you saw or heard? Even if it's really small it could be important, okay?"

"I dunno... can we go wake up Daddy now?"

"I don't know sweetie; I think I'm supposed to go on through that hatch over there."

"That's okay, Daddy needs a nap anyway, he's been grumpy. I'll just go with you then."

"I don't think that's a good idea, Sarya..."

The creature once more appeared within the hatchway, bent and peering at Longmire and Sarya. It raised a hand, beckoning them forward.

Come, it repeated, and then turned and disappeared once more.

Longmire looked down at his men, and then at Sarya, then, hitching her higher on his hip, he moved towards the hatch.

~

Day 79

Zoe and Viktor were pushed roughly out the door, blindfolded and guided only by the whispered orders of the soldiers. They walked slowly, not knowing the direction they were headed in. The freezing wind bit at every inch of exposed skin on them, especially badly on Zoe, who was not only barefoot but still only wore her ill-fitting pajamas.

Suddenly the hands at their shoulders relaxed, the whispered orders silenced. A moment passed, two breaths, three, then Zoe cautiously whispered.

"What's going on?"

A set of gentle fingers pinched her blindfold and pulled it upwards, her eyes cautiously opened towards the ground, where she saw only

408

a pair of off white pegs resting upright on the ground. Following them up she saw the pegs become yellowish before terminating at a juncture with alabaster skin covered in ridges and swirls. The skin of each extension grew together and became the body of something, her eyes creeping up its form to its neckless head, and the slightly open slit through which a sanguine light shined.

It closed its mouth and several of the soldiers immediately raised their weapons, one fired.

The bullets impacted the creature like marbles thrown at a stretched sheet, it's flesh briefly deforming before rebounding the slugs to the ground. The creature, no worse for wear, roared, its light shining out and stopping the soldiers in their tracks. The one soldier firing ceased as his finger froze holding the trigger down, the semi-automatic nature of his rifle requiring him to release and squeeze again for it to continue to cycle and fire properly.

The giant creature struck out with both hands, sending soldiers flying half a dozen yards with each brief impact, until only Zoe and Viktor remained. It reached out and grasped both of them around their torsos, lifting them up like dolls before it began moving.

The airlock to the bunker exited to the Monroe Harbor shoreline, and it was a small walk up a hill to Grant Park, where the Buckingham Fountain, and the helicopter, lay waiting. As they crested the hill the Chicago skyline came into focus, illuminated by cold starlight, as the city's power grid was long since dormant. In the open space surrounding the fountain stood nearly a dozen other human beings, and half a dozen other giants.

The people were bundled in blankets and winter clothing of all kinds, standing together in small groups of two or three, taking comfort in proximity, but not speaking. All were looking at the stars wheeling overhead, and the Moon, shining brightly in the cloudless, empty sky. The giant deposited Viktor and Zoe amongst the others, who wordlessly provided them with blankets. One brought them a crumpled sheet of paper, written on with lipstick.

"They discourage us from speaking."

The seventh giant that had brought them joined the other six, and they formed a crude circle. As they began to sway, the air was filled with a low hum that began incrementally getting louder.

~

Day 79

Linda's eyes snapped open as the rear part of the truck was split open, a jagged tear from the passenger side wall to the roof continued down the driver's side, splitting off fully half of the rear portion of the truck and allowing it to fall off to the ground. The giant stood in the midst of the gear and foodstuffs on the back of the truck, the suspension fully compressed by its weight as it stood peering down at Linda, the partition door still crumpled in its hand.

Linda quickly realized that the sky behind the creature was clear. That nothing flocked or flew, much less spelled death from observation. The thing stood silent once Linda ceased her scurried escape, peering down at her with its features twisted in... amusement...? Possibly?

She grasped the frame of the passage and pulled herself to her feet in front of it. It dropped the door over the side of the truck and gently picked her up in one spindly hand.

~

Jesse listened as the sounds from outside died away to nothingness. He bit his lip to keep silent as his fear, regret, and anger boiled up and threatened to give away his location.

Suddenly, over the sound of his blood rushing in his ears, he could hear a voice.

"Jesse, if you're still alive in there you should come see this."

He didn't believe it, couldn't believe it. It had to be a trick. Yeah... it

410

was a trick. He'd heard these things sing and hum all kinds of ways before... they must just know how to fake a human voice. Yeah, that's it. It's a trap.

"Jesse it's okay, really, it's me, you found me in a pile of bodies? We stopped because we wanted a few last sodas before they all go bad? You introduced me to tortellini?"

Well shit. Jesse couldn't figure how they could've gotten that kind of info... unless they was psychic... but hell, that's nonsense...

"I'm in this here storage room, Linda...! What's going on out there?"

"Clear skies, Jesse!"

"What!? The hell you say?"

Jesse stood and ran to the door, catching himself a bare inch from the handle and questioning whether he should really go outside.

Aw... fuck it, he thought, and he opened the door and walked through the store to the entrance, where he saw Linda bouncing with excitement, her hands clasped.

Behind her, still standing in the wrecked remains of his truck, stood the ivory giant, watching. Jesse shielded his eyes against the sunlight, looking up at the sky with not a little trepidation. All he could see was clear blue sky, a brilliant shade of robin's egg blue. The giant hopped off the truck, it's sudden movement off and the tension in the springs of the suspension making the truck jump off the ground fully four feet, and making gear and food fly every which way up into the air, to quickly rain down on the concrete, the frosted grass, and the roof of the gas station.

CHAPTER 38

Day 79

Longmire walked through the hatch, finding himself in a long passageway with only one exit, a hatchway at the other end, through which there came a shimmering blue light. He noticed a label on the bulkhead next to the hatch that read "AMDSHPS BY 3". Reaching the hatch, he looked in, seeing a large room, it's walls lined with bodies.

He pulled Sarya's head down into his shoulder, and told her to cover her eyes. A step further and he saw the origin of the blue light. In the middle of what was obviously a large cargo bay aboard the *Globe* was a shimmering figure that looked to be cut from a large quartz crystal flecked with impurities from some blue mineral. The figure was easily eight feet from base to tip and seemed to be an homage to every bladed weapon known to man.

Razor thin sheets of crystal stabbed out at every angle and juncture, some continuing for several feet, others scant inches. The edges of the sheets, rather than being of uniform line, took on hard geometrics replicating curves and cutting edges. The entire structure was suspended some two and a half feet above the ground and slowly rotating with no visible means of support.

All around the chamber there were bodies of every sort. Some looked ancient. Samurai, resplendent in their ornate armor, peasants in rags, Japanese sailors in ragged uniforms from time periods ranging from the 17th Century to World War II, American Airmen in old timey leather bomber jackets. It was like a collection of military personnel from the Western Pacific since time began.

One of the giants stood waiting. It beckoned.

Longmire steeled himself and walked forward. Even paces, confident paces, the paces of an American Fast Attack Submarine Captain without fear. Inside his heart hammered at his ribs like a rabbit in a cage surrounded by wolves. His face was dripping with sweat. His shoes fairly squished with each step. He told himself it was the unexpected heat, and not the intense terror that threatened to clench his insides into a knot.

He stopped ten feet from the titanic creature, breathing heavily. Sarya stirred on his shoulder, whispering.

"Captain... you're all sweaty... can I get down now?"

"Only if you close your eyes and keep them closed."

Sarya nodded her head and Longmire slowly eased her down to the deck, keeping hold of one of her tiny hands. The other, Sarya placed over her eyes to stifle temptation.

The creature watched passively, only moving when a hatch on the far side of the bay opened. In the doorway was another of the giants, or perhaps the same one who delivered Sarya; Longmire had difficulties telling them apart. Alongside the new arrival were two men, humans. Members of Longmire's own crew, though at the distance it was impossible for him to make out anything but that they were enlisted.

Longmire spoke up.

"I suppose I should be diplomatic about this, I know my superiors would want me to be, but quite frankly I don't have the patience. Are you going to tell me just what the hell is going on here?"

The giant appraised Longmire with what could possibly be interpreted, if it were human, with amusement.

By this point the figures approaching from the far side of the bay could be made out. The Seaman Watkins and Kellogg seemed strangely at ease.

~

Day 79

The assembled group, 21 women, 3 men, and 4 children, all boys, watched as tiny motes of silver light with colored auras began drifting from the small nodules all over the giants. The lights slowly circled the group, gradually shifting in color individually, seemingly following no set pattern. Shades of blue, pink, green, yellow, and red all made their appearances as the deep intonations continued. They began changing, going off key and atonal, discordant and grating to the human ear. The smallest of the children covered their ears.

The sparks of multihued light increased their pace, becoming a whirlwind of brilliance. The discordant tones of the giants grew louder by the moment, their swaying became frenetic, their shoulders very nearly touching even though their rough circle meant they stood easily six feet apart from each other.

The very stones beneath the feet of the observers vibrated and trembled, the sky above them grew dark with clouds, and azure lightning began sparking between them. The air they sucked in grew thick and carried a subtle taste of copper. Sensation and perception grew strange. The ancient and nearly forgotten instincts of man, the predilection to run from the strange and new, to shy from the unknown, was awoken in the observers. Fingers intertwined grew tighter, teeth were set. Children looked to adults for reassurance and found none.

414

Zoe looked to Viktor, his mouth hung open with unmindful awe. Small blue sparks were flashing from his capped teeth, his flesh fairly trembled as if a hive of angry ants roiled beneath it... and then he glowed briefly of silver threads weaving his flesh, and was gone.

Zoe could scarcely even feel a moment's surprise before she felt a twisting in her gut, as if the world had lurched suddenly three directions at once. She found herself floating in a familiar dreamscape of crimson mists shadowing beings of bizarre form and proportion.

For the first time, she knew that she wasn't dreaming, as one of the beings ceased to be there and came to be here next to her, above her, through her. Its terrible consciousness pressed in at all sides of her mind, memories more ancient than man flooded her vision, thoughts of things ghastly beyond description and emotions unlike anything she'd ever imagined wracked her brain.

She knew that she was less than an insect to this being, and yet, like a man cultivates a bee hive for honey, she sensed that this being too cultivated man, all of mankind in fact, for some minor task...

And that task was at hand.

~

Day 79

Jesse gestured up to the giant that stood behind Linda now, fully five to six feet taller than her meager frame.

"So what's your story, eh?"

The giant gazed at Jesse with ebony pools filled with golden lighting, and said nothing. It instead rose one great arm and extended a finger down the road in the direction of their intended travel.

"You telling us to get a move on? Hell we'd have done that regardless of you hadn't'a interfered. We'd have packed up supplies and done been on our way by now."

415

The giant dropped its arm to its side and turned towards the road, taking long slow steps in the direction of Beaufort.

"What? Ya ain't gonna so much as apologize?"

"Jesse, it showed us the sky's clear; I think he did us a favor..."

"A favor? Look at my goddamned truck! You call that a favor!?"

"It's just a truck, Jesse..."

"Just a...! Woman, you have no idea the blood sweat and tears I put into that thing!"

"And with a world filled with vehicles just waiting for someone to come by and claim them I'm sure you'll get a replacement soon enough. Now help me gather up some more supplies. We may be here awhile..."

"What'cha mean?"

"Do you have any idea how long it'll take other survivors to realize the skies are clear? Much less how long until somebody just happens to come by this particular stretch of the middle of nowhere?"

Jesse grabbed Linda by the arm and headed for the cab of the truck.

"C'mon, let's go."

"In that thing? Are you kidding!? That things a wreck!"

Jesse shoved her through the passenger seat...

"The box on the back ain't critical; the engine, transmission, and the cab should all be fine, now let's go see what that thing's goddamn hurry is."

He pulled himself up into the driver's seat and reached for the switches to his rigged cameras before pausing, and instead reaching over and rolling the window down instead. He cranked the truck and put her in gear, his head hanging outside the window, eyes obscured by dark sunglasses, teeth bared in a smile as wild and free as any

416

schoolboys has ever been. He immediately set off after the giant, which due to length of stride was already receding into the distance down the road.

They took no notice of the small spiky balls of grey glass that covered the roof of the gas station.

~

Day 79

The din of constant conversation would've been annoying had it not been her only real sensory input. Her view, without context, could have been considered to have an eerie beauty to it. But with context... she allowed herself the luxury of zoning out to her thoughts as frequently as possible.

"Everyvun, look!"

The German, Fritz, interrupted everyone's train of thought. Reluctantly, Angela swam back to her blurry vision of the chamber. There were giants standing around the figure in the center. They appeared to be swaying along as if some unheard tune haunted the chamber. Small pinpricks of light would occasionally spurt out of the nodules that were scattered around their necks and shoulders. They would fly chaotically about the gathered assembly then just as rapidly seek out some spot on the crystalline figure in the center.

Each spot struck seemed to ring out with its own baleful purple light before fading to black, like the iridescent blue crystal were being molded into black volcanic glass.

Bit by bit the figure and its light were extinguished, until a glossy onyx facsimile flecked with red and pinpricks of white stood in its place.

The voice of Ernheim, the British anthropologist (or so he claimed) interrupted into Angela's consciousness, as always interrogating the French socialite, his constant student and yet mental superior.

"My word... Estelle, what do you think this is now, hm?"

"I woold sey... Dey are changing the makeoop uv de object d'art to some new purpose. Just wat I woold not hazard a guess."

"Oh there you go again, thinking everything's about art..."

"Ernheim, dahling... It uhlways ez…"

Everyone's voices faded into silence as the creatures in the chamber ceased their singing and swaying. One by one they turned, until the full circle stood looking at the collection. As the last became still a subtle steam began rising off of the transformed figure in their midst.

At the same time the assembled collection lost whatever connection they had to the walls of the chamber keeping them upright and Angela saw the floor rush up at her.

Dreamy, weary, foggy, hungry, torture, panic, pleasure, whimsy... Emotions and sensations unbidden flooded Angela's mind and body. Memories of time now past and dreams of things not now to be flashed through her mind in a surge of chaos. Her vision came back. Next to her on the floor was a young woman, her ruddy young flesh only barely covered by her long rotted scarlet dress. She tasted the moldy air once more.

~

Longmire felt a surge of conflicting emotion rise within him before he pushed it back down. The sight of two of his crewman casually fraternizing with one of the creatures was something he hadn't been prepared for. Just as quickly he swallowed it back down.

"Watkins, Kellogg. Are you okay?"

Watkins looked to Kellogg and the giant that escorted them in before replying.

"Better than okay, sir."

"How do you mean?"

Kellogg decided to speak up then.

"Well, sir, uh... that's rather complicated."

"Is it something you'd prefer to keep, uh, in-house?"

"Sir?"

"Something you'd rather keep away from prying, uh..."

Longmire noticed the giants lacked anything resembling a terrestrial ear.

"...listeners?"

Looks of dawning understanding came through on Kellogg's and Watkins' faces, and Watkins answered.

"Oh no, sir! They're... our friends! Allies!"

"Just how the fuck did you come that conclusion?"

"That's a long story, sir."

"I think we have the time for a condensed version."

"Sir, it's complicated..."

"Spill it, Sailor!"

Watkins and Kellogg frowned simultaneously. Kellogg responded.

"Well, sir, they brought us back."

"You mean they guided you back to the *Oregon*, back in New York? That you didn't stumble on us by pure luck?"

"No, sir, that's not what I meant."

"Then what do you mean!?"

"Well, you see, one of them, well, kind of one of them but not really, anyway, something like them killed us."

"Watkins, what the fuck is he talking about?"

419

Watkins shifted his weight from one foot to the other before he spoke.

"It's true, sir. A giant, like them, kind of... well, it ripped us apart. I know it hurt, I remember knowing it hurt, but, I can't quite seem to remember the pain of it. Nor the feeling of being dead... 'cept I just knew I was dead... sir."

"...And then, because of them, now you're not, is that what you're telling me?"

"Yes. Sir."

"Okay. Let's just say, for the sake of argument, that you're 100% correct. How in the hell do you expect me not to see you as compromised? As biased?"

"We knew you'd think that, but, we had to tell you, they're not all alike."

"Are some more talkative?"

"No sir, what we're saying is, just because they look alike, are the same sorts of beings, don't mean they're all on the same side, sir."

CHAPTER 39

Day 79

Zoe felt, or rather remembered, herself slipping away. The feeling of one's own consciousness being chipped away and absorbed by a greater one is quite distinctive. The thoughts of the being which surrounded and subsumed her pounded through her. They weren't words, exactly, more like... feelings, impressions... determination, anticipation, some feelings with no human analog... and above all, a cold, silent fury, but at what or whom she couldn't conceive.

The being wasn't entirely present. Parts of itself existed here, with her, but far more existed in places she knew she couldn't perceive. Like a bacterium in the gut, the entire being she was aware of was only a tiny fraction of its true self.

The memories that pressed in on her were not her own, and they showed her this creature enjoyed an existence completely alien to her own. It had witnessed the birth of the solar system, already heavy with the knowledge of the eventual presence of life. It had borne witness to the expansion of the sun into a red giant, though that was eons away. It had seen this day, and was prepared.

She couldn't tell if she'd been there hours or seconds, when suddenly she felt the terrible presence torn from her. She felt the weightlessness and warmth of the void replaced by the heavy chill of winters air. Her vision returned and she could make out the ivory glow of the moon above. A moon oddly bisected by a thin dark line that stretched across the sky.

She tasted the zing of copper. Recognized it for blood. Felt the ground beneath her flow with some kind of liquid. She sat up. Around her she could make out the prone forms of numerous people. Everyone was covered in the same dark fluid now running off and forming puddles around them. She looked down at her hands, she was covered as well. The fluid writhed over her flesh, droplets leaping from the tips of her outstretched fingers.

One drop began flowing its way up her neck and into her hairline. Another stretched itself into a tiny stream encircling her wrist. She saw two droplets on her thigh form together into some kind of twisted point... which then stabbed down into her. She could feel it begin moving inside.

She screamed.

~

Day 79

Having caught up to the Giant, Jesse slowed the truck down to match its pace. The long strides of the creature made it look like it was simply taking an easy jog, but the speedometer of the truck tattled on its true speed, nearly 30 miles per hour.

The creature didn't look at the truck, but simply kept its pace going down the road. Signs flashed past indicating an intersection with State Highway 17 just a mile ahead. The Giant continued apace. The off-ramp came up, and the Giant headed off I-95 with a leap over what was left of Jesse's truck.

Jesse nearly tipped over the truck in his attempt to turn to follow. Linda rolled out of her seat down into the floorboards. A Best Western, McDonalds, and a Wendy's flashed by after they got off the frontage road. Derelict vehicles started appearing here and there, forcing Jesse to swerve around them. The Giant walked over them, or in some cases knocked them out of the way with a backhanded slap from its enormous hands.

Linda pulled herself back into her seat and pulled the seatbelt across herself, clicking it into place. They followed the Giant as it ran through Sheldon, and nearly overturned the truck again when it turned onto State Highway 21 and headed south towards Seabrook. The turn in Burton onto Parris Island Gateway and then Robert Smalls Parkway were much easier — the creature's gait was slowing down, almost as if it were trying to avoid making noise.

As they approached the Edward Burton Rogers Bridge, it's pace slowed to a veritable walk. Once on the bridge it stopped. Jesse put the truck in neutral and leaned further out the window.

"Well, now that you've had yourself a merry little jog care to reveal exactly what we came all this way for?"

The creature turned to Jesse before raising its arm, indicating a south-southeasterly direction down the Harbor River.

Jesse put the parking brake on the truck and got out, followed by Linda. They walked between the concrete barriers in the center of the bridge and to the opposite side in order to look downriver. On the northern shore of Daws Island, dozens of giants were systematically disposing of the bodies of hundreds of people, picking them up, crushing the ribcages, and then throwing them into the eastern flow of the river.

~

Day 79

Angela blinked rapidly. Her eyes were quickly moistened but the initial dryness caused lingering discomfort. Cries of surprise and alarm filled the chamber as long dormant throats found purpose once again. One of the number, a stranger, bolted. She didn't recognize his clothing. Rotted animal hides and rusted chainmail indicated he was one of the older residents, the Saxon maybe. Taking off like an

Olympic runner he threw himself in a mad dash for escape.

He crossed the center of the chamber on a long curve, giving the giants a wide berth before heading directly for the stairs. As soon as he crossed the perimeter of the circle, however, a kind of hazy red smoke began billowing from him as his steps faltered. He fell forward, his body striking the same stones Angela had landed on at the base of the stairs. There was the distinct sound of shattered bones as he fell still. The sanguine smoke seemed to curl and waft in the air a moment, neither dissipating nor condensing, before it formed a miraculous beeline for the center of the chamber, where it coalesced into a small floating piece of blue-silver glass pulsing with a tiny inner light.

The assembled crowd was silent. Most tried to use the dusty and rotten remains of their clothing to cover themselves — except for Estelle, who chose instead to cast off her deteriorated dress and stretch languidly, and not without a little lewd pride in how many of the men gawked.

An older man in a spoiled suit tried to adjust his tie but it crumbled in his hands. Shaking the remains off his hands, he cleared his throat.

"Ahem... I suppose most of you will recognize me as August Ernheim, I'm quite certain my voice sounds different than it did in our telepathic roundtables, but I hope not *too* different. Now, I would propose that we get to business."

He walked briskly up to the nearest giant and stood there quite unafraid, head high, hands at his sides looking the giant very pointedly in the eye before he began speaking.

"Might I inquire, by what right have you detained us here these long years?"

Angela stood and stretched, her clothing hardly dusty, but decidedly stiff with the dried blood from her condition previous. She watched the exchange with a curious eye. The questioned giant made no move or signal, issued no sound, but simply stared back at the erstwhile anthropologist.

424

Then, as one, all the giants turned to the stairs and began walking towards them.

"Excuse me! After so long, I feel, and I'm sure all the rest as well, that we're owed answers!"

The last giant, the one whom the steely scientist had chosen to address, paused. It turned back, the ebon orbs in its head whirling and fixing its golden pinpricks on the diminutive figure in decayed finery. In a voice both louder and gentler than seemed possible, it spoke.

"You are owed. Yes. And you will be repaid."

~

Longmire took a deep breath. The smells of mold, mildew, oil, and a strange pungent wood scent filled his nose. He closed his eyes and listened to the world around him. The drips of some far off leak, the low slow breathing of Sarya at his side, the even deep breathing of his crewmen across the way. No sound came from the Giants.

Longmire opened his eyes and looked at his crewmen, or, the men who claimed to be his crewmen. He couldn't take any chances.

"Boys, I appreciate, at the least, the attempt to put yourselves forth as advocates for an immediate peace. It's admirable, really. But I can't take you at your word given what you've told me. That being said, I am willing to listen to whatever you have to say, just don't expect me to swallow it hook, line, and sinker. So my first question is, I guess, just what are the intentions of these giants, and what are the intentions of the others?"

Watkins nodded before he spoke.

"That's fair, sir. We didn't expect you'd take us at our word. We thought, and by 'we' I refer to the Giants, Kellogg, and I, that you might need some convincing. These giants refer to themselves as 'The Freed'. As in, from service — slavery, actually. They're refugees, escaped from control. There's... well the closest thing we could call them are Gods. Things outside our understanding of time

425

or space, and they created the Giants, and the things that took the skies."

"And these 'Freed', what are their intentions?"

"Just to exist, sir. They don't want to be controlled anymore. They don't share the goals of their Gods, and so they've sought refuge here."

"By here, you mean Earth?"

"By here, they mean our reality. What we see, what we perceive, is just the shadow of what they truly are, the parts that can exist here. Like dipping your finger in a fish tank, the fish can only perceive of the part in their world, and the part outside is the larger part."

"And the other Giants?"

"They're still in service of their larger self, er, selves? Still carrying out the tasks they were made for."

"And what are those?"

"Might as well ask a hammer what it's building. Their purpose is so far beyond them they don't know. But they're aware that it involves the reducing the Earth to a planet without sentient beings."

"They've very nearly succeeded. Those things in the sky..."

"Aren't for the same purpose, at least, not explicitly. The relationship with the Shards is kind of like hammer to a baseball bat. A bat can hammer, but that ain't what it's for, and any hammering it does accomplish is incidental."

"This is raising more questions than its answering and I'm starting to get a little pissed off here."

"Please, sir... it might be easier to just... sit back and watch."

~

Zoe slapped and clawed at her thigh trying to crush the thing that was now inside her. She felt it digging through her flesh, pushing, stabbing through muscle and fat as it moved up towards her groin.

The pain was like a drizzle of red hot liquid metal was worming its way through her flesh. Suddenly she felt the liquid still crawling over her outsides firm up, resisting her movements, gripping her all over, like she was suddenly covered in a layer of shrink wrap.

The sticky, thick fluid began expanding, joining the various streams together as they flowed over her body, some ran down her forehead and up her neck, working to cover her face as she struggled to dig through her skin to get at the sizzling thread wriggling around her hip.

The fluid was forming a second skin under her clothing, covering every inch of her. Its strength overpowered her own and locked her arms out away from her body. The fluid flowed down and covered her face, closing over her eyes and ears, it pushed into her nostrils, forced its way under her eyelids, and then moved to her mouth, it's thick coppery taste nauseating. The sharp pain of the trickle moved up her side and around the swell of her right breast before coiling at base of her throat.

Her nose and throat filled with the bizarre liquid, she couldn't breathe, and actively resisted the urge to do so, lest she pull more of the concoction into her. The pain at the base of her neck cooled, becoming a solid weight hanging there. The residual pain from its path through her body deadened as well, becoming a dull awareness, a shadow of its former intensity. She felt her body twisting, bones snapping, muscles tearing... There was no pain. She felt the memories of sharing her mind with the being blossoming, expanding... There was a moment of panic as she realized she couldn't remember her own name, and then everything went white.

In Grant Park in Chicago, near the fountain, an albino giant with black eyes stood for the first time, shaking off shreds of what were once some rather fetching pajamas. It looked around at the other giants surrounding it, some standing, most still laying down, before looking up at the line of darkness bisecting the moon.

~

Jesse turned to the giant, a befuddled look on his face.

"Whad'ja bring us here for? To show us your buddies down there throwing people away like trash? What's the point of that?"

Linda reached over to Jesse, placing her hand on his shoulder she pulled him back to look again. In the waters a hundred feet downstream from where the giants tossed the bodies of their victims, lights flashed in the deep. Blues, whites, reds, and yellows flashed like camera bulbs as the waters roiled and bubbled. A coastal breeze brought a strange scent. Jesse turned back to the giant.

"What? Are y'all welding down there or something? Smells like hot metal, like the smell ya get when ya rub your hands on a bunch of copper or iron…"

The waters above the lights exploded into the air before the droplets stopped, suspended in the air before being violently sucked back down to the water. The current upstream accelerated towards the lights, the current downstream slowed, stopped, and then began running backwards. The wind quickened to a scream as the waters pitched down, unable to keep up with the roaring demand under the water. A curved black sphere interspersed with starlight emerged, the waves crashing through its surface.

The giant grunted, gaining Jesse and Linda's attention. It raised an arm as long as Jesse was tall, indicating the way they'd come.

"Go. Now."

"Hold on just a minute…"

"Go! It comes!"

Jesse and Linda raced to the truck. As Linda climbed in, Jesse turned, looking back to the bizarre occurrences in the Harbor River one last time. As he watched, a stream of multicolored light shot into the sky, but before it made it too high the lights dimmed and began coalescing into an obsidian form of angles and hard edges, glistening in the setting sun. The form arced through the air before crashing down, it's length still being formed by the flow shooting upwards from the river. The point came down into the concrete and asphalt of the far end of the Edward Burton Rogers Bridge. Debris flew every which way as the supports underneath began giving away.

CHAPTER 40

Day 79

Angela watched the giant turn back and continue towards the stairwell. One of the assembled number picked themselves up and walked after it, slowing, and then stopping as they raised their arm, seeing their fingers begin to turn dark and wither as a subtle red smoke began wafting around their form and making its way back to the form in the center of the chamber. They reversed their steps, coming back within the circle, and the smoke reversed as well, moving back to their fingers. As the smoke touched them, the skin grew from a withered and blackened leather back to a healthy and plump flesh toned digit once more.

The assembled crowd grew silent watching the events unfold. The realization that their ordeal wasn't nearly over, that their freedom was in fact limited to the circle they found themselves arranged in, was not a pleasant one. Most, in their long existence as bone-in people jerky, had come to the conclusion that their condition was permanent, and so this brief respite from their plight was just that, a respite, not a rescue. Still, more than a few had dared hope.

Angela had a sudden thought. She reached down and pulled free one

430

of her boots. Hefting its weight in her hands, she judged the distance, aimed, and hurled the footwear at the retreating giant. It sailed through the air as gracefully as a boot can before solidly thunking into the back of the giant's massive head. The creatures gait slowed, then stopped. It turned around, noticeably puzzled. Angela shouted after it.

"What are we owed!?"

The figure started, its obsidian orbs fired with shining streaks of ragged sunlight.

You are owed. To the creator. You are the medium through which their passage is charted.

"Just what in the hell does that mean!?"

You make the passage possible.

"Yeah, you said that, but how? And whose passage? Why would we matter?"

You do not. They do.

The tingle of paroxysm felt eerie after every word uttered by the giant. Like the ruby glow from its gullet carried with it the essence of the pins and needles feeling one gets from lack of blood flow in the extremities.

"Why do they matter and why don't we?"

The giant ignored her, turning back to its course, it strode to the base of the stairs. Another boot sailed through the air, this time missing completely and hitting the wall ahead of it with an echoing crack.

"You owe us answers! I may have only just arrived but others have been here decades, maybe even centuries! You took their lives from them! Stole them from their futures! They had families, friends, people cared about them, who never found out what happened to them! Don't walk away from me, you apathetic albino asshole!"

The giant paused, one foot on the bottom step.

~

Day 79

Longmire shifted Sarya from one hip to the other and rubbed the sweat from his eyes.

"Fine, show me."

Watkins and Kellogg turned to the giant behind them expectantly. It narrowed its eyes and stepped back as half a dozen other giants emerged from the shadows, forming a rough semi-circle aground the chamber. As they came to a halt, minuscule sparks of white light began emerging from the nodules which covered them, each spark leaving a trail in the vision of the human observers, a trail which shifted in a rainbow. The lights swirled, circling the group. The giants began chanting. The noise was disconcerting, like nails on a chalkboard or a child hammering on an out-of-tune piano with the fervency of a cocaine-fueled manic episode.

The motes raced faster and faster around them, becoming a blur of brilliant hues. The chaotic notes of the giants grew to the volume of a gunshot, then a jet engine, and then yet higher. The metal deck plates picked up the vibration, the walls rattled with it, pipes tore loose from their mountings. Breathing grew difficult, the air thick. Time seemed to move in jumps, or slow to a crawl.

The world twisted, and Longmire felt Sarya torn from his grasp. He reached out in the direction she'd gone, only to experience the bizarre sensation of his arm not being there to reach with. Looking down, he expected to see a bloody and torn stump, for pain to flood his consciousness. But his arm simply ended six inches below his shoulder.

Past that, he saw the universe unfold beneath him. He whizzed by planets, watched stars streak past, whole galaxies blurred by, if only for a few seconds. Then he found himself in some kind of iridescent cloud of orange with striations of brown and green. He saw something there, moving in the ether... something literally astronomical in size was emerging. He felt it in his mind. It was probing, feeling out his mood, his intentions and desires. Longmire concentrated, imagining a wall of thought, a wall impervious to any breach, a wall with no cracks or edges or borders completely encapsulating his mind... and the probing ceased.

The details of the behemoth before him grew sharper, and just as he started to form a picture of what its shape must be, everything went black.

~

Jesse hung onto the door of the truck, its steel hinges creaking under his weight. The bridge lurched, its whole surface suddenly gaining something nearing a ten-degree slant. Linda screamed from the other side of the truck as she climbed in, a wordless, shrill expression of terror.

The giant took two steps — one over the concrete barriers in the middle of the bridge — and reached out, grasping Jesse around the waist with one hand and the hood of the truck with the other. He pushed Jesse up and around the door, depositing him in the cab before pushing the truck around, its tires leaving black streaks across the asphalt. Jesse reached out to the door, grabbing it and slamming it closed as his other hand frantically pulled the seatbelt across himself. He looked briefly at Linda in the passenger seat, nodding to himself, assured of her safety, then, he threw the truck into first gear and slammed the gas.

The bridge shook and its angle worsened to near fifteen degrees. The truck lurched forward for just a moment before the singing of the engine prompted Jesse to shift into second. Twenty degrees and the concrete dividers started sliding back towards where the ebon spike was driving the bridge down. Another lurch of speed and a shift to third and they were off the bridge. Jesse peeked back through the shattered rear of the truck, just a glimpse, but he could see small nodules swelling out the sides of the bizarre column, each pulsing with an inner light reminiscent of a blacklight.

Jesse turned back to the road, just in time to swerve and avoid a

433

derelict car, the desiccated bodies of a family still inside. The giant, jogging along next to the truck, simply leapt over it. The road curved to the left, giving them a reprieve from the view of the arch and it's distended polyps. Jesse shouted through the passenger window at the giant.

"You know, we might coulda used a bit of a warning that some humongous black pillar o'evil was gonna shoot outta the river and try to drag us and the goddamn bridge down into the river!"

The giant peered over with one softball-sized eye without speaking. Linda slapped Jesse's shoulder and chided him.

"Don't antagonize him!"

"Well he coulda! "

The giant slowed its pace, coming to a walk before stopping. Jesse downshifted quickly, braking and turning the truck around to rendezvous with their erstwhile escort. In the distance, beyond the curve in the road and the forest that obscured them, they could see a beam of multi-hued light streaking up into the sky. They watched as it streamed upwards, a long, gradual curve, until the light intersected the line that crossed the sky. There, the light was extinguished and the circle ignited, taking on a deep orange glow. Jesse put the parking brake on and got out of the truck, astounded and amazed at the display in the skies above.

"Linda… did you notice that... that uh... that line... there before…?"

"No... I didn't, Jesse."

Jesse, never taking his eyes away from the sky, waved his right hand in the direction of the giant.

"I don't suppose... uh... that maybe y'all had something to do with that one?"

The giant momentarily glanced down at Jesse, and shrugged.

~

434

McGuire watched the bunker door open with no small amount of surprise. He'd given orders for the artist and the spy to be loaded in the chopper. His men should've then waited in the chopper for him to come out. There was no reason anyone from outside should be coming in, and yet, the access lights on the console had lit up in the proper order and the door was now slowly opening. He narrowed his eyes, there was something... odd... about things. He looked to the corners of the door. Each square corner should've been 90 degrees but... they weren't. At the same time, he noticed a distinct chill in the air. It took a second for him to put the pieces together, and then, he started running.

Moments later the doors parted like tissue paper as a giant tore through them. Bits of debris and shrapnel exploded through the warehouse as it barreled through the flimsy airlock as if it was made of balsa wood held together with spider web. Instantly the temperature in the warehouse dropped precipitously. Frost spread out from the giant like waves off the bow of a ship, the hard edges of the shelves and the floor of the warehouse itself distorted like they were made of runny wax exposed to a hurricane wind.

McGuire ran.

Only twenty feet behind, the giant seemed to pace itself, intentionally avoiding overtaking him, allowing the fear and panic to set in. The giant made no noise, no roars, no shouts came from its lipless mouth. Instead, as it pursued him, it threw out its arms, grasping at corners and edges of shelves to pull itself forward as it made long easy strides, each push off knocking shelves over left and right, its strength ripping up the ones bolted to the concrete sending them flying. Frozen food and various tools and detritus flew through the air like confetti in its wake.

McGuire made his way to the arms locker, a room untouched by Zoe in her stay, but unlocked and inventoried by his men hours earlier. The giant stayed at his heels occasionally catching a small something out of the air and pitching it at him. Toying with him. He fumbled with the keys to the locker, sure that at any moment the giant would snatch him up. But it didn't. He turned, it wasn't there. Even as bits of paper and styrofoam packing peanuts floated down from the last shelf it had thrown aside, it simply wasn't there.

McGuire finally jammed the correct key in the door and threw it open. Grabbing an M16A2, he slammed home a magazine, pulled back the charging handle to put a round in the chamber, and turned back, his thumb flicking the weapon to three rounds burst. It still wasn't there. And then, it was. As if emerging from behind a curtain the giant reappeared, coming arms first from whatever otherworldly void it had gone to. McGuire opened fire, pumping the trigger and fighting to keep the barrel pointed center mass as the weapon jumped and bucked in his hands.

Few Naval officers put in much time beyond the minimum with rifles, and he'd certainly never experimented with the three rounds burst setting. Still, he didn't do half bad. At least one round from each barrage found its mark. The giant stood unharmed, but with each burst some small part of its flesh had deformed before sending the rounds bouncing off in a slow ricochet. The floor in front of it was littered with the small bronze mushrooms of impacted rounds.

McGuire kept squeezing at the trigger even after the magazine was emptied, watching in horror as his efforts were wasted. The giant scratched at its chest, plucking out an errant round that had gotten caught between the ridges of its skin. McGuire dropped the rifle and went to grab something else from the locker, but the giant opened its mouth. The crimson glare filled McGuire's mind, and his purpose, his will, instantly drained. The giant moved forward. Reaching out with one hand, it grasped him by the torso, lifting him into the air before closing its mouth. The cold washed over McGuire like he'd been dunked into a tub of liquid hydrogen, he felt his skin freeze, the pain of it driving him to twist and scream briefly before the cold penetrated deeper, choking the air from his lungs. He felt his muscles seizing as they froze, felt his core go cold. His eyes froze over and his mouth iced over from within.

The giant tossed him aside, the body shattering into a dozen pieces as it impacted the floor.

CHAPTER 41

Day 79

The giant turned back to face Angela. It seemed to sigh, a noiseless raising and lowering of the shoulders, almost imperceptible, had the entire room not been so focused on its every move. It took a few slow steps back to her, stopping only when it stood directly over her, towering, such that she had to look up at it.

You... are not ready... Time is supposed to ripen you... Wisen you... Help you to understand and be prepared... But you are still raw. Unseasoned... Perhaps... Next time.

"Hold on... what do you mean time? I've been here for far too long as it is and…"

No. You have not. None of you. For some the process takes longer than others, and then there are always those who spoil when they regain motion. You, I think, have spoiled the whole of your companions. There is still time. Your kind is very resilient. You have survived two cycles. A third may yet come. Time between them will teach you.

"What the hell are you talking about?"

You will see.

Angela opened her mouth to reply but the giant stretched its mouth open, the paralysis taking hold of everyone in the room as the light shone forth from the impossible chasm within. The giant approached the tiny misshapen lump of glowing blue crystal in the center of the chamber. Reaching up to one of its shoulders, it pinched the sickly green growth there, a small mote of silvery light emerging onto one of its long fingers. It put the hand forth, pushing the light into the crystal. Immediately, Angela was hit by a wave of nausea and pain. She fell to the ground. She could hear the others falling suit, body after body thudded to the floor. Her vision grew blurry, but not before she could make out the subtle red smoke rising from her hand, then all was black.

In a chamber made of impossible stone half a mile beneath the frozen forests surrounding Lycksele, Sweden, a solitary giant watched as the last wisps of crimson ether coalesced into a glowing crystal rendition of an exaggerated womanly figure with impossibly oversized feminine features. Turning, it saw the mummified remains of the chambers residents, in their various poses they took as they collapsed. It hesitated just a moment, then, it began picking each up and placing them against the walls of the chamber, ignorant of the cacophony of screams they emitted.

After the task was done, it went around collecting the various bits and pieces that had fallen off of them in their brief flirtation with animation. A scrap of khaki cloth here, a red sash there, two boots... The chamber set back in order, it released its fragile grip on its presence in that time and place, showing itself to pull back to its true home, awakening to its true self. There, it came fully aware with all its myriad senses and portions, spread as they were. The servile portions, it's manipulators, stood by in the thousands, each distinct and conscious in only the barest sense, each more sentient then the raw materials they harvested.

~

439

Post Phenomenon, Year 5, New Panama City, Florida

A crowd of nearly a hundred stood in the morning sun, sweating. A light rain had fallen that morning, and with the sunrise the dew and few puddles had evaporated, turning the air thick and muggy. It was an eclectic bunch, jeans & t-shirts, dresses, skirts, tank tops, shorts, overalls, a few men even wore kilts. Fashion had fallen before function in the post-apocalypse.

They stood on the lawn around the old Town Hall, chosen for its records and numerous rooms and windows. When you're looking to rebuild civilization, it's a good idea to know where the pieces of the old fell. The Town Hall had all the records of all the old businesses, warehouses, and even certain records & registries of private citizens and their addresses. Maps of the utilities, water mains, gas lines, power, all came in useful. City Hall had become the primary residence of a particular band of survivors. Next door was the main branch of the Bay County Library, an invaluable resource for entertainment, as well as for critical knowledge. Certain professions and trades were completely unrepresented in the group, so in order to rebuild, they needed reference materials so they could fill in the gaps and train new people as needed.

Jesse stood on a makeshift platform in the rear bed of a truck. He held a megaphone in one hand and a steaming cup of coffee in the other. He surveyed the crowd, noting familiar and unfamiliar faces among them. He reflected once more about his decision to rebuild here. An airport and a deep water port, a fuel depot, three or four major department stores mostly untouched, but most importantly, a Navy base and an Air Force base meant high quality communications equipment. That advantage alone gave them the ability to broadcast their location and invitation to other survivors across the Southeast. Without that, they'd never have gained the numbers they had now, nearly six hundred at last count. Carpenters, Roofers, Auto Mechanics, more than a few Plumbers, Electricians, and other blue collar tradesmen... Survivors, like him. Plus a few White collars who proved worth their weight. A doctor, a computer guy (he could never remember what his "before" job title was), an architect, a few others. Then the majority were useless. Bankers,

440

clerks, lawyers... he almost shot the lawyer when they first met, just out of pure ideological altruism for the society they were building... But, he didn't. Good thing too. Turns out he was also a damn skilled woodworker.

He sipped his coffee. It wasn't very good. The beans were grown here, dried here, and ground here, but there was just something off from their beans to the stuff from before. The freeze-dried from local stores ran out the previous year. Still, the swill they had was still better than the seven months they'd gone without.

The last of the crowd was arriving. Representatives from each of the major groups the survivors had organized. Basically based on where they chose to live. Some lived in the Town Hall, some lived in a condo building by the marina, some lived in a neighborhood on the waterfront. They were spreading out, growing, recovering parts of the old to rebuild anew. To that end, they'd been discussing and debating a proposition for a few weeks, and it was time for the final tally. He cleared his throat and beeped the megaphone before speaking.

"Now, y'all know I ain't one fer words, and, y'all know what I think. We done spent the last few weeks jabberin' about it. Last night we broke for dinner and an overnight recess. Now, I'm done talking about this, I ain't got the patience for it, and I pretty much figure y'all are tired of arguing over it. And, I'm damn sure more yapping ain't gonna change anybody's minds at this point. So I'm gonna call it now.

"All in favor, say 'aye'."

A chorus of 'aye's came up like a sudden strong wind. Easily more than two thirds of the assembled crowd shouted their support. He'd come to realize that the first year was the easy part. Wandering the roads looking for evidence of survivors, building their numbers, taking anyone who wanted to go and taking down information and records from those who wanted to stay and those places where the survivors hadn't lasted. It had been the four years since, organizing and rebuilding, finding ways to settle differences, it... well it'd been a bit like trying to herd cats with a vacuum cleaner. But with this he hoped to maybe get away, get back in his element.

Jesse smiled as he finished the vote.

"Those opposed?"

A weak few voices muttered their 'nay's.

"Then by the power vested in me by, well, y'all, I hereby call the vote decided in the affirmative, and formally announce that the expedition to the former capital is to begin preparations, uh, soon, I mean... forthwith!"

Jesse looked at the beaming faces in the crowd. Most of them seemed eager and excited at the possibility of what they might find. Just the Library of Congress was reason enough to go. A treasure trove of knowledge that could be used to rebuild. Then there were the actual government buildings, the possibility of official government survivors, people who might be able to give them some answers. Linda was busily talking over the expedition with another representative, something about rescuing history from the Smithsonian. Jesse remembered the day they discovered the skies were safe, and how that first day ended.

~

Day 79

Jesse stood beside the remains of his truck, the engine still loudly idling and the single exhaust pipe — now bent at an odd angle — still wafting grey smoke into the early evening air. Eight feet away stood the giant. Eleven feet of ivory white skin and bone looking at Jesse with twin golden irises set in ebony pools.

"Ya didn't know?"

The giant huffed and turned away, its immense shoulders swinging like boulders set in flesh.

"Not no but hell no, you turn around and talk to me."

442

The giant started walking, long strides with its peg-like bone feet, the crunching thud of each step disconcerting in its stability. Jesse gave chase, the dark-haired Linda pulling at his arm trying to restrain him, her thin form barely a weight on his thick frame.

"Look, we been terrorized by your buddies up there, nearly crushed, and we're getting sick and fucking tired of it. I want some goddamn answers you pale faced, flat nosed, ridge skinned, blood gulleted bastard!"

The giant made a sound. If it were human, it perhaps would have been described as a chuckle, but from the giant it sounded more like a peal of thunder with brief interruptions by rolling gravel. The sound made Linda's teeth hurt and sent a chill up her spine. Jesse didn't seem to be affected.

"Oh you're laughing? Look Linda he's laughing! I must be some kinda comedian!"

"Jesse I don't think it's a good idea to mock him..."

"Mock him? Unh-uh, I ain't mockin' nobody. I'm asking for some fucking answers. I wanna know what the hell is going on here!"

"Jesse, please..."

The giant stopped, its head twisting to the side, like it had heard some distant sound, the flesh on one side stretching as the other side compressed, the ridges that swirled every inch of its skin acting like folds in an accordion. It slowed and stopped. It waved Jesse back, its long fingers splayed out like some strange ocean spider. Too many joints made it seem bizarre and alien... which, Linda supposed, it was.

It turned, focusing its gaze on the pair. As it spoke, the baleful crimson of its throat caused them to freeze, their every conscious effort wasted. An almost mournful tone came forth before it formed actual words.

It has come. We are done here.

Jesse advanced, his eyes narrowed, skin ruddy, fists shaking with rage.

"What the fuck do you mean you're done? What has come?"

The light in the giant's eyes dimmed, a subtle gurgling sound could be heard, and then, it collapsed. A pile of too-long limbs and twisted, ridged albino flesh in an ungainly pile in the middle of the road.

Jesse stood silent, dumbfounded for a moment, before exploding. Linda set her teeth as a string of cursing and hate boiled out of him into the evening air. His diatribe ended in frustrated babbling, discordant sounds of pure frustration and enmity punctuated by wracking coughs as he dropped to his knees. Linda knelt by his side, one knee on the ground, tiny rocks and grit digging into her flesh and grating against bone. She rested a hand on his shoulder before speaking.

"Jesse... we need to get going. Who knows what 'they' are, or why they're here? The skies are clear but... what if they don't stay that way? Do we really want to caught in the open?"

"Huh?"

"Jesse... We have to go."

Reluctantly, Jesse stood, legs wobbling as he walked back to the truck from the adrenaline coursing through his veins. As he climbed in he took one last look at the pile of a giant in the roadway, then he stopped.

~

Post Phenomenon, Year 7, the Capital Ruins

The convoy of vehicles came to a stop just as they came to the Capital Mall. Across the tall grass they could make out the Washington Monument, still in good repair even if it wasn't white anymore, stained by neglect. The driver's side door of the lead vehicle, a Mine Resistant Ambush Protected (MRAP) vehicle known as a Cougar, opened, and a leg clad in blue jeans and a black combat

444

boot extended down the step.

Jesse looked over at his riding buddy and girlfriend, a full figured brunette by the name of Claudette. She'd been working overnight security at a wholesale warehouse in Alabama when everything went to hell. Three months alone with nothing to do but read labels & memorize expiration dates. They'd found her in the first winter, when they scoured Maxwell Air Force Base. She was his other (and in his opinion, better) half.

The party collectively flinched as a rifle shot rang out in the sweltering summer air. Jesse immediately threw his hands up in the air and indicated to everyone else to do the same. It only took a few seconds for the air to be full of raised hands and the ground covered in discarded gear. Rifles, binoculars, candy bars, jerky, radios, and other bits littered the ground around each door and hatch. Soon enough, two men came into view, emerging from the Freer Sackler Gallery and walking through the tall grass to the road where the convoy waited.

~

Pre Phenomenon, 39,599 AP, 1 kilometer below the SE outskirts of New Lycksele

Angela had nothing left to say. All that could have been said, had, and they all knew it. And so the collection was silent as the giants ceased their cacophony, and the red smoke streamed out from the figure in the center. Like before, and a thousand times since, they found themselves gasping in the pungent aroma of their own bodies, and the tattered remains of whatever clothing they'd once worn. Angela stood as she always did, as the rest remained sitting or prone. One of the ivory beings came to her, as had become ritual. It's long peg like feet echoing hollow cracking sounds with each step. It stopped just short of her, her steady gaze fixed on its chest, as if she was taking aim.

Are you still proud? Still demanding?

Angela looked up into its ebon pools, raced with ever drifting jagged bolts of shine.

"I am."

Truly? You speak the words, as you have so many times before. But the set of your jaw, your stance, your hands... they do not show the fire of your convictions and determination as they have in the past. You are ready?

The attentions of the group stirred, the script had changed, and something moved palpably, the balance of power shifting in the winds.

"...I am."

The giant reached out to Angela, placing one ivory finger under her chin, bringing her gaze directly to his own.

Good.

A new sensation overtook them, pain. Then all was black.

~

Post Phenomenon, Year 7, the Capital Ruins

The two men advanced through the tall grass towards the convoy, rifles slung. One was tall, clad in faded MARPAT, with an equally faded boonie cover. His large frame seemed a size too large for the uniform; indeed, his wrists seemed to poke a bit too far out of the arms. The other man was shorter, slightly pudgy, wore glasses, and was balding. Together they seemed very much a mismatched pair. The taller one stopped just before he reached the road, still in the grass. Looking over the convoy, he spoke.

"Y'all can put yer hands down now. Who's in charge here?"

Jesse waved his right hand and whistled a short tone to get his attention.

"Uh, that'd be me."

"Name?"

"Jesse."

"Alright Jesse, my name's Frost, this is Apone, and I'm sorry to say, but if you're here to try and establish communications with the remains of the US Government, they're not here..."

"Whaddaya mean they're not..?"

"Well, they're just... not. We have satellite communications with a few far flung places where government survived — London, Moscow, Sydney, Brasilia, but DC ain't one of em. You want to trade, fine, you want to take pictures, be tourists, that's fine, we'll escort you. Only things completely off limits are the Pentagon, the White House, and Congress. The old Captain's got it in his head they should be preserved for if and when someone from the government shows up."

Jesse marveled at the peculiar way things had gone since the end of the old world. Time after time when meeting new groups of survivors, he'd been taken aback. In the old world strangers were generally met with suspicion, fear, or outright hostility. In the new, however, strangers were generally met with congeniality, even excitement, and trust. Since all the treasures of the old world were laid bare for the taking, there was no real competition for resources yet, no need for conflict between groups. So this wasn't an entirely unexpected kind of reception. A guard against dangerous wildlife was a constant component of postmodern life, but against people, nearly unheard of.

"Who's the old captain?"

"Some old Navy sub schmuck, showed up two weeks after the skies cleared with a full crew, took over, got us organized. Not the nicest or the brightest, but he's got a handle on things. Has leadership ability."

"Sounds like an interestin' fella, can't wait to meet him."

"I'm sure he'll want to meet you too. Where are y'all from?"

"Panama City, Florida. Well, now, anyway. All over, really."

"Alright, well, the Captain, he keeps quarters over at the Navy Yard. We'll escort you if you'd like."

"Sounds like a plan. Ya want the rest of us to hold here?"

"Sure."

As Jesse conferred with his group, Apone radioed in their arrival and gave forewarning to sentries on the way to hold their fire. Once the convoy was set, Jesse and Frost started the long walk to the Navy Yard.

"We'll pass by Nationals Stadium if you're interested. We've turned the field into a farm and covered most of the stands with solar panels as part of our efforts at self-sufficiency."

"Y'all ain't self-sufficient?"

"Close to, we trade with communities up and down the coast, inland as far as Nashville, mostly for parts, rechargeable batteries, things like that. Right now we're pretty dependent on the *Oregon* for power, we're hoping to change that by end of year."

"Oregon? How y'all getting power from Oregon?"

"Ha... no, *the Oregon;* she's a sub, Nuclear. The Captain's old command; he pulled her up to a pier, tied her up, hooked her up to the grid, and started her reactor on a slow burn. At first it was a nightmare; the draw was enormous. Streetlights, TVs left on, home appliances... dead people don't turn off the odds and ends, y'know? The *Oregon's* reactor isn't like a huge one, it's meant to power one ship, not an entire city. So we had to cut big swaths of the city off. We still go 'round occasionally, shutting off everything on a block, connecting it, shutting down what we missed, then clearing it out. It'll still be a few years but we'll get DC back to something usable. We know there's similar efforts underway in most of the major cities. Baltimore, Philly, Atlanta..."

"There's survivors in Atlanta?"

448

"Yep. Spend time there, before?"

"Uh… during, actually."

"Really? Hmm... Captain'll definitely want to hear about that then. He's always looking to hear stories from people who were able to move about during. Collects 'em, hear tell he's writing 'em down. Some kind of history."

"Smart. So much of what came before has already been lost... makes sense to try and get a record of everything since, y'know?"

"Heh... sure. I don't think that's why he's doing it though."

"Well, why'd'ya think then?"

"Well... you said you moved around during?"

"Yeah."

"You ever see anything... odd?"

Jesse stopped, Frost stopped and looked back.

"Buddy… the things I seen'll scare the hair right off ya head."

"Yeah... you'll definitely wanna talk to the Captain."

CHAPTER 42

Day 80

The first sensation was of heat, then pain. Sarya opened her eyes.
The light was blinding, painful. She blinked and looked away from
the light. She saw her arm; it was covered in blisters, scorched.
Sitting up, she took stock of the situation. She was in a boat of some
kind, made of dayglow orange rubber, and she wasn't alone. There
were six or seven crewmembers from the *Oregon* jumbled together
in the boat. Every bit of exposed flesh was sunburned. Those with
lighter complexions were blistering. She thought a few might be
dead.

She looked around at the placid sea. A few hundred feet away she
could see the *Oregon. P*art of her seemed to be missing. She looked
for the other ships she'd heard about, the big cruise liner and the
cargo ship, but she couldn't see them. There were other little boats all
around, and in between everything there were pieces of flotsam
bobbing in the water. She could see one near hers that seemed to be
empty except for maybe two people.

She climbed up on top of the heap of arms and legs in her boat and looked around. Under the eave on one side she found and liberated a pair of oars. She wasn't big enough to use them properly, but she locked one of them into its mounting & used it like a fish's tail, swishing it back and forth, pushing her boat slowly but surely towards the nearly empty one. She didn't have the coordination to do the task quickly, but she was determined, and after nearly an hour the two boats gently bumped into one another.

Sarya quickly scrambled from her perch near the oar mount and to the point the boats met, grabbing a rubber handle on the other boat to hold them together. Looking over the edge she saw Longmire and her father, one atop the other, her father on top.

At the sight of her father Sarya gave up any pretense of keeping ahold the boat she'd been in and climbed fully into the other. She frantically patted at her father's shoulder and chest, but he didn't stir. Underneath, Longmire groaned at the impacts. She pulled her father off and nearer edge of the boat, then scooped up some seawater and poured it on his face. He still did not respond. Longmire rolled up on one hand, hacking and coughing. He spit out a couple of good mouthfuls of some kind of yellow ichor before speaking.

"Sarya..."

His speech was raspy, a wretched croak more than a human voice. Almost as if it came from some kind hellish set of iron gears jammed up with burning coals.

"Sarya... where's the *Oregon*? Where's my crew?"

Sarya continued shaking her father, to no avail. Longmire dragged a knee underneath himself and raised up over the height of the rafts sides. Gaining a view of the other rafts and the *Oregon*, he allowed himself to sink back onto his rear briefly before crawling to Emil & Sarya. Pressing his fingers to the side of Emil's throat for a few moments, he sought out any indicators of a pulse. It was weak, and far too fast, but there. He placed a hand on Saryas shoulder.

"Stop, darlin'; your Daddy's okay. He's probably just out like I was. He'll come to in his own time."

Longmire surveyed Emil as Sarya relaxed, noting severe blisters on most of his exposed skin. It appeared as though he'd been in the sun for days. He hoped he was wrong but from the looks of things Emil might be in the extremes of heat stroke. It was critical he get him aboard the *Oregon*, and soon. He looked around the raft. All the emergency provisions were still in place. He grabbed the first aid kit and a couple bottles of water.

"Sarya, baby; would you do me a favor to help your Dad? Could you take these bottles of water and slowly drip little bits into his mouth?"

Sarya nodded and took the water bottles, opening one and setting the other aside. Longmire pulled out the sterile bandages and started covering Emil's blistered flesh. Sarya started dribbling little bits into her father's mouth, spilling a drop or two now and then. Longmire took a moment to scan the horizon for the other ships, but found only a few life rafts and the *Oregon*, adrift and listing slightly to port. He maneuvered around the raft and mounted the oars in their brackets. As Sarya continued to tend to her father he began stroking the water with long easy pulls to bring himself and his compatriots back to his ship. Calm seas made it fairly easy, and inside ten minutes he felt the raft bump into the *Oregon's* hull. Normally, a crewman would have been waiting topside to assist, but without that help Longmire had to ease the raft down her starboard side until he reached an access ladder. As he tied the raft up, he felt Sarya tug at his sleeve. Looking up he saw the other rafts, some distance away and drifting further, start to wake up, arms and heads started poking up above their sides as other crewman from the *Oregon* regained consciousness.

~

Post Phenomenon, Year 7, the Capital Ruins

Frost removed his cover as they entered the dimly lit building, indicating to Jesse that he should do the same.

452

"The Captain's kind of a stickler for protocol, still insists we do as if we were all in the Navy, Marines, whatever..."

"Aw hell, that ain't nothin', we got a guy back in PC that still wears suits. He was some kind of accountant or whatever back before, and now he's our inventory man, stays all day in a damn warehouse checkin' and rechecking what we got and what we ain't, all the while sweating bullets, ruinin' suit after suit just so's he can look like he's used to."

"Yeah, well... I guess everybody has their little quirks. Come this way, we got a few turns until we get to the Sanctum."

"Sanctum?"

Frost continued speaking as he led Jesse through twists and turns inside the building.

"It's what we've taken to calling the Auditorium. Used to be for big briefings, now the Captain uses it like a big office. Him and his girl live there, pretty much. It's filled with files and computers; he's trying to collate everything we know about the Phenomenon."

"The Captain's married, eh?"

Frost shook his head and smiled.

"Nope, he's got a daughter."

"Good, family is important."

"Yeah, but she ain't his; adopted. Don't mention it though; he gets mad. Only his original crew know the whole story, and they're pretty damn tight lipped."

Jesse frowned, considering the myriad possibilities. If the Captain just had an adopted daughter, why the secrecy? What if she was stolen, or some kind of prisoner? Any man who'd do that might not be the kind of fella he'd like dealing with or even knowing about PC.

"Well, here we are. I'll announce you, but, uh, Jesse?"

"Yeah?"

"One last bit of advice... Don't lie to him. He can smell it on you, and he hates being lied to."

With that, Frost opened one of the double doors leading into the auditorium. Like he'd said, it was huge, and filled to the brim with cabinets, bookcases, and computers. Wires snaked the floor, papers sat on nearly every surface, and down in the middle of the floor, surrounded on nearly all sides by desks, sat a hard looking man in a faded Navy Uniform. His face was craggy, his skin like leather. Cold blue eyes looked down at the papers in his hands through a pair of wire rimmed glasses. Frost spoke loudly, echoing through the chamber.

"Captain Longmire, a representative from a previously unknown survivor group from Florida, name's Jesse, sir!"

The Captain looked up from the sheaf of papers he'd been reading, and raised one hand indicating that Jesse should come down. Jesse didn't waste time, stepping smartly into one of the aisles. He came down the steps quickly, but not headlong, arriving at the perimeter of desks around the captain in short order. The captain indicated a rolling office chair along the bottom edge of the auditorium seating.

"Have a seat, son... Jesse, was it?"

"That's right."

"Alright, Jesse. I presume you've already been told the government isn't here?"

"Yep."

"Then what can I do for you?"

"Actually, I've been told you'd want me for something."

454

Longmire leaned forward in his chair, the wood and leather creaking. His cold blue eyes intense under his dark eyebrows.

"Information about the Phenomenon?"

"Pretty much, did some movin' and shakin' during."

Longmire reached over to one of the desks, pulling out a digital recorder and setting it between them.

"Alright, let's hear it then. From the beginning, if you please."

~

Day 79

Linda and Jesse rode down the road in silence, each processing just what the day's events meant. Linda was the first to break the silence.

"Jesse... Where are we going?"

"Welp, I figure survival is still first thing. So... fuel, food, shelter, arms and ammunition."

"Right, but, where we going?"

"I saw a big box store about ten miles back."

"Oh."

"Yeah. One stop shopping I figure."

"Okay... and then what?"

"Well, then we try to find some way of living."

"No, I mean... the things we've seen... the giants, that thing back there... what are we going to do about that?"

"Way I figure it, most people ain't likely to believe us about that stuff. Unless they already know something, we don't tell nothing, make sense?"

"So unless somebody comes at us asking about giants or strange fountains erupting into space, we play dumb?"

"Pretty much."

"But what if what we've seen is important? What if the giant showed us those things for a reason?"

"You talkin' fate? Intentions of the universe or some such?"

"Yes."

"Never put much stock in it m'self... but I figure if somethin's meant to be it'll be worked without much work on my part. If the universe can collude to create... whatever those things are... I gotta figure it's got ways of forcing my hands too."

~

Post Phenomenon, Year 7, the Capital Ruins

Longmire ran his fingers through his close cropped grey hair, pushed his glasses up onto his forehead, rubbed his eyes, and leaned back in his chair. Fatigue wore on his face like a second skin. The light coming through the windows set high into the walls of the auditorium was a dim pink, the last vestiges of the setting summer sun.

"...that's it?"

"Well I think I got most of the important parts..."

Really? I somehow suspect there's more.

Jesse's minds raced. He'd purposely left out the more unbelievable parts. They way they'd killed Rafei, the giants, the thing that came out of the river and shot into the sky, the rings that's disappeared

456

after just a day. He'd had to invent a few things and hoped everything meshed.

"Eh... well... I may have left out a detail or two..."

"I'm gonna be straight with you Jesse; I don't believe you. I don't believe you because I've been to the CDC in Atlanta. I've seen the remains piled in the garage. I've looked through wallets and found Dr. Rafei, with a smashed temple and broken .38 with a slug in the handle sitting on the ground right next to him. His body was noticeably not shriveled like the ones the Shards leave.

"Hell, we tried to fire up the generators there, do you know what happened? Absolutely nothing. They had fuel, they were just shorted out. We fixed that, but it didn't matter. The whole building was fried. Every piece of electronics wiped out. Had to be an EMP, but considering the wider Atlanta metropolitan area is still intact I'm not thinking a nuke. I've heard from other movers and shakers who managed to get around during the event who also saw Atlanta go dark. So let me ask you this; and, you don't have to worry about me thinking you're crazy here, but... have you ever seen a Giant?

Jesse pursed his lips before taking a deep breath, scratched his goatee and sighed.

"Yeah... I figure I might have."

"I thought so. You want to tell me why you lied?"

"Well, it all sounds crazy, you know?"

"Every time I meet someone who's encountered them, they say the same thing. 'If I told it to you straight, I'd sound crazy'. I'm trying to compile a definitive record on the events of the Phenomenon. Believe me when I say crazy is all we get around here day in day out."

"Ya want me to start from the beginning?"

"How about we just go from where you first encountered the Giants?"

"Okay, remember when I told you that Rafei and I were getting supplies together to make the journey to South Carolina, and the power went out? Well it wasn't the generators like I said before…"

~

Post Phenomenon, Day 1, North Atlantic

Longmire and Seaman Second Class Rawlings hauled on the line, their forearms straining as they pulled in another survivor. This was the second to last one. The critically injured, mostly heat-stricken, went first. These last weren't critical, but they were all so weak that they all needed assistance. He was lucky Rawlings had, like him, ended up mostly covered by someone else and thus protected from the sun.

Emil and Sarya were down below already. One of the other more able bodied crewman, an electrician named Fitz, was down there arranging the injured, putting in IVs and pushing fluids, even as every conscious crewman with any strength sipped on a half and half PowerAde and water mixture and snacked on crackers.

With a final yank, they pulled the last man aboard. The party assigned to go out and tow back the boats clambered back up the side and began hauling down the remaining men on the deck. Longmire looked out on the brilliant hues of the setting sun, it's reflections turning the water into a dancing ocean of flame, punctuated here and there by abandoned rafts, and the occasional body of one of his crew he'd been too late to save. By his count, he'd left port with 134 souls, transferred off nearly two dozen in Oz, and lost a least another 20 to this damnable phenomenon.

He remembered the great clouds in his vision, and without the mind-numbing existential terror of the moment, he was able to recognize them as something somewhat familiar. Back in the 90's with the launch of numerous new observatories as well as the fixed Hubble, astronomical photography took off. One of the greatest came from a Hubble time share. Jeff Hester and Paul Scowen from Arizona State University chose to take some pictures of the Eagle Nebula. What they got came to have a very different nickname, and that was the name Longmire knew. He looked up into the first few stars coming visible through the darkening skies, and spoke to nobody in particular.

The Pillars of Creation...

The clank of boots signified someone coming up from below. Turning, He saw Fitz's head come up through the hatch.

"Captain, you should come quick; something's happening with Emil, sir."

Longmire handed off the rigging to the deckhand and made his way carefully below. Dodging around prone crewmen, he made his way through the ship. Most subs operate on a three shift rotation, and so, outside of the officers, there were only enough bunks for a third of the crew to be laid down at any one time properly. In this situation there were crewmen laid out on tables, in passageways, anywhere they could fit.

Emil was a critical case, and as such was one of those in the actual medical cabins. They were somewhat astern of the sail and the bridge, directly aft of the main crew berth. As he approached the hatch, he could make out some kind of commotion coming from inside. Cursing and grunts could be heard. As he stepped through the hatch he saw Sarya huddled in a corner, her arms wrapped around what at first glance looked to be some kind of odd stuffed animal. She was staring at two of his crewman who were wrestling to restrain her father. Emil was a sight. Bandages covered most of his face, but his eyes and his mouth were clear. His bloodshot eyes seemed about to pop out of their sockets, and his grossly swollen tongue wiggled rapidly in his gaping, frothy mouth.

"Sir we don't know what's happening! One minute he was fine the next he's flailing about, ripping out his IV, rambling about some kind of column of salt trying to destroy the ship!"

"Get Sarya out of here; she doesn't need to see this!"

"But sir!"

"I'll take your place restraining him. Take her to the other end of the aft berthing compartment, now!"

"Aye sir."

As the Captain and his crewmen swapped places he cast one eye over at Sarya, who's quiet terror seemed to have been replaced by resignation and loss. Her eyes never left her father as she was carried from the room.

"Alright, he's seizing, he's in danger of brain damage. Do you have any idea what you're doing here, sailor?"

"Not a fucking clue, sir; I've just been going by what they seem to need. Thirsty gets water, hot gets cold compresses... I don't have any idea what to do for this guy past that."

"Well, do you know what to do to keep him still and keep him from hurting himself?"

"No, sir."

"Shit, alright. Where's the docs medical library?"

"I think it's in the computer, sir."

"Son of a... goddamnit, get him up from wherever he's at. I don't care how sick he is, get him here and have him supervise!"

"I wish we could, sir, but he's already here. He's the poor guy in the next bed. He's unconscious and taking fluid through an IV."

"Well, isn't that just the damndest..."

Longmire and the seaman suddenly lurched forward as Emil's efforts to push them away abruptly ceased. They hurriedly piled him back into the bed and put the restraining straps in place. As Longmire sat down next to Emil he reached over and opened one of his eyes, it was bloodshot and milky.

He leaned back and slumped in the chair, wondering what to do. He felt a wave of dizziness and weakness pass over him. He realized that in the time since he'd woken he hadn't had anything to eat or drink. He spied a bottle of water on the ships physician's desk and rolled over to it. It was warm but he didn't care. He opened it and drank the whole thing in one go. It only awakened his need for more, helping him realize how truly thirsty he was.

He stood, dropping the bottle into a steel wastebasket as he walked out on the way to the galley. Behind him, Emil once more began twisting and straining, this time in vain against the straps. His mouth opened and closed over his protruding tongue like a fish searching for water. His eyes stared wide open at the ceiling. He paused, jerked, paused, and then collapsed back into the bed, a long whistling breath escaping his lips. It was his last.

~

Pre Phenomenon, 39,599 After Phenomenon, 1 kilometer below the SE outskirts of New Lycksele

...Good.

"What now?"

You have no need to know.

Angela barely had time to register surprise before she felt her innards twist and the world went black. As the giants watched, each denizen of the Lycksele warren disappeared into small pinpricks of amber light. Several dozen light-years away, something vast, ancient, and

461

terrible beyond description... woke up.

In New Lycksele, more than a kilometer away, an automated system, long dormant, felt the occurrence it was designed to detect, ancient and unused mechanisms sprung to life at long last, sending warning signals to its brethren and its creators, all dust.

Around the world, in Cairo, Egypt, Lyons, France, Gary, Indiana, Phoenix, Arizona, Beijing, China, and a dozen more across Europe, Africa, & the Americas, other systems signaled their own purpose into the darkness. And each went unheard, their importance long forgotten. Only one, along the coast of what was once California, was heard by a human ear...

~

Post Phenomenon, Year 7, the Capital Ruins

Benjamin Longmire watched as Jesse retreated up the aisle to the auditorium exit. Frost met him at the door, both of their shoulders slumped with fatigue. Looking up, he couldn't see anything but darkness through the windows. As the door closed behind Jesse with a soft click, another figure emerged from the shadows by the presentation screen. A young woman, sixteen, maybe seventeen years old, with bronzed skin and deep mocha eyes, with long ebony hair in a loose braid down her back. She wore a knee length brown dress with a subtle black flower print.

"Do you think he's telling the truth?"

Longmire turned his chair, his worn shoes sliding easily across the painted concrete floor. The sound echoed like a raspy gasp through the open space.

"I think so. We've heard crazy before. This guy's eyes though... Sarya, they didn't show an ounce of deception, not after I called him out."

"He knows about the giants, even sounds like he befriended one."

462

"It's definitely different then what we've heard before, or experienced ourselves."

"We need to let Dr. Walthers hear his story, see what he thinks."

Longmire pushed his hands up, wiping his face and rubbing his eyes.

"I know, I know... we can't keep this from him."

"He's been a help before. He might know something about this "Project" thing Jesse said Rafei was a part of."

"Okay, I give up, I surrender to your indomitable will. We'll contact him tomorrow, 11am for us, 8am for him, as soon as he's at work."

Sarya gave one of her rare smiles.

"Thanks, Dad."

~

Post-Phenomenon, Year 7, Berkley CA

Dr. Henry Walthers arrived in his office-come-laboratory fully ten minutes early, and as such was starting on his first cup of tea when the satellite phone started ringing.

He hobbled in with a pronounced limp, a cane barely doing its job to support his right side. He was starting to show his age, with grey hair having migrated from just his temples to all over his head. His square jaw sported a short grey beard, only his eyebrows still bore traces of his brown youth over his grey eyes. He still wore traces of his previously distinguished career. Dress slacks had given way to cargo shorts, pressed shirts, vest, and jacket had fallen to a Berkley t-shirt... but he still carried his leather briefcase and his shoes were still spotless.

There were only three people who had access to the proper number. His wife, Nikki Thorne, a Zoologist stuck in London, and Captain

Longmire in D.C.

Since his wife was just down the hall, and Nikki had left yesterday to scout the wildlife in Scotland, there was only one person it could be.

"Good morning, Captain. How goes things out there on the East Coast?"

"Things are swell. I've got some news for you, and something for the archives. Are you set up to receive?"

Cross country satellite communications were difficult. Internet was a distant memory. In their desire to pass on large quantities of information quickly, they'd turned to the past. At each end, they'd scrounged up fax machines, which they would then plug into the phones when necessary.

"Er... not yet. Can you give me five minutes? I think I'm almost out of paper here. I'd like to refill the tray before you start sending through anything. What exactly do you have for me anyway?"

"We had a new contact yesterday, group out of Florida. The head of the convoy was out and about during the Phenomenon, had an interesting story to tell. Recorded it last night, had it transcribed overnight, and now it's ready to come to you."

"Excellent, excellent... anything interesting?"

"Very. He spent time at the CDC with Rafei, made friends with a Tall One, and witnessed the rings and what ended them."

"Jesus..."

"Right. That's why I called so early."

"Well, I'm glad you did. I've been thinking, Ben, all the things you told me about Opperthorne's research, everything we learned from the Chicago expedition. They came before, 40,000 years ago. I think they're going to come again, some 40,000 years from now. If history repeats itself, these events will be long, long forgotten."

"Most likely. What are you thinking?"

"I think we need to bring in others, pass on what we've learned, build something to send a warning down through the ages, try to make sure people are ready next time."

"Funny you should mention, this guy, Jesse, he said Rafei was involved in something like that. Called it 'The Project'."

"Send me everything, and clear your schedule for today, I have a feeling we'll have a lot to discuss."

ABOUT THE AUTHOR

R.K.Katic is a stubborn ass. He's also a father of way too many damn kids, a sarcastic, overly-literal man-child, and a fiercely efficient (read: lazy) parasite on society. He enjoys swimming, reading, playing video games, analyzing movie plots and plot holes, Reddit, and Role Playing Games.

To keep up with other projects from R.K.Katic or to send him a message, fan art, or other queries, become a fan of his Facebook page at www.facebook.com/RKKatic.